The Mystery of

The Solar Wind

Lyz Russo

P'kaboo Publishers
South Africa
2009

P'kaboo Publishers

www.pkaboo.net

First published online 2008
First Paperback Edition 2009
Revised Edition 2015

Copyright © Lyz Russo, 2008
lrusso@pkaboo.net

Cover design: Aludar8
Original cover designed by Kamino Creative

Revised Edition:

ISBN : 9780620465939

Acknowledgements

The crew and I would like to thank the following people:
Iain, my husband, co-creator and best critic, for listening to every scene as it was written, devising large parts of the plot with me, doing a lot of the research, and reviewing every last edit with me. Iain, you are amazing.
My friend and graphic designer Riana Louw from Kamino Creative, for making this project a reality. My editor Les Noble, himself a yachtsman, for his endless patience with a landlubber who thought she could write about a sailing vessel. Henning Botha from Aludar 8 for the new cover.

My wonderful family who supports me through this process in every way, and my friends' encouragement.

And especially to my children for being so patient with Mom!

This story is for you, Robin, Ray and Meggi.

0

Dublin

Running.   No: Scurrying, like rats, cutting corners, slipping and scrambling through the half-dark of the dank storm drainage system of the old harbour town.   Her older brother chasing her on from behind, her younger one scouting ahead, furtively checking each corner before they reached it, to make sure it was clear.

In a twisted way she was glad that she had cropped her hair short into an extreme brush cut, because the glorious red mane of curls she still had yesterday would have been in a hopeless mess by now.   Her face, hands and clothes were streaked with mud, reeking of rat droppings and cat urine.   She clung to her violin case and Ronan's guitar bag, as he had more than enough to carry with his Clarsach and the heavy backpack.

Shawn, who was lugging the pipes under his arm as he peered around bends, beckoned for them to proceed.   The next corner was clear.   They ought to be right under the old promenade by now, and they had to be careful, because their tunnel was half visible to the streets from here, through fairly large storm drains.   Dawn hadn't finished breaking yet.   Breaking what, she thought dismally.   Breaking her whole life, everything she'd ever cherished.   Breaking her childhood off with a deadly finality.

It had taken both Ronan and Shawney to get her pulled away from Mother's body, her hands still covered in blood.   What insanity was this?   Why not leave her there, to die too when the Unicate came knocking on the door?

Lying low at Mrs Flanagan's had been gruelling; but not as bad as spending the night down here in the drains.   And as for the reaction of relatives, yesterday morning – she didn't even want to go there.   And through it all she couldn't get the blood off her hands.   What was driving her by now, was nothing but primal fear.

"Here!" Shawney's signal was barely more than a whisper. She allowed Ronan to push past her, and found a way to hold the Clarsach for him too as he helped Shawn work on that manhole lid. They battled with it a bit. Rain and mud had sucked it into place and it was a struggle loosening it, but suddenly it lifted, and they pushed it aside.

All three waited and listened with bated breath, ready to bolt back into the depths of the storm drain system if they had to. Things seemed really silent up there. Ronan made a step ladder with his hands for Shawn, who put his foot into it and pushed himself up, peering out of the manhole.

"Coast's clear," he whispered down to his two sibs. Ronan boosted him up, then handed the instruments up to him. It was a tight fit for the Clarsach; but this square manhole was one they had tested before. Life for a young Dublin musician could be perilous at night.

"C'mon, Pae!" came Shawn's optimistic invitation.

She shook her head, unable to face the scant daylight.

"Sis, we've been there," said Ronan, almost threateningly.

Paean Donegal backed down and accepted the burglar-lift up to ground level from her older brother. Once she was out, she turned around and took the backpack from him. It took her and Shawn's joint efforts to get that heavy pack lifted out.

She lay down on the pavement and extended a hand down for Ronan; Shawn did the same on the other side of the manhole. Ronan grabbed both hands at the wrist in a mountaineer's grip and hauled himself out of the sewers, kicking against the crumbling stepladder none of them had dared to use.

All three pushed the lid back into place and stared at each other. So far so good; they were at the docks. They scanned the surrounds. Those uniforms could come breaking out of any alley, at any moment. They were not safe anywhere in plain sight.

An unkempt-looking character was idly leaning against a lamp post, watching them. It looked like a wild man, long black frizzy hair tied down around the head with a bandanna. One thing this person was decidedly not: Any kind of Unicate. There was something... he somehow looked like a sea person to Paean. On a hunch she stormed at the man.

"Sir, sir, please – are you a sailor?"

Gypsy eyes stretched wide in surprise as he took in her filthy appearance. He studied her intensely, making her wonder whether it had been a mistake talking to him at all. If he alerted the harbour guard?

"Looking for a ship to stow away?" he asked eventually with an unreadable grin.

"No, sir! We want to work! We're hard workers, have been all our lives." She hoped desperately he'd accept that. She was fifteen – work was only legal once you were sixteen. But he didn't look like the type that would care.

Critical dark eyes noted the instruments.

"Musicians, huh? *Shukar!* This way, *shey.*"

"Paean, what are you doing?" hissed Shawn.

"Getting us a job," she replied. "On a ship."

"She's right, Shawn, move!" urged Ronan.

The wild man led the way, along the docks to a beautiful white tall ship lying at anchor. Paean noticed that he moved like a predator; a feral cat or a burglar. But damn, the three of them didn't exactly arrive smelling of roses, either.

The name on the side of the two-master sailing ship, she noted as they approached, was the 'San Diego'. And the figurehead was a mermaid... its eyes seemed to follow them.

*

30 March 2116, 6:05 am

Loud banging on the white-painted door that was splintering with age. Louder banging. And an impatient grip on the door handle, forcing it.

The old lock gave way. The door swung inwards. The uniformed crew entered, with guns lifted high. Not stun guns; real fire. The little house was quiet. Too quiet.

They made their cautious way through the rooms, first the tight living-cum-dining room, the ridiculously short passage where three bedrooms and a bathroom connected; pushed the only closed door open, lifted their firearms -

"Check the other rooms! Check the bathroom! All the windows!"

7

The young charge-sergeant personally looked under the bed. There was nothing; as opposed to what was on the bed.

So she was dead. He checked the pulse of the woman lying there drenched in her own blood. Accurate. Then where were the three?

"They're not here, sir."

Damn.

6:50 am

"They're gone!"

The man in grey faced his equally grey officer's wrath.

"How did you let them get away? They are dangerous!"

"We don't know, Captain-Major. Technically there should have been no opportunity for them to escape. We were watching them this whole past week."

"Find them!"

"Yes, Captain-Major!"

30 March 2116, 9:59 am

Tights. Toothbrush. Transmitter. Tarot deck.

The girl smoothed down her sleek black hair and threw a sidelong look at herself in the narrow hallway mirror as she left the apartment. Check. Still myself. No parsley between teeth. No beauty. No big deal. She glanced back at the empty flat she left behind; all traces of her erased, as though the only thing that had dwelt here between the last tenant and now had been time. Home? No. No such a thing. Wherever she was sent, there she went.

This assignment had her excited. She had never worked on a ship before. She almost smiled as she slunk down to the harbour.

*

Paean was standing indecisively in the hatch of a *petite,* minute, tiny cabin. It had everything she needed; a pull-down bunk that came out of the wall; a round porthole with blinds – those were important; and a small, squat chest for her belongings. Neo-compounding, of course. Ronan and Shawn had been assigned a similarly small cubicle, with the two bunks pulling out of the wall one above the other.

Ronan came in and unceremoniously dumped the clothes he'd packed for her, on her bunk.

"Freshen up, sis. Don't want to present like street kids, now do we?"

She shook her head, still unfamiliar with the missing mane, and the way there were no curls to move around her shoulders but only a stark crew cut.

"Where are the bathrooms?"

He took her out of her cabin and pointed down the passage. "They call them the heads, like, on a ship, alright? We'd better wise up on the jargon, sis."

She nodded, gathered up a fresh set of jeans and t-shirt and padded to the 'heads' to get cleaned up. The heavens knew, the blood she had tried to wash off her hands for a day now was bothering her a hundred times more than the foul-smelling gutter-mud.

*

January 2116:

Two ships converge in the twilight, six hundred sea miles off Dakar. A voice calls across from one to the other. A chorus of powerful African voices answers. The national hymn of Southern Free.

Sails are furled. The two ships slow and come to a halt next to each other. Lines shoot across. A gangway extends from the blue yacht to the white trader. Muscular sailors carry goods across: Guns, heavy artillery. Closed boxes.

White teeth flash in laughter. Lines are untied, sails unfurled, the gangway retracted. The two ships veer apart, the crew of the yacht singing loudly. A pirate flag flies from the mast of the white trader. They disappear into the twilight in opposite directions, six hundred sea miles off Dakar...

*

31 March 2116, 6:59 am

"Don't know what you dragged aboard there, Federi!"

The gypsy flashed a steely grin, gazing out over the harbour. "Jon, watch these sports." He pointed at the docks. A pointless sun was rising behind a drizzly cloud cover. A Unicate patrol emerged from the ancient, narrow roads, stepping in perfect synchrony with hair-raising precision. You only heard one single marching gait. And they were headed straight for the ship.

Jon Marsden glanced over his shoulder, at the bridge. Yes, Captain also saw that patrol. He gave Federi a nod and they undid the mooring hawsers, which spun back into their holds. Captain raised the anchor. The ship started moving innocently away from the docks, gliding on solar drives.

The patrol increased its pace. Marsden glanced at the bridge and received a go-ahead signal from his Captain. Together, he and Federi peeled the neo-membrane with the false name off the side of the ship. He glanced back to the bridge. His Captain was grinning broadly. They all three watched how shock and disbelief spread over the faces of the Unicate civic military. The ship's sails clapped like thunder as they expanded. The Solar Wind cleared the port and moved out into the Irish Sea, picking up speed, sailing close to the wind.

*

1

The Solar Wind

6th of April, 2116. Rust-coloured waves, calm sea fading into the haze towards the darkening east. A minimal breeze, just enough to keep the perfectly balanced white ship moving forward dreamily, southwest towards Bermuda.

Young boy high up in the archaic Crow's Nest, playing a haunting tune on an ocarina, carried down in snatches on the wind. Young man leaning against the foremast, newly bearded and unkempt from the day's work, strumming on a Clarsach, a small Celtic harp. Ancient acoustic instruments, rare calm moment, the great sea hushed. Young sailor with red hair cropped as painfully short as her two brothers', leaning against the rail with an infuriated scowl, humming a fragmented alto line. The fast-sinking sun painting the trio orange. Three musicians, the Donegal Troubles, hired for the Solar Wind in Dublin. Dark eyes watched from the shadows of the jib stowage bay.

Blood! An ocean full of it! Paean Donegal stared at the thick red waves; and the way the setting sun lit up the blood that was still clinging to her hands right up to the elbows, blood that she hadn't managed to wash off in a whole week.

Her knuckles stood out as she gripped the rail, trying to calm herself down. There was nowhere to run; if she made any suspicious moves, the game was over. For a whole week they had managed to stay alive now without spilling their secret to the crew on this ship. But she felt trapped. By now she couldn't eat a single bite of food; couldn't keep it down. Her stomach was in a permanent knot. And it was not from sea sickness!

Her older brother's hand on her shoulder. She shrugged it off with irritation.

"You alright, Pae?"

They should have left her behind! She hadn't wanted to leave Dublin, run away like a common criminal. Here she was, travelling off into the sunset like a hero. Hired to play the happy fool and sing inane stupid little tunes and be the entertainment...

"Open yer eyes!" She made a wild gesture at the rusty sea.

"Tha's only the plankton bloom, sis," he tried to pacify. "The light catches the little plants that way at sunset. Now if you'd kindly pipe down." His eyes flitted uneasily to the bridge and the shadows at the bow, and he raised his voice to retake the tune. "An' I'll tak' the high road an' you'll tak' the low road..."

She glared at him.

"*Please*, can we be done gloaming?"

Ronan smiled placatingly. "But don't you want to be in Scotland afore me anymore, Pae?"

She groaned. "I *never ever,*" she said pointedly, "ever want to be in Scotland! Or Ireland, either. Get that, Ronan?"

Her brother scowled at her. She turned away from him, her eyes moving back to the thick, red sea, her mind compulsively returning to a place she had called home all her life, only a week ago.

Shawn Donegal came shimmying down the rigging with a monkey's agility. Old Sherman Dougherty watched him, thoughtfully drawing on his old-fashioned tobacco pipe. The ancient sailor with the thick headful of shoulder-long white hair had been listening to the angry music; now he was listening to the bickering.

"Tomorrow we land at Hamilton," he commented.

"Yay! Land!" piped the youngest Donegal. "Can't wait!"

"Shawn!" warned Ronan. Paean glared at both and turned away, disgusted. She *could* wait. She'd be quite happy never to have land under her feet again! Ronan thought they ought to get off in Hamilton, Bermuda, and restart their lives there. She didn't think so. It wasn't far enough from Dublin.

"Play the Britches full of Stitches!" she demanded snappily.

The jolly Britches! Shawn grinned around his ocarina as that old ditty spilled out of the clay whistle. Paean always demanded that tune when she wanted to punish him. Poor Pae.

Oh hey, but her temper didn't help! He wished she could just relax.

12

Everything would be fine. They were on a ship, they had escaped. Things might be a bit dubious here, but at least the Unicate would never find them as long as they stayed aboard and kept a low profile.

He watched the First Mate, Mr Marsden, and that mysterious being called Rushka, move about in the dusk. Rushka wore a black leather cap, knee-high black boots and black clothes all over. A hint of dark-red hair peered out under her cap. They were currently testing signals from the self-tuning sails, the automated winches, and the hand-holds system. Feeding back the results to Captain, on their wrist-coms. Shawn wanted such a com. None had been offered to him or either of his sibs.

Captain Radomir Lascek emerged onto the command deck and shouted something at the sky. Probably Hungarian.

Shawn briefly thought back to their first, intimidating encounter with the ship's Captain. Tall, powerful and formidable, with hands that looked like they could break a neck at the drop of a hat. His coarse black hair and short-cropped beard showed first signs of greying, and his eyes like blue steel seemed to cut through any cover-up and straight to the truth.

Except that he hadn't. They had been called to the bridge, where Captain Radomir Lascek had demanded to see their credentials. Ronan, forever the organized, cool-headed planner, had produced their identity documents and his own school leaver's cert. He was the only one who had finished his junior cert. Lascek had read the three identities with a deep scowl.

"Why are you aboard?" he had challenged.

"Sir, we'd rather be employed, and a ship is the only place that will employ people of Shawn's age." Ronan's answers were studied, self-possessed.

As opposed to Paean. She had stood there with her eyes downcast, unable to look at any of them, with guilt scribbled all over her – or perhaps depression. Until the Captain had ordered her to look at him. She'd raised her eyes, in defiance, tears lurking just under the surface, and glared at him.

"Yes, sir?" she'd barely whispered.

"What did you do in Dublin?" he had asked. She had gone pale and only stared.

"Captain, she's our essential violinist," Shawn had come up for his

13

sister. "Gigs don't work without her. We're the best harbour-side band in town," and he'd grinned, hoping desperately that the Captain would stop putting pressure on Paean. If she cracked...

He got his wish. Captain Lascek released Paean from his interrogating glare. His expression had turned cold and official, and he'd beckoned to Rushka – that same Rushka, to come forward with some documents.

"Sign here, and here, and there," he had instructed them. "You're hired. We need you to play a gig whenever one is called for, and for the rest you're deck hands and cabin boys. You shall be trained on the job."

"Works for me," Ronan had muttered and signed, his siblings following his lead.

That had been a week back, as the 'San Diego' was already putting distance between herself and Dublin, leaving a small host of Unicate harbour guards behind in her wake. Shawn had known it would be alright, as long as none of them said anything much. What was Captain going to do, throw them overboard?

Actually, what would stop Captain? Who would come looking for them? Shawn had realized since that he wouldn't want to mess with that man. Radomir Lascek had both the ship and her crew in absolute control. Watching him operate, Shawn could sometimes imagine that the crew were merely automatons responding to his signals. He trained them like that: Responses had to be instant and dead accurate.

The Captain had a military bearing, and he seemed to have an unfailing instinct where sea and sky were concerned. The Solar Wind's sails were self-tuning; but often he would override that and take an active hand, ordering 'all hands' onto the deck to tweak and influence the sails, and every time, this resulted in greater speed.

There were many rumours flying around the ship concerning the Captain. Some of the sailors said that he preferred storms to clear skies, and that there was more to Captain than met the eye; that he was ex-military, that he was an alien... Shawn chuckled. The Captain's military attitude and his alien glares at old Sherman discouraged the old storyteller from spreading such rumours. For a few hours at a time.

Shawn yawned and played the Britches one more time, in his own altered version with a beat missing, making them sound as though they were limping. It had been a long day. The break in the Crow's Nest had

14

been a respite from a lot of scrubbing, chopping, polishing, handing on tools, and tightening of things on deck. His fair, freckled skin was burnt from the work in the sun. His freckles were fusing. He'd be one big freckle soon, he thought pensively, staring at the by now purple plankton bloom and the waves that were slowly losing their gloaming as the night deepened. Surely Pae had no problem with the purple? Tonight the waves would have fluorescent peaks again. He sighed. When was this watch over?

*

Hey, Katya.

Just dropping you a line, everything's quiet now, crew's in bed, night shift is on duty...

Landed in Dublin last week. What a dreary port, rains all the time! Right under the Unicate's nose again, just like Captain likes it... was a prima getaway, too, you should have been there!

So we loaded some young sewer rats with the potatoes. Call themselves the 'Donegal Troubles', yes, I can see the 'trouble' bit. Wonder what the Unicate's up to, hunting children again? Ace musicians though. Captain's making them play a lot of what they call "Ceilidhs", which is just an Irish way of saying, make lots of noise. Yoy, Katya, when that girl plays, Federi gets homesick. Remember I had a violin once?

And Captain had to hire one more. A very beautiful girl, but – Katya, you know how it goes. When things go wrong, who has to clean them up? That brings our head count to thirteen, don't look at me like that, is not my fault! Is bad luck that!

Captain's grandiose plans are getting bigger by the minute. But seriously, Katya, he's taking too many risks now. I can't see us surviving that long.

Anyway, if we don't, I'll see you sooner.
Kathal, my sister. Missing you.
Federi

*

"Land ho!"

Paean jolted awake with a headache. The Unicate was banging on the door, sirens and flashing lights...

Turquoise light glittered and danced on the ceiling. She clung to the mattress. How she could have thought she might be back home in Molly Street... it showed that she was getting used to the constant rolling of the ship, that she could even forget about it at times when she slept.

Her blinds were pulled all the way up, all the white and blue morning sunlight flooding her cabin. She remembered. She had left them like that, watching the moonlight last night, and the red sea turning black, until she had fallen asleep. She'd been awake again for the midnight shift, the 'graveyard watch' as the crew called it, and back in her bunk at four when the early morning irrepressibles had come on duty. It was waiting for her too; she'd already had to take one early morning watch.

She swung her legs over the side of the bunk, sitting up. Except for her violin case under her bunk and the built-in white compounding chest that held her few clothes, the cubicle she slept in was bare. Frugal. No old toys lying around; no books, no music; none of her own herbal pharmacopoeia she had been steadily collecting in Molly Street. Her old friends the dolls, Shawney's collection of squishy jelly creatures in jars... all left behind. A small storage space for one small Donegal, female.

And someone banging on her door. She groaned.

"Come on, sis! Wake up! All hands on deck!"

Ronan. Taking a moment to see that his younger sister didn't get into trouble for oversleeping.

"Thanks, Ro," she called and slipped into her beaten-up old jeans and hand-me-down, faded red T-shirt. She wouldn't even have had a change of clothing if Ronan hadn't packed for her, that day.

"Land ho!"

It was Shawney's high-pitched yell that had awakened her. It cut through the ship's intercom a second time. *Land* jolly *ho?* Where the Heyerdahl did he get that expression?

She moved into the day's duties, out of her cabin and up the first set of steps – companionway, the sailors called it – to the upper crew deck, shooting a wary glance all the way down the passage towards the galley,

17

where that rainbow monstrosity of a gypsy cook was usually based. Lurking there ready to pounce on anything that had hands and give it a lot of work to do.

She had located him, that day. The wild man from the docks who had introduced them to the First Mate who had subsequently assigned them cabins. It had taken her the entire day to find him; she'd wanted to say thank you. When she'd eventually discovered the galley and realized he was based there as the person who mixed the gumbo – in itself an idea to get used to – and she'd started to say thanks for bringing them aboard, instead of an acknowledgement he'd abruptly cut her short and given her pots to scrub. Her favourite chore! - not.

She didn't appreciate his brusque order; a request would have done the same thing in a heartbeat. And his chronic sense of humour that went with his psychedelic dress code, felt forced to her. And a bit too morbid.

Paean quickly moved up the second companionway, to the outer deck, ready to call her little brother back out of the Crow's Nest – which modern ship had a Crow's Nest? Honestly, a practically forgotten concept; gone long before the ships that had supposedly floated on water with a hull made of metal – another tall tale! Ha, and she knew why Shawn hid up there: Because he knew *she'd* not be climbing up there after him! So he could play ocarina while others worked!

She emerged from the hatch to the outer deck, and stopped for a moment, to stare at the incredibly beautiful blue day out there. The sea, azure; the sky nearly the same. She breathed, and started to relax, feeling the morning sun warm on her skin, drawing out and evaporating the stress from her. She closed her eyes for a second, revelling in the sunshine. That jolly bloom had passed, thank the Infinite. And there was a nice breeze, but it was warm. That was welcome! They'd had a miserable winter in Dublin; and before it could properly be Spring, they'd had to flee.

Perhaps Shawney was right. Perhaps things really would be alright; all she needed to do was trust. Nobody. Trust nobody. But have faith that the world itself would take care of her; that somehow, they were safe. Nobody had asked them any pointed questions at all. Maybe on this ship it didn't matter and they could start anew.

And then she froze. On the horizon right ahead, a thin green line.

18

Land. They were sailing straight towards it.

What had she thought? That they'd be at sea forever? Land ho. Port Hamilton. Now she understood. Why was Shawn so infuriatingly chirpy about it?

2

Stabilizers

Port Hamilton in sight! Shawn watched in fascination from the Crow's Nest. His alert-cry had electrified the whole crew into frenzied activity, fussing with ropes – sheets, they called them – and tweaking the sails the way the automated systems couldn't. He plotted stealthily to shout "Land ho" in the middle of the ocean next time and see if it had the same effect.

And then his enthusiasm dipped for a second – Ronan was planning for them all to go ashore here, to start life over. But… maybe he could be persuaded to let them travel a bit further? After all, they were fed and had a roof over their heads – a deck at least; and you got used to all the work. There was really no rush.

Early this morning the great Genoa sail had been unfurled, to add speed to the mainsail and foresail. He had been there to watch and help, too. He had thought then that no ship could possibly go faster than she had been sailing; but now her speed picked up even more, so much that he only wanted to hold on and enjoy the rush. The Solar Wind was a Zephyr, the fastest class of ship available to traders today. She sailed lightly, like a yacht; but with a lot of added power from the enormous area of her self-tuning sails. Shawn squeezed as much information as he could out of the older sailors, whenever they had time. Particularly his countryman, old Sherman Dougherty, took time to answer his questions; and so did Federi, the gypsy cook with the illegal colour sense. That one was especially forthcoming, with information, entertainment, friendship and a never-ending load of work. The Donegals hadn't only been hired to play Ceilidhs!

The Solar Wind was an aero-solar driven Zephyr, the fastest class of ship available to traders today. The secret of her speed lay in her huge sails. Hundreds of minute sensors, smaller than freckles, optimised the angle and furl of the semi-translucent white cloth to capitalize on every slight change in wind pressure and light. The sails of the hundred-and-fifty-footer were of a practically indestructible, lightweight silicate-neosilk hybrid weave. There were miniature tensors all over those sails, tightening or slackening a tiny area of sail each, in a process involving the silk protein and artificial muscle fibrilloids. The combined effect of the electronic reefing and tacking from the CPU, and the tensor action, was that the sails were tuned in a hyper-responsive way human hands could not achieve. And still, every so often Captain ordered his sailors to do something manually with the sails that seemed illogical; and every time it turned out that he'd only pre-empted the wind changing.

The iridescent solar cells spread out like fern leaves from the axes of the two larger sails, their hair-thin goldthread connections leading the gathered electricity back to the mainmast and foremast, from which it was channelled down into the machine room to fuel the solar drives, which added just that extra bit of push and direction from under water. Shawn was burning to find out what those solar drives looked like. But the machine room was strictly off-limits for all new crew.

Military ships ran on fuel cells, he had angled out of Federi. Those were combustive drives. They had quite a bit more power than the solar drives. On civilian vessels those and all other combustive devices were prohibited. This did not bode well for the Solar Wind, since the boarding of Paean and her temper. Shawn grinned and wondered if that temper could be harnessed for drive power.

Ronan peered up at the Crow's Nest between the glittering sails and snorted impatiently. Couldn't his two unruly siblings grow up a bit?

"Shawney!" He planted himself at the bottom of the foremast, cupping his hands to his mouth. "Come down, you lazy lout! All hands on deck!" Shawn could hear him perfectly clearly, he knew it.

They had to be ready! When the instruction came that crew was dismissed, they would have to be packed and ready to go, because this was Hamilton – their destination. He was eager to find them a place to stay, with what wages he'd earned on the ship.

They'd probably have to drag Paean off the ship by her ears, because she had gone into burrow mode, hiding away when she was off duty, and talking to no-one when she was on. He didn't know his sister like that, but he guessed she had reason. But didn't she see? The longer they stayed in one place – the ship in this case, the larger the danger that they were found out. They had to keep moving. Go to ground in Hamilton for a month or so, then find another ship and travel on, perhaps to Cuba.

Radomir Lascek was suddenly behind him.

"You Donegals stay aboard."

Ronan stared at him, eyes wide. He didn't dare to ask why. That put an end to his plans! But he didn't dare disobey the Captain.

How on Earth had Captain discovered that they wanted to leave?

Radomir Lascek moved away to speak to Jonathan Marsden. Ronan's eyes followed him. There went a man who could easily be a fleet commander of some sort in the Unicate Navy. Tall, straight, authoritarian. A man to admire. Ronan had been considering a career in the Navy, perhaps even the Marines himself before everything had started going so badly wrong. And now Captain had discovered something. He was sure of it! The man to admire had become a man to fear.

They were nearing Hamilton harbour, the Solar Wind plunging through the early morning swells towards the white line of the breakwater.

"Shawn!"

Erw! Caught dreaming! Shawn grinned guiltily at the gypsy, and back at the knot he was pretending to tie into one of the tensioning lines. He was really just looking busy; and Federi saw straight through that.

"Drop that excuse of a rope," the Romany commanded. "Crow's Nest, lookout duty!"

Shawn dropped the knot with a huge grin. He clambered back up into the Crow's Nest at top speed. He didn't want to miss this landing, and he had been hoping for some lucky break so he could get back up here, where one could see everything. Lookout duty! Honestly! As though the Solar Wind with all her advanced nautical equipment needed a lookout post!

He peered at the sails that were luffing in the wind. Locked in irons, he thought; wind directly from ahead. Didn't see that often! They ought to tack that rigging by just about thirty degrees, approach the port at an angle... Funny how the ship could go so fast despite the wind resistance of the whole rigging...

Hey! It was completely wrong! Those sails were supposed to be the force that pulled the ship forward, not a resistance that held it back! What were they doing? If the sails weren't pulling the ship, what was? Whales on a leash? Why weren't they tacking? The ship was actually going straight into the wind, at full speed! And the solar drives with their bit of push could never be enough to achieve such speed against the actual natural forces... Shawn peered at the wake of the ship. What was that rising out of the water? Bubbles? Steam -?

He glanced down at Federi, who was following him into the rigging. He'd ask him. The gypsy was peering intently at the harbour, scowling.

Shawn liked Federi, despite the man's relentless way of creating work. Federi stuck out vividly, dressed like the Pied Piper. He could have been an entertainer; an actor, or a puppeteer, because no sane person would put themselves into such loud colours on purpose. Today Federi shone brightly in a light-green flared shirt with a loud orange embroidered waistcoat that looked archaic and Eastern European to Shawn. He wore this impossible set over the oldest, most faded jeans Shawn had ever seen, and topped it off by wearing a purple scrap tied around his head, from which the whole contents of a cheap jewellery stall dangled on little hooks. Like a jolly Christmas tree, thought Shawn. He wondered if Federi did it to entertain himself or others, or the younger crew, or to annoy the Captain. And he play-acted too! Once he had climbed about in the rigging with a bread knife between his teeth, grinning. This had impressed the ends out of Shawn. It impressed even more ends out of Shawn when the Captain had ordered Federi to take that darned knife out of his mouth – and the gypsy had complied instantly.

"Say, Federi – why is the ocean behind the Solar Wind boiling? We're running on fuel cells, aren't we?"

Federi threw his head back and laughed.

"And fuel cells are illegal," added Shawn pensively.

"If you say so," agreed Federi.

I don't say so, thought Shawn. They are! I happen to know my stuff! A little of the strangeness of the Solar Wind had suddenly become clear to him. He grinned.

"Okay, Federi, I won't tell anyone. But why don't we just furl those sails? They're breaking our speed!"

"Because," said the gypsy, "if we close them while we approach the

23

port, they will know, won't they? Can't furl the sails! The real question is, why is Captain going so blasted fast?" He turned thoughtful, peering at the harbour.

"Won't they figure out that the wind is blowing them the wrong way round?" asked Shawn.

"Nah," said Federi. "That's not the problem. They never look that closely – they've got their sensors and electronic binocs, with that they only see what they want to see. But we should have..." He lifted a pair of small electronic binoculars and gazed through them.

"Federi," asked Shawn, "that stuff in the harbour there that looks like black caviare. What is that?"

"Reason we're up here," replied a voice out of Federi that was altogether foreign. A quiet, dangerous voice. The clown in him disappeared completely and was replaced with something feral. Shawn watched this sudden change with bewilderment. The problem was, this was probably not a guise. The change ran deep, through the entire being of the wiry, under-tall man.

Shawn glanced back at the strange black specks – boats, he realized – that littered the harbour's waters like a hatch of spider's eggs. And suddenly he knew what they were.

"Twenty-eight!" muttered Federi, hissing through his teeth. "Whole jolly nest! Yoy..." He glared darkly at Shawn. "Stay up here, Donegal! That's an order. Don't let your brother call you down again. Watch those craft!"

The binoculars vanished into his pocket and he slid down a rat-line back onto the main deck. Shawn saw him heading for the bridge.

Quietly as a whisper, the Solar Wind turned her sails and moved away from Hamilton harbour.

*

Meeting in the galley! Paean found herself a spot as close to the door as she could, at the heavy, antique Ironwood table – the only item in this galley that wasn't light and modern. A squeaky clean galley; her and Shawn's scrubbing had a lot to do with that!

But despite the despotic drive of the Rainbow Romany for

24

squeakiness, all was not so legal and white-winged here! Shawn had discovered a gas cooker in one of the cupboards. A combustive device! Hah! And a bottle of gas.

Aw hey, she knew what this meeting was about. The Solar Wind had turned away from Port Hamilton.

Why?

She studied the gathering crew, wondering and stressing. Her two brothers: Shawn, chirpy as a chipmunk, and Ronan, tall and serious. Next to Ronan towered the blond titan Rhine Gold from Hamburg, whose real name was Reinhold Schatz; but the others were too lazy or dumb to learn to pronounce that. In 'escaper's position' right at the end of the table lurked Ailyss, the quiet mouse from the machine room. Sour-looking girl that. Old Sherman was there, fiddling with his pipe. Captain Lascek moved into the galley and sat down, folding his arms and staring searchingly at Paean. He knew nothing. She should relax. Behind him Rushka, silent and dangerous, cut off the escape route by standing in the doorway. Guarding.

Radomir Lascek nodded at Federi, who was suddenly there, leaning against the cupboard at the porthole watching them. Paean blinked. Where had he come from all of a sudden?

"Captain says I got to put you in the picture." Federi stretched lazily and moved forward into the light of the porthole. The countless jingles and gadgets he'd pinned to the scarf he kept wound around his head, glittered mysteriously. Beads, trinkets. There were even data cubes among them. Paean had by now decided that the man was a few chips short of a full processor.

So what *is* the picture?, she wondered. He smiled at her; even one of his teeth caught the light and glinted, silver.

"The picture is, we've turned. Any questions?"

Young Rhine Gold raised a hand. Like in school, thought Paean.

"What precisely happened out there, actually?"

"We jibbed," replied the gypsy cook, "*precisely* sixty-one degrees to port, catching the wind at twelve point two knots, and then adjusted the course due west."

"Why?"

"So we can round the island."

25

"But..." Rhine Gold looked indecisive, "why, Federi?"

The gypsy laughed. "To get to the other side, of course!"

"There were black craft in the harbour," Ronan spoke up. Paean glanced at him, proud of her brother's musical tenor. "It's to do with them, right? What are they?"

"The Stabilizers?" Federi asked back. "Their job is to annoy -" another flash grin. "Anyone here who doesn't know who the Stabs are?" Rhine Gold looked unenlightened. "Good. Next question?"

Yes, thought Paean. Stabilizers. The long arm of the law; the Unicate military. Their job was to escort large, fragile ships or those with precious or dangerous cargo into port. Their *other* job... she'd seen it done in Dublin, the harbour Stabs encircling and boarding a ship... if you were a criminal, or perhaps just a trader who thought he could skimp on taxes... she shivered lightly. It was hair-raising.

"So what is the Solar Wind doing running from the Stabs?" she challenged, then bit her lip.

And what were you *running away from, in Dublin?*

She blinked. It took her a moment to realize that Federi hadn't actually voiced that dangerous question. He hadn't yet answered. Was insanity contagious?

"Don't be illogical, little songbird," came his amused response. "We're not running, we're reaching. The wind is just ahead of the beam. At this rate..." A shadow seemed to move across his face. Paean suddenly had the impression that the gypsy could genuinely see the future – and the future looked grim.

"But Federi," Shawney piped up. "What are the vultures doing in Hamilton Harbour? I thought she were a free port?"

Paean nearly swallowed her tongue. Vultures? Free port? That was gangster speak! What was Shawney doing thinking in those lines? Who had primed him?

"Kaboom!" came an explosion from the crazy. "Finally, the right question! What indeed?"

It was Federi's bad influence that had Shawn thinking like a thug, decided Paean. She glared at the man, unimpressed with his aping around. No doubt Shawn would now want to grow his hair long too and hang dead birds and fish bones in it.

Federi grinned at Shawn, then glared at everyone else.

"Worthy colleagues," he announced in mock pompousness, "the situation we find ourselves in is the following. No electrics!"

The response was general confusion.

"No reheating cold coffee in the ultra-glare." He glared at Rhine Gold and Ronan. "No blip messages; no jokes shared on open blinkiethingie; in fact you switch off your blinkiethingie right now and stick it in your pockety thingie. No devices of any sort! Not even a light. They can *hear* a light being switched on." He paused, confused. "Of course they can *see* a light too. So, no lights on the ship after dark. Anyone who accidentally leans against a switch walks the plank. Understood?"

He had them all mesmerized, realized Paean. They just hung on his words, waiting for the next instruction.

"Once it's dark..." he paused and glanced at the Captain, and carried on, "some of us will go ashore in the Stormrider. *Only* those," he glared at Ronan, "with business ashore, Donegal! Anyone trying to stow away on the lifeboat will be thrown overboard!"

Shawn giggled. "We can swim, Federi!"

"There are sharks, lots of sharks," said the gypsy dramatically, his falcon eyebrows moving to emphasize the point. His white teeth flashed in a grin, flawless except for that one silver eye-tooth. "Any further questions, anyone?"

They were merely watching him in fascination.

His steely smile settled on the machine room assistant, Ailyss. She hadn't even glanced up.

"Any questions, *Ailyss?*"

She looked up, bored. "What's for lunch?"

"Lunch?" The question unbalanced him. "You're asking me, the cook? Cor, Ailyss! Let me check the menu! Yup, says fish 'n chips here, on the fridge. Again. Course this is a ship!" He grinned.

Paean scowled. There was no menu on the fridge! What *was* this?

"So in which way were you supposed to put us in the picture?" she shot. And snapped her mouth shut for the second time.

A smile; an imperceptible shake of the head.

"That *is* the picture, *dulciuri,*" Federi informed her. "Ladies and gents, this session of tease-the-dogsbody is now closed. Are all instructions understood?"

The Captain got up and nodded briskly. "Well done, Federi!" He left the galley.

Paean couldn't stand it any longer.

"What precisely is he supposed to have done well? That wasn't informative at all!" she raged. "Some real answers would have been welcome!" She glanced at the gypsy. He was gone.

"What is it you want to know?" asked Ronan sharply. "You want those silly rumours confirmed that are flying around the ship? Captain is an alien? Get real, Paean!"

She snorted. "Well, Ro, you can stop patronizing me right now! It *would* be nice to know why – aargh!"

Rushka had planted herself very suddenly in front of Paean, putting down a firm boot.

"Donegals! Captain demands to see you in the boardroom."

Paean iced. Ronan watched Rushka turn and walk off. She had an explosive way of saying "Donegals"! She was uncanny! Did she carry a knife in her knee-high boots?

"Come on, Pae, Shawn." Ronan and his sibs followed the unfathomable Rushka.

"Think it's that serious?" Radomir Lascek studied his gypsy with a scowl.

"They're frozen solid with fear," replied Federi. " 's got to be serious! Captain, think Hamilton is about them?"

Lascek laughed without humour. "We should be so lucky! *You* know what Hamilton's about! Keep an eye, Federi. Here they come."

Shawn scanned the Solar Wind's blue boardroom as they entered. He had been in here once, investigating, and Federi had found him and given him something to do in the galley, with a warning that the boardroom was off-limits. The door to the boardroom was always closed. It was reserved for officers' meetings.

A long pine-coloured meeting table and chairs dominated the room, along with a plush dark-blue neofibre carpet, smelling slightly musty from the damp air. A great flat screen was mounted on the stern-facing wall;

tiny black gadgets in all the top corners. Shawn knew what they were: Closed-circuit cameras. A wooden-looking cabinet was mounted on the other wall, with a safe combination lock. He wondered what was hidden so securely in there. Treasures? Drugs? Secret instructions to world domination?

The remaining wall space, where it wasn't housing closed cupboards, was decorated sparsely with woodcarvings, one here, one there. Ship scenes; battles on the sea, lighthouses submerged in tidal waves; one scene of a Zephyr – the Solar Wind? – flying off into the sunset. Yes, flying. Having lifted off from the waves.

The Captain was waiting for them. Rushka had positioned herself at the door again; Federi, in a corner, cross-legged on an office chair, assembling something small. Being inconspicuous. How had he got to the boardroom without passing them? Was this ship riddled with secret passages?

Blond Rhine Gold was there too. So, all the new crew. But not Ailyss. Shawn wondered about Ailyss.

Ronan tried to move to a position from where he had an overview of everyone, and found he couldn't. Either he lost sight of Federi, or Rushka, or his younger siblings. It was maddening.

Paean watched in trepidation as Radomir Lascek got up and walked past their ranks with slow, measured paces. He stopped right in front of Rhine Gold. The young German swallowed, his blue eyes round. He was half a head taller than the Captain. Paean wondered why he was looking so guilty, if he was perhaps a fugitive too.

"This is too important to discuss in the galley," said Lascek. "And you should hear it from your Captain, not your cook. Federi did a marvellous job."

Paean couldn't stand it any longer. "Captain, in which way was he supposed to put us in the picture? We've learnt nothing!" She glared at the gypsy. He smiled innocently at her.

"That's right," replied Lascek genially. "But we have. What's for lunch, Tzigan!" Federi grinned. Lascek's smile dropped away and he glared at the crew. "Sailors, the one who leaks any of this to Ailyss walks the plank."

29

Ailyss! This was about Ailyss! Paean started releasing a pent-up breath.

"As for you, Paean Donegal…" said Radomir Lascek.

The breath stopped in her throat. Paean stared at the Captain, frightened.

"Would you dare to repeat that question you asked Federi?" demanded Lascek with an intimidating frown.

"No," she said shakily. "Sorry about asking."

Lascek and Federi exchanged puzzled glances. Federi laughed brightly. What on Earth did Captain Lascek see in this madman, that he allowed him so close to the core secrets? Or had knowing those secrets driven Federi insane?

"Paean Donegal, repeat your question!" commanded Radomir Lascek. "It was an interesting question."

"Why… are we running from the Stabilizers?" muttered Paean, wishing she were elsewhere.

"Thank you, Miss Donegal! And there's another question you are burning to ask."

She stared at them both in fear. How did they know? This mind-conjuring was rattling her chains.

"Get on with it!" barked Lascek.

"The ship I boarded in Dublin was the 'San Diego'," she said.

Lascek nodded at Federi.

"Was a false identity," replied the gypsy cook.

Paean gasped.

"Why were we using a false identity, Captain?" asked Ronan quizzically.

The Captain laughed aloud.

"Welcome aboard, Donegals, and Mr Schatz," announced Captain Radomir Lascek. "Aboard my pirate ship, the Solar Wind!"

3

Port Hamilton

"The problem lies right here," said Captain Lascek, pointing to Port Hamilton on the map on the boardroom's console screen. "What on earth are the Stabs doing here in such force?" He tapped the flat screen thoughtfully with his pen, gazing at his gathered officers. Port Hamilton zoomed in and out behind him with every second tap.

Silence met him. They stared back at him indecisively: Rushka, Federi, old Sherman Dougherty, Jonathan Marsden, Dr Jake, Dr Judith – and Shawn. ("Why me?" the boy had asked Federi, and the gypsy had replied: "Captain moves in mysterious ways.")

The Captain folded his arms. "Well, we'll find out tonight what they're up to. Blasted nuisance!"

"I'm concerned!" Rhine Gold was helping Ronan coil up lines. Extra lines. Their function was not clear, as the tensioning of the Solar Wind's sails happened automatically, via electronically controlled coils on the large scale, and the micro-tensors for fine-tuning. "One is hired on a ship and finds oneself entangled with pirates! *Verbrannt*, Ronan!"

Verbrannt indeed, thought Ronan. Not bad enough that the Unicate was hunting them. It would be practically impossible to disappear now, if the ship they arrived in was a pirate.

"It's a tough one," he agreed, wishing he had a solution for himself and his sibs. Actually, Rhine Gold had the easier deal. "Didn't he give you the option of getting off here? And with a spotless record?"

"A spotless record?" The tall young man from Hamburg shook his head sadly. "Joking, Ronan. The Unicate is going to find out sooner or later that one has spent time on such a ship. He can forge my travel documents all he likes. They will pick it up. The safest is really to stay aboard until we're in the uncivilized regions."

31

"You're staying on until Hawaii?" asked Ronan.

"That seems like a good plan. I only have to keep my hands clean though. I won't be involved in any looting or shooting or whatever."

"Fair," said Ronan.

He wished he could make a similar resolution. Essentially he also saw himself as law-abiding and good, like Rhine Gold. Only he had the nasty feeling that he'd never be given that choice. After Dublin... Captain knew something. They had become prisoners on the very ship on which they had been hoping to flee. He worried what Captain was going to do to them.

They ought to jump ship at the very next port where the Solar Wind landed, and hang the wages!

"Pirates, huh!" Shawn was dicing vegetables with new aplomb. The officer's meeting had been over for an hour now. Lunch was overdue. Suddenly, *not* going ashore because the Solar Wind was hunted, was a lot more exciting than going ashore.

It also meant, and he understood this clearly, that for now the Donegal Troubles were safe from the blasted Unicate. By a simple function of being in the right place. Clearly Captain had experience getting away, or he wouldn't be a pirate still. This was altogether good news. Maybe if they could just stay on as extra pirates... He wondered what it would be like, boarding and looting vessels. Whether he'd be given a real bolt gun, like the police wielded in Dublin.

But coming to think of it – you couldn't be a pirate with only a bolt gun! They only immobilized people. These pirates probably had guns that shot something more tangible. Bullets or laser or fire or something. And knives. And... silver teeth!

Federi grinned darkly. "Pass me that – never mind." He fetched the egg lifter himself. There was a pile of newly peeled potatoes sitting on the Ironwood table. "Shawn, don't get your hopes up. There won't be any bloodshed."

Shawn blinked, puzzled. "Why not?" How could you be a pirate and not do bloodshed?

"Because Captain doesn't believe in unnecessary killing," said the gypsy. "We're not that kind of pirate." He started filleting one of two

32

metre-long deep-sea tunas that Wolf Svendsson, the assistant engineer, had pulled out of the sea earlier. Shawn watched, fascinated. He picked up one of the translucent little scales that were coming off under Federi's expert knife.

"Fancy," he said.

"There are classified documentary chips no larger than that," commented Federi, glancing briefly at Shawn's intent face. The kid was on a track about spies, technology and danger. Perhaps those topics would throw the young boy off the track of boarding and looting, slashing throats and keelhauling. Federi frowned. That had been psychologically ingenious of Captain! Telling a young boy of twelve that they were pirates! Inaccurate, too.

Outside, the turquoise waves splashed against the Solar Wind's white hull. The ship turned a little on its anchor chain. The sunlit island came into view through the starboard-side porthole. The knife sliced the fish-belly open.

"Evisceration," said Shawn with a grin.

"Next time, your turn," replied Federi. "So observe!"

The paradise of blue sea and green shore lay smiling in the afternoon sun. A breeze blew here on the outer deck, by the bowsprit with the not-quite-figurehead, where Paean was standing staring into the hazy distance. It was nearing four o'clock. The afternoon seemed endless, working on her overstretched patience.

Oh hell, the Solar Wind was a pirate ship! Hadn't they just boarded the ship so they could get away from being hunted? Now they were stuck in one place, fixed targets, and... They ought to escape! But she couldn't even discuss it with her brothers.

She had finished scrubbing all the heads, not that she'd had orders to do so. She had tidied and swept all the cabins on the lower deck, and the infirmary – a glum, cluttered little yellow cabin on the starboard side of the lower crew deck. It sported two bunks on opposing walls, a too-small porthole covered with a pale grey vertical blind, white metal medical cabinets mounted against every available wall – bulkhead, they called the walls; a drip stand that was clipped to the wall, fixed-mounted machinery with touch-buttons and knobs and so many indicator needles and displays, and a wall-mounted flat screen. The infirmary, for all it was cramped, was clean, well-equipped and functional; but it gave Paean the creeps.

The crew cabins weren't any larger, on the lower deck. Her own was two doors down from the infirmary. The lone door on the port side, across the passage from her cabin, was always closed; on the rare occasions she had tried the handle, it had been locked.

Her own frugal little cubicle was by no means a skimp. All cabins on the lower crew deck were that small. She kept the pull-down bunks opposite her own, and the one overhead hers, secured to the bulkheads to have a bit more room to move. Not that her room at home in Molly Street had been that much larger.

And now she'd run out of things to do. It wasn't her watch anyway; she was supposed to be off-duty. So she could stress herself into shreds. Ooh, and the sea had to be so darned blue, and the day so sunshiny! Belying what was lurking beneath the surface.

"What's eating you, girl?"

Paean turned and stared at Federi, rattled.

So it was interrogation time? For one who jingled and squeaked when he walked, he'd crept up on her without a sound! Blooming stealthy. And his dress code was a walking disaster. Sometimes she wondered if he were a ghost.

"Och," she said listlessly and flashed him an insincere smile.

Federi returned her smile and took a spot leaning against the rail next to her; there above the mermaid figurehead that wasn't really one. Just a blob of compounding. In Dublin she'd thought the Mermaid's eyes were following her around. Another illusion.

"Missing Dublin?" he asked gently.

"Where's Dublin," replied Paean acridly. Gentleness was the last thing she needed now. She'd left a lot of friends behind in Molly Street. Blast him!

"Sorry I gave you trouble, back in the galley," said Federi. "Wasn't in a position to answer you. You heard the Captain."

Ah yes. Because of Ailyss.

"So what's *she* supposedly done?" snapped Paean.

Federi smiled regretfully. "Classified, young lady. Sorry."

Paean snorted. "So if this is a pirate ship, does this mean everyone's a pirate? The whole crew?"

"That's what it means, little songbird," smiled Federi. "Unless you'd rather be a hostage...?" He peered at her. "Thought not."

She clamped her mouth shut. They *were* hostages.

They both stared across the deck and at the sea and the island, where the gulls were circling. And Paean sighed. She wished there were a chance of living, again.

She thought back to countless rainy afternoons in her old schoolteacher's musty living room. A room lined with genuine old bookshelves, with ancient books made from original paper, and slightly newer ones on permaprint, on every conceivable topic. The old teacher didn't believe in electronic literature; she used to say that the Unicate could control what you read, that way, and could even erase it. Mrs Flanagan, the rebel teacher, her grey hair in a tidy knot, subversively reading history or philosophy to the children of Molly Street who were gathered on her carpet.

Mrs Flanagan, who had hidden the Donegal sibs in her study and concocted a wild story for the Unicate police, charming them old-lady style while the sibs had pressed their ears to the door trying to hear what she was saying.

"I miss her," she muttered, not even aware that she was speaking aloud. "She taught us such a lot!"

"Your old teacher?" asked Federi.

She inhaled sharply. What? She hadn't told him anything! Either he was sharp as a flaming laser, or he could jolly well read minds!

"She taught you things you didn't learn in school?" guessed the gypsy. "History? Culture?"

Subversive content. Paean knew very well that Mrs Flanagan ran a huge risk. The Unicate had outlawed all knowledge and culture that dated back more than thirty years. They discouraged remembering even five years, and if they found you keeping records...

"So when last did you attend actual school?" asked Federi with a knowing smile.

Oh, for crying out loud!

"We're done with school," she announced defiantly. "It's only compulsory until age sixteen. And I'm... sixteen."

35

"Give or take," laughed Federi. "So, *shey*, how many months short of junior adult status?"

"I *told* you, I'm…"

"Not a very practised liar," completed Federi, winking at her. "You were raised to be honest, *dulciuri*, that is your biggest problem here. Relax, little bird. Got my own secrets. Won't give yours away. Never heard of honour amongst thieves?"

Paean rolled her eyes.

"So," prompted Federi, "fourteen?"

"I was born the thirteenth of August, *on* the century," she said angrily. "Year Zero. It's twenty-one-sixteen, so work it out, won't you?" She ground her teeth and added, annoyed, "I'm not a child, Federi! Just not very tall."

Federi's gaze wandered into the hazy distance. For a moment he seemed miles away. Probably trying to do the calculation she had just challenged him to. The ship turned slowly on its anchor chain, rocking gently on the waves.

"You're lonely and sad," he diagnosed. "Could try telling Federi about it?"

"Or I could try falling off the face of the Earth," she replied moodily. "Sorry, Federi. Just – I don't think you can help us." She glanced down at her hands. The blood was still sticking to them; ghost blood that would never go away. And she looked up and noted with fright that he'd followed her glance. "Don't think anybody can help me," she said under her breath.

"Captain might," replied Federi quietly.

She stared disbelievingly at him. Captain would not even bother to wait for the next port before throwing them off the ship.

"Captain's a dangerous man, in't he?"

The gypsy bared his teeth. "The Pirate Captain? Most dangerous man I've ever come across!"

Paean nodded. She'd thought so.

"Wish there were somewhere on this ship where my brothers and I…" Another sigh; another gloomy shrug. Hells, she couldn't tell him!

"Ah," said Federi, brightening up. "For a sibs' meeting. *Minunat!* But not in the cabins, little hummingbird."

36

"Didn't think so," agreed Paean. "People listening in?"

"Electronic eyes," said Federi. "Go check. In the top corners. And hidden microphones. The whole ship is riddled with them. Safety measure. You keep this to yourself, *hai shala?*"

"Course," said Paean seriously. "Is there any place…"

Federi laughed softly. Was like picking a porcupine's pockets, talking to this one!

"Come," he said, leading her away from the prow, down the steps of the small elevated jib deck onto the main deck. "Let me show you a spot!"

Captain Radomir Lascek, on the bridge with his Second-in-Charge Jonathan Marsden, frowned and watched how his gypsy out there on the deck showed the Donegal girl the one place on the ship that was unsupervised. Well, the only one that was accessible to her. In the jib storage area, at the prow, under the small rain deck with a roll-down gate. Between crates and vats and sails. No sensors there.

A solution still had to be devised concerning those three mischief-makers! The Donegal Troubles, the youngest had called their band. Lascek needed to find out their secret.

Rushka arrived back on the bridge. She followed the Captain's gaze.

"Nearly time to get the Stormrider ready," said Lascek. He pointed at Federi, shaking his head. "The faithless rogue! He's making the Donegals aware of the eyes."

Rushka laughed softly.

"You're finding this funny?" the Captain snapped at her.

"Very!"

"Well, you would," growled Lascek. "He's covered for you often enough!"

"This is *really* funny," said Rushka, watching how Federi and Paean rounded up Ronan and Shawn.

"Yes! Right where I can see them plotting and scheming," retorted the Captain. "I suppose I should see it the other way. At least I'll know when their conference will be finished!"

"They're not plotting and scheming, they're coming to grips," Jon Marsden, the First Mate pointed out from where he was busy at the console. "Most honest people are a little bit shocked when they find out they have just turned into pirates!"

"Honest, those three?" wondered Lascek.

"Are you sure this is a good spot?" asked Paean doubtfully.

" 's good as any," said Federi. "Make yourselves comfortable. Captain can see where you've gone, but he can't hear what you're discussing."

"But you can," grinned Shawn.

"Well observed," said the gypsy. *"La revedere!"* He strolled off.

The glint of something small caught Paean's attention. She picked it up. It was a minute electronic gadget, no larger than a lentil.

Shawn had a look at it, squinting in the low light, and then Ronan did too.

"A microphone," he said with a grin.

"Thieves' honour," laughed Paean.

No Ceilidh tonight. Bermuda's lights glittered in the post-gloaming gloom. Paean hung onto the rail, the evening breeze blowing spray into her hair.

She felt somewhat better than this afternoon. According to Ronan, it was alright to shelter on an illegal trader for a while provided that nobody exposed their secret to anyone. It helped the invisibility along; such things as customs police checks didn't apply, which solved a lot of problems. He was going to try working it through Rhine Gold that the three of them could also get clean papers from Captain when they arrived in Hawaii. The concept of jumping ship without Captain's agreement was not viable anymore; the authorities would pick them up. The most important thing now was to be excellent deck hands and cause no trouble. And possibly, to build good relations so that nobody wanted to dig up dirt about them. Doubtlessly every single crew member – barring maybe Rhine Gold – had some or other reason to evade the law on an illegal trader. Paean noticed that Ronan absolutely refused to speak the word "pirate".

Good relations. Shawn had no problem with this, Paean knew. Already her little brother had become very friendly with the gypsy, and Ronan, too, had made firm friends with Rhine Gold. She herself was a little out of the water there; if she could decide to *like* anyone on this ship, she'd maybe try to connect. But it felt rather pointless. How ironic, she thought, when she, Paean Donegal, had been the main socialite and organizer on the block back in Dublin!

Her eyes followed the Stormrider, the silent electric motorboat that was headed for the shore, carrying Captain, Marsden, Dr Judith and Federi. She feared them, at least, most of them; but her fervent wishes went with them. Let them be safe, let them return soon, so they could weigh anchor and sail away from this fraught island!

Another presence next to her. She turned and saw Ailyss leaning against the rail too, studying her. And she thought of the Captain's warning.

The dark-haired girl said nothing, just studied her. In the very near dark each recognized the fear in the other's eyes.

Whatever the other girl was hiding, she was not going to tell. And Paean herself – she'd have liked a friend, but sharing her own secret? Friends, Paean Donegal realized, were something of the past. She couldn't do it. She sighed and moved off towards the hatch. Sorry, Ailyss. Sorry, Ronan.

Paean descended to the galley where Sherman had gathered the young crew around Federi's Ironwood Table and was telling fabulous stories in the dark, his voice hushed. Ships drowning in tidal waves. Rocks ripping holes in hulls. Submerged debris floating about, banging into a ship. Huge quakes…

As though they didn't have enough disaster in real life! Paean recalled how Ronan had tried picking some of Sherman's stories apart for their glaring logical inconsistencies. He had ended up scrubbing decks until midnight, a result of Federi's wrath. It seemed as though on this pirate ship, the entertainers stuck together.

By that logic the Donegals should stick to old Sherman and Federi as well. She shrugged impatiently and took herself off down the unlit passages, back downstairs to her cabin, sitting on her bunk in the dark wishing she had brought her diary with her. Although that was pointless. What she wanted to write, must never ever be committed to paper. It would be her end, and that of her brothers.

39

Down in the machine room, Wolf Svendsson was checking on the various drives with Ailyss by the dim light of torches. Dr Jake's workplace was a calm, organized area; where most ships had some damp in their bilges, the Solar Wind's were kept clean and dry. Most apparatus in here was stowed safely in white metal casings, with all sorts of indicator switches, needles and mini-screens to keep the engineers informed of the status. There was a terminal of the ship's processor where Wolf spend a lot of time programming; metal cabinets housing the diving gear and other necessary gadgetry; and the water desalination system. The Solar Wind, like all modern vessels, derived her drinking water straight from the sea.

Some of the back parts of the machine room were also used for storage. Great plywood crates were stashed against each other, containing mostly torpedoes, ammunition and other everyday necessities. Federi now and then took the liberty of storing food there, if his pantry as well as his little storage area on the main deck got overloaded. This didn't suit Wolf all that well. The harbours had a way of selling one roaches along with those food crates. And today's roaches were descended from the poison-proof survivors of the nuclear wars of the Sixties. A roach in the works could cause all sorts of electronic nonsense, and mostly, of course, more roaches. Wolf kept a slipper at hand for just such emergencies.

It was the first time since Ailyss was hired that the two colleagues were really alone; Dr Jake, the ship's engineer, was always there guiding and teaching and supervising. This way it was nearly impossible to get into conversation with the dark-haired mystery girl.

"So, are you enjoying it on the ship?" asked Wolf.

"It'll do," shrugged Ailyss.

"How old are you anyhow?"

"Twenty," said Ailyss.

"I'm twenty-two."

An awkward silence followed. Wolf was discovering that Ailyss was not the talkative type.

"Where did you graduate?" he asked, trying again.

"You wouldn't recognize the name," replied Ailyss.

"Oh."

Another little silence ensued. A disjointed thought of dentists and pliers crept into Wolf's mind.

"Got any sibs?" he asked.

"Is this an interrogation?" Ailyss shot back.

"Crypts!" said Wolf, put out. "Sorry I asked!"

They continued their work routine in silence.

At stroke eleven the shore party met back at the Stormrider with their various purchases. They had only managed to take on enough food supplies to last them a few days, more was not possible with this small manual mode of shopping. Few shops had been open; it limited what they could get. This meant they had to restock somewhere else within the next week.

"Found out anything?" Jonathan Marsden asked Federi.

"They're all out drinking," replied the gypsy. "Not that they'd be making sense when they're sober. Heads full of girlfriends, mum about job. 's a pretty good team that," he grinned approvingly. "Dratted pity they're on the wrong side!"

"And that's not all," prompted Marsden.

"Darned right," agreed Federi. "Will tell you the rest on the ship. 'Fraid you might not believe it!"

Half an hour later, with everyone back aboard, the Solar Wind set sail for Plymouth. Paean heaved an enormous sigh of relief to be turning her back on Bermuda. She spelt the Unicate with four letters. D-e-t-h. Mrs Flanagan would have made her sit and write it out twenty times if she had known.

Shawn sat in the cool, misty Crow's Nest, the night wind tousling his hair, finally being allowed to play his ocarina again. The moisture added a muted, somewhat fuzzy quality to the sound of the clay whistle.

It was dark up here; the small guiding lights that studded the foremast at the handholds, had been dimmed down to a minimal glow, barely more than reflectors, to allow for better outward vision. The only reason they were not simply off was deck safety. There were no lights on the Crow's Nest itself.

While the Zephyr tuned her own sails to the wind, under the electronic control of the CPU and the command of the bridge, there were still tasks to be done on deck. Jon Marsden and Rushka were down there, along with Rhine Gold and Ronan, checking things and degreasing the winches which had a bad habit of becoming tacky if you left them – a function of the compounding greasing mixture, and sea salt. But the activities were all low-key and muted – no Ceilidh tonight!

The presence of those Stabs in Hamilton Harbour worried them all. Captain expected an attack from the Unicate; Shawn's responsibility was in the Crow's Nest, as early warning system.

He had been equipped with all sorts of nice gadgetry. A wrist-com was one; another, an advanced set of electronic binoculars. Federi had given him a glass-lens one too, pointing out that they were traversing an area prone to electric storms. Electronic gadgetry wasn't always completely reliable here. There were several such places on Earth's oceans, the gypsy had explained. Shawn was to ask Sherman about it.

The gadgets were for his job. Shawn was now part of the alert system of the ship, a human high-tech sensor. Sitting inside yet another sensor. Because that was what the Crow's Nest was. No other ship had such a structure.

The Crow's Nest was the one visual feature the Captain kept flaunting in the Unicate's face. Ships these days were identified by satellite, not by sight. A reason why they had not been pursued from Hamilton. Usually by the time someone cottoned on that the ship that was just leaving had a Crow's Nest, the Solar Wind was well beyond reach.

Shawn had learnt that Captain enjoyed allowing people sightings. He usually removed the false name and identity just as they left a port. Sometimes this resulted in interesting chases, but according to Federi the Solar Wind was the fastest ship moving on today's oceans, so there was no real worry unless they sailed into a trap. And to prevent just that, Shawn had been stationed in the Crow's Nest.

"Oh, hi, Federi!" Shawn watched as the gypsy climbed into the rigging. "Was the shore fun?"

Federi shot him a wry grin. "Don't like land much," he commented. "But, yes, eat your heart out, Donegal, I've been to a pub."

"Pooh, I can smell it," laughed Shawn. "Smoke all over! Any good

42

music?"

"Nothing like the Donegals," said Federi. "Spotted any whales yet?"

"Nope!" This got Shawn's heart racing. Whales? He had thought they were extinct! "Are there whales here?"

"Course there are whales, boy! This is the Ocean!" The gypsy laughed.

Shawn peered at the dark waves with his fancy binoculars.

"Found out why the Stabs are in a free port?" he asked, only listening with half an ear. What if a whale surfaced while he was not paying attention?

"A pirate port, in Unicate speak," added Federi. "Fact is, they haven't attacked Hamilton yet. She's still a free city." He stared over the dark sea, into the distance.

For how long would Hamilton remain a free port, now that the Stabs had given her attention? How many other free places would be brought under the merciless rule of that corrupt organization now?

"Federi," said Shawn, "why are we pirates, if we don't do bloodshed?"

"Because the Unicate calls us that. We don't exactly stick to their laws."

A disappointing answer. Shawn had hoped for treasure, boarding and looting, daring stunts and glorious sea battles.

"But if they call us that anyway, and if they hunt us anyway..." The boy got an evil little grin. "Shouldn't we exploit that a little bit?"

"Oh, Donegal!" Federi laughed. "You worry me! You're more of a pirate than Federi!"

Lascek had business partners and suppliers in Hamilton and other free ports. Federi wondered whether one of those business partners had been a bit too eager to make a buck out of Radomir Lascek. Perhaps some of them were trying to palm in the small fortune the Unicate promised for his capture? But somehow his gypsy radar, his internal sense of truth, told him that the answer lay closer. Much closer. On the Solar Wind herself, in fact. And perhaps this time, worried Federi, the spy they had loaded along with the new crew had been one too many. It had gone badly wrong in the past.

"In the Pacific," he said dreamily, "where there's less Unicate and

43

more Freedom… there you might understand. We are basically just traders, like everybody else!"

"What do we trade?"

Federi laughed. "Not going to tell you! Should ask Captain, if you're so curious!" He was not going to inform Shawn that they laid traps for and captured Unicate military vessels, put the crew ashore and sold the ships to the Rebellion; or that they trapped and caught Rebellion craft, corrupted or unloaded the crew and sold the vessel to other contacts inside the Unicate! But all that was just a day-job. Captain Radomir was a big picture person. He had a much larger plan.

"Federi," said Shawn, "what are we going to Hawaii for?"

The gypsy considered. The Donegals had been briefed. Briefly. But disclosing Captain's plans – he wasn't authorized to do that.

"Trade, of course," he said lightly.

Shawn grinned. Evasive gypsy!

But at that moment something else drew his attention. Was that a light in the distance? Shawn peered through his electronic binoculars and got only disturbance. He moved the binoculars through their various options – no use. Och, dratted electric storm! As predicted! He grunted impatiently and reached for his glass lens binoculars.

Federi trained his own set of glass lenses on the light as well. Shawn activated his wrist-com.

"Captain, ship sighted about – er – twenty degrees starboard. Can't see anything through the electronic binoculars, can't see enough through the glass ones. How do I get an identification?"

"Satellite," came the answer. "Good work, Donegal. She doesn't show on the Solar Wind's radar. Probably shielded. I'll identify the vessel."

Shawn kept his binoculars trained on the other ship. It seemed to be getting bigger…

"Captain, they're coming towards us! At a rate!"

"I know, Shawn. I've nearly got the identification."

Shawn strained his eyes. The other ship was darker in colour than the white Solar Wind; more Shawn couldn't really be sure of in the treacherous partial moonlight. The other ship's speed was surprising. The

44

vessel probably ran on fuel cells. Therefore, probably military. He glanced at Federi, concerned. The gypsy had transmuted into that sharp, sinister entity again. A subtle shift. It scared Shawn.

"If Captain identifies them by satellite, can't they identify us too?" he asked, worried.

"They have, long since," said Federi darkly. "Can bet on that!"

Not by satellite, the Romany refrained from adding. It was more complex than that...

If Federi could have had a glimpse from a bird's eye view, he'd have been a lot more worried still. Hamilton Port was where the main force of Stabilizer T-craft lay. Small, agile motorboats built for all sorts of fast manoeuvres in the comparatively shallow waters of a harbour. But all around the islands, in regular intervals with their radar fields overlapping, military speed-ships were positioned, Pursuers, which were equipped with fuel cell drives running on hydrogen gas. These vessels were built for bursts of extreme speed over short distances, and their spacing was such that once in view of Hamilton, the Pirate could not escape without registering on at least one Pursuer's radar screen. The Solar Wind had sailed into the Unicate's net.

"Donegal, come in!" came the Captain's shouted command over the wrist-com. "Come down from there instantly! All hands below deck! Shout it to them! Leave nobody out! Hurry!"

"All hands below deck!" yelled Shawn as he shimmied down the rigging like a monkey, followed by the gypsy who grabbed a rope and slid down it. "Captain's orders: All hands below deck!"

"All hands below deck!" bellowed Captain Lascek over the intercom. "Boardroom! Accounting system! Roll call!"

Seconds later everyone was gathering in the boardroom. Jonathan Marsden was already taking roll call, making marks at the voices that weren't yet responding and reading them again at the end of the roll call. All were accounted for. All were below deck. And the Unicate vessel was still bearing down on them.

"Marsden! Make sure nobody moves a foot outside! It would be lethal!"

Rushka and Federi were leaving the boardroom at a run.

"What are they doing?" Paean asked, at no one in particular.

"Checking that all portholes are closed," said the elderly Doc Judith. "Run, Paean, help them! See there, over the doors? Those electronic displays? Run to the galley, Paean, check those two. Make sure they're good and tight."

Shawn was running after his sister.

"And now?"

"Checking portholes, bro! Come!"

Aboard the Unicate MS Hun, Captain Anya Miller blinked. Was it possible?

"What the hell is that maniac doing?"

Just a second back she had everything fixed to capture the entire Solar Wind, crew, Pirate Captain and all. What a fortune she'd be palming in, along with the deep satisfaction of having outwitted Radomir Lascek! Now before her eyes the white sails of the Zephyr folded up like bat's wings, disappearing into the booms as the latter lifted up to align with the masts, which telescoped a bit and laid themselves down gently on the deck. Something glinted. She peered, trying to see what it was, and got a better view as her search-beam brushed the Solar Wind with the lift of a wave. It was hooks – springing up out of the deck to secure the folded-up rigging down. The next moment the entire ship simply – sank! She saw a vague glow vanishing under water.

4

Undertow

Anya Miller cursed. The Solar Wind had got away from her before, merely by speed. But at some point she had been promoted into a position where she could choose her own ship; and that was how she was Captain of the Hun, the fastest craft in the entire military force. By normal conceivable means the Solar Wind could not outrun her. But then, Radomir Lascek wasn't normal. He had just provided new proof.

"Get a grip, ladies!" snapped Miller. "Get a fix on that boat and follow! Move!" She gazed at the spot where the Solar Wind had vanished. "And close your damned mouth, Anyhow! This time the old crook is not getting away!"

She had positioned herself perfectly. She had been accurate with the assumption that Lascek would not be able to stock up the way he needed to in Hamilton, and would therefore try to make a dash for the next pirate port. Which one was not quite clear; Cuba, Venezuela and Nicaragua all had some unconquered harbours, hidden bays that the Unicate was still trying to bring to light. It was, after all, the major trade route to the Pacific, the great domain of the Rebellion. And then there was Barbados. Though unconfirmed, Anya Miller was personally convinced that Barbados still had a pirate port somewhere. If it were true, she'd bet he'd head for Barbados!

She knew the old pirate! He'd try for the one that was slightly out of the way rather than carry on straight, to throw pursuers off track. But Radomir Lascek was never completely predictable; it was this element that made him so dangerous. So she had taken the precaution of stationing ships all around the island while placing herself squarely between him and Barbados. Her calculation had been on the money.

She had known that he was off the satellite. How the old crook managed that, the devil alone knew; *nobody* circumvented the satellite ID!

But his ship being radar-cloaked had come as a surprise. This explained the lethargy of the Stabs. Anya Miller's sharp wit alone had resulted in her seeing him at all: The Solar Wind had practically tripped over the Hun on her way down to Barbados. She had been spotted visually.

"Got to go deeper," muttered Radomir Lascek. "She's still on our tail. Risky." He punched another sequence into the console, and the Zephyr descended further. He activated the intercom to the machine room.

"Dr Jake, we need the fuel cells. Solar drives not fast enough."

"Yes, Captain!"

The fuel cells blasted into action. The Solar Wind surged forward. Quite a few new crewmembers sat down suddenly.

Shawn had followed the Captain to the bridge. This was another playground full of technological wonders. Shawn couldn't get enough of all the beautiful electronics! The ship console and all the controls took up the width, more or less, of a piano. The "mixing desk", as Shawn thought of the panels of buttons and indicators, was flat to allow the Captain or the helmsman a clear view to the outside, from the bridge over the main deck, to the prow, and to the ocean beyond. If all electronics failed, Shawn realized that one could run the Solar Wind manually, by visuals and wind. Basic; effective. He was impressed.

The Captain was monitoring the helm that was on autopilot with his left hand while his right moved over the keyboard of the console. Readings showed on the various screens.

"Who is this ship?" asked Shawn, pointing to the blipping dot that showed on the electromagnetic grid. The reading was somewhat clearer from down here. The Unicate ship had a huge electromagnetic presence; it had to carry all sorts of charge.

"The Hun. Ship of Anya Miller." Lascek grinned, a cold light in his eyes as the console reflected in them. "Old enemy of mine. Very ambitious woman, Unicate navy officer. She tends to bend the rules. I caused her a ruffle from her superiors once. Been following me around ever since. Let Old Sherman tell you that story some time."

Dr Judith was walking amongst the crew in the boardroom with oxygen masks for those who needed it. "Don't panic, this is normal," she told the newcomers. "We're just evading some troubles on the surface. Would you like some oxygen? Oh my, Ailyss has passed out. Ronan Donegal, won't you please revive her?" She handed him another oxygen mask to hold over Ailyss' face.

The Captain kept his eyes fixed on the dot on the screen.

"Blast! We're not losing them! Going under is usually enough for most other ships."

"Do they ever try to follow us below, Captain?" asked Shawn.

Radomir Lascek studied the witty Donegal Trouble for a second. Shawn gnawed his lip, hoping Captain's sense of humour was active tonight.

"That Anya is a tough customer!" The Captain peered at the screens and muttered a Hungarian expression. At least, Shawn hoped it was Hungarian. "We should mask. Be ready, Donegal. Don't get scared now." He punched the intercom to the machine room again. "Dr Jake, we're masking. Be ready. Shawn, sit down!"

"Yes, Captain." Shawn obeyed, wondering what that 'masking' entailed.

Lascek waited until the Hun was nearly upon them. Shawn held his breath. Nerve-racking stuff! Was the enemy ship going to send a torpedo? The Captain hit a sequence of buttons. Everything went completely dark. The Solar Wind blended into her surrounds. Her radar-diffusing coating, paired with the absence of any electricity or light made her invisible on the enemy ship's varied detection systems.

"Worried, Doc?"

"Very! Captain hasn't disengaged the electrics underwater in a long time!"

Paean's ears peaked at the whispered conversation between Doc Judith and Sherman Dougherty.

"Enemy must be right overhead," said the old storyteller.

Paean felt someone take hold of her sleeve in the dark and nearly lost her balance with fright. A firm hand closed its long wiry fingers around her wrist and guided her own hand to the back of a chair. The Solar Wind

49

was still listing and rolling a bit.

"Sit down," ordered the gypsy's voice by her ear, almost inaudibly. "Could hurt yourself!"

She found the seat by touch and complied, a bit put out. She had been doing fine before he pulled her off-balance!

"Why are the lights off?"

"Don't worry, sunshine," whispered Federi. " 's a standard procedure. But we all have to be dead quiet!"

He ponged of pub! Smoke and alcohol! Not ale though, that smelt subtly different. Something stronger, sweeter. Rum perhaps?

"Federi, you're drunk!" she hissed, annoyed. Sheesh!

"Am not! You'll also smell like this after a seedy gig!"

"What was the mission – fratting with the enemy?"

What a little spitfire! Federi's falcon eyebrows lifted as he tried to work out how he had deserved that attack.

"Why is it so important?" he asked.

Paean laughed softly. "It's not! Go stink to yourself in the dark, why don't you, Mr Thieves' Honour!"

"Ah!" So that was it. A broken promise! Federi grinned to himself. "Think you'd want to give me back my microphone?"

"Nope," said Paean. " 's a handy little item."

"Can't do anything without its other half," Federi pointed out.

"Neither can you."

"I can hear everything you say."

"Can't, either!"

"You were singing some opera music this afternoon," said Federi.

" 's your imagination," said Paean. "Ro has disabled it! With a hammer."

Federi paused. She could tell that he was – well, a bit doused. Like a drenched poodle. She grinned with glee.

"Well…" the gypsy said tentatively, "will it help if I say I'm sorry?"

"I'm not upset," smiled Paean. "Anyway you're fickle. I'll accept your apology, knowing that you'll do it again soon. There's no curing you."

"Will you two be quiet back there," hissed a voice. "We're masking!"

"Sorry, Jon," the gypsy hissed back. His sinewy hand briefly closed

50

over Paean's wrist once more. *"Kathal,* Twinkletoes!" Then he was gone. Gone off to stink in the darkness. Paean shook her head, puzzled. Twinkletoes -?

They waited. Ronan had managed to revive Ailyss with the oxygen mask, for which he had received a venomous look just before the lights went out. Now he stood in the dark feeling slighted.

Rhine Gold was counting down time in his head. One a potato, two a potato, three a potato... how long was this still going to go on? He wondered if any of the female crew were in any way approachable for a little tête-à-tête in the dark. Let's see. There was Ailyss – no, she was certainly not approachable. Rushka plain smacked of danger! Who else was female? Doc Judith was surely a bit old. Sixtyish, he'd guess. He was wary of her too. The last time he had encountered her by accident in a dark, lonely passageway, he had been overpowered with a Vitamin B injection! He always looked both ways now before venturing to and from his cabin on the lower deck.

Sheesh, not much of a choice on this boat! All the females were dangerous!

And then he remembered there was also little Paean. Young, childish, and a tomboy too, but if one thought about it, actually really the only one who was in any way a possibility. Perhaps if one chiselled at her she might get more ladylike. He'd have to work on it quite a bit though; this ship with all its hard work turned every sailor into a man, even the girls. See Rushka. So he'd have to get at it while Paean wasn't yet a proper sailor. Then again, Rhine Gold liked such mathematical challenges. He began to work on a plan. It never occurred to him that perhaps she was more dangerous than all the others put together.

Wolf and Dr Jake were down in the machine room by the smallest ray of a micro-torch. They had to see what they were doing; they were getting the other drives ready for when Captain needed them.

Sherman Dougherty cooked up a brand new story in his head. And then he designed the holes into it, especially for Ronan Donegal. He was rather disappointed that the young man hadn't picked his last one apart. And he had built in such beautiful inconsistencies! He'd have to tell Federi not to punish a questioning young mind for being a critical thinker.

Shawn was on the bridge with Captain Lascek, learning the ropes of a pirate escaping the law.

"Quiet, Shawn," whispered Captain Lascek. "They have sound detection on. But they won't pick up a whisper, not over the noise of their own ship. We're drifting away from them now. Anya must have forgotten that there are counter currents down here, flowing opposite to the surface current. Or perhaps the Unicate Marines don't have that information."

"Pardon, Captain?"

"We're in an undertow," explained Lascek. "That's why we had to go deeper: To get ourselves positioned in it. I suspect it's in fact part of the oceanic conveyor belt. That flows south, right here, and it comes surprisingly near the surface. Would be interesting to find out why. Could be a thermal current too though. The Solar Wind picked up the turbulences. Anya's on the surface, where the Gulf Stream is moving her north. The currents are moving our ships apart without me doing a single thing."

"But won't they just follow?" worried Shawn.

Lascek laughed silently. "They've passed us, and they were going at an ape velocity when they did, and it took them a good few seconds to stop their own movement, and now they're not sure where to look for us. Even if they cease their engines to listen for us, we'll simply drift away from them."

"What are they listening for?" breathed Shawn.

"Well, any sound at all; any light; any slightest signal. The electric disturbance outside is working against them. Fudging their signal a bit. Dr Jake and Wolf are working on an electronic shield for the Solar Wind, but it's not yet ready for use. Son, you'll love this ship once you know everything about her. You won't want to leave."

"I already don't want to leave," whispered Shawn. "I'm crazy about this boat and everyone on her. Well, everyone except – that is –"

Captain Lascek chuckled soundlessly. "Out with it, boy! You dislike Verushka Lascek?"

Shawn paused. "Verushka – *Lascek*? Is that Rushka?"

"She's my daughter," said the Captain, and Shawn clearly heard the pride in his voice. Lucky Rushka, thought Shawn. She has a dad and he's proud of her!

"No, Rushka's cool," he said. "*Really* cool! But Ailyss. I don't think I like her very much. She's *strange*."

"Good instincts, Donegal. I wonder about the older Donegal, though."

"Ronan? He warned me of her. But he didn't have to, I've got my own sense of danger. Captain, if we're pirates, what are girls doing aboard?"

Radomir Lascek laughed softly.

"Aren't you glad that they are? Or your own sister would have had to stay behind!"

"Och, but – she's not a *girl*," said Shawn. "That's different!"

"She's not a girl?" The Captain was amused. "What is she then?"

"Och, just – one of the guys," said Shawn.

Lascek smiled. "So, Shawn, what's your sense of danger telling you right now?"

Shawn listened for a moment. The Solar Wind rolled a bit, shifted a bit, listed a bit on the undersea current. She was also very slowly turning, he thought. Drifting without drives. He reached out with his "sense of danger" to detect the foreign vessel. It was far away, out there somewhere behind them, circling and steadily moving away in the wrong direction.

"They've lost us," he concluded. "I may be wrong, Captain. It just feels like that."

"I second that, Captain," came Rushka's quiet comment behind them. Shawn jolted with surprise.

"Good, both of you! Now let's test your theory."

Lascek sent a single, minute satellite blip in the surmised direction of the Hun. The signal came back, somewhat distorted, but still confirming what both the Captain and Shawn had sensed: They had practically shaken off their pursuers. The Hun was bobbing about in the far distance trawling for submerged objects with loud satellite and radar signals.

Captain Lascek activated the com. "Dr Jake, come in!"

"Captain," came the quiet response from the machine room.

"Empty the ballasts. Get the nu – the *special* drives ready but don't activate until I give the signal. We rise to the surface quietly, no sound, no light, minimal power. They're searching for a submarine now."

"Alright, Captain," Dr Jake's hushed voice acknowledged.

The Captain turned. "Shawn! Go find Mr Marsden and relay these orders: When we surface, still no lights or sound. We're sailing due east. Will turn later. Don't trip in the dark!"

"Okay, Captain!" whispered Shawn. He felt his way to the companionway that led from the bridge directly below deck.

Slowly the Solar Wind rose to the surface in the pitch dark. If Anya Miller the Hun had known where to look, if she had been close enough, if there had perhaps not been any haze, she would have witnessed a reversal of what she had seen before: The beautiful white ship surfacing, raising its two masts, stretching out its rigging like arms after a good sleep, keeping the sails furled though, and then – there was a flash of light and the Solar Wind shot away across the ocean.

As it happened, Miller did see the flash of light.

"What?!" What were they doing that far south?

"If that was the Solar Wind, we'll never catch her now," said her First Mate.

Captain Miller was furious.

"Follow!" she snapped. "We'll catch her! We're on a Pursuer, for crying out loud!"

A cheer went up on the Solar Wind when the lights went back on. Shawn went looking for Federi, and found him in the galley, alone, clearing up and making coffee for everyone. He told him about the currents.

"If Captain Lascek knew about the currents, didn't that other ship know too? Why didn't they compensate and calculate it in?"

"That is the beauty of the Solar Wind," said Federi with a grin. "You were so lucky to be on the bridge with Captain!"

"What do you mean?"

"The Solar Wind is not your usual ship," said Federi. "Other ships have functions built into their processors that find the path of least resistance on the ocean, consistently and reliably. The processor plots the smoothest course. Is a case of humans too reliant on their technology for their own good. You're still going to see how our Captain exploits that! Ditto with our getaway from Hamilton harbour!" He laughed softly. "Fact is that Captain uses this kind of information consciously where

54

others let their ship's computer do the work. *That* is what!" He handed a mug of hot coffee to Shawn. "Captain knows most minor currents on Earth's oceans personally. He actively seeks them out. Part of what makes this ship so fast!"

"But how does he know about the undersea current? Is it on the map?"

"Doubt it. Old maps perhaps." Federi rolled his eyes. "Donegal, if you must know. The Solar Wind is a very special ship. Her outside is – shall we say – like skin. There are sensors everywhere. She knows every current, every change in temperature, every shark that comes nibbling. The ship computer is constantly processing the information from the sensors. We know a lot more about Earth's oceans than any other ship out there. But you keep that mum!"

"Captain is a genius," said Shawn, marvelling.

"That's why he's a pirate. Nobody must tell Captain 'You can't have more sensors on your ship, you must have a license'. Nobody must say, 'You can't hire Shawn Donegal, he's too young.' Captain doesn't like walls."

The Captain appeared in the galley's doorway.

"Just so, Federi," he agreed, accepting the mug of coffee the Romany handed him. "She'll tail us for days now. She's a tough one to shake. But she won't catch up. Not now."

"How many days, Captain?" asked Federi apprehensively. They were only stocked for four or five. And when they landed in Plymouth, what was to prevent Miller from bringing down the local forces on them? Sometimes he wished they could just sink the woman. Couple of torpedoes ought to sort it.

"Not scared, are you, Tzigan?" Radomir Lascek narrowed his eyes at his gypsy, amused.

"Just worried," admitted Federi. Shawn watched the Captain and the cook. Two contrasting attitudes to danger!

"We'll double up on fishing," decided Lascek. "Don't worry."

When Shawn got out onto the deck the next morning, he noticed the Captain was in a great mood.

"That Hun is still following our trail," Federi explained to Shawn when the boy reported to the galley and asked about it. "We're leaving a trail for her to follow."

"What kind of trail?" asked Shawn, fascinated.

"Potato peels."

Potato peels! "Why?"

"Because after she follows them, the squid can eat them. Captain doesn't believe in pollution."

"And then we eat the squid," laughed Rhine Gold, who was peeling potatoes again. Mostly for the peels, Shawn realized.

"But why is he leaving a trail?" he insisted.

"Let's just say, he likes playing games," grinned Federi as he chopped an onion with a virtuoso staccato movement. Shawn watched, impressed. He had a sinister notion that Federi would have preferred it to be Anya Miller there on the chopping board.

He seated himself across from Rhine Gold at the huge, heavy Ironwood table. Federi had secured that table for the galley at an auction many years ago. The table dated back to the early pioneers' days of Ovimba, in Southern Free Country. The Ironwood table had been fastened to the floor with serious bolts, because anybody who got squashed by this solid piece of furniture during a storm or sudden manoeuvre would be gravely injured if not killed.

"What is the Hun's problem?" asked Shawn.

"Well, she's Unicate," said Federi. "And of course, injured pride. Captain Radomir and Anya Miller have a feud on as old as the sea. 's been going so long it's almost a love affair."

"Och no," commented Shawn, disgusted. "That's so – urgh!"

"With you there, Donegal," said the gypsy, frowning. "Federi thinks it's a huge risk. She wants us dead. She's a bounty hunter, thinks that's how she's going to make her fortune. 's a lot of cash. Probably wants it to retire from the military. Course by now it's personal." He glanced up from the onions. "Shawn, we know how to deal with bounty hunters. The problem is that she's a bounty hunter with the whole Unicate military at her fingertips."

Shawn said nothing for a few moments. Then he looked up.

"So the Captain of the Hun wants to have Captain Lascek put to *death* for *money*, and because he hurt her *pride*? And Captain doesn't want us to defend ourselves because he's in –"

"Quiet!" Federi held up his hand. "Haven't you been listening to Sherman, boy?"

"What do you mean?"

The Captain peered into the galley.

"Coffee, Captain?" asked Federi, getting up.

"No, that's fine, Federi," replied Lascek with a grin. "Just checking…" He went off, whistling. Shawn stared after him, rattled. "Sheesh! Who's the pirate in this equation?"

"Us, always us," said Federi lightly. "Never get that mixed up. Aargh! I detest onions, yodiho!" He wiped at his burning eyes with his colourful flared sleeve.

Shawn reached out and took over dicing the onion, starting to cry right away.

"There aren't that many potatoes left," said Federi. "Got to get to Plymouth soon!"

"And if she follows us all the way to Plymouth?"

"I think the potatoes will run out before that," said Federi. He glanced up at Shawn's confused face and laughed. "Don't worry! Captain would never let her sink the Solar Wind!"

Don't worry? Shawn iced. Suddenly it felt to him as though it weren't a joke at all.

Federi watched him. The chill had reached him too. He feared that Captain was underestimating the Unicate viper. There was something terrible aboard her ship. He had sensed it last night.

"But why should it be personal?" asked Shawn, dumping the chopped onion in the electric wok.

"Complex question. She was demoted because of him," said Federi. "She bends the rules, abuses Unicate resources. Deserted her post, I suspect. What do you suppose that bunch of Stabs at Hamilton was about?"

"Not about us, surely?" asked Shawn.

"Can't be ruled out, can it? But I fear they are in fact taking over Hamilton Port. Manila went that way, last time we passed there. Worrying that, in the Pacific. That's not even Unicate territory! Wonder if the Rebellion has conquered that place back yet."

"But why is the Unicate doing that?"

57

"Clamping down on deviants," said Federi. "They're just following their program. World domination."

The Crow's Nest beeped on Shawn's wrist.

"Sorry, Federi, can't do the onions," he exclaimed, dropping his knife and running down the passage towards the companionway to the hatch.

Federi stared after him, wondering. Those three Donegals! He couldn't piece it together. The oldest, Ronan, was reserved and very responsible, if completely unforthcoming about his past. Shawn was downright chatty and light-hearted, although there were topics he shied away from like a cat from something rotten. And the girl – whatever haunted her was eating her alive. Every time he spotted her she looked a bit more harassed and less sane. And – she wasn't allowing him to help. Skittish. No trust.

Whatever she had done, he knew Captain would get to the bottom of it. He heaved a sigh. Then what in hell had been the point in rescuing the three of them from Dublin?

It would probably not matter, in the big scheme of things. Captain was playing a far too dangerous game with that Mad Miller woman. Federi knew he had to get behind the truth of what was hiding on her ship, before it killed them all.

Even as Shawn scaled the ropes, he spotted the small dot in the distance. He activated his wrist-com.

"Captain, ship approaching fifteen degrees port."

Captain Lascek was already on the bridge next to his daughter Rushka, having received the Crow's Nest signal too. He keyed a few variables into the ship computer.

"Well done, Donegal," came his answer on Shawn's com. "Friends on their way. The vessel is the Sea Eagle. Ali Hlabane's boat."

"It was the Solar Wind who spotted her, sir, not me," said Shawn.

Captain Lascek punched in a few more figures. A blip from the satellite answered his question. The Hun was far behind, but still tailing them. She'd catch up with them in two hours if they stopped.

"Blast that woman!" he muttered. "This is going to be tricky! No time for visiting." Anya Miller would not be following the Solar Wind if she didn't have the facilities to disable the ship.

"She didn't shoot last night," Jon Marsden pointed out. "She didn't use shock either although she was practically on top of us! She could have, even without knowing where we were. It would have fried our processor. That would have killed us, because we would have had no way of surfacing. We have to look into that, Captain. We must find a way of emptying the ballasts manually. It's a weak point of the Solar Wind."

"Clearly," said Lascek, "she didn't want that to happen. I wonder why not!"

"Didn't want to lose the prize money," said Marsden. "She needs to bring us in, dead or alive, as proof that she captured us. She'd never have found us if she had sent shock. We're radar cloaked."

Radomir Lascek nodded gravely.

"That's not the same as not wanting us dead," Marsden pointed out.

"Dead or alive, Jon?"

"That's the contract, Captain. You know it."

"Right! Of course, if we're already badly damaged and immobilized, and all she has to do is walk aboard and collect us…"

"Piratical," grinned Jonathan Marsden.

"Ancient trick," replied Radomir Lascek.

5

Abandoned

Federi listened up. There were voices, singing! A powerful chorus of voices he knew could only be from one place...

He dropped the knife and the onions and headed for the deck at a fast stroll. Hell, they had started without him! The crew was already throwing mooring lines across to the beautiful blue hundred-foot Penbrook yacht with its triangular aero-solar sails that had drawn up alongside the Solar Wind. Its automatic gangway extended across the gap. Wolf was on the deck along with the other sailors, waving madly and singing loudly with Captain Ali's crew – the anthem of Southern Free. Ronan was listening intently, and Shawn was picking up on the harmonies.

Federi glanced up into the rigging. The Crow's Nest was empty. Usually it was him, up there, shouting those first words of the anthem. And them answering! Arw hell, and he had missed it!

Captain Ali Hlabane, a short, powerful African man in a white playboy suit with keen, highly amused eyes, walked across the gangway first, leading the way for his crew. The five Africans streamed onto the Solar Wind, laughing, shaking hands, clapping arms, collecting hi-fives from the Solar Wind's crew while the new sailors looked on with wide eyes.

"Federi," asked Shawn by his side, "what's so special about these people?"

The gypsy glanced at him with a five-mile grin. "What's so special? Shawn, just look at these guys! They've got Freedom all over their personalities and they bring it wherever they go! Besides they're great friends of the Solar Wind. Hey there, Vusi!" He moved into the melee, joining in the greetings.

Shawn watched. Captain Ali was very well dressed; his yacht also smacked of luxury. On his hands he wore several heavy gold rings. His left wrist sported not a wrist-com but a classic Swiss luxury watch. And his face, a grin second to none.

Captain Lascek clapped a hand on Hlabane's shoulder.

"How are you, old pirate?"

"Glad to see you too, Radomir, old sea-devil," replied Ali. "What are you up to?"

"I've got the Hun on my tail," said Lascek with a grin.

"Bummer," Ali grinned back.

"She'll be here in another two hours. You in the mood for some sports?"

The visiting Captain nodded enthusiastically.

"Let's get the supplies out of the way first, my friend," said Ali. "You're short, you say. I can help you out."

At the orders of Captain Ali, the crews of both ships began to carry crates aboard the Solar Wind and stow them in the storage deck.

"Got my goodies?" Ali asked as he and Lascek watched from the Solar Wind's bridge. Lascek opened a cabinet.

"As promised. Now what can I offer you, Ali?"

"Nothing alcoholic, Radomir," said Ali. "Give me a Coke. Got to keep my wits sharp too if the Hun decides to question me."

Coca-cola, the favourite drink of the 20th and 21st centuries, had made it into the 22nd. Despite nuclear wars and the Unicate. A resilient beverage. Lascek poured a glass and handed it to Ali. He paged Doc Judith to the bridge.

"Hamilton Port, taken by the Unicate," said Hlabane, turning serious. "They're forcing us back into the Pacific!" He mulled. "That complicates things. I can't restock there any more than you can. We must make another plan for more provisions. But at least, if we both keep on fishing, you should make it through to Panama and I should manage until Rabat."

"Ali," said Lascek seriously, "not trading girls, are you?"

Captain Hlabane grinned. "Are you making an offer?"

"I seriously hope that's a joke!"

"Radomir," laughed Ali, "the only girl I've got aboard is my own personal property! I'm not trading her! Not even for Rushka!"

"You've laid off the slaving?"

"You injure me, Radomir," said Ali. "I've never been a slaver! You

61

took all those jokes seriously?"

"You never know," growled the Captain sheepishly. He had believed Hlabane about the slave trade. Even now he wasn't entirely sure if he ought to believe the denial.

"I only trade guns," replied Ali. "Just breaking into a brand new market. Highly specific electronic weapons. Potent enough to sink a city. Just learning the ropes. Got a marvellous mentor."

"Should introduce me," said Lascek.

"I will, one day! She's sure pretty enough for you!" The Southern Free man grinned. "Still trading ships, Radomir?"

"Of course!"

"That was no joke?"

"No."

"And they still haven't caught you?"

"Not that they didn't try!"

"You're not the Unicate's favourite civilian then, are you!"

"You'd be surprised," smiled Lascek. "They keep throwing money in my direction! What concerns supplies? I think I have an idea! Ah, here's Dr Judith."

The doctor handed a small metal case to Captain Ali. He disengaged the safety lock and peered inside. Two neat rows of little vials sat embedded in a wooden frame. He whistled softly through his teeth.

"Nice! This stuff works?"

"All of us have already had ours," said Dr Judith. "This stuff is gold. Don't lose it."

Ali nodded. "Thank you, doctor," he said, extending a hand which she gave a brief shake.

"Welcome, Captain Hlabane." She left the bridge to return to her work.

"Now," said Ali. "As for your plan?"

"Have a seat!"

Shawn watched all the highly excited activity on the deck and between the ships from the hatch. It seemed as though things were being printed and pasted and painted and programmed. Data cubes wandered back and forth. The gypsy cook was suddenly next to him.

"Supervising them, Shawn?"

"What are we doing now?" Shawn asked back.

"What pirates do best," grinned Federi. "Watch and learn!"

Aboard the Hun, the officers watched a worrying scenario on the electronic screen.

"Looks as though another ship has spotted Lascek and has opened fire," commented young Johnny Anyhow, the First Mate, locking onto the second ship's electronic identity. "Aha. Satellite identifies her as the Santa Anna. She's famous," he added. "Name rings a loud bell. Captain is – it's on the tip of my tongue –"

"Phineas Skebengo," read Captain Miller, annoyed. Was someone else going to palm in her reward? "Depraved bounty hunters!"

"Ah yes, Skebengo." Johnny Anyhow nodded sagely. "Heard a lot about him."

"Such as what?" snapped Anya Miller, paging impatiently through the spotless history of the Santa Anna's captain.

"Good guy. Has stopped a drug-syndicate in Oceania. Or was that Captain Hawkins from the Espagnola?"

"Stop gabbling, Anyhow!" Miller glared at him. "How did you come by such a name, anyhow? One can't really use it!"

The First Mate shut his mouth, rattled. Head Office had assigned him to her, not by her own choice. First Mate at age nineteen! But she had accepted it without a complaint, even welcomed it. He suspected that Miller was so ambitious she didn't want anyone with too much experience as a second-in-command. It wasn't a comforting position either – her prior First Mate had disappeared mysteriously.

Captain Anya Miller watched the battle of the two ships ahead of them with a sinking heart. Skebengo was a damned civilian! How had he got his filthy hands on such sophisticated firepower -? Enormous electric discharges were flying to and fro, invisible to the eye but recorded by her systems. She wasn't going to ask where Lascek had got hold of his stun charges! Her console showed that even under water, torpedoes with electric hypercharge were hitting the Solar Wind. Clearly Skebengo was after the bounty money: He didn't want to damage the hull of the ship, just disable the processor and stun the crew. She laughed cynically.

Without his precious processor, Lascek had only one way of submerging the Solar Wind – permanently.

Then a distress signal came from the Solar Wind, probably sent automatically by the ship's system itself as the processor failed.

"Ha! The old crook! He's met his nemesis!" growled Captain Miller. "His ship's in trouble. He can't move!" She got angry. "Nobody else must get to him first! I'm the one who must turn him in! I've worked years for this moment!"

Her ship com activated. She listened with amazement to the patchy signal from the Solar Wind's dying com system.

"Anya," came Radomir Lascek's voice, deep and resonant, but sounding somehow broken. The signal certainly was. "Help! I know you're there! Save us!"

What! He was begging her for help? The old pirate thought she would actually step in on his behalf?

"My crew is out cold," pleaded Lascek. "These guys are taking us apart! If they board we are finished! You're our last hope, Anya! You're Unicate! Have a heart! In the name of fair play!"

He was delivering himself into her hands? Captain Anya Miller smiled as she hit the button.

"I don't believe it! Are you surrendering? I'll take you to Headquarters, you know it!"

"Anything! Anything you say! It must be better than watching my crew be slaughtered by these bounty hunters! They're a good crew, Anya. They don't deserve to die!" Another shockwave travelled between the two ships. "Aargh," said Radomir Lascek.

"Hang in there, Radomir," called Anya Miller. She switched the direction of her intercom, pushed a sequence, and the Hun charged forward.

"Attention, Santa Anna," Miller sent to the other ship's intercom. "Thank you for intercepting the Solar Wind. We'll take it from here."

"Acknowledged," called Captain Skebengo with a strong African accent. "Captain Miller, this is Captain Phineas Skebengo of the SFS Santa Anna speaking. We have apprehended the pirate Radomir Lascek of the Solar Wind. You will ensure that we get our remuneration?"

"It's already on record. I'll see to it personally," lied Miller. There

64

was no way she was going to share her prize money! She'd deal with Skebengo when she'd finished with Lascek. Easy enough to concoct a story of Skebengo being another lawbreaker, which he probably was, in fact, who wasn't? Her crew were behind her, they'd back her story, especially if it could be fortified with some grains of truth. It didn't take Miller a second to plot this manoeuvre.

The Hun circled the Solar Wind, wedging the pirate between her and the Santa Anna. Ropes shot across, hooking onto the Solar Wind's rail and pulling the Pursuer up alongside, closing the gap. Captain Miller and her officers boarded the Solar Wind, leaving only the technician aboard the Hun, holding the bridge.

There was no one on the Solar Wind's deck. Nobody on the bridge either; the console was dark. This was most disappointing!

"Lascek, come out! You're surrounded! Give it up, old villain!" Anya Miller got no response. Absolutely nothing stirred aboard the Solar Wind.

"You're finished, Radomir," said Anya, more to herself. "Time to negotiate for the lives of your crew, I think."

It had occurred to her a moment back that she could win both ways in this one. Radomir Lascek himself was rumoured to have considerable financial resources. She wondered how much he would pay over to her for the freedom of each of his crewmembers. She could arrange that freedom easily, just place them all on his motorized lifeboat and send them off; the Unicate only had a reward on his head and the actual bringing in of the ship, not on the rest of the crew. But she might as well force the money out of him and then have them all executed for the criminals they were, anyway; bribery or its attempt was illegal in itself.

Radomir Lascek had to care about his crew a lot if he were prepared to deliver himself into the hands of the Unicate in a futile effort to spare their lives. This worried her. It was, in fact, an illogical move she couldn't quite understand. She understood her own response to it even less. She didn't want to dwell on the idea that perhaps he had some gentleness in his character, or perhaps she ought to admire his courage. It complicated things, and interfered with her plans.

"Radomir, come out! Don't you want to negotiate? Aargh, the old coward!"

It was disappointing. She had expected at least a heroic show of resistance from her old enemy – or perhaps she would have enjoyed seeing the look on his face when he admitted that she had won. This – all of them cowering below deck in fear – this was almost demeaning. It certainly took the sparkle out of the capture! Anya Miller entered the hatch and descended the companionway into the upper deck, aware of her crew following right behind her.

It was dark down there. Doors were closed; blinds covered any open portholes. She had left the hatch open; light filtered into the passage from above. The Santa Anna had indeed scrambled the entire electrics of the ship with her shockwaves.

Right by the companionway a young girl lay groaning. Her eyes were shut. Miller kneeled down, looking closer. The shockwaves had not only damaged the ship. Could this be the explanation for Lascek not responding to her summons – that he was stunned too, senseless? Or even dead? Unfamiliar panic crept over Miller.

"What's your name, girl?" she asked.

The little redhead moaned. "Watch," she mumbled vaguely. "Watch out…"

"What do you mean, girl?" Anya Miller leaned over her to hear her better.

"Pirates!" said the girl, sitting up suddenly and banging her head against that of Captain Miller. "Ooh! Ouch! Rats!"

The pirates descended on the officers of the Hun from all sides. Anya Miller felt strong hands restraining her. Not that she could have moved, currently; she was seeing stars from the collision. The girl's head had caught her right across the eyes.

"You can't do this, Lascek!" she protested. "You're surrounded and you're outnumbered."

"I can do," came his voice right by her ear, "whatever I like, Anya. Don't forget, I'm a pirate."

The pirate Captain grinned at her out of the darkness. "Now, allow me." She found her wrists tied behind her back and her feet tied together. Captain Lascek picked her up and put her down in the big comfortable swivel chair in the ship meeting room. He tied a few more ropes around her.

He had said it himself! She mustn't forget that he was a criminal! She wouldn't forget it ever again, this she promised herself.

"I shan't speak for you in the Unicate court," she said acidly.

"Comfortable, my dear?"

"You'll regret this," hissed Miller. "Captain Skebengo is right behind me."

"My friend Phineas Skebengo?" asked Radomir Lascek. He flicked a switch and the lights came on. All five Miller's marines were tied to chairs around her.

"Anya," said Radomir Lascek, "thank you for heeding my call for help. It tells me that there's a soft spot somewhere in your embittered little heart. You said something about negotiating earlier?"

"For the lives of your crew," Anya ground out through clenched teeth. "It occurred to me that you called for my help so that your crew can survive. You know that you're a dead man walking, don't you. But there's no particular reward on their heads, so I thought you might want to buy their lives!"

"Anya!" Lascek smiled. "How thoughtful of you! They're good pirates, you know. Loyal to the last soul! Even our little spy. I'd never hand them over to the Unicate, never. But I'm willing to make a trade anyway, for your sake. My crew goes free, and in exchange we help ourselves to your food supplies. It seems as though we can't restock at Hamilton anymore."

"You wouldn't dare -!"

"Thanks, Anya! Kind of you," smiled Lascek.

Ronan held a cold pack against his sister's head.

"You're a hero, Pae. Well knocked!"

She laughed. "I don't think I've ever had such pleasure hurting myself! Thanks, Ro, that's better!" She picked herself up from the deck. She did indeed feel fantastic. It was hugely empowering to knock out the enemy.

"Hey," said Ronan, pointing down the passage. "What's with him?"

Paean followed her brother. Wolf Svendsson was sitting on the floor, holding his head in both hands. Paean crouched down, a hand on the scruffy young engineer's shoulder.

"Are you okay, Wolf?"

"Will be in a second," muttered Wolf, keeping his eyes closed. "Blasted Unicate and their blasted stun guns!"

"Someone stunned you?"

"Hells, yes. Feels like my brain's been rewired!"

"Come, Wolf," said Ronan, helping the muscular young sailor up. He and Paean supported Wolf down to the small yellow infirmary, and onto one of the bunks.

"Sorry, guys," said Wolf with a grin. He shut his eyes again.

"Nothing!" retorted Paean. "You couldn't help that! They shot at you! Is there something I can get you? Glass of water? Painkiller?"

"Nah," replied Wolf. "Thanks."

"Want me to stay here a bit?"

"Nah, don't worry," said Wolf. "I'll get over this in a second."

The two Donegals left him and made their way back up the dark passageway. Paean thought that she'd have to come back in a while and open all the blinds and curtains. She hoped Wolf would be all right.

Shawn stood in the Crow's Nest, watching the goings-on between the three ships with delighted fascination. The Sea Eagle had circled to the other side of the Hun, and both crews had boarded the military ship. The helmsman who had stayed aboard the Hun was tied up. The crews of the Solar Wind and the Sea Eagle looted the food stores of the Hun, which had just been replenished at Hamilton. Anya Miller had known that the Solar Wind was headed for the Pacific, so she had stocked up well. Practically all of the Unicate guns went to Captain Ali, boosting his trade. Then Captain Ali and his men helped Lascek's crew put Anya and her officers back onto their own ship, on the outer deck.

Federi was on a mission of his own, trailing through the enemy ship. She was a beautiful vessel; speed and economy of design was written all over her. The crew cabins were larger than the cubicles of the Solar Wind; the Captain's Quarters downright spacious. But there were only eight crew cabins. Each could house four crew, with two sets of pull-down stack bunks on opposing walls, like those of the Solar Wind. A force of thirty-two? They could accomplish things, actually! But Miller

68

only had five. Clearly this bounty hunt wasn't too well supported by the military headquarters.

Five? And she set after the Solar Wind? It told him more than that. Firstly, she must know how under-crewed the Solar Wind was. Not counting the Donegals, there were ten – and she couldn't know about the Donegals, as Captain had kept them hidden in both Dublin and near Hamilton. Though Federi had no doubt she knew about Rhine Gold, and seeing that she was a Unicate insider, probably about Ailyss too. If Ailyss was indeed a Unicate spy, as Captain suspected.

But more, it told him of her intended strategy. With only five marines, you didn't plan to board a pirate. No. Miller's main aim had been to disable the ship from a distance. And then? Call in reinforcements, no doubt.

The Unicate's favourite colour was unfortunately grey; the compounding that lined the decks and the colour of the hull and walls was grey. It saved the compounding the effort of fading to grey over time.

The bridge was slightly more spacious than that of the Solar Wind. Federi cracked the code on the safe following a hunch. As it opened, he grinned smugly. Anya Miller was so egocentric that the password she had used was an anagram of her own name! He rummaged a bit; inside the safe there were various interesting-looking items, data chips, cubes, quite a bit of money, some rings and a sealed capsule that radiated evil. He slipped everything into his pocket.

On the deck, Anya Miller fumed while the pirates had amiable conversations with her marines.

"Tell me one thing," said Johnny Anyhow good-naturedly. "How on Earth did you guys survive such blasts?"

"It's an illusion," replied Jon Marsden with a smile. "We've cooked your detectors with long-distance program overrides. Want to join us? I'll show you how it's done."

Johnny Anyhow shook his head, shocked. He had just been invited to become a pirate! If these pirates only knew how numbered their days were, with or without today's fancy manoeuvre…

In their position today, he would have killed Anya Miller and her crew to the last man. Plain survival. Why were they taking such care not to harm anyone?

Captain Ali's ship departed first, with the two ships' crews waving madly at each other and wishing each other fair winds and happy trading. The Sea Eagle would sail off in another direction, then change course as she changed her identity back to the original. Ali Hlabane was especially gleeful about the false name he had picked. It wasn't really an African name. But Anya Miller wouldn't know; she had never been to Southern Free. Skebengo meant vagabond. But the digital history of the fictitious Phineas Skebengo was that of an angel.

Radomir Lascek was keeping Anya Miller company on the Hun. He had sent his sailors back to the Solar Wind; once everything was organized and Captain Ali had a decent head start, he was going to release Anya Miller and return to his own ship himself, and set sail. He waited for the signal from his First Mate. Finally he got impatient. He punched a button on his wrist-com.

"Jon, what is the situation? Can we sail?"

"Still waiting for Federi, Captain. He's still aboard the Hun."

"Aargh! What's he doing so long?"

"Probably picking all the cabins clean," commented Jon Marsden unkindly.

Federi was by now in the bowels of the enemy ship. In his many years as a fugitive he had learnt one thing more loudly than anything else. You ignored a hunch at your peril.

The machine room of the Pursuer was like the rest of the ship: Sleek, frugal, minimalist. And grey. Federi's eyes darted to the water desalination system – smaller than the version they had on the Solar Wind, but newer. The huge hydrogen drives, powered by fuel cells, were mainly situated near the stern, with smaller drives for steering bursts lining the sides of the machine room. A highly manoeuvrable craft! Federi sighed. Almost, a man could dream.

Between the side drives, torpedo guns were mounted into the hull. That made sense, for a military craft. Federi investigated the nature of the

70

torpedoes. There were conventional ones that merely ripped holes into the enemy vessel by exploding on impact; there were electric discharge torpedoes that could fry a ship's electrics when fully charged, without destroying the hull. He also found a more sinister type of torpedo, the kind that hooked into the hull of a ship, drilled a hole and released poison gas. All of those missiles were heat-seeking, and capable of homing in on vibrations. He shuddered. She could have killed them any number of ways last night, by disabling their machinery or poisoning them while they were under water if Captain hadn't switched off the power.

But none of this accounted for the horrible feeling of foreboding, the evil presence he sensed. The hair in the back of his neck stood on end. He had to find that threat, disable it… kill it if he had to. He closed his eyes, listening for his gypsy radar's message.

His eyes flew open. The presence was right next to him! Bristling, he turned and stared at it –

A grey metal box, standing as tall as himself, mounted into the prow of the machine room. And it whined softly. Federi reached out carefully and withdrew his hand before it got too close. That thing was charged with evil! It radiated cold. He moved to its other side and understood. It was the shock gun. He shook his head. This was odd. He never got a whiff of danger that turned out to be nothing! But they were aware that Unicate ships disabled the processors of other ships using electric shock…

He read the voltage.

He read it again to make sure. The fear that streaked through him was grey and icy. Disable the computer? This lightning bolt could wipe out the whole crew, fry them all to a cinder with one single directional discharge! No compounding hull could protect them from this! And it was charged up and ready to fire. Only awaiting Anya Miller's command.

Potato peels and trails -! Captain had no clue of the magnitude of this woman's hatred!

There was only one right thing to do. He had to find out how this thing worked. He investigated the panel of the gun. It wasn't exactly user-friendly, but Federi had experience with weapons. Even a Unicate stun gun needed to be serviced at times. Even a Unicate technician could get himself fried fussing with something like this. There had to be a safety catch somewhere for the technician. He searched and found it, and released it. The lightning gun wasn't going to go off unsolicited now. Carefully he opened the panel, unscrewed the plate and laid bare the gun's innards. And there was the heart of the weapon: The hyperconductive generator coil, hermetically sealed and deeply chilled by liquid nitrogen, shimmering slightly in the half-dark.

Federi took a small piece of something soft and malleable out of his pocket with fingers twitching in stress, pushed it snugly around the coil's casing with his pocket knife, inserted a small gadget the size of a thumbtack into it, stood back – and detonated the explosive.

It was a small, accurate explosion. Liquid nitrogen leaked out of the casing; the hyperconductive super-pure coil was blackened and bent, its hair-thread coils fused together. Excess voltage fizzled along the wires that connected it to the ship console, and into the processor, which responded with a resolute pop. Queasy apprehension streaked through Federi's gut a second time; what if it had triggered anyway? He should have waited until the Solar Wind was well out of range, and then discharged the shock gun and taken the life boat back to the Mother Ship.

Anya Miller had that thing charged up all the way, last night. He, Federi, had sensed it. There was no more doubt that she meant to kill them all. She had to be prevented from coming after them again. He disabled all the drives, collecting wires and parts as he went. His bag got heavier by the moment. To fail now was to send the entire Solar Wind down the chute to hell. He'd have to tell Captain.

Jon Marsden's signal came. Radomir Lascek grinned to himself. He hadn't seen his Tzigan leave the Hun, even though he was on the outer deck with the hostages! How did that gypsy do it?

"Right, Anya," he said. "You are free to sail. I'm untying your hands. Help yourself with your ankles, there's a big girl. You may do the honours for your crew. Thank you for providing us and our friends with fresh food – and such nice food, too!"

The moment Anya's hands were free, her elegant fist connected with his nose. He caught her wrists and laughed.

"I'll be going now. It was nice to see you again, Anya."

"You'll burn in hell, Radomir," snarled Anya Miller.

Radomir Lascek crossed the gangplank to the Solar Wind and

withdrew it. Anya fumbled with the ties on her ankles, and one by one the knots came unstuck. Finally she was free. She charged to the bridge, to lock onto the Solar Wind and pursue – and found the system down. She ran back to the deck to catch a sight of the Solar Wind sailing away. The crew waved to her; amongst them on the deck stood Radomir Lascek, blowing her a kiss. The absolute gall -!

Anya Miller returned to the bridge and examined the console. It was dead. Someone had disconnected the power supply and stolen the adaptor; beyond which there were traces of soot and the acrid smell of fried circuitry. There was no resurrecting this processor in a hurry.

Captain Miller took in the situation. A Pursuer had no sails; they would interfere with speed. The fuel cells only responded to the electronic command. The back-up solar panels, for the event of failure of the fuel cell, were implanted in the roof. They too responded to electronics only. Except for the fuel cells and their slow solar backup, there was no other way of propelling the craft forward. In summary, they were stuck, drifting on the currents at random. Too late she realized that no matter how fast the Hun was, its complete reliance on electronics was a weak point. They were marooned on their own ship.

6

Federi's Amends

"You *WHAT-?!*"

The Captain's voice thundered across the deck. Jonathan Marsden ducked behind the console. Rushka vanished. Ronan and Rhine Gold looked supremely busy suddenly. Shawn fled into the Crow's Nest. Paean, emerging from below the deck, got stuck in the hatchway and stayed rooted to the spot, gaping in horror at the confrontation between the Pirate Captain and the gypsy cook.

Federi glanced down at the bag he held in his hands, and back at the Captain.

"Captain, I've only disabled her ship," he said. "She won't be able to follow us. I've taken the sting out of her shock generator too. When that ship is running again, she won't be able to fry us."

He failed to add that disarming a time bomb was probably a safer task than what he had achieved there in the Hun's bilges. And how he had nearly collapsed with relief on returning to the Solar Wind and finding his friends alive and uncooked.

"You left Anya sitting helpless and immobilized in the middle of nowhere," raged Lascek, "and you fail to see the problem? Here, what's this?" He dug in the bag. "By Stravinsky, Federi! What all did you loot? Information! And cash, too! You corrupt Tzigan! Anya will be in such trouble!"

Anya! Ratted Anya! Fry Anya in hell! Federi frowned and refrained from informing the Captain that the cash in the bag was petty change as compared to what had gone into his pockets without detours. He also omitted to mention the personal effects he had stolen. They weren't in the bag. One day his larcenous habits might get him into trouble, he thought. Only he hadn't thought it would be today, after saving the scalps of everyone on the ship! He stood speechless, surprise frozen on his face as his Captain let rip at him.

Lascek was Hungarian. This accounted for it, thought Federi. Hot temper. Just like his daughter Rushka; except that the poor girl was so regimented by her authoritarian father that her outbursts of temper had turned in on herself. Every now and then, Federi quietly cleared away the shards of a broken mug out of Rushka's cabin and spoke gently to her until she simmered down. He had experience. And mugs were a regular item on his shopping list.

He ought to have looted some mugs from the Hun, he thought absently. There had been one with a bunny on it in the machine room, and "Anyhow" scribbled in indelible ink on the bottom. He hadn't had the heart.

He caught the terrified blue stare of little Paean, in the hatchway, and pulled himself up straight.

"Captain, if you don't mind," he interrupted the Captain's loud tirade. "I'll fix it."

Captain Lascek's mouth got stuck open. His face registered a complete blank. Five seconds passed in silence.

"How?" asked Lascek, stumped.

"Simple," said Federi with an easy smile, "I'll put the money back!"

Another three seconds. Then the Captain exploded into laughter. Federi winked at Paean.

"You useless rogue," laughed the Captain. "But you're dead right, Federi. You *are* going to fix things! She could have a collision, sitting there on a major trade route without lights at night! She could get looted by pirates!"

Federi bit his tongue. The woman had just been looted by pirates!

"You know yourself how inefficient the Unicate is," said the Captain. "They'll take their sweet time rescuing her! Especially if she can't call for help! You've disabled her radio com too?"

"Particularly her radio," said Federi. "Didn't want her reporting Captain Ali!"

"Well, we won't need to go shopping for replacement cables and electronics now," sighed Lascek. "I don't want to say well done, Tzigan! I was curious to see how far she'd trail us into the Pacific. Now we have to rescue her!"

75

"She'd have cornered us at Panama, Captain," said Federi rationally. "She'd have alerted the military there. With all those sluice gates we'd have been sitting ducks."

"We might still be," said Radomir Lascek, troubled. "The Unicate taking over Hamilton! Panama is already Unicate territory. I wonder how we'll slip through this time!"

"We could round the Cape," suggested Federi.

"Get real, Tzigan! We're on a time schedule!" The Captain smiled grimly. "Here's what, my good Federi. We attach the Hun to the Solar Wind. We sail into Hamilton Port and drop Anya off, under the guise of a harmless trader who happened across this disabled ship. This way we, the Solar Wind, don't endanger our reputation, and she doesn't lose face. And it's *your* project."

Now it was Federi's turn at staggered silence. Had he heard right?

"Tow her into Hamilton, Captain?"

"Exactly."

"With all those Stabs we've just escaped?"

"Precisely!"

"And Federi co-ordinates this?" asked the Romany disbelievingly.

This was bad. This was crazy! The other thing that Federi had learnt in all his outlaw years was this: Never underestimate your enemy! A real enemy was never stupid.

"Afraid, Tzigan?"

"Petrified," laughed Federi. Ye Stars, he wanted to run away! He glanced at the little redhead who still stood transfixed in the same spot with her shocked blue eyes. "So what are we waiting for?"

You don't think Miller wants you dead, he thought as he took the bridge. You didn't see that gun! Good and well for Captain to be infatuated with the Solar Wind's arch-enemy. But Federi thought he detected a deep instability in her. And an uncanny coldness...

The Solar Wind turned.

Night fell over the Hun. Captain Miller's furious command to "fix it" had resulted in several hours of trying to find enough wiring to get the drives reconnected, and trying to hot-wire things between the solar cells and the console. It was hopeless. The ship's engineer Tony had ended up opening the fridge and using its inside wiring, twisting it into longer leads, only to find that there wasn't enough. She'd need about ten times as much. And she had no idea what she was supposed to use to replace the subionifyers and the ZITs that had been stolen.

Next she had tried to resurrect the radio com with the wire ripped from the fridge. This tested her capacities to the extreme; eventually she had something that might have worked – except that a crucial bit of machinery was missing. The encryptor. Tony raked her hands through her short black hair. She dug in her intellectual resources. Could the anchor chain be fashioned into wire? The image of it being fashioned into nooses for all of them intruded on her. Could she use anything – anything aboard to "invent" something that could replace that encryptor... like, for argument's sake, her belt buckle... She knew now that she was not cut out for the military. She'd get out the moment they got back into port. Anya Miller was in any case a madwoman.

"Here, Tony!" Johnny Anyhow descended down the steps with a burning piece of plank as torch. "Don't sit down here in the dark feeling sorry for yourself! All is not lost! Come out on the deck! Tomorrow is another day."

Johnny Anyhow, the trusty ex-sea-scout, was prepared! An empty wooden crate had been taken apart and the planks made into flaming torches, fastened to the deck of the Hun to make her more visible to passing ships. He was boiling water for coffee on one of those planks. At least the pirates had left the supplies of coffee, and the mugs. And accurately enough provisions for two days, and the fishing rods. The water desalination with its separate small solar power supply had been left intact too, where everything else had been destroyed. It gave him food for thought. They really didn't want Captain Miller and crew dead! Why not?

A tiny light approached in the distance.

"Ship astern," called Johnny Anyhow.

"Which one?" snapped Captain Miller.

"Lock on and get identification," said Anyhow innocently.

"We can't, you idiot! Just look at her outline. What type of ship is it?"

"Light patterns look like a Zephyr or a Frigattina," said Johnny, peering through his electronic binoculars. One of the few items that hadn't ended in Federi's bag. "There she comes – come on – move a bit closer…. Got something stuck in the rigging, it seems. Something boxy."

Anya Miller took the binoculars off him and peered through herself.

"It's the damned Solar Wind," she exclaimed. "She's coming back! Oh hell!"

"Why is she coming back?" asked Johnny, feeling left out of a crucial part of the conversation.

"To kill us all, of course!" Anya Miller was panicking. "Anyway, you don't understand!"

Some of the key data cubes had been stolen. Lascek now knew about a lot of the movements Headquarters were planning. And here they were, unable to flee or defend themselves, unable even to send a warning or call for backup.

"So far Captain Lascek hasn't hurt any of us," said Johnny rationally.

"Radomir Lascek," said Captain Miller, "is a first-rate criminal. He is extremely dangerous! If he steps aboard, each one of you personally has my orders to terminate him. Am I understood?"

"Yes, Captain," replied a shocked crew.

Anya Miller glared at them. Had they perhaps not quite understood what they were dealing with? Had they misread her willingness to save Lascek from Skebengo as a concession, rather than a practical measure, keeping the end in mind? Had it led to them underestimating the pirate? Thinking him harmless, perhaps even kind? She recalled the gallantry, the kiss he had blown her, and went cold. Did the crew have the impression that she had some sort of emotional attachment to the murdering villain? In which case, could she still rely on them to comply? Were they still taking their mission and their Captain seriously?

This could lead to grave complications, she realized. If her crew took a humanitarian stance and began to disobey her concerning Lascek, it might cost them their lives – especially hers, with that data capsule in his hands. She had to recover that! She would have ordered them to start shooting at the pirate vessel the moment it came into range, if all their weapons hadn't been looted!

A little while later the two ships were in shouting distance.

"We're towing you to Hamilton," Lascek called across. "It seems as

78

though one of my crew has disabled your ship. This is regrettable. It leaves you in my responsibility."

The crew listened up. So he didn't mean to execute them?

"Careful," Anya told her crew. "It's a trap."

"Come, Anya," laughed Radomir Lascek, reading her body posture against the flickering firelight, "don't be afraid. If I had wanted to kill you I would have done so earlier. We're towing you back to Hamilton! Can't just leave you here!"

"I'm not afraid of you, pirate," shot Anya Miller, annoyed.

"Good! Then you'll catch the lines and fasten them onto your ship."

A line came flying towards them, shot out by the Solar Wind's mooring mechanism.

"Let it drop," commanded Captain Miller. "If they get close enough to board, we throw them off the ship with our bare hands if we have to."

The crew were military men and women, trained to obey orders instantly. The line was dropped into the sea.

"You're being stubborn, Anya," shouted Captain Lascek. "Now be a good girl and catch those lines! You're invisible to commercial craft and this is a main shipping route. You might have a collision."

Anya Miller dug in her heels. Hamilton? Back to her superiors? She wasn't ready for that encounter! And with a damaged ship! Besides, there was no way she'd give an inch to the old pirate after believing she was rescuing him this afternoon and walking into his trap. The line came flying again. Once again Captain Miller ordered her people to ignore it. The metal mooring clip caught on the Hun's rail.

Tony reluctantly freed it and threw it back into the sea. She scowled. Pirate vessels like Lascek's, who snared other ships, were equipped with looting chains that had grappling hooks at the end. He hadn't sent them one of those, only an ordinary mooring line leading a hawser. The whole scenario failed to make sense to her. Lascek didn't seem aggressive at all; he genuinely appeared to be extending a helping hand. If she had to rely on her judgement of character, she'd say he rather liked Captain Miller.

"The military will pick us up," Captain Miller told her marines. "We don't need to go along with the machinations of this outlaw. Do you believe him? I don't! Head Office keeps permanent tabs on where every ship is, and they'll see on the map where we were last. When they don't reach us by radio or satellite signal, they'll come looking for us."

She knew that what she told them was only partially accurate. Head Office could be very inefficient, especially if their record showed that she had loaded provisions recently and no distress signal had gone out, therefore there was no sense of urgency. The last routine communication had been that morning, but she hadn't informed anyone that she had located the pirate. She didn't want to share her reward if she didn't have to. This failure to be a team player proved to be a mistake. She could lose her career now, or her life. Depending on how they managed to fend off Lascek. She wasn't overly hasty to confront Headquarters.

Being positioned on a major trade route could be good or bad. A collision, though highly unlikely, couldn't be ruled out entirely as they were radar-shielded. More likely they might receive help from a passing trader. Then again they might encounter a Rebellion ship. In their military uniforms, the chances of them being slaughtered were only exceeded by the risk of being taken hostage and traded off, like so much merchandise, back to Head Office. That would certainly spell the end for her. Unicate dealt efficiently with inefficient military leaders.

Lascek turned to Jonathan Marsden.

"What do we do?"

"We could harpoon her," suggested Marsden.

"Causing further damage to her ship," Lascek pointed out. "But the principle is sound. Ha! Marsden, Donegal! Come below deck!"

A short while later, out of sight in the dark of the sea, looting cables and mooring lines were secured to the screw of the Hun. Then Jon Marsden and Ronan Donegal re-emerged on the Solar Wind, dripping wet and with satisfied smirks.

"Captain, this thing's going to fly. Haha!" Ronan was enjoying himself immensely.

"Good work! Set sail for Hamilton!"

"Set sail for Hamilton," called Marsden.

"And hand over to Federi, blast you all!" added the Captain. "It's *his* project! Got to organize everything myself for the man! What's this?"

Anya Miller watched how the Solar Wind's huge white sails unfurled in the moonlight. A small burst of power from her solar drives, and she started moving. Away. Anya Miller allowed herself a sigh of relief. They were going to be left in peace. How she had managed to talk the Pirate off her back, she didn't quite understand. But she and her crew were safe for now, and a bit of time had been bought. She had to find a way to explain the loss of those files to Head Office. And the devastation of her ship. She knew what to expect if the truth came out. Perhaps the military was the wrong place for her to be, now. Perhaps she ought to reconsider the proposal her brother had made, not too long ago.

The Solar Wind's sails opened fully, and the night breeze punched into them. The wind was at their back; she plunged ahead, her large mainsail and huge foresail "goose-winged" to each side to catch the most air. The solar drives switched off as wind power took over.

There was a bump as the lines pulled taut. The Hun was not half the size of the Solar Wind; she turned back-to-front and got dragged along, the wrong way round, in the wake of the pirate ship. Anya Miller turned as white as a sheet.

"Captain? What's happening?" asked Johnny Anyhow, just in time to see her collapse on the deck.

~

Wolf opened his eyes through a zingy red haze. Across on the other infirmary bunk crouched Paean Donegal, her eyes stuck on his face.

"You okay?"

He probed tentatively for the headache that was still lingering just under the surface. It was survivable. His sight cleared as he finished waking up.

"I'll live," he grinned.

"Coffee for you," said Paean and pressed a mug into his hand.

"Aw! Thanks! That's thoughtful!" She was cute!

"And painkiller," she added, handing him a strange powdered substrate. Wolf sipped his coffee and eyed the powder with deep suspicion. Not so cute!

"Don't need that, thanks," he said.

"Alright." Paean got up from the second bunk. "I've got to get back to

81

work."

"Sherbet, so do I," exclaimed Wolf. "How long did I sleep?" It was dark outside!

"Few hours," replied the redhead. "But you were booked off injured. So it's okay."

"What? I was just knocked out by some oaf's stun gun, that's all! Who booked me off?"

Paean grinned and pointed to herself.

"Don't do that again!" growled Wolf. "Thanks all the same."

"Any day, Wolf," called Paean, already halfway out of the door. "Later."

Wolf shook his head as he collected himself and got up.

~

Federi looked up from the console. In the door to the bridge hung a worried little redhead.

"You okay, Federi?"

The gypsy laughed.

"Fine, Paean. Except that Captain's making us sail into a – oh, hell's gadgets, it's fine! We'll be fine. Federi's an old coward, that's all! Anna bottle…"

"Coffee for you?"

Federi smiled broadly. "Now that's going to make all the difference," he stated. "Thanks, little carer!"

"Any day," said Paean and handed him his steaming mug. "Got any decks for me to scrub?"

What? With death hanging over all their heads? He didn't think so!

"Funny thing that," he said, then trailed off. He could see how she'd had a lot of friends in Milly-Molly-Mandy street. Anyone who cared for their friends like this, had friends. He frowned. It made no sense. This was her true nature, he sensed it. Whatever she had done that was weighing on her like that – it had been a fluke, a mistake. When Captain decided to drill down to the truth – he'd be there protecting her, he decided. And he glanced at her hands.

The skin was abraded away right up to the elbows from scrubbing. He

82

knew he'd been giving her a lot of decks to wash, and she'd taken on extra heads-scrubbing duty for reasons only she understood, but this... it was something else. He locked the steering and grabbed her hands to take a closer look. And observed how she shrank away, her breath hissing between her teeth as she inhaled sharply.

All that blood...

"Got to get that seen to, *shey,*" he said. "Put something on it. Captain will think Federi's working you to death. Wait..." He dug in his pockets and unearthed a small flat tin, and slid its lid open. There was something grey and greasy-looking inside. He picked out a gob of the stuff and slapped it on the back of her left hand.

"What's that?" she asked doubtfully as she spread it over her abused skin.

Federi hesitated. "Neomer polycarbon thixotropalene."

She gawped. *"What?"*

"Motor grease," he grinned and pressed the tin into her hands. "What! You expect me to carry medical supplies in my pockets?"

She stared at her hands in horror.

"It works." provided the gypsy. "Keep it, I can get more from the machine room."

Paean pulled a face, but obediently spread the dreadful stuff over her hands and forearms. Federi was right; people would notice. Good that he only thought it was from washing the dishes. She glanced uncertainly at his face and caught him staring moodily into the dark beyond the bridge.

"Doesn't matter anyway," he muttered.

"What?" asked Paean.

Federi scowled. He'd seen it before. But by now it really was irrelevant. They'd die in Hamilton, regardless what she was guilty of. And if by some strange luck they survived tomorrow, there was Panama waiting for them, inevitably...

Did she sense about the horror he had found in the machine room of the Hun? How could she sense, he thought. And about the irony of Captain being prepared to rescue his arch-enemy... sail right into the death trap that was Hamilton! With all his crew.

"Störtebeker," he said.

"Pardon?"

"Pirate called Störtebeker. You should ask Sherman about him. Federi can't tell a story quite the same."

"Tell me anyway," pushed Paean, still rubbing at the synthetic compounding lubri-squatch he'd made her put on her hands.

"Aw, alright. Störtebeker must have been a bit like Captain. This is long ago. In the days before mineral fuels. He and his whole crew got captured by the law, and of course piracy carried the death penalty even then. So Störtebeker negotiated with the government that all of his sailors could go free past whom he could walk after he was dead."

"That's dumb," commented Paean.

"Wait for it," said the Tzigan. "I said I can't tell it like Sherman! So they line up his crew and chop off his head. Paean, *atenţie!* He walked past his entire crew with his head chopped off. All of them! Before his dead corpse fell to the ground."

"Whoa!" commented Paean disbelievingly.

"Is true," said Federi. "Was a historical figure. Go look it up in the Sher…" He sighed impatiently and stared out to sea. "Go to sleep!"

Paean gaped at him in shock, then she shrugged and left the bridge. Federi glared at the sea some more. In his mind's eye he saw Captain walking past the Solar Wind's crew with his head chopped off. Aw hell… and now he'd snubbed the little mockingbird! For what?

The next morning dawned bright and blue. Another borrowed day, thought Paean as she got out of her bunk, today amazingly without a headache. Maybe they'd make it through to Hawaii, if they could just keep it quiet, like now. Definitely if she was allowed to knock the Unicate one on the noggin, like yesterday! She peered through the porthole.

Suddenly she felt observed. She turned and glared at the electronic eye in the top corner of her cabin. Federi was right: The darned ship was studded with them! There was no cabin without closed-circuit camera. Couldn't even change a T-shirt!

Paean padded the few paces to the Solar Wind's infirmary in her pyjamas and raided the First Aid Box. She returned to her cabin and pasted a plaster over the electronic eye.

"Nobody watches Paean Donegal change!" she muttered through clenched teeth.

Shawn's optimistic tunes carried down from the Crow's Nest. Captain's orders were that he stay up there a lot, and definitely with every landing or sighting of a ship; because of his acute gift for being observant. Federi stared glumly up at the boy. No amount of observance was going to change their fate today. He climbed into the rigging with another of Captain's nonsensical orders. The warm breeze was blowing, it was promising to be a marvellous day. It was hard to be morose in such gorgeous weather; impossible to be upbeat in the face of what waited for them in Hamilton. They had been towing the Hun for ten hours now, and another four lay ahead. Four more hours of being alive. Federi had no illusions as to what the Unicate would do to them. And no matter how he turned it, there was no getting away out of that spider's nest. What he needed most now, was a paranormal phenomenon rescuing them. His eyes had acquired an insane glitter.

"Get down on the deck, Donegal," the gypsy ordered with a mirthless grin. "Captain wants a Ceilidh. I'll put Rhine Gold on the lookout. Anna potato."

"Sure," smiled Shawn.

Federi climbed down, black eyes darting across the deck. He still had to organize the pasting of the false name on the Solar Wind's hull. Marsden had taken care of the programming of the false identity. The gypsy took in the blue sky, the turquoise sea. A beautiful day to die! Hells and jingles! He'd remember it all his – er... What had got into him to take the Captain up on this challenge? He had to be crazy. His business was to survive!

Anya Miller had arrived at some sort of strategy. All was not lost. After all, she was bringing the pirate into port! It didn't matter who towed whom, in the big picture. The Solar Wind had spotted the Stab craft in the harbour, the first time. She knew this from the reports of the ship turning away. Clearly though, Lascek wasn't aware of the wider net of Pursuers stationed around the islands. Bit of a challenge that she could not contact her lieutenants yet and prepare them. She'd have to act fast, once in the harbour. Doubtlessly Lascek would put her ashore and turn tail right away.

Contagious Irish reels and airs carried over to the Hun, where some of her marines uttered wistfully that they would like to have a party too.

"Any of you who wishes to be on the pirate ship can go," said Captain Miller.

"Really, Captain?"

"And when I turn them all in, in Hamilton, you can be judged as renegades and buccaneers too!"

~

In the afternoon the civilian trader Santa Marguerita sailed innocently into Hamilton Port, a crippled military craft in tow.

"Just thought we'd give this lady in distress a lift," signalled the small, dark-haired captain to the harbour authorities. The river-boatmen converged on the strange twosome, helping with the untying of ropes from the screw of the Hun. Quite a few of the military men and women peered curiously up into the Santa Marguerita's rigging at that strange boxy structure.

Captain Miller got onto the leading T-craft. She was wearing a grin a mile wide.

"Gomez, we've done it! Look! That ship is the Solar Wind!"

"The Solar Wind? That ship is the Santa Marguerita," argued Gomez. "Well known private trader. Their record is spotless. You're lucky they're the ones who picked you up, Captain!"

"It's the Solar Wind," insisted Anya Miller. "We tracked her down and got into a battle. Very nearly sank her. Came a bit short, but here she is." She fired an impatient glare at the T-craft captain. Gomez. Not one of her hand-picked ones. But he'd have to comply anyway.

Captain Stefano Gomez regarded her with narrowed eyes. That sounded like a wild yarn! He had seen who was towing whom! Besides he knew what Lascek looked like – and the Captain of the trader didn't look like Lascek in any way! What was Anya Miller playing?

Gomez had been placed under Miller's command for the duration of this project. He was the commander of the Stab craft in the harbour. Technically he ranked higher than she; how she had achieved this reversal of the power structure, he wasn't quite sure. It certainly reeked of some unethical goings-on. He wasn't too happy about it; Anya seemed unstable to him.

He punched a few more buttons. "No, Captain, sorry, that ship is definitely not the Solar Wind but the Santa Marguerita. The identity checks out."

"Just arrest them, Gomez," ordered Anya Miller. "You'll see."

Captain Gomez had enough.

"Captain Miller, you have an obsession. You'll never get this past Head Office. You can't arrest the nearest civilian and try to palm them off to Head Office as the Pirate. I've been observing you and reading up, Miller. This is not the first time you've abused Unicate resources. But you aren't getting me entangled in that, lady! I'm booking you off, as of now, and putting it down to a nervous breakdown. Three weeks reprieve in a top nerve retreat sound good to you?"

"No," shouted Anya Miller, finally boiling over. "That does not sound good! It sounds like subversion, mutiny! I'll report you to Headquarters! The notorious pirate Radomir Lascek is aboard that vessel over there!" Her voice was striking a hysterical coloratura as Gomez's fingers moved calmly over the keyboard. "I found him, I, me, me! I want to turn him in to the authorities! I want to collect my reward! You're not sabotaging me, you nobody!"

"I've just booked you for a stay on the Canaries, Miller. Subtropical island paradise, all expenses paid courtesy the Unicate Navy. Three weeks."

Anya Miller tackled Gomez and tried to choke him. Two of his marines had to take her away forcibly and organize her into the harbour's private nerve clinic for observation. Gomez cancelled her island holiday again.

He peered at the outline of the white Zephyr that had rescued her. What a mindboggling hag that Miller was! He couldn't believe she had tried to turn in a civilian who had just saved her and her crew! His First Mate Gina Nevada re-emerged out of hiding from the minute galley compartment. She levelled a gaze at the trader that was sailing out of Hamilton Port.

"What are they doing now?"

"They're removing something —" Gomez trained his lenses on the ship. He started laughing.

"What?" asked Gina.

"It *is* the Solar Wind!"

"They've saved that Miller harpy's life," said Gina.

Gomez smiled. "Shall we give her a decent head start?"

"We're going after her?"

"Sure! That's a lot of money!"

The men on the Solar Wind were laughing too. Loudest laughed the Pirate Captain, back on his bridge.

Federi had withdrawn to his cabin. He sat cross-legged on his bunk, just staring, his fingers clenching and unclenching subconsciously. He felt sick. Captain could laugh now, but in his mind the gypsy could still see the horrible little black craft closing in all around the Solar Wind like spiders, Unicate marines crawling aboard, his friends being brutalized, gutted, murdered…

The trick had relied completely on psychology. But that wasn't all. He had a hunch that though this prank had gone well, it had been the first sea mile on the long, dark voyage into oblivion.

*

Katya

Very nearly, your brother joined you today. Captain must be off his mind. He outwits that Anya Miller, and then, when Federi has made doubly sure that all danger is past and she can't come after us and fry us with her lightning bolts, Captain catches a virus and orders me to rescue her! Right back into that nest of Stabs! After such a beautiful getaway yesterday! It's enough to drive a man twitchy! Katya, sometimes I really think Captain is a madman.

He's protecting our three little musicians, and that's great – haha, the little songbird's pretty upset with Federi bout that thieves' honour thing, can't accept that I'm not an honest, ethical, upstanding – Katya, are you laughing as hard as Federi? Maybe Federi's not laughing all that loudly anyway, rats in pyjamas...

Pretty impressed with Shawn, the kid's got wits. Was the first to figure out we're pirates, even before Captain told them.

Captain talks about Donegal magic. They have an amazing effect on us all. We're laughing more than in a long time. And that music... Cor, my heart-sister, I'm tired of being a morose pirate! Want to be a happy Tzigan again! Haven't had much chance at playing the clown since the Princess is all grown up. Hells, Katya, but I can't laugh after I've seen the voltage of that woman's hatred... Can't stop thinking of headless old Störtebeker!

Going to pass out a bit and then make everyone coffee. As though they need it, blasted crew of hyperactive monkeys!

Kathal, my sister.
Your wrecked little brother.

7

Old Sherman

Shawn came shimmying down the rigging in the early dusk to join his sister and old Sherman at the rail. Paean had her violin out and was playing a few tunes to Ronan's accompaniment; but her heart wasn't in it.

"That was an ace trick today," Shawn laughed. "Wonder what that Anya Miller is doing now!"

"I don't like wondering about psychopaths," replied the old storyteller.

"Och, won't you tell us a ghost story, Sherman?" begged Shawn.

"You like your ghosties, Shawn," laughed Sherman Dougherty. "Are you three planning to tour around the world playing music?" He pulled out his pipe and started cleaning it.

"Och no," said Paean, giving up on the tune she'd been attempting. It didn't want to.

"But why not? You three are good, Paean!"

She studied the old man, with his wild white mane and his huge, somewhat tobacco-stained beard. An old leprechaun. Not even the Unicate had managed to edit leprechauns and shenanigans out of Irish folklore.

Almost she'd like to trust the grandfatherly old sailor and give him a real answer. But... yeah. That was suicide. A low profile!

"Och, Sherman, we didn't make it in Dublin, and that's the world capital for music."

"Made a good deal of money though," piped Shawn happily. "Up until..."

"Shawn!" Paean frowned at him. It was bad luck if Shawn wanted to talk about the past right now! Couldn't he just keep on shutting up until Hawaii? Anyway, what did he call a good deal of money?! "It was *Ronan* who was earning money, remember? We just went along!"

"Sure," came a cryptic comment. The gypsy had appeared out of nowhere and was leaning against the foremast, watching them. Paean peered back at him critically. He was in a lime-green flared shirt with a sky-blue waistcoat and a mauve paisley headscarf – a combination that hurt the eye, even in the dusk. He must be feeling better.

She had changed her mind. She wasn't going to give Ronan's plan of making friends another go. Making friends on this ship was not only darned tricky; it was pointless, too. She couldn't really see why she bothered. Ro could carry his plan out alone. And Shawn. Friends were dangerous. You ended up telling them things.

Quite a few of the sailors were out on the deck by now, drawn by the beginnings of the Ceilidh. There was an air of elation. They wanted to party, having pulled one over on the Unicate.

"Yup, that's right," grinned Shawn. "They kept on just giving Ro all the money! And we did just as much of the work! Played weddings, funerals, seedy pubs…"

"Ceilidhs," corrected Ronan sternly, putting his Clarsach away in its weatherproof bag. Mist was beginning to rise. The wind was picking up. The Ceilidh would have to move below the deck. "All you two ever played was Ceilidhs. Paean, pack up your violin, it's going to get wet! We're a law-abiding family, Shawn. Don't know where you got all those other ideas! Sir, he dramatizes!"

"Stands to reason, he's Irish," said Wolf Svendsson. Paean glanced up from putting her violin away. So Wolf was back on deck!

"Now, Svendsson, what precisely do you mean by that?" asked Sherman Dougherty sharply.

"Och, Sherman," begged Shawn, "a ghost story, please?"

"Wouldn't you rather tell us about your own ghosts, Shawn?" replied Sherman. "Why are you at sea, when you ought to be at school?"

Paean hissed under her breath. The Donegals had last been to school in September. It was not a topic she wanted to discuss. "Sherman, what is the Solar Wind's mission in Hawaii?"

A small sound caught her attention. Federi was laughing quietly to himself.

"Might as well ask how a Dougherty gets by the name of Sherman," said Ronan, trying to get the conversation back onto safer ground. Drat Paean and her sharp wit! He didn't want to be put ashore in the next port!

The plan was to get to Hawaii, not stay in Plymouth!

He had his hands full with his sibs. Shawn had to be pulled in line all the time, telling people too much, while Paean had developed a style of communicating that was – well, loudly suspicious.

"How a Donegal gets by the name of Paean," countered Sherman. He had the pipe lit by now and puffed on it, studying them all.

"Mother picked it," said Paean defiantly. She turned away, walking along the rail towards the prow. The Ceilidh was over.

The Solar Wind was cutting her way south-southeast towards Plymouth, another free port. Captain Lascek, Marsden and Rushka were on the bridge, holding a conference.

Radomir Lascek summarized the situation. The Unicate had been swarming all over Hamilton harbour. Discovering that Hamilton was a pirate port, they would carry on searching now until they found more pirate ports. What Federi had found out that night on his pub mission was disturbing. The Unicate was systematically checking every last port now. Hamilton was gone; Manila was gone. Several ports in the Gulf and along the Florida coastline, including Key West, had already been discovered and taken over. Nicaragua, a resilient free country, had folded to the Unicate days ago. It would be in the World News now. All in all the Unicate had suddenly become a lot more vicious – but why? What lay behind it all?

Some answers would await them in Hawaii, this they knew. Jonathan Marsden had been working on the decryption of those data sticks and especially the high-security capsule Federi had picked off the Hun – with little success. It seemed as though whole parts of code were missing. What single glimpses emerged, made no sense as yet. This was no small project.

The Solar Wind's concerns for safety lay closer still. Had the Unicate discovered Plymouth yet? Unicate was like a bulldog – once they had a grip on something, they never let go until they had finished it. The Unicate was a fearsomely thorough conqueror.

But Plymouth was only the first stop on Lascek's map of concerns. They would have to cross the Panama Canal to get to the Pacific. Anya Miller knew of their course, that was clear. She had been too accurate positioning herself. So the Unicate would be waiting for them in Panama.

"It's madness," said Marsden.

"Good," replied Captain Lascek. "So, any ideas yet?"

Rushka shrugged. "Go around the Cape?"

"For all that's going to cost us in delay," replied her father, "it's not that much safer. Unicate's all over the Atlantic. You know this."

"At least we won't be delivering ourselves right into their hands," said Rushka.

Radomir Lascek's eyes narrowed. "Right into their hands, you say?"

Jonathan Marsden shuddered. There was a plan brewing in that formidable mind! All he could do was modulate the Captain's risks down, try to make it a bit safer.

"A year ago I would have said, go north," he suggested. "Even now – wouldn't that be better?"

Lascek shook his head. "The passage is frozen again."

"Blast our way with the nuclear drives?"

"Not doable, Jon. The ice is finally recovering. Sea level has dropped."

"Submerge and pass under the ice cap?"

Radomir Lascek leaned back and folded his arms, mulling.

"For all it's possible," he said, "it would cost nearly as much time as going around the Cape. Now that the Unicate is hatching something, I feel there is more need to hurry. We'll just have to find our way through Panama."

"If the sea level has dropped, Lake Gatun will be a challenge," warned Marsden.

"It will be a challenge anyway," said Lascek.

Rushka nodded. "Stabilizers," she said.

Lascek's glance fell on the little Irish waif out there at the rail, under the occasional spray of the prow wave. She stood as tall as her tiny frame allowed and met his eyes across the whole length of the deck with Donegal pride in every inch of her stance.

"Rushka," he said, "remind me!"

"*Igen*, Captain."

For now, he needed to focus on the Panama Debacle.

Sherman Dougherty had his audience gathered around himself now. The ship's deck lights lit up automatically just as he took a breath to start.

"Shawn," he said, "you know where we're going, now don't you?"

"Sure," said Shawn, "Hawaii!"

"And do you know how we're going to get there?"

Shawn's face was a blank. It was on the tip of his tongue to say, "by sailing ship", but clearly this was a loaded question. He waited.

"D'you know your geography, Donegal?" asked old Sherman.

"No, but I will," said Shawn happily. "Give me five years or so at sea!"

"Plymouth in about four days," said old Sherman, smiling. "We restock, and then we pass through Panama – that should be sports! From there –"

"What kind of sports?" asked Shawn, riveted.

"Unicate," said Sherman. "Now listen! Don't get so excited! You think you're a pirate? You don't know anything! Probably read too much subversive literature! You want some real pirates, go to the east coast of Africa. The Indian Ocean coast. Mayotte. Dzaoudzi. Reunion. Slave trade, Donegal! Right into this century! Why do you think there's a place on the northern tip of Mauritius that is called, to this day, Cannonier's Point?"

Shawn nodded, impressed.

"In any case that's the most dangerous stretch of ocean ever designed," said Sherman Dougherty.

"I thought that was south of the Cape of Storms," interjected Ronan.

"Storms, ha," said Sherman. "The Agulhas comes down from India along the East Coast. Warm water pushing south. The Oceanic Conveyor Belt goes up that coastline, but of course deep down. Storms? You get lots there. Great cyclones. High waves. Ships tend to disappear without leaving a forwarding address…"

"The place must be littered with wrecks," commented Shawn.

"Sherman, won't you tell us the one about the Bronberg?" asked Wolf Svendsson.

"Which one -? Oh. All right!" Sherman puffed on his pipe and settled comfortably on the deck. The ship rolled as she ploughed on through the dark. Fine salty spray settled on them. The crests glowed a bit with bioluminescent plankton.

"The Bronberg was a Namakura, Class fifty-seven," said Sherman, leaning back against the starboard rail. It was the holes that worried him. He hadn't yet had a chance to build holes into the Bronberg's tale for Ronan. Well, he'd just have to do it as he went along. "Blue ship. Now wasn't she beautiful as the evening breeze? A steamship from the mineral fuels era; ran on what they called dirty oil. Unrefined oil. And was it dirty, now!" He frowned and went silent for a moment. He had been there. "You kids have no idea what rubbish was thrown into the atmosphere by those old steamers! And all other transport! Why do you think the ice caps started melting? If the Unicate ever did one thing right…"

"What?" asked Shawn, surprised. "The Unicate stopped the use of mineral oils?"

"We don't really know, do we?" replied Sherman. "I believe it did run out. The Unicate wasn't responsible for Nemesis II either."

"You sure?" asked Wolf Svendsson with a grin. Nemesis II had been one of a pair of meteorites. It had hit Earth in the mid-Atlantic. Nemesis I had been caught further up the solar system by Neptune.

Sherman had been alive at that time, too.

"Oy! That was a tense time for Earth, wasn't it!" he recalled. "Tidal waves, earthquakes, volcanic outbursts. Luckily it was a comparatively small hit; Nemesis I would have sliced our planet in halves. Geography shifted."

"How?" asked Ronan, eyes narrowed. Here it came!

"The Mid-Atlantic Ridge? Boys, you should see it now! Used to be a nice fault line. Now it's a real cliff. And hasn't the east side sunk a great bit lower?" He grinned and drew on his pipe.

"Ah." Had it, now? Ronan smiled and considered whether scrubbing the galley floor was a worthwhile option tonight. It had to be a tall story! If the east side of the ridge had sunk any lower, Ireland would be where Tir Nan Og was! And probably, half of Europe too!

"What about that dirty fuel, and the ice caps melting?" asked Shawn, ears hot.

"You're talking about another story now," said Sherman. "And they didn't exactly melt, did they? Just thinned a bit. The ice receded a wee bit. Unicate blasted a passage into the thinned Northern Ice Cap in the late Eighties to promote traffic between Tokyo, New York and London. But it has iced over more every year now, as the atmosphere recovers from the Greenhouse effect. Soon it won't even be open in summer any longer, and what a pity that will be for the sea trade!"

"And the sea levels?"

"They've been dropping, but not too dramatically," said Sherman. "Don't you Dublinites know? All harbour towns were built up quite a bit in the fifties, with the sea levels at their highest. Harbours were raised and dykes were built higher every year. A lot of technology went into that! You think you had a problem? Should have seen Holland, and Florida!"

"Lowlands," muttered Ronan.

"Now that the sea level is dropping again, there are places where one can see the old submerged buildings resurfacing," said Sherman. "Old highways. And so on. Isn't that the plain truth!"

"Och," said Ronan and bit his tongue. Decks!

"I wonder if Dr Jake is ready with his electronics shield." The Captain pressed a few buttons on his wrist-com. "Dr Jake, come in – how far is that shield?"

"Incomplete yet, sir, but we can use it for partial disturbance."

"Thanks, Dr Jake. We'll use it. Can't disturb them enough, where I'm concerned!"

"Obviously we'll have to sail under a false identity," said Marsden. "The San Diego?"

"Paean Donegal busted that one," smiled Lascek. "And the Santa Marguerita will be all over their records now. Got to create a new one."

"Captain, can I go listen to Sherman?" asked Rushka.

Lascek studied his daughter for a moment. Well, she was only nineteen, and these heavy survival issues shouldn't strictly be her concern. Other girls her age were having fun at University!

"Only I find that I get better ideas from his stories," said Rushka.

"Go, little rogue," laughed Lascek. "Go play with the other kids! Jon and I will take care of the Panama business."

"Thanks, Papa."

The ship's ghost peered at the single little figure up there on the jib deck by the bowsprit, in the wind, catching the spray of the prow wave. Sherman's probing had cut close to the truth. Federi could sense the stress radiating from the little redhead.

Should he go and tell her that she shouldn't worry, everything would be alright? But what if it wasn't? What if her deed was so awful it broke all rules of humanity? There was really no way of telling. In reality he didn't actually want to know, either. It was up to Captain to deal with that kind of thing. Or to choose not to.

"The Bronberg," Wolf prompted.

"Now, the Bronberg," Sherman agreed. "Beautiful ship. Beautiful crew, too. Black as ink, tall, straight marines."

"I thought a Namakura was a coastal guard?" asked Shawn. He had been reading!

"In the same way that the Solar Wind is a Trader," agreed Sherman grinning. "At any rate, pirates. Mwali. Mutsamudu."

"Incantations," grinned Wolf Svendsson.

"Places," corrected Sherman. "The Unicate suspected goings-on in those regions. So they sent the Bronberg, from Southern."

"But I thought Southern Free is a free country?" There. Decks after all. Luckily Ronan was practiced with scrubbing by now.

"Is, and was even then," smiled Sherman. "They were currying favour with the Unicate though, those were the early days. And didn't the Unicate send the Bronberg of all ships to Mayotte to investigate what is going on there? O' course, this is right after the strike of Nemesis II, so the Earth's crust is unstable. Volcanoes all over. New uncharted islands springing out of the sea."

"*Uncharted* islands?" asked Ronan sceptically.

Wolf had told Shawn at some point that Sherman was over a hundred years old! Well, that would account for the holes in the stories! Paean with her sharp tongue had of course told Shawn not to believe everything Wolf Svendsson said...

"Of course," said Sherman. "You'd think, a place like the Mozambique Channel... Nobody goes there! Only slavers and drug dealers!"

"It's a major trade route," said Ronan.

"Today, yes, today," said Sherman. "In those days… anyway, the Bronberg goes in. She travels up the coast – now, the Captain of the Bronberg's no fool. The Agulhas runs south there. But there's a counter current, known to the ships of old, closer to the shore. The Captain's a dare-devil, he –"

He glanced up at Rushka, who had suddenly popped up out of the floor.

"What about the Captain, Sherman?"

"This is another captain," laughed Sherman. "Sit down, Rushka! Mustn't be so sudden! You'll give an old sailor a heart-attack!"

"Sorry, Sherman." Rushka settled in the general vicinity of the Donegal brothers.

"So every now and then a new island pops up out of the sea," said Sherman. "Covered with seaweed and dying anemones and rock-pools full of starfish. And sometimes a whole sunken ship is raised to the surface that way, full of ancient treasure."

"But why uncharted?" pressed Ronan. "Wouldn't that information be available instantly on the Net?"

"Och, the Net," said Sherman Dougherty. "They didn't have the Net in those days, now did they?"

"Ouch," said Wolf. Sherman's bushy white eyebrows lifted. He'd have to be subtler with his lies. Wolf was in on the ploy, but this had been an instinctive reaction.

"But shouldn't they be visible from the satellites?" insisted Ronan.

Sherman Dougherty rolled his eyes. "Complicated. Volcanic islands are very small."

"Come on! Ships in Tokyo Harbour are visible from satellite! Saw a photo back in…" Ronan trailed off.

"I'd love to be that high up," said Shawn enthusiastically. "What a feeling!"

"Back in…?" asked Sherman, studying Ronan critically.

"The Bronberg," prompted Wolf again.

"Och all right, the Bronberg," said Sherman, who realized that no matter what he did, he wasn't going to get out of telling that story. "Now

98

o' course, isn't that area prime habitat for whales?"

"Whales?" asked Shawn excitedly. "They still exist?" Despite Federi's assurance that this was the Ocean, he hadn't yet spotted one.

"Hear me out, Donegal! Sheesh, Donegal Minor and Donegal Major! Whales are known to do battle with giant squid. Humboldt squid."

"Why?"

"Why? They eat them, now don't they? Either way round, depending who wins! Now, the suckers of giant squid are ten centimetres across. The squid themselves are fifteen to eighteen metres in length. Work out the size."

Ronan got up and paced out fifteen metres.

"I don't think so," he commented. Shawn watched, with eyes wide.

"Fifteen *feet,*" corrected Wolf.

"There's that," said Sherman. "And what about the whale shark? Size of a whale, rises out of the twilight zone at night to feed. I'll tell you, things grow bigger down there! Leftover species from the Pleistocene. Who knows what all lurks in the deep?"

Blond Rhine Gold sounded as though he had a coughing fit. Within seconds they all knew he was trying not to laugh too loudly. He had settled close by with a pile of potatoes and was calmly peeling them while listening. Duties were duties, tall story or not.

Paean had gone to her cabin to put on a jersey. Despite the tropics she suddenly felt chilly. Cold and alone. She hung about the frugal cubicle for a while, sitting on her bunk, trying to think of something to do. She could have done with her old weather-beaten teddy bear now, but he had stayed behind in Molly Street like everything else. Like Mother. Her mind shied away from that.

She switched off the light and tried to sleep. It was hopeless. Images haunted her. Ten restless minutes later she got up impatiently and left her cabin.

There was still light and movement in the cabin across the passage. Paean peered in through the for once open door. Usually the Doc kept the door closed religiously; all Paean had glimpsed so far was a fridge at the far end.

White equipment and clean surfaces met her eye everywhere. She

99

marvelled. Red displays on great square metal appliances gave what seemed to be temperature readings. There was a translucent machine with a jelly-like substance in it, with many little orange lines travelling across it. There were columns of reinforced silica-plex, sporting bands of colour along them. Everything either bolted into place, or placed into wells, holders and clamps to keep it steady. An extractor fan operated ceaselessly over the workspace.

"Paean," said Doc Judith. "Come in!" She handed Paean a paper mask. "Put this on. Don't contaminate the air!" She grabbed a spray-bottle and sprayed at Paean. A very cold, sweet mist. Paean sniffed and her eyes started tearing.

"Don't breathe that, unless you want to get drunk," said Doc Judith. "It's seventy percent ethanol."

"Can I lend a hand?" asked Paean, finding her bearings. "I'm feeling useless."

"There's not much to lend," replied the Doc. "But you can keep me company. Sit over there!" She motioned to a compounding barstool that had been bolted into place next to a work surface. "Did you have chemistry in school?"

"A bit." Paean took a seat and studied the elderly lady doctor. Doc Judith had to be sixtyish. Her hair was tied back into a loose bun; this was clearly for practical purposes, but Paean had never seen her wear it any other way. It made sense. "But what I really want to learn is medicine. Want to be able to heal people."

"Really? It's a tough field," said the Doc.

"Och, I'm tough as well," said Paean. "And I already know some herb lore."

"Herb lore!" Doc Judith paused. "You know *herbal* medicine?"

"A bit," said Paean.

"How did you get by that knowledge?"

Paean went silent. This was dangerous ground.

The Doc read her worried expression.

"All right, I won't push," she said. "I only hope you're over your addiction?"

"Addiction?!" Now Paean Donegal was incensed. "Hell, no! There's no addiction in *our* family! Doc, do I look like a girl who would

100

voluntarily drink or smoke her brains away?"

"No," laughed Doc Judith. She was relieved. So that was not where the herb lore had come in! "Which herbs do you know?" she asked.

"Well, the most important is probably willow bark," said Paean. "Aspirin by another name! I know they don't have aspirin as a drug in the pharmacies, but it does everything. Breaks a fever, kills pain, protects the heart... so I extract my own out of willow bark."

"Beauty," commented the Doc. "And -?"

Paean thought a bit. "Nettle, for detoxing the kidneys. Cranberries against migraines."

"Didn't know that one," said Doc Judith, surprised. "Does it work?"

"Like a bomb," said Paean. "What else do I know? Basic stuff, Doc... Chamomile and fennel for upset stomach, Valerian for sleeplessness and anxiety..."

"Elder," said the Doc, enthused. "For...?"

"Antiseptic and antiviral," replied Paean without hesitating. "But it doesn't always work."

"It does," argued Doc Judith. "It used to be the sacred tree of the gypsies, did you know?"

"And the druids," agreed Paean. "St John's Wort for depression..." She grinned nastily. "Foxglove for poisoning people's espresso..."

"Paean!" The Doc shook her head. "That's not particularly funny. And have you brought any of your herbs aboard with you?"

"Only a bit of hemlock," said Paean casually.

"I hope that's another tasteless joke," said the Doc. "And why this interest in herbology?"

"Doc, we're from Molly Street," said Paean. "That's not a rich place. We cut corners. We grow our own potatoes in our gardens. Medications are expensive. I was the neighbourhood herb witch. Used to make remedies for everyone. Mother and me. Our remedies always worked." She went quiet, frowning. Battling.

"And where's Mother now?" probed the Doc.

Paean turned away. "Excuse me, Doc, I need the bathroom," she said and made her escape.

"It's called the heads," Doc corrected in her absence. She activated her wrist-com. "Captain, a free moment?"

"Certainly, Doc."

"About the Donegals."

"Ah, yes," said Lascek tiredly. "That's one I've been putting off. They're nice kids, actually. Did one of them say something?"

"I'm afraid it may be rather sinister," said Doc Judith.

"So, the Bronberg, Sherman," Wolf pushed.

"You know, the sad thing? I can't really remember what happened to the blue Bronberg," said Sherman. "She went in to investigate the slaver situation and uncovered an illegal nuclear testing site. Was already on her way back to Cape Town when she disappeared."

"What!" Now he had their attention.

"We think it was a rogue wave," said Sherman. "Happens a lot, in that Channel."

"Rogue wave," said Shawn. "What's that?"

"Where the surf from a storm collides with a major current," said Sherman. "They can get thirty metres high. They swallow ships."

"Thirty feet?" guessed Ronan.

"Hundred feet," said Sherman. "Thirty metres. Fourteen stories on a mid-city flats block. You Donegals haven't yet weathered a proper storm at sea. We've had surprisingly fair weather so far this passage. Wait and see! And the Bronberg was sighted about two years back, off the Cape of Storms. Work that one out!" He got up. "Please, kids, excuse me. I can't focus on my tall tale. That Panama debacle's worrying me too much." He moved towards the bridge.

Ronan got up and followed him at a run.

"Sherman, I'm sorry! Didn't mean to break your speed."

Sherman chuckled. "You didn't, Donegal! I was waiting for much more from you, actually. But I'm serious. Panama's a death trap. We'll have to try talking Captain into rounding the Cape. We'll not make it through Panama this time."

"That bad, huh?"

"Worse." Sherman walked off to the bridge, leaving Ronan standing worrying. This was a lot worse than any ghost story. This was their life!

He turned, and nearly tripped as he came face to face with the very sudden Rushka.

"Captain demands to see the Donegals in the boardroom!"

8

The Donegals' trial

Cold spotlights irradiated the blue boardroom from all around the tops of the walls. The huge flat screen against the stern-side wall was off; not in use. At Captain's fake pine boardroom table, Jon Marsden and Doc Judith had taken seats; Federi was in an inconspicuous corner, apparently absorbed in assembling some or other small gadget. The door was closed; but Paean knew that Rushka was guarding, outside.

The Donegal sibs were standing, lined up for execution. The large, carved analogue clock over the screen was ticking softly, tick, tick. Carved out of compounding. Strange how such details stood out when it was your last hour that was ticking away. Oh hell, oh hell, she should have had the sense and stayed out of that lab! And kept her loud trap shut! Paean Loudmouth, she berated herself. Rats all over!

She thought back to the blue early this morning; to the way things had almost normalized in her mind, with their predicament almost forgotten, and such issues as recalcitrant friends taking her attention. She should have realized. Her guard had slipped. Their borrowed days were up; all three of them were going to pay with their lives for her carelessness.

Radomir Lascek paced before them, measured, grave.

"When I hire new crew," he said eventually, "it's always a surprise packet. Donegals, let me first apologize. I as your Captain should have taken care of this the day you boarded. I might say in my defence that I had my mind on somewhat larger things."

Paean's eyes darted to the gathered older crew. Witnesses, that was all they were. And of course Doc Judith, the prosecutor. She saw Federi's mouth twitch at the "larger things". But when she looked at him, he avoided her eyes.

"Take this to heart, Donegals," announced Radomir Lascek. "The Solar Wind is a pirate ship. Does this mean we have no law? No! On the

Solar Wind, I am the Law! I make the law, I enforce it; I deal with who oversteps it."

Paean heard Ronan swallow.

What form would their execution take? Would Captain hand them over to the Unicate? Would he kill them himself? She hoped that her brothers would forgive her.

"Paean Donegal," said Radomir Lascek, bending down to eye level with her, placing a firm, authoritative hand on her shoulder. "One of my most important laws is that of secrecy. No secrets from the Captain, on the Solar Wind!"

She nodded, her throat dry.

"What are you hiding? What have you done?"

"She's done nothing, Captain, she's innocent," said Ronan.

Radomir Lascek shot the young man a single glance, then returned his attention to Paean.

"If you are innocent, why do you fear execution?"

Paean stared straight ahead and said nothing. If she said nothing, nothing could be held against her. It was a silly notion.

The Captain straightened out and glared at Ronan.

"And you? Speak up!"

"Captain, we're innocent," said Ronan.

Lascek shook his head. Paean watched him, then glanced again at Federi, who was studying her. For once there was no humour in his black eyes, only – sadness? Almost a friend, she thought glumly. If she had trusted him and told him? Could he have turned things? Or would he have turned them in? Would he have kept mum and she'd simply have had a friend for a few days?

Radomir Lascek's cold glare brushed Paean once more, then he turned to Shawn. The boy would have grown into a man taller than Captain, thought Paean. And a better man! How low, to cut him down now while he was still small and defenceless! She took in how her little brother stood proud, fearless, facing his Captain with confidence.

Aw hell! How could she allow Captain to ruin that? As Radomir Lascek drew a breath to speak, Paean interrupted.

"Captain..."

He turned back to her.

"Will you let my brothers go? I'll tell you all."

"Paean, no!" exclaimed Ronan. "Captain, she's done nothing! She's innocent!"

"Donegal, quiet!" thundered Lascek. "Let your sister speak!"

Paean took a deep breath. Here we go, she thought. "Captain, do you promise you'll let my brothers go? After all the Unicate only needs one guilty party."

"Paean –" started Ronan and flinched from the Captain's glare.

"Paean Donegal, this is like the proverbial dentistry. State your case and then we shall decide! Dr Judith mentioned that it might have something to do with you giving your mother unwholesome herbal preparations. Paean Donegal, tell me everything."

Paean nearly felt the electric shock that went through the gypsy. She glanced. He turned his head away. She blinked, confused. *What* was that Captain had said? "Captain, pardon?"

"You poisoning your mother," repeated Radomir Lascek patiently.

"Poisoning Mother!" This was one too many. It started as an exclamation and ended as a great, heartbroken sob. "No! That's not true! I didn't!"

Mother, lying grey and emaciated in her bed, bleeding, bleeding ceaselessly, from her nose, her eyes, her mouth... Blood all over her, over the sheets, the pillow, Paean's hands... Mother had died in her arms. Tears came down in a torrential deluge. She couldn't stop them. The box had been opened. The nightmares spilled out of it, there was no way to put them back and ram the lid back into place. Paean covered her face in her hands.

A gentle hand touched her shoulder. The elderly Doc was there beside her.

"I misunderstood, didn't I?"

Doc Judith had no idea. Guilty as charged. Herbal home-remedies were illegal; and with reason. Sometimes they went wrong.

Radomir Lascek studied the scene of the nervous breakdown, and then the other two sibs. He wouldn't push Shawn with a feather right now; the boy looked as though he were going to go the way of his sister in a second. There was no information to be got out of him now. Ronan remained standing, straight, proud – and mightily angry.

Radomir Lascek focused on the older brother, frowning. They could cover all they liked, with anger and tears and emotional breakdowns – but he would get their dark secret out of them! He had to! He didn't ship a crew of pirates around the world out of sight of the Unicate only to endanger them with the presence of real criminals!

"So Ronan, if that's not what happened, would you care to enlighten me? Why are you three on the run? If your mother wasn't poisoned, what did Paean actually do to her? Was it an accident? Was it drug-related?"

Ronan took a deep breath.

"Captain, with respect. That was unnecessarily cruel! My sister has suffered the most of all of us. How can you accuse her of something so vile?"

"Without knowing the facts, Donegal?"

He could literally see the cogs working in the oldest Donegal's mind. The young man was clearly weighing up the risks of telling him the truth against the risk of remaining silent. If they refused to talk, he'd turn them over in Plymouth, he thought. Send in Jon Marsden, or Federi… But they would talk! He had experience in making people tell him things.

Clearly the truth won out. Ronan's shoulders lifted in a hell-with-it expression.

"Captain, in brief, here's what happened," he said. "I don't know what the regulations are in the rest of the world, but in Dublin you need a medical care license if you want to be treated by a doctor when you get ill. Our license was up for its yearly renewal and we didn't have the quid. So it lapsed. My sibs are under age and we hadn't yet figured out that if we play a gig I'm the earner and they're just there for the fun. That's legal."

"And your father?" asked Radomir Lascek.

He could see how the boy had to restrain himself from spitting on the deck. "What's a father, Captain?"

"Do carry on!" prompted Lascek. He had thought so.

"So our mother came home ill from the factory the one day," continued Ronan. "Once you're ill, you can forget it, they're not renewing the license without a fine the value of your head. We think it was a virus. But on second thought, it may have been poison. Paean and she tried fighting it out with herbal medication, but it was no use. She bled to death, eventually. Was not pretty!"

107

He sniffed loudly but kept staring defiantly at the Captain. Radomir Lascek nodded.

"So it wasn't your sister's herbal concoctions that killed your mother?"

"Captain, we're from Molly Street," said Ronan proudly. "Mother was our neighbourhood healer. Who needs doctors?" He glanced at Doc Judith. "With respect, Doctor. But Paean and our mother cured a lot of common colds and flu's and tonsillitis and stomach upsets – a lot of things with their herbs. I would say, Paean and our mother knew their herbs too well to make mistakes. In any case they never used the really poisonous ones. Too risky."

"So then if you are innocent, why did you run?"

"We're legally liable for her death because in those six months we couldn't raise the licence penalty money," replied Ronan. "Maybe the hospital could have saved her. Unicate came looking for us the day she died."

"That same day?" asked Lascek.

"Yes." Ronan shrugged. "We've broken many laws, Captain. We stopped school. We all three worked under age. We used herbal medication on a dying person. We evaded justice. We had to leave her there…" He stared straight up at the ceiling, fighting for his voice back. "So, Captain, if you want to put us to death for that, pick me and spare my sibs. I'm the adult in the equation."

"How long between her getting sick and her dying?" asked Jon Marsden, worried.

"Six months," said Ronan.

Radomir Lascek started pacing. This was grave! He exchanged troubled glances with Jon Marsden, who scowled back; then with Federi.

" 's the truth," mouthed the gypsy.

"I know," replied Lascek dismally. "Easier if it weren't! Ye Powers, and what do we do now?" He turned to Doc Judith, who was talking softly at Paean, trying to pacify her. "Doc, what do you make of that?"

"Pardon, Captain?" asked the doctor. "I wasn't listening."

Radomir Lascek repeated the essence of Ronan's story.

"Haemorrhagic fever," said Doc Judith. "Bio-engineered to stretch over six months. The original wipes you out in forty-eight hours. Those bio-engineered viruses defeat the strongest immune system. Paean, there's nothing wrong with your herbal remedies. You had no chance from the beginning. A shot of highly specific antiviral along with interferon would have fixed it."

"That's what the Unicate withheld, via the expired license," commented Lascek. "Doc, so the Unicate hunts them for the death of their mother, and they step aboard and damn the whole crew of the Solar Wind?"

Doc Judith fell silent. The clock ticked.

"None of us caught it in six months," said Ronan. "Paean was working the closest with Mom, she was helping her, practically the whole time."

"The incubation time might be even longer," the Doc pointed out. She stared darkly at the three siblings.

Ronan cleared his throat.

"So, Captain, what happens now? Will you turn us over to the Unicate in Plymouth?"

Radomir Lascek turned to his officers. "Conference on the bridge," he ordered. "Who stays behind with the Donegals?"

"I shall," volunteered Doc Judith.

"No, Doc, I need you in the conference. Federi?"

"*Shukar,* Captain," said the gypsy.

The Captain, Doc Judith and Jonathan Marsden left the boardroom, taking Rushka with them who had been on guard outside the door.

Silence descended in the boardroom. The three sibs stared at each other, frightened. They dashed suspicious glances at Federi.

"It's going to be okay," said Shawney eventually. "I'm sure Captain thinks like a fair man."

"He's going to make us walk the plank," argued Paean moodily. "Sorry, you two. My loud mouth!"

The gypsy's eyebrows went up, and he smiled at Paean.

"Least you're innocent," he said. "See it that way."

A bio-engineered virus! She sighed and shrugged, close to tears again. Innocent. Months of shaky guilt released her slowly, one by one like a swarm of disinterested piranhas. It had looked like a common flu at first, and Paean had made Mother their own home-mixed flu remedy as she always did; but it didn't go away, and so Paean had upped the strength and

109

frequency of the tea, uneasily because she knew that it also thinned the blood. Then the nose bleeds started; Paean immediately stopped giving Mother any further willow bark based tea and started her investigation into other herbs. Cat's claw, kava kava… they all had side effects, and not all were equally available. She peddled small favours with a Roma family in lower Dublin to entice them to get hold of some herbs for her via their relatives and contacts in the Free Gypsies – a highly risky endeavour for both her and the Roma. And with each of the herbs, new symptoms emerged. It was a nightmare!

The more frantically she tried to help Mother and doctor her back to health, the worse things got. Eventually she didn't give Mother any herbs at all, in a hope that it would all go away – but once more the disease was ahead of her and turned for the worse, so that Paean resumed the herbal fight. In the same time she and her brothers pulled out all the stops to earn enough money to get that licence restored – in vain. Several times they were close – but the Unicate wanted the whole amount in a single go, and every time they went in, there was some inflation and the goal-post was once again just out of reach.

In those months she had started fearing that Mother was sick because of her herbal teas, and especially too much willow bark tea. Or that perhaps a poisonous plant had slipped into the harvest – how, she could not imagine, but who knew. Mother died literally drowning in her own blood. Paean remembered having blood on her hands permanently those final two weeks. It haunted her at night in her dreams. Sometimes in the daytime too.

"Federi," Ronan's voice interrupted her troubled musings, "what's your position? What landed you on the Solar Wind? I'm not aware that Roma mingle easily with the *gadje!*"

"Not a Rrom," replied Federi, "Tzigan. Difference."

"What's the difference?" asked Ronan.

"Tzigany are Free Gypsies."

Ronan stared at Federi in surprise. The man was a Free Gypsy? Those were so elusive and secretive, few people ever met any in their lives! And they *never* mixed with non-gypsies! What on Earth was the man doing working on the ship, solitary, amongst *gadje?*

"But –"

Federi smiled. "I'm an outlaw," he said with a shrug. "Aren't we all? Good enough, Donegal?"

"What do you think Captain will do to us?" asked Paean despondently. "For bringing the virus aboard the ship?"

Federi sighed and glanced down at the gadget in his hands.

"Don't know, little songbird. Was a mistake. Should have told him, got yourselves quarantined. Can't see how it should make much difference anyway..."

"What do you mean, Federi?" asked Shawn.

"Panama," said the Tzigan grimly. " 's a death trap. No way round it. No way through it. End of line. Captain won't listen!"

"Federi, I'm sure those are officer's confidences," said Ronan. "Why tell us?

"What's the point?" replied Federi with a shrug. "Going to die anyway, all of us, in another five or eight days. Six eggs if I tell you."

The Captain, Doc Judith and Jon Marsden returned to the boardroom with grim expressions, Rushka with them this time. The mysterious girl took up her post standing by the closed door, gazing a hole into the air. Guarding again, thought Paean.

"Donegal," said Radomir Lascek to Ronan, "you come with me. Federi, you supervise Shawn. Doc, as discussed."

Doc Judith approached Paean.

"Come with me, Paean. To the lab."

Paean grabbed onto the closest chair, eyes wide with alarm. They were to be separated? Killed one by one?

"Captain," she begged, "please..."

"What now, Miss Donegal?"

"At least – can we have a bit of time to ourselves first? To say goodbye?" Tears were threatening again. She fought them down, thinking frantically. If she could only get her brothers alone, they could maybe come up with a plan, a getaway...

"To say goodbye?" repeated Radomir Lascek, frowning. "What's this?"

"Why are you executing us separately?" sobbed Paean. "What's Shawney done to deserve it? He's just a kid! And Ro is innocent too!"

"*Execute you!* What kind of a man do you think I am?" exploded the Captain. "Execute you! For the Unicate murdering your mother and then hunting you for it! There shall be no executions! I'm protecting you! The only thing I have to consider is how to protect the rest of my crew too!"

Paean wailed loudly and hid her face. Doc Judith put her arm around her shoulders and led her out of the boardroom.

"Sedative for you, girl," she declared. "Did you honestly think for a second that Captain intended to put you all to death?"

Paean nodded.

"He's a fair man," said Doc Judith. "He runs a tight ship; but that's necessary. We wouldn't survive any other way. But he never hurts innocents. You and I, Paean, we are going to do like you said you wanted to. We'll look after people's health. We're going to try and isolate your virus, and clone an antiviral."

"Genetics," said Paean. "Is that not illegal?"

"Then again we're pirates," Doc Judith pointed out with a smile.

"Why did Paean have to go with Doc?" asked Shawn anxiously.

"Taking care of the medical crisis," said Radomir Lascek. "I hope we're in time. We've been everywhere spreading it! Hamilton Port. Anya Miller and her crew! Ali! How on Earth are we going to contain this one? It's all over the place now!"

"Captain, if the mother of the Donegals had it, it's all over Dublin in any case," said Federi.

The Captain nodded thoughtfully.

"You're right, Federi. And if it is over Dublin, it ought to be over the whole world by sunset. Ha! That may in fact sort our problem in Panama! Maybe it spreads more slowly than that. Well, back to work, men! Federi, check up on Doc Judith's progress every half-hour and report back to me."

"Yes, Captain."

Paean watched in apprehension as Doc Judith drew blood from her. The sample got fed into a small, sleek machine, and Doc pressed a series of buttons, programming the machine.

"The Genitron," she explained. They waited. Doc Judith paged in the lab's console, pages and pages of what looked like scientific text.

"There we go," she said eventually, "haemorrhagic fever. Now we feed that into the Genitron…"

The small, sleek machine emitted a beep.

"We've got a match," said Doc Judith with a completely uncharacteristic grin. "Lookie here!"

Paean bent over the screen of the Genitron. All she could see was long rows of letters.

"There," said the Doc and pointed to a highlighted red area where the letters were doubled. "Now we analyse! *In situ!*"

She focused on her work, typing in variables and reading, and typing some more, and reading again. Eventually she sat back.

"Paean, listen. This is very strange. I don't know if these data are reliable; we'll repeat it in a second. But what it means is this. You carry the virus all over you; probably by now, all of us do. But according to this none of us is going to get sick from it. Not you either, nor your brothers."

"Why?"

"Because it's a disabled virus."

"But – my mother died from it!"

"Yes," agreed Doc Judith. "You have to understand the mechanism of this piece of artillery. It's broken now. It broke when it got out of your mother – what was her name?"

"Annie Donegal," said Paean softly.

"This virus is a Unicate design, specifically created for Annie Donegal," said Doc Judith. "They didn't want it spreading and wiping Dublin clean, that's why they built in the safety catch. Exposure to air breaks it."

Paean stared at Doc Judith, only taking in half of what she was saying. "I don't understand."

"We'll clone an antiviral anyway," said Doc Judith. "To be safe and put Captain at ease. But there's no risk. Nobody got this virus. Your mother was assassinated, Paean."

Ronan found that he had been included in the discussion on the bridge about the crossing of Panama. This surprised him immensely. For now he tried to say nothing and only listen.

"The Crow's Nest will have to come down," said Radomir Lascek with a sigh. "Now they know we're radar cloaked, they'll be looking at our outline, visually. Makes a false identity so much more difficult!"

"Can't we submerge all the way?" asked Ronan.

"Those sluice gates," replied Sherman Dougherty, who had been holding the bridge during the Donegals' trial and was still at the console. "They only let ships through that obtain authorization. That's the whole problem!"

"Captain, I'd much rather round the Cape," said Rushka. Ronan nodded. That sounded a lot more sensible.

"I know that, Rushka," replied Lascek. "That's why you're not the Captain!"

Rushka shut her mouth.

"We're landing at Plymouth," said Lascek.

"If she's still a free port," commented Marsden.

"Working on the assumption that she is," said Lascek. "That should give us some space to think. Time to do the Solar Wind's face change."

"Here I am, Captain." Federi had gainfully employed Shawn in the galley, along with Rhine Gold, and was now reporting in for the officer's meeting.

"Good that you're here," said Lascek. "Should we call the Doc too? I suppose, not the Doc. Find out for me how things are going in the lab."

"Yes, Captain!"

Federi appeared in the door of the lab, watching silently as Doc Judith operated the machinery. Paean raised her gaze to him, feeling drowsy and warm from the potent non-herbal sedative the doctor had given her. She was thankful for the medication; it blunted all edges to all feelings and made her too sleepy to remember.

The gypsy was studying her out of his dark eyes.

"Hi, Federi," said Doc Judith, glancing up from the console.

"Captain wants to know how things are going," said the gypsy.

"Smoothly," said Doc Judith. "Tell him, we're creating the immunization as we're speaking. We'll come round and inject everyone tomorrow through the day."

"Will tell him. Can I borrow Paean for a second?" asked Federi.

"Certainly."

Nothing happened for a few seconds.

"Paean?" prompted the Doc.

"Uh?"

"Go," said the Doc, motioning.

"*Shukar,* Doc," muttered Paean. She followed the gypsy uncertainly. He only led her as far as the passageway.

"Where did you learn that expression?" pounced Federi.

"Heard you use it."

"I see." He frowned. "Are you alright?"

"Fine, thanks," said the little redhead. "Just Doc gave me a sheda... a sedative."

Federi grinned briefly at her slip of tongue. "Feeling better about things?"

"Shomewhat."

"Shee? – er, see?" He laughed and shook his mane. "Captain's a fair man!"

Paean smiled. Since the Captain's verdict, her entire outlook had taken a leap. They were not living on borrowed time anymore. Their time had been given back to them, all the way: A present from Captain Radomir Lascek. They didn't have to fear the Unicate, any more than the rest of the crew did. They didn't have to fear execution by the Captain anymore, either. Instead he was keeping them safe. The man was her hero.

"Thanks for looking after Shawney," she said.

"Sure. Stole this for you in Hamilton." Federi handed her something turquoise.

"Oh wow, a moonbag!" Paean beamed and fastened it around her waist. "Thanks!"

"Pleasure," replied Federi. "You'll find it handy. Get back to work now! Shoo!"

Paean smiled and returned to the lab.

"He's a shweet guy," she said to the Doc.

"That he is," agreed Doc Judith with a smile.

Only then did Paean find the fly in the ointment. Had he said he'd *stolen* it for her -?

*

9

Stalling in Plymouth

Paean opened her eyes. How she had got to her bunk, she had no recollection. She did remember vaguely about the Doc coming in the middle of the night and giving her another injection, after which she had slept some more. Now she was awake, if still lethargic.

She recalled about all the blood. She'd had a horrible nightmare about blood. Her mother's blood, all over her, not only her hands but her face, her mouth, her eyes; the live virus crawling into her via the blood; the sea, moving and churning blood; and then a still, cold lake of grey-green water devoid of life. The end of the world. A name. Lake Gatun.

Somehow that eerie, empty place had spooked her worse than all the violent blood in the dream before. She had woken up screaming hysterically. Which was when Doc had given her the second shot of sedative.

The antiviral! Paean swung her legs out of her bunk, noticing the soft leather moonbag she was clutching like a fluffy toy. Turquoise teddy bear, she thought. Yes, it would indeed come in extremely handy. She loaded her pennywhistle into it and strapped it around her waist before she even changed shirts. Time to report to Doc.

Half an hour later Doc Judith and Pacan went around injecting the crew with the antiviral. The doctor had briefed Paean to not tell the sailors what it was for. It was vitamins, and period. She didn't want to precipitate panic. Of course Paean braved the first injection; then she found Ronan on the bridge, being taught the console by Rushka, and gave him his, while Doc Judith took care of the older sailors and the Captain. After Ronan, Paean injected Rushka, who simply bared her arm without a comment and accepted the sting.

"Hurt?" asked Paean.

"No," said Rushka and returned to the instructing of Ronan.

Not talkative, thought Paean. She went down the steps and trotted along to the galley and found Shawn, Rhine Gold and Federi busy preparing meals again.

"Who goes first?" she asked, brandishing her syringe with a maniacal grin.

"Go for it, sis," grinned Shawn and presented his biceps.

Paean punched him. "Relax that muscle, kiddo! Otherwise it hurts!" She injected him nicely, the way Doc had shown her. He was already her third victim, so she was picking up experience.

"Who's next? Reinhold?"

The huge blond sailor blinked his sky-blue eyes in surprise. "You said it right," he commented.

"Course," she replied. "Ready?"

Rhine Gold looked a bit squeamish. Paean found it funny that such a powerful young guy should cringe from an injection.

"Come on, Rhine, it doesn't hurt," encouraged Shawney. Federi glanced back from his frying pans, where tomatoes were being singed.

Under protest and bellyaching, Rhine Gold received his injection. Paean moved on, loading the next disposable syringe from her turquoise moonbag. She looked up and caught Federi's grin.

"That coming in handy?"

"Very," she smiled. "You next?" She reached for his left sleeve.

"Hang in there," said Federi and ruffled up his right sleeve instead.

"Ah," said Paean sagely. "You're left-handed." She scowled at the scars that marked the olive skin of that sinewy arm. He looked as though he'd made personal contact with a meat shredder at some point in the distant past.

The gypsy grinned and said nothing.

Ailyss was alone in the machine room when Paean entered. The redhead had hoped that Wolf would be there too. Oh well. She loaded a syringe.

"What is this?" asked Ailyss suspiciously.

"Vitamins," replied Paean. "Got to have them. We're all getting them. Doctor's orders."

"I don't need vitamins," said Ailyss. "No, thanks."

Paean sat down on a square metal box. It was a bit warm.

"Don't sit there!" yelped Ailyss. "That's radioactive!"

"Yow!" Paean got up again. "What I meant to say, Ailyss, you'd better take this injection. It covers you against the nastiest disease I've ever seen."

"What is this?" asked Ailyss again, putting down the copper wires she had been twisting. She was alone in the machine room, and there was nothing much happening, so she amused herself with metalwork. A spy novel was lying next to her, with a bookmark about halfway. Paean found this strange. She knew that her brothers thought Ailyss was an agent. She thought they must be wrong. Which agent would read spy novels?

Sure, Ailyss was cagey and hedgy, but so had she herself been up until yesterday! Ailyss was only a bit better at it, that was all! Who knew what tragedy lurked in the older girl's story?

Well, there might be one in her future if she kept refusing the injection! Doc had said it was unlikely, but it couldn't be ruled out that the disabled virus recombined with a common cold or flu or other everyday jinx to mutate into something disastrous. Virus did that, sometimes.

"If you want to die from a haemorrhagic fever virus about seven months in the future, then refuse this injection," said Paean. Never be vague when applying pressure; this she had learnt from having two brothers.

The older girl studied her intently.

"You're serious!"

"Dead serious. Ailyss, our mother died from that. We Donegals brought it aboard. The Doc is taking preventive measures, doesn't want the whole crew to die!"

"So that's why you've been so cagey!" Ailyss rolled up her sleeve and presented her shoulder. "Inject away," she said. "Sorry I gave you resistance. You never know."

"You're right, you got to be careful," agreed Paean. "Can't just go trusting any old one. There, I hope that didn't hurt too much?"

"Not a bit," lied Ailyss, smiling. "Paean, seems like you're a sensible girl. Are you aware that this is a pirate ship?"

Paean paused. Ailyss had not been in on that briefing.

"You're kidding," she said.

"You're lying," replied Ailyss, smiling. "I can tell. You already knew."

"Got to go," said Paean. "Still have twenty other people to inject!"

"Twenty?" Ailyss counted in her head. There weren't that many sailors on the Solar Wind. "Well, have fun!" Strange kid, she thought.

Weird girl, thought Paean as she made her way up out of the bilges.

The Solar Wind sailed into Plymouth's harbour later that week, under shade of night and a false identity. The Bronberg. Ronan grinned indecently about this.

"I promise that's the first time the Solar Wind has used that name," old Sherman insisted. They stood on the prow, watching Plymouth's lights. Ronan had asked Sherman whether he could have a puff on his pipe and had instead got a vicious lecture about never taking that first drag.

To the crew's relief the port was still a free-trading town. A beautifully Stab-free harbour greeted them.

They docked and moored the Solar Wind, Ronan and Rhine Gold receiving instruction from Federi and Wolf on how to fasten the mooring cables on the ship by the mellow glow of the deck lights.

"This harbour is deeper than it was when it was originally built, too," mentioned Sherman. "The water level is higher by a number of feet."

"A few feet," said Shawn, helping Ronan securing a hawser to a cleat with a huge metal clip. "Do a few feet matter? A metre or two?"

"Do they matter! Those two or three metres caused Holland and Florida and Japan and various other flatlands to build enormous dykes! The coping mechanisms on the Pacific tropical islands were unbelievable. And Samoa was submerged. But we're talking a good few decades ago. The sea has dropped back to within half a metre of its original level. And many of the islands have recovered."

"How can they recover from that?" asked Ronan, puzzled. He suspected another tall story.

"They were actively repopulated and replanted by the Rebellion," Federi threw in, glancing up from coiling up deck lines. The sheets, lines used for the sails, were self-coiling – those that needed to be coiled in the first place. "The original population was rescued and taken to Australia."

"So the Rebellion are the good guys?" asked Ronan.

Federi got a thoughtful look. *"Nu,"* he said softly. "Don't really think so."

The Captain allowed the Donegals to go ashore, along with Wolf and Rhine Gold. They sat in a plush coffee bar and sipped espressos with their first wages from the Solar Wind. Paean could see clearly again; the long night's sleep and the work in the early morning had restored her brain back from the sedative. And her mood had improved by a hundred miles.

"Nice to have wages to spend," she grinned.

"Even nicer that one doesn't have to spend them," growled Ronan, who was drinking only water. Having had the responsibility of running the Donegal household on their meagre takings from gigs, his sense of financial freedom had received a severe knock. He was too thankful that someone else had to worry about provisioning the ship!

"Och, relax, Ro, I'll sponsor you for this one," Shawn offered generously. "Get yourself something!"

"Sweet that they allowed us ashore," said Paean.

"Why?" asked Wolf. "Why should you not be allowed to go ashore?"

Paean glanced nervously at Ronan. Her loud mouth again!

"I think it's safe to tell him now," said her brother. Paean explained.

"Oh," said Rhine Gold. "That's why we got those injections!"

"Exactly."

"That was an interesting one there in Hamilton," said Wolf, changing the topic.

"Could have gone wrong," replied Ronan. "What if they had cottoned on? Are there any other ships that have Crow's Nests?"

"Only on the virtual records," grinned Wolf.

"What do you mean? – Oh!" Shawn laughed. "All the false identities of the Solar Wind!"

"Exactly. Someone who hasn't been operating the system too long can easily assume that a Crow's Nest is an optional add-on for Zephyrs!"

"So how are we going to get through Panama?" asked Rhine Gold.

Ronan smiled.

"You!" Rhine Gold rounded on him. "You sit in on the officer's meetings! Won't you leak a bit to us?"

"Nope," grinned Ronan. Wolf grinned too.

"So you're in on it as well?" asked Rhine Gold.

"Let's say – trust our Captain," said Wolf. "For that matter – how long have we been sitting here wasting time?"

"Have another cappuccino," prompted Rhine Gold.

"Not as good as Federi's," grumbled Wolf.

"But a lot more expensive!" replied Shawn with a bright smile.

The shore party returned around eleven, with Rushka moodily waiting for them aboard the ship. The Captain's daughter had once again been forbidden to go ashore.

Federi watched from the shadows. He thought he'd really have to take that up with the Captain again soon. Ever since the girl had started developing some frontage six years ago, her father had kept her locked on the ship, not allowing her ashore anywhere, ever. He didn't want the strong-willed teen to get into trouble. This had of course resulted in secretive, insubordinate escape episodes. Federi had repeatedly helped her get out; he had also talked her back onto the ship once or twice. He'd fielded several confrontations with the Captain about this Rapunzel situation, meeting a brick wall every time. He shook his head and grinned wryly. Well, the next one was due. He'd give it some real steam this time. It might be Rushka's last opportunity to go ashore, ever.

The night passed; the morning dawned; they were no closer to raising anchor. The officers and the Captain met at erratic intervals, sharing their new ideas. Doc Judith returned to the lab. She was pleased that she had a little apprentice she could train; Panama was a hair-raising debacle, with or without a distracting manoeuvre. She felt, along with Rushka and the rest of the officers, that they should round the Cape. Even with painting the hull of the ship royal blue, as the crew was doing right now, and giving her the identity of Bronberg, the Doc couldn't see how they could con the Unicate. The Crow's Nest was going to be dismantled too, closer to Panama, on the open ocean. The Captain was wary of watchers. But even so! That stunt in Hamilton had no doubt served to turn the full attention of the Unicate on the Solar Wind.

Doc Judith locked the lab at five in the morning, and was suddenly aware of a dark gaze.

"Hi, Federi."

"Hi, Doc."

"You're up early again," she mentioned. "Checking on everything?"

The gypsy nodded. "Not early, Doc. Late."

So he'd been up the whole night again!

"Sleepless?" guessed the doctor.

Federi grinned. "Can sleep when I'm dead!"

"Worried," concluded Doc Judith.

Federi nodded gravely. "Doc, I wish Captain would listen! The officers are unanimous that we should round the Cape."

Doc Judith sighed. Panama had them spooked. Even Captain. If it didn't worry him, they'd be on their way by now.

"And you have no plan either?" she probed.

"I do," said Federi. "Cut and run. Best plan ever! Then again this is not a democracy," he added with a grin.

That was right. And they were all feeling it acutely. The whole crew was scared of Panama; the more informed they were, the more it scared them. A death-trap. But Captain wasn't budging from his plan. And Captain's word was law. Basta.

Another bright blue morning. But the light-heartedness of yesterday was gone. It felt to Paean as though the blue was only a prop, and if you peeled it off the sky, behind it there was darkness. If she stared into the sky long enough, she could actually spot the black behind the blue.

" 's the universe," laughed her little brother when she pointed it out to him.

"Yeah, sure…" That wasn't what she meant. Since she could relax about her own past, she had been observing the others. And the older crew slunk about with terrible frowns and stressed eyes. Doc Judith was downright morose about Panama. This stopover in Plymouth wasn't a holiday. It was Captain, out of plans.

Urgh! Something had to happen; something had to give. Paean knew that they were dressing the Solar Wind up as someone else, meaning to sneak through the Channel and all the gates. From what she had learnt about satellite identities, the harbour authorities considered them infallible. This did give her hope, because Jon Marsden clearly knew how to reprogram the Solar Wind's satellite ID. But it wasn't going to be enough, she knew. Captain knew too, or they'd be on their way by now. He needed more.

It worried her relentlessly as she went through the drill of dissecting a raw chicken some time later that morning, and sutured it up, a skill a young paramedic had to have, as Doc Judith insisted. Paean wondered vaguely how many chickens got into scrapes on pirate vessels and had to be stitched. And if she'd be stitching the surviving crew after Panama.

"This is terribly shoddy work," scolded the Doc. "I can see your mind's not on it."

"I know," replied Paean with a sigh. "Worried about Panama."

"I'd leave the worrying to the strategists," said the Doc soothingly. She would be in that strategic meeting right now, but she had nothing to bring, today.

She studied Paean thoughtfully and wondered about three young people who had somehow acquired a lot of learning without attending school. She was intent on finding out how Paean had learnt about Sophokles and Descartes, and in which way her more detailed than average view of history coloured her political perception.

"Shall I show you how I cloned bioluminescence?" she offered to take Paean's mind off Panama.

"Oh yes, please!" Paean was highly excited.

"It's really simple," said the Doc, leaving the remains of the chicken carcass in the galley for Federi to cook for lunch, "it works like a puzzle. Say you have an organism here," she said, grabbing a writing pad. "Let's take an Ecoli. And you want it to do something for you. Say, glow in the dark. Bioluminescence. What you do is go look for something that does that naturally. You read up until you find the gene that causes it. That process has been simplified for us by the researchers of the twenty-first century, before the Unicate. They set up huge gene libraries. And Sherman Dougherty rescued those data for the Solar Wind!"

Paean's eyes widened. "Sherman was a geneticist?"

"Sherman was an information technologist," said the Doc. "He survived the Unicate Takeover. Now he's a source of knowledge and joy."

124

"How did he come by a gene library?" asked Paean.

"He predicted which way the wind was blowing and copied down a lot of data from the international files. On all sorts of what they call subversive topics today. All openly available in those days of freedom, Paean! He kept all those old memory sticks, and drives from those days that can decipher the ancient data. Sherman was right! The Unicate closed access to all that information, first thing after their takeover."

Paean listened in shock.

"Jon Marsden adapted the Solar Wind's processor so she could access all those ancient files. It's been invaluable! They knew a lot in those days. Today a few top secret places know it all, and the rest is kept in darkness."

"So there's a lot of stuff I could learn simply off the ship computer," said Paean, ears hot with excitement.

"Now focus, Paean," said the Doc and showed the young girl how to program the Genitron. Genetics, which had once been complicated, had been simplified to extremes by the pre-Unicate scientists and simplified further by Doc Judith and Jon Marsden. The Solar Wind's processor did a lot of the actual work.

"I'd like to clone a bug that keeps Panama running to the loo for as long as we're in the Canal," said Paean viciously.

"Paean!" The Doc was shocked.

"They can't catch us that way," said Paean.

"You never, never ever release a GM organism into the wild," said the Doc angrily. "The results are completely unpredictable! That's why genetic research was outlawed."

"Well, the Unicate does," muttered Paean. "Case in point, Annie Donegal!"

"Well, you won't!" ordered the Doc.

"Not even if it only makes them drowsy a few hours?" asked Paean. "Just long enough for us to pass unnoticed?"

"Laughing gas!" exclaimed the Doc, staring at her. "Paean, you are a genius!" She left the baffled teenager in the lab and hurried off into the strategic meeting she had been bunking.

Paean stared at the Genitron. And the gene library on the console. She knew she could do it! But she knew too little! Doc had only shown her the rudimentary basics. She paged back to the method on the console screen and read through it. Let's see if she could get it right alone with the example Doc had just shown her.

Actually, she suddenly understood, it was really simple! The element of chance, trial and error, had been completely removed from genetic manipulation, as long as one knew exactly what one was looking for. If she could get it programmed correctly on the *computer,* like Doc Judith would, and then just press the "de novo" button on the little machine... the last step in the chain was to make the information into a ring-shaped plasmid, something the *de novo* function could be set to do automatically, and shake up the plasmid with an Ecoli of choice...

"Just for interest's sake," she muttered, "Solar Wind, what is an Ecoli?" She typed the word into the console and pressed the look-up function key. "Ecoli – not found! Ecology... all that goes with that... Egoli – Place of Gold," she read, "central in Southern Free Country! Mined out of gold and uranium in 2064, insignificant mining town survives as largest town in Southern, blah, blah... Oh, well."

The "Gold" had drawn her eye. She paged through the gene library.

"Hey," said Shawn. "Still down here, sis? You'll get square eyes! You haven't been out all day! Going to get all pale and cheesy! Did you sleep in here last night?"

"This is so intriguing," muttered Paean, stalling him with a hand. "You should read the console, Shawn. Gee, there's a lot going on here!"

"Captain says we can go ashore again," said Shawn. "The seniors and Federi have decided that it's okay."

"Go ahead without me," said Paean absentmindedly. "Gosh, Shawn, this stuff is incredible! And look!" She pulled a small stopped-up tube out of the incubator. She blended it gently by turning it upside down a few times. "Switch the light off!"

Shawn complied. The tube glowed orange in the dark.

"Bioluminescence," said Paean. She grinned. "Now check!" She dug back into the incubator and fetched another tube. This one glowed green.

"The first one's Doc's recipe," said Paean. "This one," she held up the brighter, green tube, "is *mine!* What do you say to that, Shawney?"

126

"Wow," said her brother, his face greenish in the light of the tube. "Can you also program one to sing?"

"Need a lullaby?" laughed Paean. "Go, Brother! You're disturbing my circles!"

"Sure you don't want to come? Wolf's going to be there!"

Paean laughed mellowly. "Scoot, brother! Give the old ruffian my regards!"

"Not in love with him, are you?" teased Shawn.

Paean laughed again. "If I were, would I be telling you? Be off, wastrel!"

Shawn went off, worried about the way his sister was suddenly immersing herself in learning. It struck him as unnatural.

"Woof," said Paean with another laugh and shook her head. She had to admit, if she thought about it, that the young nuclear engineer did have nice eyes! Green ones. But it took more than eyes…

"They've been docked here for five days now," said Gina Nevada. "Captain, how long before you contact the forces?"

"I'm not contacting the forces!" Gomez laughed. "Want to share the prize money with everyone?"

"You're beginning to sound like Miller, Captain," said Gina. "It worries me."

"Don't worry! I only have to cook up a suitable ambush. I'm thinking, for now, let's collect information. Let's follow them as far as they can go."

"And when they're cornered at Panama, we take the prize," said Gina as though she had a logical plan for this.

"Something like that," said Gomez. He had parked the T-craft, the "Stab" vessel as civilians called it, in a boathouse out of sight. He and Gina had booked into a hotel and were watching the Solar Wind under plain clothes cover.

Paean drifted into the Solar Wind's bilges.

"Oh, hi," she said uncertainly.

Wolf looked up.

"Hello," he said shortly and returned his focus to his work. Ailyss was

127

ashore; the young crowd had insisted on taking her along, strongly supported by Federi. Wolf wondered irritably what Federi wanted from Ailyss. And Rushka had actually been allowed to tag along for once. How Federi had got that right, was a mystery. Marsden and Federi both had gone along as supervisors. And Doc Judith was taking a well-deserved rest, after which she wanted to go ashore too. She had been surprised when Paean had declined; but she had put it down to the girl still being afraid of being spotted by the authorities. Here in the free port of Plymouth!

"Aren't you going ashore?" asked Paean.

"Someone's got to baby-sit these drives," said Wolf. "Paean, you shouldn't be down here, there's classified stuff!"

"I'm a pirate, Wolf," said Paean. "There's honour amongst thieves, so I'm told. Got my own secrets too."

A smile lingered in the corner of Wolf's bearded mouth. He'd heard that line before!

"Tell me yours and I'll tell you mine," he offered.

"Really?"

"Paean, despite what you seem to believe – Wolf Svendsson doesn't lie. That was perhaps my biggest problem, that's how I ended here. Unicate requires a certain amount of lying. I couldn't do it."

Paean digested this. An honest pirate!

"We Donegals of Molly Street have always been honest," she volunteered, making herself comfortable on a metal box. "That's why it's difficult…"

"Don't sit there!" cautioned Wolf. "If you want your guts slowly grilled from below…"

"Eww!" Paean slipped off the nuclear drive casing. "That dangerous? Where can I sit?"

Wolf pointed at a wooden cabinet. Paean cleared herself a space on top of it.

"Please just don't scramble those cables," said Wolf, too late again. He sighed. "Oh well, I'll just have to do it all again."

"Sorry."

"So why haven't *you* gone ashore?"

"That's what I wanted to ask about," said Paean. "What's the plan

128

with Panama?"

"There isn't one," said Wolf. He bent over the console and wrinkled his face.

Ooh! Wolf Svendsson didn't lie? Paean knew from the smug way her older brother had been carrying himself that there was *some* sort of plan. She couldn't get it squeezed out of Ronan. Well, perhaps it was only part of a plan, she thought; that might explain it.

"So how are we going to get through?"

Wolf looked up.

"Lookie here, Paean. I know you're the ship's little candy girl or something, but I haven't stayed aboard tonight to baby-sit you! Got work to do! Isn't there someone else whose ears you could talk off their heads?"

"Thanks," said Paean and removed herself from the machine room.

What a horrible character! Nice eyes? Well, you could be a mass murderer and happen to be born with pretty irises! Pretty is who pretty does, thought Paean acidly.

She padded to the galley, helped herself to a cup of coffee and went back to the lab. No point in practising violin while she was in this mood! With what had she deserved that?

She'd show them! She was properly peeved now! If there were medals for peeving, Wolf Svendsson had just earned himself one. Little candy girl! Just because she was small and light, and had stopped growing a year or two ago. She was mere months away from legal junior adult status, for the love of luminous tubes! Well, she'd show them that the most dangerous poison came in the smallest containers! Very small in fact… She gazed at the Genitron with a calculating smile. Hemlock by another name.

On the morning before they set sail for Panama, Federi was on the deck with Wolf and Marsden, lighting fireworks. Shawn and Ronan gathered close excitedly.

"What are you doing?" asked Shawn.

Federi smiled brightly.

"Look!" He handed one of the missiles to the boy. Shawn studied it in detail.

129

"Wow, Federi!"

It was a rum bottle with wings, mounted on a rocket, with a matchstick model of a ship inside it. The ship looked suspiciously like the Solar Wind. Shawn looked closer and saw that "Solar Wind" had been penned in minute letters on one of the matchsticks on the hull.

The Crow's Nest looked vaguely electronic.

"That's an electronic transmitter," said Federi. "Now observe!"

The design of the rocket was conceivably simple. It operated like a firework.

"Isn't the heat of the rocket going to ignite the insides of the bottle?" asked Shawn.

"No. It never gets there. See, the rocket is *behind* the glass bottle. These wings stabilize the whole thing, let it go nice and far, and when the fuel is up, the last bit lights a fuse, and the fuse lights the material of the wings, and they burn off. The bottle can withstand that! By the time the wings are gone the bottle is at sea level. Wolf has worked it all out, done the strength tests and so on."

Shawn stared at Wolf with wide eyes.

"Wolf is a genius," he said, awed.

"And so say all of us," agreed Federi. "Credit to Marsden too, Shawn, he thought of it all!"

"And Federi built the little Solar Winds inside the bottles," completed Marsden.

"Wow," said Shawn. "Can I have one?"

"No," said Federi. "These are all for a purpose. But I'll make you another one."

"Wow," said Shawn again. He pointed at the bottle. "Isn't the glass going to break when it hits the sea surface?"

"Only if it strikes a young volcanic island springing out of the sea," quipped Ronan.

"Nah, don't worry, the bottles are sturdy," said Federi. Wolf had done strength tests on various bottles, and they had selected the one brand that would survive such an impact.

"What are we doing this for?" asked Ronan.

"Fun and games, *amigo*," said Federi with a grin.

"What if one lands on an island?" asked Shawn.

Federi laughed. "That should puzzle them!"

"This is very interesting," said Gomez, peering through his binoculars. "What are they doing now?"

"Lighting a whole bunch of fireworks, it seems," said Gina. "Wow! Look at it go! Wonder why they do it by day! Gosh, doesn't the thing come down at all?"

"This is very interesting," said Shawn, training his binoculars on Gomez. "There's a man watching us with binoculars!"

Federi looked up. "That one? Stabilizer! Followed us from Hamilton! Wonder what he and his little girlfriend intend to do against a whole ship full of pirates!"

"Does Captain know?" asked Shawn.

"Is the Pope catholic?" Federi asked back.

"They've spotted us," said Gina.

"I know," said Gomez, grinning. "Our presence doesn't seem to worry them!"

Gina was worried, though.

"There you are," came a voice behind them. Gomez's heart sank into his shoes. Gina had the urge to flee.

"Miller," said Gomez. "I hope you are well recovered?"

"I see you're on the job?" said Anya. "I'd better come with you. Knew I'd find the pirates in Plymouth. We'll corner them in Panama. There's no conceivable way they'll get through that Canal!"

"Where's Johnny Anyhow?" asked Gomez.

"Having details seen to," replied Anya Miller. "How close is the pirate to setting sail?"

"For now they're just amusing themselves," said Gomez. "See there!"

Anya Miller squinted. "Wonder what the old villain's up to!"

10

Panama

The Solar Wind had left Plymouth and was sailing on a fair wind, due west to Panama. For three days, at regular intervals, Federi and Marsden lit more missiles and sent them off over the sea. Nagging at the very edge of vision, carefully tracked by Shawn from the Crow's Nest, followed a weird black tadpole-shaped craft carrying Stefano Gomez, Gina Nevada, and to the distress of both, Anya Miller.

"Blast this," said the Captain at some point and asked Dr Jake to activate the fuel cells. The Solar Wind shot forward, out of sight and out of range of the Stab vessel.

On the fourth day, before the stars had faded in the dawn, a distress signal came from the Solar Wind, just off the coast of Haiti. Instantly the coastal guard was alert. What luck! The pirate ship practically delivering itself into their hands! They started zooming in on the signal.

Quietly as a whisper, a beautiful royal blue Zephyr by name of Bronberg slipped into the Canal. The control tower checked out the identity via tamper-proof satellite signatures; it was all authentic. Bronberg had clearance for the Canal; she was a legal trading vessel on her way to Adelaide.

The Unicate had installed this modern system in backwater Panama two decades ago, when a lot of political movement had taken place between the Pacific and New York. Today, in fact, if they hadn't been expecting the Solar Wind, they wouldn't even have bothered to man the control towers, which operated automatically.

The junior operator okayed the system to go ahead, confirming the Tower's electronic identification with a sigh. This drill had been carrying on for nine days now. It was jolly tiring to sit up here hour after hour confirming identifications that were fireproof anyway!

He sent a signal through to the other towers of the approach of the blue Bronberg. The first sluice gate opened, letting her in. She began her long wait for the water to rise up to the next level.

It seemed to Captain Lascek as though they were going to go through the Canal without a hitch. His skills in programming hadn't let him down yet.

Quieter even, a porthole opened and a small hand extended out, pouring something into the Canal. *De-fluorobacter valeriensis* would survive the seawater; but it would actively gravitate towards sweet water, and that in a matter of minutes. All the hours of reading up had paid off. The little green bug was a masterpiece. Streamlined to perfection, it had a very small genome and only needed about thirty seconds to replicate. All non-essential genes had been deleted. It was covered in flagella that enabled it to swim extremely fast. It had nothing in it that would make people seriously sick. The nth division was abortive, self-limiting the bacterium.

Off the coast of Cuba, another distress signal started beeping. It seemed to the Cuban Coastal Guard that the Solar Wind, the notorious pirate ship was just offshore and experiencing trouble.

"Ha!" said Salvatore Rodriguez, Captain of the Day Watch. "Now we've got you, old fool!"

Haiti was experiencing trouble finding the ship. Then the report came that she was lying outside Cuba.

This was annoying. Haiti sent their coast guard out straight away, along with the Stabs that were already looking. Cuba wouldn't palm in that reward!

Tortuga got the next call. By now the coastal watches of three different countries were all getting into each other's hair trying to locate that blasted ship that seemed to be moving around madly despite its damaged condition.

And then came a call just east of Cayenne. The Solar Wind seemed to have been moving south, headed for the Cape. And having some difficulties. And another, from the Northern Atlantic, at the height of Jacksonville, heading back towards Hamilton. A signal that caused great excitement amongst the Stab forces in Hamilton.

More satellite signals came. The authorities were confused and hunting in circles. A whole fleet of Solar Winds seemed to be adrift in the radius of about fifteen hundred sea miles from Montserrat. More than twenty signals riddled the satellite tracking system. Then they all died down. An hour later, Cuba picked up on their original signal again. Then the merry chase began again.

The Unicate derived that the actual location of the Solar Wind must therefore be at Montserrat, and fine-combed those islands.

In the first control tower of the Canal, the junior operator fell asleep over his freshly made coffee. It had been a long, boring shift. The first sluice had closed behind the Bronberg, which was now properly locked into a chamber, waiting for the water level to reach the correct height for the second sluice gate to allow her passage.

Aboard the "Bronberg", Paean was pacing up and down passageways wearing a terrible frown. With all the brilliance of her plan there was one obvious thing she had overlooked. The Solar Wind derived her drinking water from the sea. As long as none of the crew actually drank any water...

She drifted into the galley, casting troubled glances out of the starboard porthole.

Federi was drying dishes, for once not helped by Shawn, who was on lookout duty on the deck. The Romany looked up as she walked in.

"What's eating you, my girl?"

Paean stared uncertainly at the colourful entertainer. A sweet guy; a dicey ally. Would he keep her secret if she told him?

"Federi, what was the plan with Panama?"

"Little bird, I can't tell you. Captain would have my hide."

"It's my life too," said Paean. "Federi, Lake Gatun is Panama, isn't it?"

"Yes, why?"

"I had a dream. Lake Gatun is the end of the world. It's death."

The gypsy with the mauve headscarf full of data cubes and earrings put his drying of plates down. He planted himself in front of her, arms folded, his black eyes boring into hers.

"You've got the sight," he stated. "Why does it surprise me, actually? Listen, Paean. The plan is that we fight our way out of Panama. Our electronic shield fudges our signals and protects us a bit from the Unicate death bolts. We have torpedoes too. We should have gone around the south, the Cape, but there's no time..."

"How do you rate our chances?"

Federi frowned. "Bad," he said. "We're going to die."

"And what if..."

She couldn't tell him. What if he told Captain? Och, it was hopeless.

A light appeared in the gypsy's eyes.

"What have you done?" he probed with a slight grin in the corner of his mouth.

"Nothing," said Paean, rolling her eyes in desperation. She had turned him down once for sharing her secrets. She still didn't know how good an ally he would have been... but he looked after Shawney, that counted for a lot, and he'd been sweet and concerned with her before... if they were all going to die anyway... "Federi, can I take you up on that Thieves' Honour thing? For real, now? I need someone who's on my side..."

"You've really done something," stated the gypsy in amazement. "Spit it out, girl, let's see if Federi can help you fix it!"

"Only..." She petered off.

"I've helped Rushka many times," said Federi.

That tipped the balance! "Och, okay! Is there any way you could rig it so nobody drinks any water? Specially not the Captain!"

Federi's eyebrows lifted. "You want me feeding them all rum?"

"No! Just not water, and not anything that gets made with water – coffee for instance..." Her face fell. It had been hopeless from the start. "Oh, blast!" The entire crew of the Solar Wind was addicted to coffee.

"Cor!" Federi shook his head. "No coffee! Could you explain?"

She sighed. "Federi, I never finished thinking it through, I thought I had, but now there's this hole in it..." She told him what she had done.

His reaction floored her. Federi laughed until tears started down his cheeks.

"Federi...!"

He stared at her and packed up laughing again.

"Oh, you little genius!"

"What's so darned funny?" asked Paean, upset.

Federi sat down on a chair at the Ironwood table, wiping the tears of laughter and relief out of his face with his green flared sleeve. Brilliant, brilliant! Maybe there was not going to be any shoot-out.

When Plan A had consisted of a showdown of firepower, Federi had known that his Captain was out of plans. An unbelievable risk; the Solar Wind against a fleet of Unicate.

Captain had tried to avoid it. But the active way in which the Unicate hunted them now made going around the Cape no safer. They would have had to field battle after battle all the way down South America's eastern coastline. It was like Lascek to risk everything in one single, highly dicey manoeuvre, hoping to break through fast, rather than face ten potential battles in locations they couldn't predict.

But Federi knew. Based on stealth alone they would not make it. He had seen it. Lake Gatun was swarming with Stabilizers, just like Hamilton Harbour had been. They would not be conned by the Zephyr being blue and having taken down the Crow's Nest. They would send shockwaves first and sort everything else second. And when the Solar Wind submerged, which she was definitely going to do to get away, they would have their suspicions confirmed beyond any doubt.

Unless they were all asleep. The little genius had just given them their lives back!

He glanced up at the girl's shocked face, grabbed her wrist and pulled her down onto a chair too.

"You are a brilliant star, little luv," he told her. "Got to tell Captain right away."

"Aargh!"

That beaten, betrayed look on her face! And right after she had saved all their hides and given them a fighting chance! He couldn't leave it like that, even if it cost him precious time.

Federi pulled something lime-green out of his pocket and unravelled it with quick fingers. Paean watched his prestidigitation, mesmerized.

"Paean, welcome aboard! You're a real pirate now!"

"What?!"

"Because there's not a pirate aboard this ship who hasn't breached the law in the name of survival – or treasure."

"Och Federi – you're just saying that to make me feel better!"

Federi solemnly shook his head. "Take me, for instance!"

"Take you?"

"Bin in deep water so often I've lost count," said Federi. "Mostly for treasure. Last time for survival, you saw that one... Come here!"

The fluorescent green thing in his hand turned into a scrap of material; he tied it around her head, gypsy-style. To her dismay it was also covered in stolen spangles.

"Aargh!" said Paean. "Now I can be an eyesore too!"

"You see?" smiled Federi, looking mightily proud. "Now you're a real pirate too." He nodded, satisfied. "And now we tell Captain."

"No!"

This was serious. She hadn't understood. Federi took her hand in his and caught her eyes.

"Little luv, see here. I got two questions concerning the bug itself. Firstly, is it dangerous?"

"No," said Paean. "I've taken all the dangerous genes out. It only carries the sedative from the Valerian plant."

"You know your herbs," commented Federi. "Second question. Does it work?"

"I haven't tested it as such, not on anybody," said Paean. "I don't really know."

"Okay. So you release a GMO into the sea. Did you consider that it could mutate?"

"Yes," said Paean, "but I've made it self-limiting. The nth division is abortive and kills both daughter cells."

"Beautiful," smiled Federi. "Sleek, small, dangerous. Does it also have red hair?"

Now Paean had to laugh.

"It has flagella, it can swim," she said.

"What does it eat?"

"Are you joking? We're in Panama!"

Federi grinned. "Oh, yes. Paean, listen. How old are you?"

"Going on sixteen," said Paean.

"Nearly an adult," agreed Federi. "*Atenţie*. Nuclear physics and Unicate shoot-outs and genetic engineering – those are all adult games.

137

Why? Because they are dangerous. Not just for yourself but everyone around you. You want to be an adult, you'll also have to learn to carry the consequences. What you have done was very daring, and I think you've saved our lives. But you got to tell Captain! If you don't, it could go badly wrong!"

She stared at him, frightened. She had understood.

"Federi – can't you rather…"

"No," said Federi. "That would be playing outside the rules. Got to do it yourself, young woman! Do you believe for a moment Federi would spill your secrets to anyone – even the Captain?"

"You wouldn't?"

"Of course not! Paean, that's sacred ground. People who do that don't deserve friends."

Paean sighed.

"Och, alright. What the hell. In for a penny…"

"That's my girl!" said Federi proudly. "I'll go with you. Federi shall protect you!"

He studied his masterpiece. The green certainly complemented her skin tone. And she did look becoming covered in stolen treasure.

The first control tower operator was asleep. The others only had to see that nothing unusual occurred.

For nine days and nights, nothing unusual had been occurring all the time. It was a boring process. The radio operators who had been temporarily employed for this felt abused. After all, the electronics did all the identifying anyway. No one could hope to sidestep that system. The past sixty ships had confirmed their opinions.

"Blue Zephyr with no Crow's Nest passing through, and two American yachts," yawned a colleague a bit further down the Canal, looking at the image of the Solar Wind on the side screen and comparing. The irony was that the Solar Wind on the image carried the name "Santa Marguerita". He had checked by zooming all the way in.

He yawned. These early mornings were the worst… His head sank onto his arm. His mouth dropped open as he began to snore. Perhaps a more exciting job would have kept him awake at this moment.

"A moment, Captain?"

Captain Radomir Lascek turned from the console where he was analysing the sluice gates with Rushka, to look at the colourful rogue. The Romany had Paean Donegal in tow, with a hair-raisingly green head covering that contrasted fiercely with her flaming red hair. Punch and Judy? What was going on here?

"Federi, you know this is no time for comedy."

"Not comedy, Captain. An interesting development." Federi pushed Paean forward. "Speak, little hummingbird!"

Paean stared at the Captain, terrified. He studied her. How much did she guess? Did she understand that he was sailing his crew straight into hell?

"Make it short," snapped Lascek.

Paean swallowed.

"Captain, I've released a bio-engineered bacterium into the harbour. It puts everyone to sleep who drinks water."

"*What?!*"

"Or coffee," she added.

Radomir Lascek gaped at her, rattled. It took him several moments to assess the whole situation. Did that bacterium actually work? Federi looked as though he thought it would! And the Romany had a pretty fine sensor for such things.

This might turn out disastrous! But it might also be exactly what they needed. What a brazen little wildcat! And then that forsaken green lighthouse she was wearing...

"Do you have any idea what you've done, girl?"

Paean stood silent, petrified.

"Go tell everyone," thundered the Captain. "They must not drink any water or coffee or anything else! Call a meeting! In the boardroom! Federi, empty the reservoirs! Get Wolf on the job to help you! Snap to it! If we fall asleep, that's it!"

"Yes, Captain," whispered Paean and turned tail and ran. She jingled as she bolted. The Captain and Rushka stared after her.

"We're not asleep," said Federi. "She's given us the edge. If enough Unicate forces fall asleep... even if they just get drowsy..."

"Get on with it!" bellowed Lascek. "Empty the reservoirs! And Federi

_"

The gypsy was already halfway out the door, but he stopped short.

"Yes, Captain?"

"Keep an eye on her! Donegal Black Magic! Hemlock! That girl is dangerous!"

"Yes, Captain." Federi vanished from the doorway.

Rushka and Radomir Lascek exchanged a glance.

"Especially with that glow-in-the-dark headscarf," added Rushka, and they both exploded in peals of laughter.

"She deserves a medal," exclaimed Lascek, catching his breath. "What a head start! No wonder the towers have been so placid!"

"Still insubordinate," Rushka pointed out. "She should have cleared it."

"Right. She's a fully qualified pirate. We'll have to watch her carefully."

As it turned out, only about half the crew was up and chirpy. The rest had already had their coffee. To Paean's intense relief, Dr Judith had had coffee too. There was another confrontation she dreaded.

Paean called the meeting, and Captain informed them that nobody was to drink anything that was made with drinking water.

"This might turn out to our favour," said Lascek seriously. "If we need to mask suddenly, we need not worry about the sleeping crew!"

Rushka disappeared suddenly from the boardroom.

"It poses a real problem though," continued the Captain. "How are we going to get through the sluice gates if the operators are asleep? Have you thought of that, Miss Donegal?"

Miss Donegal had hardly any shade left to go paler to. Her complexion almost exactly matched her scarf. She shook her head mutely, her treasure beads jingling softly.

"A suggestion, Captain," Federi spoke up. He was leaning against the wall of the boardroom, arms folded, mainly observing and feeling ill at ease. He suspected that Captain held him responsible for the wild idea of the Irish girl. Only because he had backed Paean a bit. He had to deflect the entire situation, and fast. "If one of the gates gets stuck, Shawn and I will go ashore, get into the control towers and open it."

140

Shawn nodded enthusiastically. He was highly delighted with his sister's coup. He couldn't wait to get a turn at input, too.

Radomir Lascek frowned. "And if you get caught?"

"We won't, Captain."

The Captain's eyes narrowed. Federi had a point. Federi never got caught. And if he did, he got away. It was the definition of who he was: The one that got away. It was good luck having him on the Solar Wind.

He wouldn't let them catch the boy, either. This idea was quite safe. In any case, thought Lascek wryly, the point was not gates getting stuck. He and Marsden had hacked into their control mechanisms and could override them from the Solar Wind if they needed to; Federi wasn't even aware of this. The point was teaching Paean Donegal consequential thinking!

"Very well, Federi," he said, rolling his eyes. "Do what you have to!"

Paean's timing was perfect: It was still so early in the morning that people reached for something to drink either as they surfaced, or in order to stay awake the last hour of a long shift. The bacterium spread down the Canal; helped along by four further dosages by Paean's hand, on Captain's direct orders. As they passed through the Canal, the morning wore on. The automatic system worked beautifully, even better without the manual interference of control-tower operators. To Shawn's disappointment, not a single gate got stuck.

"How long is this thing now going to spread around the world, sis?" asked Shawn.

"It's got a self-destruct built in after 24 hours," she replied. "The nth division is abortive, so each strain self-terminates as it reaches that division. That is, unless there is a mutation."

"What happens then?"

"Who knows!" She shuddered. "Anything's possible. But luckily nearly all mutations result in cell death. So they're self-limiting. So the chances are actually quite low that one survives. – Then again, there are a great many cells out there, oh boy... actually the chances are quite good!" She thought about it some more. "On the other hand – they do have that self-destruct built in, so there would have to be at least two viable mutations for it to be dangerous – one mutation would have to be

141

specifically the disabling of the terminate-switch. And they'd have to happen this side of the 24 hours. So I'd say –" she did some fast multiplications in her head. "The chances are – just about – one."

"One out of a hundred?" asked Shawn.

"No. One. Out of one."

Shawn took a second to digest this. "Hoo boy! I can see why it's illegal! And how long are they going to snooze?"

"Well, at least three hours after taking in the valeriensis. But when they wake up they may just self-dose again, because they'll be thirsty…"

Shawn laughed. "Brilliant, sis! And if there's a mutation disabling only the self-destruct – and the same bacterium just carries on and doesn't stop? Does Panama sleep for 100 years?"

"I hope not," muttered Paean, not finding her brother's questions particularly funny.

On the deck, Federi unpacked his stock of Coca-cola, straight out of the boxes in his storage area.

"Hope everyone likes this. I've also got Raspberry – ohmigod, and greengage – oh boy! Who packed these? – Hlabane!" He shook his head. "The pirates aboard Captain Ali's ship have a kindergarten palate!"

"How about ale, you stingy fiend?" suggested Wolf.

"We're not out of danger yet, Svendsson. Let's first get to the Pacific, and then we celebrate! Meanwhile you can have ginger ale."

Wolf growled.

Aboard the T576, Captain Gomez was wishing he'd left what was well enough in Plymouth. That Anya Miller was a right pain in the neck.

"They're going to go through the Canal, I'm telling you!" She was nagging. "These distress signals are decoys! I know the pirate!"

"Personally?" Captain Gomez couldn't stop himself from asking. He really didn't want to know; but anything to rile this obnoxious female was a good thing to say. He wished she hadn't found him in Plymouth! What pleasure it would have been to follow the pirate to Panama just with little Gina.

Of course the distress calls were decoys! Out of sheer curiosity, for having his suspicion confirmed, he zoomed in on one of them that was coming from close to the entrance of Panama. It wasn't easy; there were intervals when the dratted thing would stop sending any signal and he had to continue the course on hunches. But eventually he was right on top of the signal, and he found – nothing!

"*Something* is making those signals," insisted Gina.

"All I see is a bit of rubbish floating about," said the Miller.

Gomez looked again.

"That's not rubbish!"

Gina opened the hatch and fished the bottle out of the sea. They looked at it in detail. They marvelled at the minute matchstick Solar Wind inside it, complete with Crow's Nest and almost-mermaid figurehead.

"Awesome," said Gina.

"Awful," corrected Anya's loud voice. "Awfully dumb to fall for this! Just listen to me! Lascek is going through the Canal! So are we going to waste more time drifting around aimlessly?"

"No, no, Miller," said Gomez tiredly. "Of course Lascek is in the Canal! Do you believe for a moment that he'll actually get through it? How do you envision that?"

"He does! He will!" How could she explain that nothing was impossible to Radomir Lascek? It was this trait that made him so dangerous!

They headed towards Panama.

Some time later, Gomez muttered, "This is strange!"

"What is?"

"Our people manning the control towers aren't responding!"

"I told you! He's killed them all!"

"Come now! How can he have killed an entire city?" asked Gomez, eyeing the shore which was suspiciously devoid of movement.

"I told you! He always finds a way!"

The First Mate had taken flight to the galleyette. She re-emerged now with a tray of coffees.

"Great idea, thank you, Gina!" said Gomez and accepted a cup, putting it down distractedly. Whether or not the control towers responded, the automatics should kick into action any moment now. After all, this was a Unicate craft; that meant automatic clearance everywhere. And then they'd see how far Lascek had made it into the Canal.

Anya took a cup of coffee as well, sipping it in frustration.

My, it had been a long chase! The weariness of all the past days suddenly descended on her. This coffee had a melancholy taste, reminding her of home and her teen years...

With a sigh she put her coffee down and took a chair.

"Sometimes it feels so pointless..." she sighed before she fell asleep.

Gomez and Gina looked at each other, then at Miller's cup.

"Clever girl," said Gomez. "What have you put in there?"

"Nnnnn..." denied Gina, sank down to the floor and nodded off.

"You're beautiful when you're asleep," Gomez complimented his First Mate. He glared at his coffee cup. He wasn't going to sip that dangerous stuff. Clearly it had some sort of drug in it, although it had nothing to do with Gina, or she wouldn't have drunk any herself. Gomez wondered. It was a long shot, but...

Suddenly he understood what was happening in Panama. He started laughing. He laughed so loudly he nearly hurt himself.

"Old fox," he laughed. He took a subconscious sip from his cup. Realized it. Looked at the cup.

"Oh, bug..."

11

Lake Gatun

"I only have half of my crew, Paean Donegal!"

They were gathered in another emergency meeting, on the bridge. The Gatun Locks had gone smoothly; they were in the last chamber, and the gates would open soon. The water level was still rising, regulated by the sluices. The bad part was that they couldn't see through the sluice gate what was awaiting them in Lake Gatun.

The Solar Wind had crossed through the Panama strait many times; Radomir Lascek could navigate the sea bridge backwards with his eyes closed. The nuclear wars of the sixties, at the time of the Unicate takeover, had destroyed most of the Canal. It had been painstakingly rebuilt, all but the parts through Lake Gatun, which were considered less necessary. The Lake was a natural body of water. The nuclear bombs had blasted sinkholes into the lake in places, lowering the bottom at erratic intervals. With the increased ocean levels and the warmer climate of those days, great torrential rains had swept the beleaguered Panama, and the Lake's levels had risen significantly, nearly submerging the island in the lake. Though this was decades in the past, the lake's levels hadn't at any point sunk low enough again for Panama to take action. Ships could still pass comfortably.

Traders such as Captain Ali trod a fine line though. Many illegal vessels had contacts inside the Panamanian Unicate, bribing their way, usually by offering favours or bits of their merchandise. The Unicate kept a half-awake eye on such dealings. When it suited them, they suddenly sprung a trap on such an illegal trader. Usually not on his associates though, as they tended to provide leads to further pirates.

Possibly, nothing waited in ambush for the Solar Wind. Alternatively, if Federi's hunches were anything to go by, a hefty Unicate fleet. How far had the green bug got? Lascek had ordered Federi to find that pesky

Donegal girl and bring her to the bridge.

"How fast can you multiply that green nonsense-bug?" asked Lascek.

Paean relaxed a bit. She had expected another ruffle.

"The problem is more of slowing the multiplication down, Captain," she said.

"How fast can you make a volume that would fill – say – a Spiffy bag?"

A small sandwich-bag that sealed. "Ten minutes, Captain."

"Get started!" ordered the Captain. "Federi, call Wolf. Bit of engineering there."

The water was still gushing from the sluices into the chamber when five missiles were launched from the deck of the Solar Wind. Five Spiffy bags filled with teeming green bacteria, spinning their flagella in eagerness to get their furry little bodies into the lake. The bags broke as they hit the water surface, and their gooey contents spread out. It was good enough. They had quite a bit of time from here. It would take another half-hour for this gate to open.

Paean returned to the boardroom, where the remaining crew sat discussing their options. She glanced at them. Shawn was awake and chirpy; so was Wolf – the lout! Luckily, Dr Jake and Marsden as well. And that was all. Captain was on the bridge with Rushka; Federi was out on the deck, checking the functioning of something.

Wolf, Marsden and Federi had had an interesting time carrying all the sleeping crew members to their bunks. The Doc had fallen asleep in the lab over an article she was reading onscreen. A complicated, scientific article – who could blame her! Ailyss in the machine room, watching the drives. Ronan and Rhine Gold in the blond giant's cabin where they had been playing a game of cards. Must have been a bit of a slow game. Old Sherman had sipped his coffee on his graveyard shift on the bridge. He had been the first the Captain had come across, not being in a position to explain it at the time. Lascek had first thought that he should stop relying on the centenarian for a full shift. He'd had a bad conscience. Old Sherman was so resilient and brave, one forgot his advanced age.

Of course, the moment he had the full picture, his guilt had transformed into anger at Paean. How dare she cause him to feel guilty

146

about a standard procedure on the ship!

He appeared in the boardroom's doorway now, scanning his scant remaining crew. Rushka was holding the bridge; he couldn't leave her alone for long now, as the sports were about to start.

Federi entered the boardroom just behind him.

"It's all set, Captain."

"Good. Tune in the cameras. We're sealing now; it can be hoped that the lake is still deep enough to submerge."

"Will do, Captain." Federi moved off to the bridge.

"You," the Captain snapped at Paean. "Why didn't you tell me about this before you released it? We could have kept everyone awake!"

"Captain, I –" Paean swallowed, hot panic in her stomach. "I was doing this against Doc Judith's wishes!"

"What!" Lascek was genuinely angry now. Breaching orders from a senior crewmember!

"I'm sorry," peeped Paean.

"You had better stay under supervision for now," commanded Lascek. "Stay close!"

"Yes, Captain!" She wished she could rather stay far, far away.

"Captain," came Federi's voice on the Captain's wrist-com, "the gate is opening."

"On my way, Federi." The Captain beckoned to Marsden, and the two headed for the bridge. Paean obediently tagged after.

Wolf and Dr Jake left for the machine room. Shawn moved to follow them; Wolf turned and forbade him. Shawn stayed behind indecisively; all alone in the boardroom. He toggled after all the people who headed for the bridge.

"There!"

A vast expanse of blue water became visible through the opening gates. And with it, a host of gleaming black T-craft, Stabilizers, like volcanic sand grains on a mirror. All lying in wait for the Solar Wind.

"The Canal is too shallow to submerge," growled Lascek. "Have to move out into the Lake, right into their range!"

An electric shockwave frizzed through the ship. The screens jumped for a split second and stabilized again. The electronic shield held up. The

Captain activated the sequence for the rigging folding up, even before they were out of the last shattered remnant of the old Canal.

It was as Federi had predicted. The Unicate was sending in shockwaves first and sorting the details later. Couldn't the Tzigan have predicted plain sailing instead?

"They're not asleep," said Lascek scathingly. He glanced at Paean and Shawn. "Rushka, could you take the nursery school down to the galley please and give them something to do? The bridge is overcrowded!"

"Yes, Captain!"

"Some of them are asleep," said Federi quietly as only five of the thirty-something Stab vessels converged on the Solar Wind. "Most of them!"

"Lake not deep enough here," muttered Lascek. "Dr Jake! Nuclear drives! We need the speed!"

The ship lurched forward into the lake.

"Captain, they're closing in faster than we can submerge," stressed Federi.

"I can see that! We'll ram them out of the way."

"Wonder if the Solar Wind can handle that," commented Jon Marsden. "Compounding hull like hers!"

He leaned over the Captain's shoulder and hammered a sequence. One of the nuclear drives ignited the torpedo that had been on its way to the Solar Wind before it could reach her.

"Sheesh," said Federi, pale as chalk under his horrible headscarf.

"I'm scared," said Paean, in the galley. "I thought they'd have fallen asleep too!"

"Only the ones who had something to drink," Shawn pointed out. He headed straight for the starboard porthole. Paean followed suit. Rushka stared through the opposite one.

"Can't we force them to drink something?" asked Paean.

"Look, sis," said Shawn. "It did lame most of the force! Oh no!" This last comment at the water level rising past the portholes. The Solar Wind was submerging.

"This is worse!" Paean watched in horror how a flame leapt out from the Solar Wind and fried a torpedo, and the whole ship rocked with the shockwaves of the explosion. Another high-voltage attack zinged through the equipment and their heads.

Rushka keyed some variables into the microwave's console with flying fingers. The microwave screen became a radar screen.

"There," she pointed out, "another torpedo!"

The Solar Wind lurched forward, shooting and blasting at the five Stab vessels. One stopped moving. A rare species of water bug surfaced carefully out of the murky water of Lake Gatun and had a good look around.

"That's better," growled Lascek as a complete picture of the positions of the Stab vessels appeared on the console screen, sent back by his bug. "Can finally see them clearly!"

"Target practice," grinned Marsden. "Our turn!"

He launched a torpedo at the nearest T-craft, aiming for the rudder. The round Stab vessels looked different from down here. From above, they had resembled floating black eggs with squat, square-ish tails. From below, the deep, blade-like triangular keel was clearly visible, half of which was rudder.

Marsden's aim was good. The rudder broke off the T-craft with the torpedo's impact. The solid little craft leapt out of the water; but it was heavily plated. Even a frontal impact might not have damaged it enough to sink it.

"Blasted Unicate!" Lascek was raging. "Those are good young men and women aboard those boats! Throwing them into the fire like that!"

"Always hits the innocents," commented Federi, keeping the visual sensors trained on the enemy craft. The Solar Wind was submerged now; some of the screens showed the surrounding T-craft from below, and one – the periscope – located the enemy from just above the water, giving just that little bit extra visibility.

"You're right, Federi," said Lascek thoughtfully, studying those screens. "There are only four moving now. That green bug has done a lot!"

"Three now," said Federi as Marsden's next torpedo hit its target. More electric shockwaves fizzed across the screens.

"Hells, if that damages our processor!"

Dr Jake and Wolf in the machine room were fully occupied too; they

149

could have done with Ailyss helping. Dr Jake directed the drives, and Wolf shot nuclear blasts at any torpedoes that approached the Solar Wind.

There was a jolt. They were hit. The Solar Wind's alarms went off. Rhine Gold and Ronan woke up groggily.

Another shockwave zinged through the systems. This time the lights dipped.

"Surface!" The Captain hit the sequence just as Rushka came storming onto the bridge with eyes wide. "Back to your post, Rushka. Round up whatever Donegal Troubles you can and find that leak!"

"Two more Stabs, Captain," said Marsden. "If we can keep her down about six more seconds..." He released one torpedo while he was speaking and searched for the last T-craft. Federi helped by paging through the different camera views at high speed. Another electric shock ran through the ship.

"Can't, Jon," said Lascek darkly and surfaced the Solar Wind. "We'll drown!"

The safety catches released and the masts stretched out. A last huge shockwave rolled across the ship, and all the lights went out just as the rigging fanned out.

Paean, Shawn and Rushka had found the leak. It was in Wolf's cabin. As the Solar Wind surfaced, much of the water that had been gushing in began to recede. A lot of it also ran down the passage into the bilges, where Wolf and Dr Jake cursed and swore at the way everything had gone dark. Now their shoes were getting wet too! They knew what that meant for everything in the machine room. Dr Jake hoped fervently that the Captain was surfacing the ship.

Dark was not entirely dark anymore though. It took the eye a few moments to adjust; but soft orange bioluminescence in jelly glowed in jam jars that had been mounted to the walls. Federi had done this while they had been stalling in Plymouth. He had decided that a teen crew like theirs was tough to keep under control in the pitch dark when they submerged; besides, it was high time that Doc's sweet little creation got put to daily use! It was one of Paean's tasks to feed the glow-bacteria. By the dim light of these, Wolf and Dr Jake began to assess the damage.

The fuel drives were still active; they had to be operated manually now.

The nuclear drives did what they were designed to do in such an event: They were shutting themselves down, with safety mechanisms quenching the reaction. It would take time to get them restarted. But first, the processor would have to be checked, and repaired if necessary. Dr Jake hoped that the Captain had been in time to release the safety catches – or they'd be as marooned as that Anya Miller outside of Hamilton.

Marsden and Federi were out on the deck. The last T-craft was pursuing them relentlessly. Marsden handed Federi his long-range rifle.

"Time, my friend?"

"These are innocents, Jon," replied Federi. "Not their fault they're employed by crooks!" He disappeared below the deck and re-emerged, carrying two airguns, giving one to Marsden.

"And what now?" Marsden had a close-up look at the guns and the ammunition. His eyebrows shot sky-high, and he laughed. "My word, Tzigan, have you been busy these three hours!"

Federi grinned. "Five minutes, my friend. Didn't take long."

A grappling hook shot out from the T-craft. It caught on the Solar Wind's rail.

"They're darned well going to damage the ship!" growled Federi. He leopard-crawled at top speed towards the hook, freed the heavy polyramic structure from the rail and hooked it onto the nearest cleat.

"What the hell are you doing, Federi?"

"Play along!" hissed Federi. "We don't want to get hurt!"

Marsden reflected briefly what luck it was to be the best friend of the one who got away. He followed Federi's example. Both lunged to the deck in the storage area, hiding behind crates of food. They waited, guns ready. The Captain watched this manoeuvre from the bridge. Federi gave him a thumbs-up. Everything under control.

"How many are we expecting?" he asked his friend.

Marsden trained his handgun on the rope that connected the grappling hook to the Stabilizer.

"Don't shoot that!" interfered Federi. "We want them to step aboard! Ah, there they come!"

A young officer, smart in his Marine uniform, came up the ladder and looked around. Federi waited until he was well on the deck and shot.

The man crumpled, a surprised look on his face. The woman behind him emerged, brandishing a stun gun. She followed suit. Marsden and Federi waited for more. None were forthcoming.

"Only two?" asked Federi, surprised.

"These T-craft aren't particularly big," replied Marsden. "There are bunks for four, but the Navy prefers to man them sparsely and rather use more craft. More fire power. Makes sense."

Federi nodded and retrieved the tiny syringes he had looted from Doc Judith's supplies, and cut to shape to fit into the air guns. They had delivered their little green payload. Now that he knew of Paean's brilliant bit of piracy, he'd invest in dart guns. Being a pirate had just become a lot more fun!

Marsden helped Federi tie the two marines up. They scanned the lake. None of the Stab vessels moved. Those who had been immobilized by Marsden's torpedoes had been left behind out of range; those who had had coffee, were in any case out for the count.

"I know this one," said Marsden. "He turned down an offer to become a pirate."

"Yup," said Federi. "Johnny Anyhow. Anya Miller's Second." He narrowed his eyes. "I'd say he has potential, but he'll need some work."

"For one," said Marsden, "we'll have to teach him to drink coffee!"

"Don't say that c-word!" protested Federi. "I've got withdrawal symptoms!"

The Captain emerged from the bridge.

"Good work, all of you! We can cross the lake now, I think! Are any of those lazy louts awake yet?"

"I'll see whom I can round up, Captain," said Federi. "I'll make them some coffee."

"Tzigan! Watch your step!"

"Yes, Captain," grinned Federi. Clearly the Captain was suffering too!

"And if you see that little green bandit, do tell her to report to the bridge," added Lascek.

"Yes, Captain." Federi went on his way. Poor little Paean!

The last leg of the crossing was Panama City itself. There was another series of automatic sluice gates, and more Unicate waiting for them, no doubt. Lascek called Federi and Marsden into a meeting on the bridge. Paean was present too, awaiting orders. The leak in Wolf's cabin was not yet completely repaired, but there were others taking care of that. The passage through Panama was becoming a harrowing experience for her.

Radomir Lascek looked back over his shoulder at the little green light-bringer, from overriding the first of the Pedro Miguel Locks.

"Miss Donegal, get back on a pack with Wolf Svendsson and make us more Spiffy bombs."

"Yes, Captain."

Waiting for the water level to sink in the first chamber, the Solar Wind launched several more small missiles into the Canal at Panama City, the Pacific end. They released their payload into the water system of the Capital.

"Now we wait," said Lascek over the ship com, stretching and leaning back, hands behind head. "Take a break, sailors! But remember – no coffee!"

"This is getting tedious," growled Federi in the galley. He'd start chewing coffee beans if he couldn't have his dosage soon!

Eventually the sluice gates opened one by one, over an hour, as the hydraulic Canal system did its work. From thirty-three feet above the current sea level, the Solar Wind descended the steps down into the Miraflores Locks.

It was the strangest event the city had experienced in recorded history. Like in a fairy-tale, Panama fell asleep. It was lucky that the tropical city was not really awake at that hot, drowsy hour anyway. It was a rather extended siesta.

Doc Judith surfaced and was informed by the Captain. She was so taken aback, she failed to deal with it at all. She had to admit that she felt wonderfully rested.

Wolf and Dr Jake began the repair to the processor. Not everything had been levelled. Dr Jake's shield, though not yet powerful enough, had done a lot to protect the electronics from that last lethal wave.

"We'll have to get components in Panama City," said Dr Jake. "Five of her infra-lateral pointsel orbitors are gone. And two PUPSs."

"Go ashore? You can't be serious, doctor?"

"Well," smiled the nuclear scientist, "we can always send Federi to steal them for us!"

Though the remaining Unicate forces in Panama were alert to the Solar Wind being in Lake Gatun, on last report she had been hit by a torpedo while submerged. The last shockwave had been reported to blow out her electronics, having got past that mysterious shield she seemed to have against such electric assault. If it had erased the ship's electronics, the calculations were that the crew had to be stunned too, if not dead. Johnny Anyhow had reported that they were boarding her and bringing her in. All was in hand.

Teatime for the Navy.

"Now," said Lascek. He engaged the intercom, which was up and running again. "Dr Jake, all ready?"

"Mostly, Captain. We'll get through to the Pacific on what we've got."

"And the fire power?"

"We've lost the nuclear drives for now, Captain, but the torpedoes are ready."

"It will just have to be good enough. Set sail," decided Lascek. "Let's get this over with."

The smaller and noisier of the two motorboats, the Lawnmower, cast off from the Solar Wind, carrying Federi and Marsden, and two unconscious Unicate marines. They unloaded the two sleeping officers onto the quay.

Federi stayed behind on the dock.

"Sure you guys can spare me?"

"Federi, I'm not happy about it," replied Marsden. "Having you aboard is a necessity. We'll pick you up in an hour."

"If the Unicate captures you guys, I'll rescue you," promised Federi.

"Course you will," smiled Marsden. "Go well now, Tzigan. Good luck!"

"You too," said Federi. "*Kathal.*"

Marsden's gaze followed him. Within seconds, the gypsy had disappeared, merging into Panama's shops and streets like a rogue colour

154

into a rainbow.

Still life of a sleeping city. Shawn watched in fascination from the rigging, where he was on lookout duty. Tourists sleeping at wharf-side café tables. Single motor vehicles moving along the empty streets, those deviants that refused to hold siesta or take lunch. Shops standing open, unattended, the assistants out for lunch. So were the shoplifters, clearly. There were Unicate ships in the Canal, amongst traders; but they showed no response.

"There's Federi," shouted Shawn. The gypsy was on the wharf, waving wildly. The Solar Wind slowed; Jon Marsden mobilized the Lawnmower a second time and picked him up from the dockside.

"If Shawn hadn't seen you?" he asked, tongue in cheek.

"Jon, I've got my wrist-com," laughed Federi.

"Has the electric shockwave not wiped yours?"

Federi checked. "Fry me, it has! Got to ask Wolf to fix it."

"So what would you have done?"

The gypsy bared his white teeth. His eyes narrowed. He peered over the Canal.

"With all these speedboats on sale?" he asked. "Are you joking?"

Once back aboard, Federi headed for the bilges.

"As specified, Doc!" He emptied his bag of loot out onto the cabinet. "Are these the right ones? I could go again."

"No, they're perfect," said Dr Jake, smiling appreciatively. Federi had secured the very newest kind of pointsel orbitors. They were a lot more powerful than the old ones.

"Great," said Federi and left for the main deck.

"Is that the Pacific out there?" came Shawn's call from the rigging. "Ocean ahoy!!"

The Solar Wind was suddenly out on the open sea.

"We did it!" A cheer went up from the ship. The entire crew, with the exception of Ailyss who was still asleep, and Dr Jake in the machine room and the Captain on the bridge, was out on the deck. Federi brought out bottles of champagne and uncorked them with a lot of splashy mess.

"Here's to the Bronberg," he announced loudly. "Here's to our undemocratic, dare-devil Captain, and to our cannoniers, Marsden and Wolf, and here's to our hero – Paean!"

The little green pirate glowed over her whole face.

"Why are you a hero?" asked Rhine Gold, puzzled. "And why are you wearing that green thing on your head?"

"Aw," said Paean with an embarrassed grin. " 's a long story!"

12

Storm

The open sea awaited. Panama slept behind them.

The Solar Wind was restored to herself. Ronan and Rhine Gold, under Federi's direction, washed the blue neo-transpoxy paint off her hull by pouring biodegradable soapy water over – the sea would do the rest. Marsden reinstalled the original identity chip. Radomir Lascek added the latest transgression to the ship log with pride, describing Panama as "an amazingly sleepy town with incalculable opportunity for those who know how to look". Shawn, Federi, Ronan and Rhine Gold rebuilt the Crow's Nest back into the rigging. Jonathan Marsden clambered about with a voltmeter checking the reconnected wires and sensors. Every last Crow's Nest signal was tested to make sure it was all fully functional again.

The moment he got the thumbs-up for it, Shawn climbed into the Crow's Nest and played a tune on his clay whistle. Ronan joined in on his tin whistle, hooking his elbows around the ropes of the rigging.

It was their first taste of real freedom in seven months.

Radomir Lascek watched from the bridge. He felt so good about the won battle, he wished he could arrange it more often!

Next to him, Sherman Dougherty swore softly. Radomir Lascek glanced down.

"Making progress?"

"Wish I'd started on that earlier," growled Sherman. "Some very sinister stuff coming out of here! But it's clearly missing a whole part. I can decrypt every tenth word or so, and that's on guesswork." He bared his tobacco-stained teeth. "Maybe we should have hung onto Johnny Anyhow as a hostage!"

"That bad?"

"Look there, Radomir."

The Captain bent down over the console, studying what his veteran had been able to pull out of Anya Miller's data capsule. His face clouded over.

"We've got to take every turn we can to get to Hawaii faster," he mulled.

"Skip Atuona?" suggested Sherman.

"Hell, no! That would be disastrous! We'll just have to hurry, that's all."

"And you?" Federi prodded Paean, who had watched the whole Crow's Nest procedure from the rail. "Don't you want to join in the Ceilidh?"

"Och, no," she said, turning away. She leaned on the portside rail and stared at the receding land, behind and to the left.

"Hey!" Federi inserted himself between her and her view. "Are you alright?"

"Feel sick," said Paean. The Romany peered at her, worried. Seasickness boded no well, on a pirate vessel.

"Not the sea," she clarified. "That ratty green bug. Federi, what if it mutates anyway? Doc forbade me to release anything GM into the wild!"

"Doc forbade you?" Federi frowned. "Bad news, little pirate. You'll have to face the music."

She nodded. "I know."

"What does your sight say – will it mutate?" asked Federi.

Paean went quiet. The gypsy could see how she was listening for that gift of hers. He wondered how well she had developed her gypsy radar, whether she had used it back in Molly Street. Whether her gift – and Shawn's – had anything to do with Annie Donegal's execution.

"No," she said eventually. "It self-terminates much faster than I thought. Three to five hours. That's all. I think. Got to simulate it in the lab."

"Good. Now go and report to Doc."

"Can't I have five more minutes first?" asked Paean, her blue eyes pleading.

"Alright," laughed the gypsy. "Five more minutes leaning on the rail with Federi. I'm timing it!" He glanced down at his rewired wrist-com. The Captain was calling him. "Sorry, little sunbird. Without Federi.

158

Kathal!"

"You're a sterling friend," said Paean quietly as he sauntered off. She thought he hadn't heard it; but a broad smile spread over the gypsy's face.

The day turned glorious, the tropical afternoon sun beating down, the sea wind blowing and the ship surging ahead on the gently rolling waves. Panama had long since disappeared beyond the hazy blue horizon. Ronan sat on the prow of the Zephyr gazing ahead, enjoying the cooling spray that splashed across his face every now and then. They were headed west-southwest now, towards the Marquises Island Group where they were going to stop over before setting course for Hawaii.

Federi and Shawn were in the galley preparing lunch. A very late lunch. The portholes were open; the blue of the afternoon blew in balmy and just short of sticky.

"One thing we could do a lot more on the pirate ship," commented the Romany sleepily, filleting a celery stalk. "Loaf around!" He yawned. It had been a darned long run! Shawn agreed heartily.

"Should we cook the veggies in Paean's special water?" asked Federi with a grin.

"Oh yeah, and when everyone's asleep, we take over the ship," Shawn played along.

" 's called mutiny," Federi said, decapitating a carrot with a swift stroke. "Never do that unless you're prepared to kill the Captain, first mate and everyone else who isn't on your side."

"Like, my sister." Shawn yawned. "I could do with some of her concoction now." He had been up since well before dawn, as they all had, and he was beginning to feel it.

"I don't think you need any," laughed Federi. "Go on, boy, go sleep. I think I can peel enough potatoes myself." Rhine Gold, incidentally, was loafing around, as was Ronan Donegal. Fair was fair. The younger brother shouldn't be made to work harder than the older one.

"I'll sleep in the Crow's Nest," said Shawn. "Cooler up there."

"Scoot off then. Shoo!"

Federi wiped the sweat from his forehead with his flared sleeve. It was an exceptionally hot day. In the excitement of moment-to-moment survival he had failed to notice it earlier. He followed Shawn briefly onto the deck and watched him climb into the rigging and settle himself in the newly reinstalled Crow's Nest.

The sky was a hazy blue, the sea warm. The air had that specific tang to it that you only got here in the Pacific. Called Freedom. But hang on –

He activated his wrist-com. "Actually, Shawn –" Federi stopped himself. Plenty of time still to call the boy back down from there if his suspicions came to bear.

"Yes, Federi?" came the answer, and the red shock of hair popped up over the Crow's Nest rim.

The Romany gave him the thumbs up. "Watch out for those seagulls."

Federi joined Ronan on the jib deck at the prow. "Fine hazy day." The spray whipped up at them.

"Strangely warm, this sea," said Ronan. "In Dublin the sea is always cold. Funny to have warm sea water."

"Too warm," commented Federi.

"Why?"

"Watch that squall develop!"

Ronan nodded.

"You get on well with my sister," he commented.

Federi smiled. "Poor girl needed the moral support."

"Poor girl! Dratted naughty girl! Cloning something and setting it free! Still going to box her ears for that," growled Ronan. "She's out of hand!"

"You're not going to," said Federi. "She's already had a ruffle from me, and then Captain, and then the Doc. She needs you to be a brother now, not a father figure!"

"Is that an order?" asked Ronan.

Federi smiled slyly and stared up at the taller young Irishman.

"Would you like it to be one?"

The Captain came up to the prow too. He peered into the distance.

"Anything yet, Federi?"

Federi nodded. The Captain smiled. "Good!"

Two hours later it was upon them. The muggy haze boiled up into billowing sulphur-coloured clouds, partly obscuring the sun, and still thickening. The wind picked up, transforming the gently rolling tide into choppy surf, reflecting the evil glow of the clouds in yellow crests. The light compounding hull of the Solar Wind was beginning to dance upon the waves like a young horse.

Federi was checking the repaired leak in Wolf's cabin. The torpedo had caused damage to one of the tubes that made up the ballasts of the Solar Wind when she submerged. The Solar Wind's hull was a double hull. When Radomir Lascek had converted her into a submarine, one of his alterations had been to line the whole outer hull with inflatable compounding tubes that were usually empty and flattened out; when she sank, they were pumped full of water via pumps in the keel, and when she surfaced, compressed air was forced into them from the top ends to force the water back out, helping the pumps along. As the last water was removed and the valves closed, the air was sucked back out of the tubes, back into the compressor tanks. Those were hiding in the two crew cabins furthest astern, on the lower crew deck. Federi kept the cabins locked; the tanks comprised part of his round when he checked on everything on the ship.

It had been a huge and tricky job, he remembered, removing and repositioning the network of sensors on her hull onto the slightly flexible outer hull that was added on after the tubes had been installed. It had taken days testing and fixing the functionality of each sensor. That outer shell of the Solar Wind was layer upon layer of ship compounding, lined with wire mesh. The ship type compounding came as a gooey liquid that set to a tough, somewhat elastic solid on contact with air. The Solar Wind's hull was tough. A torpedo could at best hope to make a crack.

This torpedo had cracked both layers of the hull. The repair kit Rhine Gold and Ronan had used, contained a compounding spray that foamed out and filled all crevices and then solidified. He'd need to clean that out and repair it properly in Atuona, so that the tube could resume its normal function. But it was a watertight repair; he could hardly see the seam.

"All flyers on deck," came the summons over the intercom. Federi straightened out, content that should the Solar Wind need to submerge, the cabin wall would stay intact, and that only one ballast had been sacrificed, for now. He made his way to the outer deck. So Captain wanted to fly this one!

161

This was where the ropes came into play. Shawn had wondered about them a few times, and their function, as the sails of the Solar Wind were electronically controlled. Federi had always replied: "Wait and see!"

"Shawn," yelled Federi in a panic. The ship was beginning to buck dangerously, and he had forgotten about the young boy sleeping in the Crow's Nest. He tied a lifeline around his own middle and climbed into the rigging.

Shawn was surfacing, groggy and confused, falling about in the hard Crow's Nest. He couldn't understand this. He stuck his head out and very nearly went over as the ship pitched.

"Whoa!"

Tough wiry hands gripped him. "Steady now, boy! Hold onto me!"

Shawn hung onto Federi's sinewy arms, taking in the storm. Oh so. That was why one didn't fall asleep in the Crow's Nest! A huge breaker roared towards the ship and broke against her hull, the impact sending a shudder up the Solar Wind's rigging, the spray flying nearly all the way up to them. Shawn could feel the mist.

"How do I get out of here?" he asked and started climbing out.

"Stay put!" snapped Federi. Ronan arrived by the gypsy's side. Between the two of them they tied lifelines onto Shawn. Ronan tried hooking his elbow around the rigging to free up both hands. Federi shook his head vehemently.

"One hand for the ship and one hand for yourself," he shouted over the surf. "Never forget that! Rule One! Shawn! Why didn't you tie on a life-line when you came up here?"

"Forgot! Sorry!"

Rain came down suddenly, arriving with a great sigh. From the first fat splotches to the deluge took less than ten seconds. An enormous wave wandered over the deck, submerging the hooks. The Solar Wind's deck vanished. There was nothing but ocean for a second. They were marooned in the ship's rigging and the rest of the sailors were standing in the sea, hanging onto handhold lines, drenched with rain and seawater. Shawn stared, awestruck. Thunder clapped.

"Aargh! I hate these tropical storms," yelled Federi. "They come aboard uninvited!"

Shawn climbed out of the Crow's Nest, hanging onto the supporting hands of his brother and the gypsy. Once he hung hands and feet on the ropes of the rigging, they began their precarious descent. The rigging bowed and waved like a famous actor after a show. And they were the fleas, thought Shawn with a grin. It was the first really exciting thing that happened on this ship, excepting the sea battle they had braved earlier today. And that had perhaps been a bit too exciting!

On the deck, more activity was happening. The breaker that had washed over had been a single; most of the waves stayed meekly below the level of the deck, although they roared and splashed impressively. Shawn watched how the older sailors tied more handhold lines. Ropes criss-crossed the deck. The Captain was watching the procedures from the bridge.

"Move it, Shawn," prodded Ronan. The youngest Donegal unfroze out of his fascinated trance and shimmied the rest of the way down the rigging to the deck.

"Captain's orders are," shouted Federi as they finally reached the deck and the handholds, "all hands below deck except the flyers." He untied Shawn and sent him below. "Go close all portholes, Shawn!"

The young pirate grumbled but obeyed. It wasn't fair. He wanted to be out in the rain too, flying the storm!

Ronan, Rhine Gold, Wolf, Marsden and Federi set the sheets of the mainsail and foresail to just forward of beam reach positions, but let those of the big staysail and the jibs fly free. The Captain activated the furling gear for each, and the sails wound up on their revolving stays to become narrow sausages, so that there were no sails flying in front of the foremast. They clipped their lifelines to running lines secured to the foredeck, just ahead of the foremast. Federi collected the ends of four ropes from a hatch at the base of the mast and showed the younger sailors how to lead these lines, which he called the flying sheets – or brake sheets and speedbar sheets – through the electronically-assisted extra pulleys that had risen out of the deck; how to wind the ropes twice around their hands and hook one foot under hoops fitted to the deck, which he called toe-straps. Marsden checked each of the four active winches personally.

"We usually have at least six," he commented. "But it will just have to be good enough. I'll be co-ordinating the set of the other sails from the flying console, as usual. Federi, port speedbar sheet, Svendsson starboard. Schatz, starboard brake sheet. " He instructed the beginners how to control the sheets – pulling was straightforward but if they had to feed out, they needed to loosen the lock on their winch by tugging the winch line at the same time as giving a slight pull to the flying sheet before allowing play. The hand with the winch line had to hang onto a handhold line too; you tugged the winch line without releasing the handhold. Only a slight pull was needed; it had to be done firmly though, while another tug would re-engage the lock.

Marsden gave a whole lot more detailed instructions. Ronan battled to envision what precisely the First Mate meant.

"It's your first time, Donegal. Do you understand what you're supposed to do?"

Ronan nodded. He didn't really follow; but he figured that he would copy what the others did and learn as he went along. It had worked so far.

"You've got the port brake sheet there," repeated Marsden, not satisfied. "You pull that, it bends the port end of the wing downward. You need to watch the wing very carefully, adjust the sheet the second it goes the slightest bit out of shape with the rest, and listen out for Captain's orders. If he says pull, pull until told to stop. That steers the kite, among other things. If he pulls the kite closer you have to take up the slack immediately, and if he lets out you have to pay out the sheet to match."

"Yes, sir." Wing? Kite? What wing and kite?

"Ready, Donegal? Ready, Schatz? Svendsson?"

Rhine Gold grinned hugely and nodded at the First Mate. Wolf gave a thumbs-up. Marsden waved a signal back to the Captain on the bridge.

The Solar Wind dipped into a trough and came back up. Something shot upwards like a rocket out of the base of the foremast, dragging cables out of the deck behind it. It missed the upper parts of the stays with their furled sails by only a breath and snapped open in the wind with a resounding crack, shaping itself into a huge batwing filled with air. Its wingspan was easily twice that of the whole height of the foresail. The Solar Wind leaped forward.

Federi grinned at Ronan. "Meet our kite sail!"

Ronan gaped.

" 's a parafoil wing really," added the gypsy. "But we call it a kite."

The kite sail flew well above the height of the masts, where the wind was supposedly cleaner. Right now the Solar Wind felt as though she had more wings than a swarm of dragonflies.

There was a strange sensation as if the sea level were dropping under the ship. Ronan, who had dutifully been gazing at the kite sail, got disoriented, lost his balance and staggered, and hung onto his brake sheet. The huge kite pulled sharply to one side, suddenly shorter on one end. The ship got dragged sideways; the deck tilted. The sea came a lot closer again; some water from an annoying breaker spilled around their feet. The kite skimmed the water.

"Donegal! What are you doing?" shouted Marsden. "Let out the line! Let it out!"

Ronan let go of his flying sheet in consternation. Federi lunged for it and handed it back to him.

"Pull your winch line and feed the flying sheet to the winch," he explained, and supervised that Ronan did it right. The kite rose again, one wing-tip painting a spray of seawater against the clouds.

"Thanks, Federi."

"That was Captain pulling her back up with her risers," commented the gypsy. "Take in the slack! ... Good. You've got to feel the ship through your feet. No time for looking down! If you stumble, grab the handhold lines, don't tug your brake sheet!"

"We've lost the momentum," Marsden threw in. He waved at the bridge. Captain's voice came through the com on the mast, shouting something unintelligible.

"She's going up again," translated Marsden.

The kite sail strained at her rising cables as though she were trying to break free. That sail was aptly named. It was really like trying to control an extremely big, capricious kite. And Radomir Lascek's commands over the ship com on the mast, often repeated and translated by Jon Marsden, didn't make sense.

Marsden grinned at Federi without any humour. "This one is pure dentistry," he remarked. "Bleeding green team!"

The breakers that gushed across the deck every so often made things more exciting. These were high seas!

"Why are we doing this?" shouted Ronan to Federi.

"This is how we fly a storm!" Federi emitted through his teeth. "Yippee! Yee-haw! Anna bottle of rum!" He never took his eye off the kite sail.

"Are we having any success?" Ronan shouted back. "Feels like we're just slipping around!"

"This is a tricky one," shouted Federi. "Can't seem to catch that stream. Not flying yet. Not really going anywhere!" He started singing loudly and slightly off key. "Daah dee daah beedee dabeedee daah, YO-HO-HO..."

Ronan grinned. "Want singing lessons?"

"AND a bottle of RUM! RM!@*!" A faceful of spray drowned the Romany's song. The result of not keeping his eye on the sea. And he was the one who had drilled into all three Donegals that you never, never turned your back on the sea!

Ronan peered up at the huge kite sail. It was being whipped to and fro, and they with it. He couldn't be sure if the tip he was supposed to be watching had the right shape or not. Horrible turbulences up there! That gigantic bat darting about above them looked far too large for the ship. In which way was it controllable?

The Solar Wind lifted onto a crest, and beyond, and that sensation of being right out of the water, was repeated. What was happening? Ronan lost his bearings as the ship moved in a way she should logically never be able to. He staggered, tripped on the toe-strap, and fell, taking the sheet with him.

"Donegal!" thundered Marsden, turning. The kite sail dived into the water. The Solar Wind lost her extra height again and crashed down into a trough, and the sea came aboard. Jonathan Marsden lost his footing and scrambled back onto his feet with salty brine shooting all around his knees.

Ronan tried to figure out whether it was his fault again. He let out his line. More breakers were opportunistically wandering across the deck now. Someone closed the hatch from inside.

Great! So they were stuck out here, come hell or – suddenly the whole effect wasn't funny anymore. Ronan glanced at the gypsy and recognized the reason Federi was yodelling off-key like that. Fear.

And if the veterans were afraid…

Another order crackled over the ship com. It was unintelligible again. Marsden and Federi exchanged glances.

"All flyers below deck," translated Jonathan Marsden for the sailors. "Captain's orders!"

Ronan breathed his relief.

"What!" shouted Federi, flashing a grin. "Just when it was getting jolly! AND a bottle of RUM! RUM!"

The kite sail rose again from the waves and pulled upwards. Ronan's eyes followed it. Its cables shortened and it was hauled in. The Solar Wind crashed down into another trough, and spray gushed aboard. Ronan suddenly worried about all the slack on his line and lost hold of it in his eagerness. He lunged for it, releasing both the handhold and winch line, and went down, flailing for a grip on anything, just as Marsden was yelling: "The sheets look after themselves when we take the kite in." Federi, Wolf and Rhine Gold released their flying lines too at that moment, and the sail collapsed into a heap of cloth which was sucked back into its place, disappearing into that hatch in the deck. Wolf was already fighting his way to the bridge. Another wave washed over the deck, dragging Ronan along. His lifeline pulled taut. He splashed about wildly, gasping for air. That darned line was so tight, it was cutting his breath off. And when he managed a huge gasp, it was full of salt water. He coughed and retched, and panicked.

Someone grabbed Ronan under the arms and yanked him back to his feet. It was Rhine Gold. As Ronan caught his breath he saw that Federi had also started battling his way towards them.

"Thanks, Mate!" gasped Ronan, hanging onto the huge German to steady himself while he found the handhold ropes again. The ship rolled heavily. He fell back against the lines; this time he didn't lose his footing though.

The sailors fought their way up to the bridge, as the hatchway had been sealed off against the crashing tide. One by one they passed through the door and down the stairwell onto the upper crew deck, Marsden last, after he and Federi had finished removing the flying sheets from their winches while leaving forestay and jibs still furled.

The Captain glanced at his First Mate.

"Are they all in?" asked Marsden wildly.

"All that I could see," said Radomir Lascek. "Solar Wind registers all wrist-coms. Roll call, right away."

"Yes, sir!"

"Roll call," announced Marsden when they were all gathered in the boardroom.

"Roll call," Radomir Lascek's command boomed over the ship com, loudly audible in every last part of the ship.

A few crewmembers still came trundling in, holding onto all the railings along the passageways as the ship was whipped and tossed this way and that by the storm. Ailyss, emerging from deep below the decks, looked very green, nearly resembling Paean's scarf. Dr Judith handed her a piece of chocolate. Ailyss looked at it and charged towards the porthole.

"Don't open the porthole!" chorused the crew. Marsden glanced up from his roll-call. Paean moved to Ailyss's side and put her arm around the girl.

"Got something that's going to sort that," she said. "Come!" She led Ailyss off to the infirmary. "Breathe deeply, slowly, Ailyss. Tell me about yourself."

"Don't pry!" gasped Ailyss.

Paean snapped her mouth shut, shocked. Then her good sense won out. The older girl was probably feeling so sick she didn't want to communicate at all.

"I'm not prying," said Paean gently, "I'm helping you. Talking will make you feel better. Tell me your favourite colour."

"Green," said Ailyss through clenched teeth. She looked it.

"Panama went well, don't you think," prompted Paean.

"One up for the Solar Wind," retorted Ailyss. "Blasted sea!"

Why would the girl take a job on a ship if she got seasick? But perhaps she hadn't known.

"Your first job on a ship?" the little redhead asked.

"And my last one," snapped Ailyss. "Damned! When we get to Honolulu I'll be off the ship so damned fast!"

"I'll miss you," said Paean.

Ailyss stared at her in blank surprise. "Why?"

Paean shrugged. She hadn't known that she felt this way; she had begun to regard the Solar Wind's crew as a family, and especially all the younger members were like a litter of sibs. She had never felt as closely tied to her friends in Molly Street, although she had known them a lot longer. Maybe it was something about nearly having died together, all of them. Having survived that death place, Lake Gatun. Maybe it was because they were all fleeing from the Unicate.

"Cause you're my friend," she said instead of a lengthy explanation. She doubted the brunette would understand, or even want to listen at this point. "See, here we are. In the infirmary. Sit down a spell. Don't look down. Fix your eyes on that sea battle there. Here, hang onto that!" She stuffed a pillow in Ailyss' hands.

"Urgh," commented Ailyss. "Colour scheme honks!" Paean could see by her complexion that she was feeling better. The little herb witch rummaged in the Doc's drawers.

"Now where did I see those vomifenes... Fry that!" She scrambled off towards the galley, and moments later she was back with something bulbous in her hands. "Chew this, Ailyss. Will make you feel better!"

Ailyss had stretched out on the prow-wards bunk and had closed her eyes. Now she opened them to eye that root with suspicion.

"Ginger," said Paean. "Fresh as anything. Trust me, it works." She sat down on the rim of the bunk. "I'm a herbalist, Ailyss. My remedies work." And suddenly her eyes stood full of tears, recalling just how well they had worked. And how they had failed the one time she most needed them to work. She sniffed.

Ailyss accepted the root and bit into it. It took her breath away with its "freshness".

"Ow!"

Paean smiled, swallowing back those tears.

"You'll feel better in no time flat," she said. "Shall I go?"

"No, stick around," said Ailyss, waiting for the burning to stop. "Just please don't talk, okay?"

"Promise," said Paean, took the thick Physiology volume off the pull-out shelf under the sternwards bunk and made herself comfortable. She had received an unexpected treasure earlier today – a friend. It was her

169

turn to be one.

"How you can read in this, I don't know," said Ailyss.

Paean smiled and stayed true to her promise of not talking. Ailyss bit into the root again. Amazingly, it did make her feel better.

Everyone was accounted for. Nobody had gone overboard. Radomir Lascek punched the submerging sequence into the console and watched the rigging through the lashing rain. The sails closed; the rigging started folding up. But then it got stuck. Radomir Lascek peered out into the storm, trying to fathom what was going on. The problem seemed to be the Crow's Nest. It wasn't collapsing the way it should. The Captain stared at it, worried. This was no good! Without the Crow's Nest flattening out and the rigging folding against the deck, the masts could not be secured down. And he couldn't submerge the Solar Wind without the rigging secured. The sea would annihilate it!

Merry hells! He'd have to send someone out there, into that hurricane from Hades, to sort it out!

"Federi and Schatz," he called into the intercom. "Need you back on deck to fix up the Crow's Nest! And be careful, men!"

Rhine Gold beckoned to the gypsy and led the way up to the bridge, out into the torrential weather and down the steps. Slippery stuff; but he was wearing his heavy sea boots that he had procured in Hamburg before setting out. They were really good stuff. They were specially designed for extra grip on compounding decks in heavy weather. In the North Sea they had already given him good service in a few of those icy storms. He wondered if Hawaii would have any of those boots – he'd like to get some for Ronan, too.

He shook his golden curls out of his face, splattering like a wet dog, and peered up into the rigging with its half-closed booms, hanging onto a line. The sky was grey with dusk now, darkening the clouds further. The white Crow's Nest contrasted starkly. Yes, that thing was indeed stuck. They'd get to that in a second!

He forged his way forward along the handhold lines, ignoring the water that gushed around his boots. He was a born and bred Hamburger! Bit of sea didn't frighten him! He dashed a glance over his shoulder to see if

170

Federi was following, wondering how the scrawny man stood up to the job in times like these. And yet Federi was one of the toughest sailors on the ship. Rhine Gold supposed that he compensated for his physical shortages with sheer willpower.

"Lifeline!" barked the Romany. Rhine Gold grinned and tied a lifeline around his middle. Almost he'd forgotten! Pirates or no, he'd make Captain proud of him! He started up into the rigging of the foremast.

Radomir Lascek watched from the bridge. He also hoped that Federi would handle the situation, if young Rhine Gold got into trouble.

The two unequal sailors, the tall and the tough, climbed into the rigging, securing extra knots like mountaineers as they went. Federi stared at the gigantic waves boiling towards and around them and grinned. There were moments when they hung almost below the waves; only to get whipped back upright the next second. The rigging with its slight elasticity! He'd never get used to this! In all his years on the Solar Wind he hadn't yet. It terrified him anew every time. And yet there was a streak in him that loved the very fear of it, every second.

"DAY-O, Da-aaa-ayo!" he bellowed. Singing lessons? He thought he'd like some! For added volume.

Rhine Gold heard the gypsy's voice and glanced down.

Suddenly his life paused. There was an enormous wave moving across the deck, nearly the height of the bridge; it passed what looked like inches underneath Federi. The ship tilted as the wave moved on. The rigging rose up towards the darkening skies. The deck cleared of water – and the descent began. They went down with the rigging in an arc, towards that gaping void of black water – and another monster thundering towards them, reaching for them…

"Three BANANA," Federi yelled delightedly, nearly level with him now. "How're you holding up, mate? Come on, not far now!"

Rhine Gold stared at the unlikely man with the drenched purple scarf around his tatty black tangles. He wanted to give an answer, but his jaw was clenched and wouldn't release. Ditto his hands. They hung at forty-five degrees for a moment, then the rigging rode up again. He could feel his whole body beginning to shake, but he couldn't unclasp a hand from those ropes.

"Come on, old buddy," yelled Federi. "Got to do this! We'll finish it and go back below deck!"

Rhine Gold managed to get his jaws unlocked, but what came out had him cringe with fear and embarrassment.

"I'm going to die!"

"You're not!" came a shout from below. Ronan was right underneath him. "Come, man. Ronan Donegal's here. You saved my life just now. I won't let a friend like you drown!" Ronan was beside him now.

"Donegal!" shouted Federi. "Thank the Stars! What?"

"Captain's orders," said Ronan, grinning. "Yow-wee! Roller coaster's an understatement!"

"Federi!" Jon Marsden was right behind him. "Good to see you, mate! Donegal, Schatz – below deck! Federi and I will sort the Crow's Nest!"

Federi climbed higher, nearly floating with relief. That had been a nasty moment there! For a second he had wondered how he was going to get Schatz back down to the deck! But if Ronan could stabilize Rhine Gold… He glanced down at the two young men. If Ronan hadn't managed by the time he and Jon were done with the Crow's Nest, they'd pick up that blond pussycat by his ears and his toes and carry him back below the deck! He turned his attention to the Crow's Nest.

It was a hinge. A single, forsaken little hinge that had been installed the wrong way! Federi hooked his elbow around a rope the way he had forbidden Donegal to do earlier, took out his pocket knife and started loosening screws. Jon Marsden was there beside him, securing three more lifelines before releasing the rigging altogether and helping with his small toolkit that he had brought up here for the job. The gale lashed around their ears, the surf crashed over the deck, the ship pitched and rolled, tossed about like a ball by the waves. Not losing the little screws was the trickiest part of the whole job.

Federi was bored with the banana boat song by now. Jon Marsden ground his teeth. He knew what was next.

"Ma-haaaa-la -!!" bellowed Federi, delighted. He grinned and listened. Ronan feared that the mast might break. "Blast, it doesn't work! It never works on this ship! Should have heard them on Captain Ali's ship!"

"We did hear them," growled Marsden. The national hymn of Southern Free. Federi did the same little act every time!

The Solar Wind pitched forward steeply. Ronan's fears for the mast and rigging were shared by the Captain. He watched from the bridge and wondered if he ought to abandon the steering to Dr Jake and go out there to help them. But nobody could hold the Solar Wind as steady as he could in such a situation. He would not be doing them a favour.

It took Ronan longer to get Rhine Gold down from the rigging than it took Federi and Marsden to sort out the problem with the Crow's Nest. The two young sailors arrived on the bridge only moments before the salted men. The Solar Wind sealed. The Crow's Nest and rigging folded up neatly now, the hooks secured it to the deck. The four mavericks watched from the bridge with the Captain. Another huge wave rolled across the deck and foamed right past the bridge. Ronan grabbed onto something in fear. The water rose, and rose...

"We're submerging," Federi pointed out. Ronan breathed again.

As the ship dropped well below the surface, the wild thrashing and churning calmed down into steadier rocking. Radomir Lascek wasn't content until they were deep enough that the ship was a lot steadier. Then he released the console, turned and grinned at his men.

"Well done!"

Federi had escaped to the galley. He had ordered the sailors to get into dry clothes; now it was time to prepare supper. He sat down at the Ironwood table, his own clothes still dripping, his mind a blank. He needed to think up a meal. All he could think of was that horrific storm outside.

Why had Captain tried to fly this one? It had been far too choppy, the wind hopelessly too unsteady! It had nearly cost them two sailors, that attempt at flying, and then closing the rigging too late.

Captain's judgement in storms was better than this! Federi scowled and stared at the one eye in the Ironwood table that had originally made him buy the antique. It stared back at him without an answer. Why on Earth would Captain want to fly a storm like this? Why take such a risk?

Was it the aftermath of surviving Lake Gatun? Or was it something deeper? Something darker? His gypsy radar clamoured about this. He'd have to find out.

Shawn stuck his head into the galley.

"There you are, Federi!"

"Help me, Donegal," said the gypsy bleakly. "What the hell am I going to make them for eats? Ratted crew wants to eat all the darned time!"

"Pancakes!" cheered the young boy. Federi lightened up.

There was no staying gloomy or scared with those two younger Donegals around, the chirpy twelve-year-old and his impish sister.

Far behind them, Captain Gomez was being flung about in the storm. The T576 had headed straight into it; being an exclusively motor-driven craft, though, at least she didn't face the risk of losing a mast.

"He can't survive this," said Gomez to Gina, tapping at the screen with the vague positronic trace signal of the Solar Wind. "There is no way a sailboat can come through this kind of squall!"

A huge wave very nearly capsized them; but given the rounded nature of the T576, this hardly mattered. These sturdy little craft didn't have outside decks at all; they were shaped a bit like a cross between flying saucers and tadpoles. Their windows were large, all thick armour glass that bullets could not penetrate and even a cannonball would have trouble cracking. If they were turned upside down by a gigantic wave, a thirty-footer like this one coming towards them now – aargh!! – the craft would simply right itself again, by the hugely disproportionate weight of the triangular fin and with a blast of all the correct drives. The people inside the craft – well now – if they got hurt it was their own fault for not fastening their star-shaped seatbelts! Gina rubbed her head where she had banged it on the wall.

"Glad about one thing," she said.

"What is that?"

"That we managed to put that Miller hag ashore in Panama."

"Ha," said Gomez. "If I hadn't woken up minutes before her, and dosed her with another sip of coffee before she was properly awake…"

174

In a plush hotel room in Panama, expensive linen pillows were being torn to shreds and crystal decanters were being flung at crystal mirrors with gilded frames.

13

Terror of the Pacific

That night, Ronan lay awake. The images of those dreadful mountains of water wouldn't let go of him. Every time he tried closing his eyes, another of those monsters came growling towards him.

Ronan Donegal had grown up in Dublin. As a child, he had often watched the sea; when it stormed and the surf was high, he had hung in wharf-side canteens to watch the waves, fascinated. How often had he dreamed of being a sailor!

Now he wished for nothing more fervently than dry, solid land under his feet. Preferably far away from any shore. Knowing that they were inside rather than on the waves was even worse. If something went wrong, if one of the portholes didn't seal, if pressure pushed the hatchway open, there was no escape. It was a cold, deadly prison.

He got up and out of the cabin he shared with Shawn – who was sleeping like an innocent. He moved out into the passage, weirdly lit in orange bioluminescence. All was quiet on the lower crew deck. Soft radar blips carried over from the console in the infirmary and the one in the lab. He knew that in the machine room someone was on night shift – possibly the taciturn Dr Jake, whom one only saw occasionally at mealtimes. The machine room was off-limits to all new crew; besides which Ronan didn't feel like pulling conversation out of the scientist like a starling pulled worms out of the ground.

He started moving north, towards the upper crew deck. Everything was quiet here too, except for more soft radar blips from the galley and the boardroom. Ronan cast one glance along the whole long passage from the stern-side stairwell to the open but dark galley and shuddered. He went one turn further up the staircase, and found himself on the bridge.

"While you're at it, lad," said Sherman Dougherty, looking up, "make us some coffee, will ya. Put a shot of rum in it."

"But – Ship's Rules –"

"Captain knows," said the old man. "In times like this – it's what the stuff is for. Make it a stiff one, won't yer?"

Ronan poured hot water and rum into the cups with coffee powder.

"You boys were grand out there today," said Sherman, moving the pointer pointlessly around the console screen. It looked as though he was on the Net. "Real hero-craft."

"We nearly bloody drowned, din't we just?" said Ronan tonelessly.

"Now you know why sailors swear," agreed old Sherman. "And why they chase every skirt in the harbours. We're going to land in Atuona, Donegal. I want to make the Captain's rules clear. While at sea, no drinking." He motioned to the coffee. "Situations like this excepted. When ashore, no womanising! Land wind messes with a sailor's mind. Captain needs his crew coherent. I mean that both ways."

"Thanks," said Ronan. "Wasn't going to go womanising!"

Sherman Dougherty drummed his fingers on the console. Ronan sipped his Calypso coffee and stared out into the glum darkness. The Solar Wind's deck lanterns were on, making an eerie green glow in the black water. For the first time Ronan understood just how waterproof everything was on this ship. It amazed him.

"How long are we staying down here?" he asked.

"As long as it takes."

"And if the air runs out?"

Sherman smiled.

"Can't," he said. "Our water desalinator produces oxygen. And we've got a store of it in the machine room, and then there are our rebreathers from the diving gear. We can stay down as long as we like."

"How long is that?" asked Ronan.

"Until the storm breaks. This one might take days, we're going the same way as it is."

Ronan groaned.

Morning did dawn eventually, a green bottle-dawn. Ronan's eyelids were finally beginning to sag. Sherman Dougherty was burning up with frustration. While the young man was sitting next to him, he couldn't decrypt any further! He had talked on about pointless stuff – cannibalism on Hiva Oa and sea levels rising and falling – but it had failed to get the young man tired enough to go back to sleep. Old Sherman could understand it though. He had watched on the screens how the sailors had battled the sea yesterday evening. The fear had to sit very deep in Ronan's bones! Sherman wondered if he would have held up so bravely himself.

Captain Lascek walked onto the bridge. He checked the screens.

"That Gomez still on our tail?"

"Yum, Cap'n," said Sherman around a blob of chewing tobacco. He missed his pipe.

"Means they've got more detectors than radar," mulled Lascek. "Wonder what their newest trick could be! Storm anywhere near abating?"

"Looks like she's slackening down a bit."

"Could we ride her now?" Lascek glared at Sherman. "No spitting, Dougherty!"

"Washn't gonna, Capt'n." Sherman obediently spat his chew tobacco gone tasteless into his empty coffee cup.

"That was *my* coffee!" objected Ronan.

The Captain looked at him critically. "You're a brave man, Donegal. Go catch some sleep."

Ronan dragged his tired self off the bridge.

"Sherman," said Radomir Lascek the second he was gone. "Any progress with that capsule?"

"Poor lad was here all night," said Sherman.

"You go get some rest too, Sherman," suggested the Captain. "You've done your best. Marsden and I will take it from here."

Rain was still lashing the bubble windscreen of the T576 in grey veils. Gina Nevada stared out into it vacantly. Stefano Gomez glanced at her profile.

"Funny thing they're radar shielded," she ventured.

He nodded silently. He would shield too, in their position! But that wasn't going to throw him off. The positronic pattern detection system gave a signal not half as clear as sonar, but it was a signal against which

178

the Solar Wind couldn't shield. As yet.

That Anya Miller was right about one thing. The technology aboard the Solar Wind had to be extremely advanced. All the deadbolts in Lake Gatun hadn't killed the ship and crew. And now the ship was moving on ahead, although her signal came from under the sea. Odd. A faulty reading, or another mechanism to throw his detectors off track?

Gomez wasn't going to let go of what had happened in Hamilton. Why would the pirate tow his worst enemy into the harbour, right into the flotilla of stabilizers under his command? And why would Anya react so violently?

There was something cooking here that he needed to lay bare. He suspected that it was somehow connected to the corruption in the hierarchy of the Unicate.

He understood of course that he was on his own. He had delegated the command of Hamilton Harbour to his First Lieutenant. He doubted he'd ever regain that position; in fact he wondered how legal his status inside the Unicate was at current. But it didn't matter, because if the whole structure was corrupt, it was all only a matter of time in any case.

He peered at the console screens, wondering.

"Here's a problem," muttered Radomir Lascek, just as his First Mate arrived on the bridge.

"What, Radomir?"

"See there, Jon? She was supposed to wait for us here! There's absolutely no sign of her!"

Great grey waves were rocking the ship, and rain still lashed down. The Solar Wind had surfaced, though her rigging remained secured.

Jon Marsden nodded gravely. He was literally the only one aboard who knew about this rendezvous. The reason Captain couldn't have gone to Hawaii first and left the contacts on Hiva Oa waiting. Plymouth had already cost too many days.

They were now at the exact coordinates where the RY Angelfish ought to have waited for them; where they ought to have taken the informant aboard. But there was no sign of the private yacht. Not on the radar, the sonar, the electromagnetic sensors – no signal either...

"What's that over there?" asked Marsden, pointing.

Lascek squinted into the rain. Something white was floating on the surf.

"Hang in there, Jon," he said and stormed down the stairs to the machine room. A few seconds later he resurfaced with a fishing rod.

"Can you get her closer?" he asked. Marsden navigated the Solar Wind close to the piece of debris, then stalled the engines. Radomir Lascek ran out onto the deck into the lashing rain, tightened a lifeline around his middle and descended down the rungs on the side of the ship. He reached out with the fishing rod. It was just too short.

"Hang this!" He hooked the fishing rod into the rungs and jumped into the high waves, swimming towards the floating board. There was a bit of lee in the lifeline. It allowed him to reach the huge piece of white compounding and hang onto it. By now he spotted various such pieces, scattered over the waves.

He swam back to the ship, the piece of flotation board in tow. He climbed back up the rungs, carrying it. Compounding wasn't heavy. He laid it on the deck of the Solar Wind.

"Over there, Captain," Jon Marsden called on his wrist-com. The Captain glanced to the bridge, to see where his First Mate was pointing; then followed the directive.

There was an orange buoy floating on the waves a bit further out.

Radomir Lascek descended those rungs once more. He untied his life line and swam out. The orange buoy had something attached to its bottom. He drew it up by its line. A sealed black box, half the size of Federi's toolbox.

"No!"

He swam back to the ship with it, returned to the bridge and broke the seal with a horrible, sinking feeling in his gut.

Right on top there was a hand-scribbled note.

"*Radomir,*" he read. "*I hope you'll find this. Get this into the right hands – go through it, you decide. Careful – Rebellion divided. Watch out for Semanchio Sancho – he's here, I'm dead. Good luck. Angelina*"

In the box, the processor of the Angelfish.

Radomir Lascek stared out into the rain, at the floating remnants of the white RY Angelfish, his heart a blank.

Jon Marsden sealed the door again. "What now, Captain?"

Radomir Lascek gave an impatient hand signal. Jon Marsden understood. Submerge again. Angelina was dead; her yacht blown to pieces. She had clearly thrown the black box overboard before her ship was annihilated.

And with her, the informant had been murdered. By whom? By that violent brute, Semanchio Sancho. Who was a pirate and a gunrunner. Neither Rebellion nor Unicate himself, double-dealing both. What had he done that for?

He would pay for it. If that Sancho was still in the area, he, Radomir Lascek, would sink him. He stared grimly into the pelting rain, watching the waves fold over the deck of the Solar Wind as she submerged.

Rushka came into the galley. The gypsy was already up, getting everything set up for breakfast. The Hungarian beauty watched him and got a mug of coffee stuck into her hand.

"That was touch and go out there, twice, yesterday," she said.

"Yup."

"Saw it from the bridge."

"Uh-huh."

"Can't understand why Captain doesn't allow me to fly anymore. Been part of the flying team since I was twelve!"

"He's just protective of you," said Federi, taking a seat across from her and sipping his own coffee.

"Och, you're always shielding him!" shot Rushka.

"Och?" probed Federi with an arched eyebrow.

"Those Donegals are contagious," grinned Rushka.

"Och aye," agreed Federi, smirking too. "Aren't they, lass?"

Shawn poked his nose into the galley. Rushka pulled her black leather cap into her face and lapsed into silence.

"Hey, hey! Can I have coffee too?" asked Shawn.

"Shore," said Federi. "Och, Dunnigall, won't ya bring old Sherrman a mug too? He's on the earrly shift on the bridge."

"*Shukar*, Federi!"

Shawn went on his mission, a coffee in each hand. Federi shook his head with a broad grin.

181

"I'm tired of being jolly Rapunzel," Rushka said.

"Well, did you enjoy being Sleeping Beauty yesterday?"

"You know exactly what I mean!"

"Yes, I know," agreed Federi with a sad smile. "You just want to be let out of the cage a bit. Be a normal teen. Party, go dating dirty young rogues without any cash flow. Get yourself into scrapes and marry and settle and have ten babies and get divorced. Och, it'll never fly, Princess! But if you want, I'll work on your father some more…"

"Whose side are you on?" lashed the young Hungarian fury. "You sound just like the Captain!"

"Och, noo, wee lass! I soond loike the Dunnigalls, now don't Oi?"

"I think it's time I started fighting my own battles," retorted Rushka sourly.

"O boy!" Federi didn't look forward to that. Rushka was just as dangerous, stubborn and hot-tempered as her father. A lot of mediating lay ahead for him.

"When you were nineteen, where were you?" asked Rushka.

Federi's eyebrows lifted. "Hah! You know where I was! Southern Free! Getting ready to board the Solar Wind!"

"Ensorcelling lots of girls," gnashed Rushka.

Federi laughed. "Sadly," he said, "no. Never ensorcelled anyone."

"Yeah, I'll believe that," growled the Captain's daughter. She downed her coffee, got up and left. Federi stared after her, then he gathered up the cups with a sigh.

"Was already dead then," he said softly. "But you knew that, I thought."

Shawn arrived on the bridge with two mugs of coffee. He glanced out into the bottle-green undersea dawn.

"Hey! Wow!"

Jon Marsden took one of the coffees. The Captain ignored Shawn completely.

"What's that?" asked Shawn, pointing to the radar screen. Marsden blinked. A second dot had started blipping there.

"Donegal, go and help Federi in the galley," ordered the First Mate. As the boy padded off, having lost a bit of altitude, Marsden locked onto the second dot.

"What the hell…"

Radomir Lascek peered over his shoulder.

"That's them," he said.

A large ship appeared on the T576's radar. Stefano Gomez frowned and locked onto the ship identity. Its satellite emission was disabled, by the looks. He dug into the ship's own processor via the universal security override codes.

The Sue Jenkins.

The Sue Jenkins? The name stuck out like a lighthouse in his mind. He'd been fifteen when that passenger liner had gone missing on its way to Hong Kong. It had eventually been presumed sunk.

"How is that possible?" he muttered. "That ship has been missing for decades!"

"Maybe she's empty?" wondered Gina.

"Going too fast for that," said Gomez. "Unless it's one of Lascek's tricks."

His forehead creased in consternation. The signal of the Solar Wind was coming from underneath now. How was that? And yet she seemed to be moving at a steady speed, so it was unlikely that she was damaged. The Solar Wind, a submarine? That changed the ballgame! He could suddenly understand Anya Miller's frustration.

"Look!" said Gina. "Lascek's stopped!"

Gomez smiled grimly.

"We'll catch him up in a few minutes. So will the Sue Jenkins. Wonder if he has a rendezvous with her?"

"Then why stop? And he must know we're behind him!"

"Maybe it's a trap?"

"We're armed," said Gina fearlessly. "This boat is no Pursuer, but there's not a ship we can't disable with our bolts. If it's a trap for us, let's show them whom they are dealing with!"

Gomez smiled and shook his head. Oh, Gina! The bolts that were available on standard T-craft like this one were harmless. They killed nobody and only stunned for a moment. The electric equivalent of the rubber mace. A means of intimidating civilians. And the Solar Wind had come through Lake Gatun, where each of the T-craft had been armed with a Pursuer's dead bolts on Anya's orders! Miller had been unable to stop herself ranting about it.

He peered at the huge vessel that loomed ahead in the grey rain. The Sue Jenkins was a passenger liner without sails, purely solar driven. Her compounding had faded to grey – if that was compounding! Suddenly Gomez wondered. T-craft were mainly of volcanic glass/neoplex polysynth. But apart from that and compounding, he wasn't aware of other materials for modern hulls. The Sue Jenkins turned her flank.

"What now?" asked Gina.

"Let me speak to them." The Captain engaged his ship-to-ship com.

"This is Captain Gomez from the T576. Identify yourself," he demanded.

An answer came back in a language he had never encountered before. Creole? Aztec?

"Careful now," he heard the other Captain give orders to his crew in Spanish, not even bothering to switch off the intercom. "We don't want to damage the boat."

Whoa! Those pirates were hoping to capture them!

"We are armed," warned Gomez. He reversed the T-craft. The tadpole started back-paddling. But not fast enough. The Sue Jenkins came straight towards them.

"Fire," Gomez told Gina. She engaged the firing sequence. A massive electric shockwave fizzled around the hull of the Sue Jenkins.

"Is that the best you can do?" jeered the other Captain. Gina discharged another wave, with the same result.

"They seem to have some sort of protective shield," said Gina.

Gomez peered at the grey ship. That was a layer of some or other metal over their hull! Metal deflected electricity!

He addressed the other ship again.

"If you are in league with Captain Lascek, be warned that there are forty more T-craft behind us. They'll be here in minutes."

Another salvo of laughter echoed over the intercom. Harpoons with grappling hooks shot out from the pirate ship. There was a jolt, and the T-craft turned sideways.

"They've got us," said Gomez.

Gina stared horrified at the wild men appearing on the Sue Jenkins' deck as they were dragged towards her. She had a sudden, very clear impression of what the rest of her future held.

"Get our guns," Gomez ordered. "We're not going down lightly!"

She went to fetch their stun guns. Compared to the automatic fire power these men were carrying, the stuns looked pathetically like toys. She suddenly understood that the Unicate didn't equip all of their military the same. Her Captain Gomez, despite having been the commander of the Stabilizers in Hamilton, seemed to rank quite low in their favour. It made her irrationally angry.

The sonar beeped. Something was approaching fast – from below.

"Come, look," said Gomez to Gina.

"Torpedo," she breathed. "Massive one! Heaven help us!"

"It's not aimed at us," said Gomez. "Look at that!"

The pirate ship suddenly rocked violently. They heard the impact, and the explosion. A scream went up from the Sue Jenkins's crew. Then a message came through both ships' intercoms. In heavily accented, bad Spanish.

"Semanchio Sancho! This is Captain Radomir Lascek of the Solar Wind. That was a warning shot. Cut the lines to the T576."

"Your warning shot has ripped a hole in my ship!" roared Sancho.

"It was meant to," said Lascek. "I mean my warnings. Cut the lines to the T576 or I'll fire the second shot. I'll give you ten seconds."

"Hold your fire, Lascek," screamed Sancho. "We're cutting! You're dead! Why are you siding with the stabs now?"

"I'm not," said Lascek, a malicious smile in his voice. "I'm applying pest control."

That smile chilled Gina. No matter what Anya Miller was like – perhaps she was right? Perhaps Lascek was indeed a psychopath?

They would have to be prepared. They had made the mistake of underestimating the pirate, just because of an unpredictable action. But if Lascek always consistently did evil deeds, he wouldn't be unpredictable! And who knew why the pirate had saved that Anya Miller? Surely he had his own agenda!

They owed Lascek their lives now. She wondered what the price would be, and if the Solar Wind's pirates would apply "pest control" to the stabilizers too after finishing Sancho? She glanced anxiously at her Captain Gomez. Did he have any plan? He was smiling grimly, his hands poised over the controls.

The crew of the Sue Jenkins sawed through the lines holding the stabilizer craft. It was no mean feat. Those lines were reinforced metal cables. But thirty pirates' lives dangled on those cables – and more importantly, their boss Semanchio's!

Once those lines were free, Sancho called over the ship com.

"Your little pets are free, Lascek! Where the hell are you?"

"Behind you."

Radomir Lascek watched the pandemonium that broke out on the Sue Jenkins' deck. He scanned for any sign of Angelina and her contact – but that was hopeless to begin with. Semanchio Sancho had a modus. He didn't take hostages. He brutalized and murdered wherever he went, human life was cheaper than dirt to him. Sometimes he murdered brutally simply for the pleasure. His crew was hand-picked – all of them as cruel as he himself. The only reason they had so far been left alone by the Unicate and the Rebellion was because they traded with both – and in both organizations, human life was a cheap commodity anyway.

All that frantic running around was going to bring them nothing today, thought Lascek. Justice had arrived.

14
Hey, ho, ho

The craft was free. Gomez revved the drives. Nothing happened.

"Screw is stuck," said Gomez, adding a juicy expression in Spanish. "Hold the bridge, Gina. I'll go and see what I can do."

Lascek's voice came over the intercom. "Gomez, get out of the way. You can catch me later."

Gomez looked at Gina and she back at him.

"It's all a game for him," said the Stab Captain incredulously.

"You're wrong, Gomez," retorted Lascek. "This is no game. Get out!"

"We can't move, Captain Lascek. Looks like Sancho disabled our ship," said Gina.

"Then doggy-paddle!" came the impatient answer.

Gomez got out through the hatch to look at the damage. Gina waited nervously. Gomez came back in, shaking his head.

"Dry dock," he said. "The steering mechanism is wrecked. Parts are wrenched off."

Radomir Lascek hammered a sequence into the Solar Wind's console, and the second torpedo got released.

"That's for Angelina, you swine," he muttered softly. His fingers ran across the console. The Solar Wind submerged once again.

The Sue Jenkins opened fire on the Solar Wind; too late. The white sailing ship was sinking back beneath the waves. On the radar she was invisible. Sancho swore.

One of his sailors arrived panting on the bridge. "Captain, we're sinking!"

"Then get into the lifeboats! Don't stand there yammering!"

"Aren't you coming?"

187

"I'm coming," snapped Sancho, "just – as – soon – as – I've – sunk – the Solar Wind !"

Semanchio Sancho ground his teeth and tried again to get a lock on the Solar Wind. She had disappeared. Another torpedo slammed into his ship. His crew were abandoning ship, mobilizing the rubber lifeboats. They had left one lifeboat for the Captain. How fast things could turn at sea!

"My mistake," growled Sancho. "Shouldn't have assumed that dog Lascek was sunk! Should have known it's one of his party tricks!"

There was one thing he could still do. Instead of the remaining lifeboat, he took one of his jet skis that was fastened on the deck. He unbolted it, slid it into the surf along its lubricated rails and gave it a moment to surface. He jumped onto it, his marine submachine gun slung over his back.

The T-craft would make a better lifeboat than a rubber dinghy. An easy target, too. For his personal satisfaction he'd slit that Gomez' belly open, for buddying up with Radomir Lascek and bringing ultimate doom on him! And that sharp little woman – a bonus. Third today. He was in the mood.

He knew how T-craft worked. He had hijacked so many of them, cracking their security locks was like opening a can of beer. Sometimes he had hijacked one, sold it to someone and then hijacked it again from the buyer. Balanced on his jet ski, he fished the slim stiletto blade from his boot and inserted the tip in the exact right spot. The thick glass hatch opened silently, smoothly. Sancho abandoned the jetski and climbed aboard the T576, into the small machine room. Waves splashed in after him. He pulled the hatch closed.

"He's aboard," Gomez whispered to Gina. "Get into the galley!"

Gina obeyed silently. She had seen the artillery this man carried. Stun guns? They had to be mad!

Gomez pulled her into the small pantry cupboard and closed the door. They stood silently, listening, breathing. She felt her Captain's breath in her hair.

Gomez pulled something out of his pocket and held it up for her to see in the nearly complete dark of the cupboard. A handgun. A real one.

"I'll only get one single shot," he whispered close by her ear. "Got to get it right. We'll wait in here until he's in the galley." He held his finger up to his mouth, indicating complete silence.

Gina nodded, leaning against him. He was clutching her with his left arm, hanging onto a shelf with his right, with the gun. She started praying for that split second advantage her Captain needed over the pirate Sancho.

Sancho moved out of the tiny area at the hatch that led down into the machine room, and through the folding doors to the cramped little sleeping quarters with the four bunks, stacked on both walls. He shifted open the second folding door and walked into the cockpit just in time to see his own ship sink. With a great sigh she suddenly pitched, lifted her great old prow right out of the water and steered away backwards into the depths. Enormous air bubbles burped to the surface.

"That Lascek's going to pay!" Sancho said between clenched teeth. "I'll take the Solar Wind from him!"

"Ha, ha, ha," came Lascek's tired voice over the intercom. "Look at you, Sancho. How are you going to do this? You've given yourself into the hands of Stabilizers! All they need to do now is tie you up and take you to Panama to be hanged!"

"I'll kill them first!" hissed Sancho. "And then it's you!"

"Oh, I know, I know!"

There was a jolt. Then the craft started moving. It lifted clear of the waves, tadpole tail first. Sancho was knocked off his feet and landed face first on the windscreen.

"Aargh! What now, Lascek? What devilish trick have you planned now?"

"Just winching you up," said Lascek. "To make it easier for you to get aboard the Solar Wind to take her off me."

Sancho screamed in rage and opened fire. He shot the T576's console to pieces, tried to damage her windshield, failed, turned around and laid waste to her interior.

"Where are you, Gomez, you cowering son of a bed-sheet?" he screamed. "Where's your woman? I've heard that the Unicate sluts are the tastiest!" He laughed viciously.

189

Gomez moved. They had both fallen against the side of the cupboard, with tinned goods and cereal boxes crashing on top of them.

"Are you hurt?" he whispered into Gina's ear.

She shook her head. On the contrary, she had found something very handy. Forget sissy stun guns! Her hand had fastened around a highly pressurized bottle of caustic drain cleaner. All she needed was one shot and good aim.

Their survival chances had just gone up by fifty percent. One of them would definitely see it through. Maybe both.

"This is unreal!" Sancho reloaded his automatic. The T-craft swung face-down above the waves. He stood on the volcaniplex bubble windshield. He could see all the way up to the hatch; it opened, and Radomir Lascek stuck his head in.

Sancho blew that head off with one burst of rounds. His temper derailed and he carried on shooting quite a bit after.

Small pieces of pale yellow compounding rained down on him. And then, with a thump, the whole pirate Captain came through the hatch and landed on the glass next to him. Right into his rain of bullets!

Semanchio Sancho panicked. His gun shot the wildcard pirate's body full of holes; but the man just kept coming. Like in his early childhood nightmares, the bogeyman. He had known something when he was five. He regained it now, in the last moments of his wild and irresponsible life. He had known that this would be the way he'd go. The Devil would come and fetch him, and no amount of fire power would stop him.

He stared into the Devil's steel-blue eyes, unable to move anymore. His gun had run out of rounds. They hadn't helped. There was icy judgment in the Devil's eyes. Semanchio felt himself grabbed by the hair; there was a flash of light on metal, and then his senses ran away in a rush. His hand went up to his throat and registered wet.

"You've murdered your last victim," said the Devil and stepped back, allowing him to collapse to the glass. Semanchio Sancho watched the sea far below; as he breathed his last, it occurred to him that the Devil hadn't shot at him once.

It made sense. The Devil didn't need a gun.

Radomir Lascek turned from the crumpled, blooded form of Semanchio Sancho and waved an impatient gesture at the Solar Wind's crew. They lowered the T-craft back into the water. Lascek walked past the galleyette to the hatch.

"You can come out now," he shouted at Gomez and Gina, and left their T-craft.

Federi was shooting the pirates out of their lifeboats with uncanny precision. It only took him one shot per pirate with his long-range rifle.

"Why are you doing that?" asked Shawn, shocked.

Federi didn't turn. He aimed, shot. Splash, went another dead pirate into the high surf.

"But Federi!" protested Shawn. "You said we're not that kind of pirate! You said there would be no bloodshed."

"This isn't bloodshed," said Federi curtly. "This is pest control."

"I don't understand!"

Federi turned and nailed Shawn with a very loaded stare.

"*Atenție*, Donegal," he said darkly. "These are criminals. Murderers. Dirt. They rape and kill. We've terminated their captain. They'll come for revenge when we're not looking! Want your sister murdered by them?"

"No," said Shawn, shocked.

"There, you try," said Federi, pressing the rifle into Shawn's hand.

Shawn aimed and shot. One of the lifeboats deflated and bubbled away under water.

"No, man, Shawn! It's much harder to hit them when you can't see that much of them!" scolded Federi. "Did you mean to hit the boat, or the pirates?"

"The boat," admitted Shawn.

"Good shot then, boy!" Federi took the gun back and kept on executing, with undiminished accuracy, one criminal per shot.

"Lascek!"

Radomir Lascek looked back from the Solar Wind's deck at the disabled craft that was once again bobbing on the waves. Stefano Gomez was calling him through the hatch.

"Save it," shouted Radomir Lascek. "I didn't do that for you!"

"Wait! Gina and I want to talk to you!"

"Catch us up in Atuona," said Lascek curtly.

"Our drives are broken!"

Radomir Lascek turned disgustedly and made a hand signal at his crew. Jon Marsden organized Rhine Gold, Ronan and Shawn into helping the Unicate Captain get his craft moored onto the Solar Wind. Captain Lascek disappeared below the hatch.

Gina stepped aboard first, still clutching her weapon – the drain cleaner. Jon Marsden helped her onto the deck, then shook the hand of Stefano Gomez and demanded that he hand over his gun. Gomez complied.

"Are we hostages?" asked Gina, concerned.

"That depends," said Jonathan Marsden pleasantly. "Please follow me."

Radomir Lascek had finished changing. He returned to the bridge and activated his com.

"Where are they, Jon?"

"In the boardroom."

"Leave them in Federi's care," said Lascek. "Report to the bridge."

"Federi's still cleaning up, Captain. But these two don't seem hostile…"

Lascek bared his teeth. He could hear how the mind of his First Mate made a U-turn. Regardless of what they seemed, they weren't allies. Never underestimate an enemy.

"There's Federi now," said Marsden over the com. "I'm on my way."

Moments later he was on the bridge.

"These two are a nuisance," said Radomir Lascek. "What do we do now? Can't carry on decrypting! And I need to know what Angelina left me…"

Marsden nodded bitterly. That one would smart for a long time.

"Aw, hell, we'll turn them into pirates," said Radomir Lascek with a decisive grin. "What choice do they have? Marsden, I'm counting on you and Sherman to get that stuff decoded. I take it you've informed Federi and Doc of Angelina?"

"Yes."

"Come. You take the bridge. Course to Atuona is clear. We'll take turns keeping them busy. Use every minute on the bridge, Jon. I'll do the rest."

Radomir Lascek stood in the door of the boardroom, taking in the scene. Gina and Gomez had sat down at his fake pine table; Paean was serving laced coffees. The ship was still tilting quite a bit with the swells, which was why the cups were of the closed, thermos kind. Paean left the room straight after handing out coffees. She was still in disgrace and had more decks to scrub. Rushka had assumed her usual position by the door, taciturn and dangerous, her luscious red mane tucked out of sight under her black leather cap. Good girl! Radomir Lascek was inordinately proud of his daughter.

"Federi," he said, "you can carry on now, I'm here."

The gypsy, who had assumed an unassuming spot in the corner again, got up and stretched. All his double-jointed limbs crackled.

"You don't need me in here, Captain?"

"No, it's alright. There's a lot to do."

"*Shukar.*" Federi disappeared out of the door.

Radomir Lascek sat down at the boardroom table, making himself comfortable.

"So, Gomez! What brings you all the way from Hamilton into the Pacific? Surely the bounty money can't be that good!"

"If I may ask, Lascek," retorted Gomez. "Seeing that you are a hunted man, why help your pursuers? This is the second time I've seen you rescue Unicate marines!"

Lascek smiled. The Irish game! Answering a question with another question! Maybe keeping them occupied wouldn't be as tedious as he'd feared.

"How did you get rid of Anya Miller?" he asked.

Federi looked up from drying dishes. A little ghost with red hair and a lime-green scarf that needed a wash, hovered in the galley's doorway.

"Hello," said Federi. "Still alive? Or has all that detergent dissolved

193

you by now?"

"I'll never clone an illegal organism again," said Paean with feeling. "If I'd had any idea how much cleaning it would cause me... and she doesn't want to train me any further!"

"Aw, no!" Federi frowned. Maybe Doc Judith didn't quite understand the implications? Paean's spell of cloning had been her revenge on the Unicate! But she needed to learn medicine, so she could come back from the dead.

"That's no good! Let me speak to her!" offered the gypsy.

"Och, I don't know, Federi... " She fiddled with the ends of her shocking-green headscarf. "Don't really know if I'm cut out for medicine anyway..."

Despondency. If she only knew how much she was echoing his own state of mind... he didn't have clearance to tell her about the demise of the RY Angelfish. Wouldn't do her much good in any case. He sighed.

"Listen, little luv. If there were someone who was really glum. What would you do about it?"

"Ailyss?" asked Paean, her red eyebrows raised. "Give her St John's Wort. Make a strong tea from it! Better, a tincture. Actually I ought to clone that herb into a bug as well, to concentrate the active stuff – really worked for the Valerian, didn't it?"

Federi laughed. "See? You're cut out for medicine. You can't resist it! 's in your blood! I'll talk to Doc. Let me make you some coffee."

"Och, thanks, Federi, but no – got to talk to Ronan, he was wondering where I am."

"Uh-huh. Well, good luck, little songbird."

He followed her with his dark gaze. St John's Wort. He'd secure some in Atuona. And then he'd darned well season the food with it for the next three weeks!

"Gomez," said Radomir Lascek, tired of the Irish game, "you understand one thing. I'd hate to become known as the babysitter of the Unicate's long arm. So I shall tow you to Atuona, under condition that it's a plain-clothes operation. There's a shipyard there. Get your craft fixed up."

"Lascek, it's appreciated," said Gomez. "Let me ask you again: Why

194

are you doing this?"

"You have just abandoned your post and followed a pirate into the Pacific on a bounty hunt," replied Lascek. "What will the Unicate do if you come back empty-handed?"

"Lascek," replied Gomez, "this is the thing. Anya Miller gets pardoned and promoted for such acts, but someone who is her superior in the structure, such as myself, can still face a traitor's death. Explain this to me?"

"How does that work?" asked Radomir Lascek, puzzled. It wasn't an Irish question.

"That," said Gomez with emphasis, "is my whole point. What is going on inside the Unicate? Lascek, you're an evasive old rogue. You've dealt with the Unicate for years now. Haven't you noticed anything strange?"

"If *you* don't know," said Radomir Lascek, "how should an outsider find out?"

"I believe there's a whole level of dealings there that even high ranks like myself know nothing about," said Gomez. "Will you help me unravel that?"

"So you don't want me writing a terrible ship log for you and launching you back into your career where you left of?" asked Lascek with a wink at Gina.

"You could do that?"

"I've done it before," smiled the Pirate Captain.

Gomez nodded approvingly. "There is of course no going back," he said.

Gina stared at him, shock written across her whole face.

"Getting into the navy was a mistake," said Gomez. "There is no way out."

"This wasn't about the Pirate," said Gina, devastated. "Not the prize money and nothing!"

"You're right, Gina," said Gomez with a tired little smile. "I'm sorry I dragged you into this. It's between me and the Unicate."

"Gina," said Radomir Lascek, "Miss Nevada, is it?"

"Yes, Captain."

"I can offer you safe passage back to civilized lands," said Lascek. "We can concoct a story about a storm and a death and a passing trader picking you up. Your military career and record need not be touched by this episode!"

"*That* is thoughtful!" said Stefano Gomez. "Lascek, I'd appreciate it if you could arrange that for Gina. All this is not her fault. I never gave her a choice."

"No," said Gina. "Please don't. I'll stick with Captain Gomez. Didn't know he was going to desert, but he'll need the backup."

Lascek looked from Gina to the staggered Gomez and grinned.

"That's the way I like it!" he said. "True love!"

He moved to the drinks cabinet and unearthed a bottle of brandy. It seemed to him that Gomez might be a useful contact after all.

Later that night there was a knock on the Doc's cabin door.

"Come in," she muttered distractedly. The death of Angelina had shaken her too.

The Captain entered.

"Could I ask you to have a quick look at something?" he asked. "If you don't mind, Doc." He led the way to the infirmary.

The Doc followed, concerned. She noticed him walking with a very slight limp.

"Right," said Radomir Lascek and pulled the door closed. He sat down on the sternwards bunk and pulled up the one leg of his trousers. High up above the knee. He unwound a make-shift pressure bandage.

"That's nasty!" said the Doc. "Doesn't it hurt?"

"I thought I could deal with it," said the Captain.

"That was one of Sancho's rounds, right?" She looked at the bullet that had ripped into the Captain's thigh. "I'm surprised you could walk at all!"

Lascek grinned.

"You men," scolded the Doc. "You pirates with your fragile egos!" She took scissors and cut the seam of the Captain's trousers open to get to the wound more easily. "Lie down! I'm operating this right away. Oh, hell, it would have been nice to have an assistant! Had such high hopes for Paean!"

"Can't you forgive her?" asked Lascek, stretching out on the bunk. "She's added an amazing secret weapon to the Solar Wind's arsenal. Jon

196

had a look at the construction of that bug. It's so small, it can't mutate. Any mutation causes cell death. And it self-terminates. She took precautions! She wasn't all that irresponsible!"

"But," said the Doc, "she didn't get clearance first."

"You're right of course," said Lascek, "but don't punish that by killing her talent. I'd punish it with increased supervision and more work. Of the medical type," he added. "She scrubbed herself to a standstill today. Drew the line at the rigging though. I believe the girl has a fear of heights."

"Federi also spoke to me on her behalf," said the Doc pensively.

"He talked me into allowing Rushka ashore," growled the Captain. "In principle! Is the man on a knight-on-white-charger mission?"

"With Federi you never know," said the Doc. "Alright, Captain, if you wish it, I'll take Paean back under my wing. She does have a natural talent for genetics. And a passion for medicine. She's a carer, essentially."

Radomir Lascek smiled. "That's better."

"We'll have to work on bullet-proof pants for you," said the Doc. "That was a risky manoeuvre. Just a few inches to the left…"

"I know," laughed Lascek. "The thought smarts!"

15

Atuona

The Solar Wind was eating miles of azure sea between picturesque green mounds. Shawn hung in the Crow's Nest in the mellow afternoon breeze, playing his ocarina. Federi came up the rigging and climbed into the lookout next to the boy.

"Nice islands," commented Shawn, pausing in his play.

"The Treasure Islands of bygone eras," said Federi. "Used to be paradise."

"Used to be? And nowadays?" asked Shawn.

"Today they are crawling nests of all sorts of predators," said Federi with a far-away look in his eyes. "There is bloodshed nearly every time we land here. Half of the time it has nothing to do with Captain's ethics."

"What precisely are his ethics?" asked Shawn.

"Never commit a crime. Unless you've got to," said Federi. "More or less. There's lots more, but I don't want to overload you. We'll still sit here tonight if I get started." He glanced down. "There's Gina!"

Gina Nevada, tired of listening to the politicking of the two Captains, was ascending into the rigging too.

"Gonna get cosy in the Crow's Nest," grinned Federi.

"Want me to leave?"

"*Nu*, for heavens' sakes, Donegal!"

It wasn't as much of a squeeze as the Romany had predicted. The Crow's Nest was roomy enough for three more people, thought Shawn.

"Have you been in Atuona before?" Gina asked Shawn.

"Nope. My first sea voyage. But he has," and he indicated Federi.

" 's a filthy place," said Federi dreamily. "Don't go roaming on the beach, 's dangerous. Don't get separated from the others. Don't go drinking alone. Shawn, Gina, Captain's orders: No womanising when ashore!"

"So womanising aboard is okay?" grinned the boy.

"Manising," said Gina. "Captain Lascek says there's no Unicate on these islands."

"That's right – they can't get their drugs sold there," said Federi.

"Drugs?!" gasped Gina, shocked.

"But Precious," said the Tzigan, "where do you think the name Unicate comes from? A unification of all the drug syndicates on Planet Earth!"

"Shawn, don't listen to him," said Gina, incensed. "It's not true! The Unicate is all the governments of the world, they got together one day and decided to stop all war, and we've got peace ever since! That's the truth! I've studied history through Harvard!"

"This was the correspondence course?" asked Federi with a smile.

"It's exactly the same as the full-time course on campus," replied Gina tetchily. "What are you implying?"

Federi gazed out into the distance, where the hazy sea met the hazy islands. His hand pulled something out of his pocket; he began to carve at it with his spring-loaded jack-knife.

"I'm a Romanian Tzigan," he said without looking up. "We're part of that history. We *know!*"

"So's everyone on Earth," retorted Gina. "What do you have against the Unicate anyway?"

Federi stared out to sea. What did he indeed have against the Unicate? Except that they had hunted him relentlessly, and his family... except that they themselves were a huge wrong, and someone somewhere would have to fix it... except for what they were doing to Tzigany and Rroma as a group, fine-combing for a certain element...

"I'm Tzigan," he said. Didn't that girl get it?

"Oh, an *ethnic* gripe," said Gina disgustedly.

"Federi," asked Shawn, "what have they done to your family?"

...his family, ripped to pieces...

Blood, everywhere.

"Federi, you've cut yourself!"

He stared at his hand, detached. His arms and legs climbed him out of the Crow's Nest and down to the deck, and his feet walked him down through the hatch.

Shawn stared after him.

"He was shaking!" commented Gina. "What did you ask him?"

"Nothing," replied the young pirate. "Leave it!"

Ronan was helping Dr Jake with the stock-take for the engine room. It was surprising how many things needed to be replenished. Even more amazing that the nuclear scientist actually talked!

"We're working on ways of deriving most of these substances from our surroundings," explained Dr Jake. "Take the hydrogen for the fuel cells now. So expensive to purchase! Meanwhile it could be derived from the distilled water our desalination system generates. That's what all those components are for," and he pointed at Ronan's list. "And we're using organic refuse for the fuel cells too... the way they were originally designed, which has become a hushed-up secret. Not much longer, and the Solar Wind will be completely self-sustained."

"Even the nuclear drives?"

Dr Jake shot Ronan a sharp glance.

"Don't you ever mention those to anyone, understood?" he ordered.

"Okay," promised Ronan, eyes wide. "And when we're fully self-sustained, we'll never need to go ashore again, right?"

Dr Jake paused in the stock-take. He frowned at the Donegal, horrified. Never go ashore again? Up until this moment it had not occurred to him that that was what Captain might have in mind. Now it hit home.

It would be right up Lascek's alley, wouldn't it? Frequenting Unicate-haunted pirate ports would not be a necessity anymore. Nothing to look forward to than more wind, sun and sea... He shuddered.

They landed in a blue lagoon surrounded by a green, jungle-covered island. The Solar Wind's sails furled. The anchor descended down into the depths.

"Welcome to Hiva Oa," declared Shawn loudly, seeing it for the first time himself. Rhine Gold and Wolf gravitated to the prow of the Solar Wind to gaze at the lush vegetation and sloping volcanic peaks.

"Time to get down from here," said Gina.

Shawn looked around for his gypsy friend. Federi was nowhere in sight.

"Federi?"

The Romany looked up from putting the last dishes away. Paean Donegal, green scarf and all, hovered in the doorway watching him.

There was such an intensity about that girl! He smiled at her.

"Coffee for you, little sunbird?"

"No, thanks. We're going ashore, Shawney and I. Are you coming too?"

"Nah."

"Not?"

"Don't like the land much," said Federi. " 's a stinky place. You'll see."

She hung there, studying him. He smiled at her again.

"But are you going to be okay, Federi?"

He chuckled. "Little luv, this old piece of junk is in the habit of being okay."

"You're not old, and you're not junk," said Paean sternly. "And there's no harm in asking! Is there something I can get you?"

It was very difficult to stay down around this little sunshine. She bullied one back into a better frame. Those people in Milly-Molly-Mandy Street had lost a treasure, Federi thought. Lucky Solar Wind.

He shrugged. "Nothing really."

"Wanted to say thanks," said Paean.

"For what? What have I done?" Federi glanced about wildly. The redhead giggled.

"For talking the Doc round. She's taken me back into training."

"Aw! Great!" He grinned. "So that's why you've been so scarce! Captain spoke for you too, you know."

"*Captain* did?"

That smile was worth pure gold. Federi nodded, satisfied.

"Look after your little brother, see? Don't let him get up to trouble. 's a dangerous island for those who know how to look!"

"Och! Trouble is his middle name!" Paean declared dramatically. "Later!" She waved and moved off. At a rate.

"*Kathal*, little sunbeam," said Federi quietly to her retreating back. He smiled. This time it actually originated from his insides.

Unicate was death. Land was death. Damned Sancho was death – luckily he was dead now himself. Because too many people had died. There was death here in Atuona too. Sometimes death was like a cage around Federi. Part of life, sure, but just enough to make living impossible. But she helped him see past the bars to the outside, where the sun was shining.

Jonathan Marsden supervised the two boats being crewed and casting off. Practically the whole young crew was on the boats, with the exception of Ailyss, Ronan who had volunteered to keep an eye on Federi for his concerned sibs, and Rushka. Of the older crew, Doc Judith and Sherman were going along with Captain; and the Solar Wind's guests, Gina and Gomez, on a mission to organize the repairs to the T-craft.

He as First Mate was left in charge of the Solar Wind. It suited him, because he hadn't yet given up trying to decrypt the stolen data. Jon Marsden didn't give up easily on something like that. It would be insulting himself; furthermore it would be letting Angelina down, who had lost her life trying to tell them something.

Behind him, Rushka appeared on the deck. She pulled her black leather cap off and shook her whole cascade of red hair free. They watched the boats move off.

"Keep your eyes and ears pitched, Rushka," said Jon Marsden. "Anything suspicious."

"That's all I ever do these days," said Rushka.

"And believe me, it's essential," Marsden assured her. He gazed out at where the two boats were heading for the shore. "Captain predicts that he'll marry those two before we set sail for Hawaii."

"He can only marry one of them," laughed Rushka. "And I know they're Unicate, but they're not all that cute... Think I'll have to call Gomez Mama?"

"You know what I mean, little good-for-nothing!" grinned Marsden.

"I know." Rushka's smile faded. "You know, Jon, when I was younger, I was allowed to make myself useful and scrub decks and help peel potatoes and all sorts of things. Now I'm allowed less and less!

Shawn's more useful than me, and he's the ship's mascot! Not even Federi will allow me to get my hands dirty with galley duty anymore!"

"He's following orders. You're being groomed for Captain," said Marsden. "Be patient, Rushka! One day the Solar Wind will be all yours, and the crew will be at your feet!"

"Ha, yes – when I'm old," said Rushka. "The Solar Wind is my father's ship. When he's as old as Sherman he'll still be captaining her!" She sighed. "Lucky Gina! I wish I could plot my own course!"

"But do you want to leave us?" asked Marsden. "Don't you like us anymore, Rush?"

"Och, you guys are my family, I love you all," said Rushka. "But I only also want a deal like Gina! Freedom and a nice guy who loves me."

"Och, and I deduce the nice guy has already been selected?" asked Marsden, amused.

Rushka blushed and confined her hair under her black cap again.

Federi had said that land was a stinky place.

Paean understood what he meant! On the ship there were smells too; from the frying fish in the galley to the chemical smell of the infirmary to the slight damp in the machine room. But over everything there was the constant, clean smell of the sea wind.

Here? They had hardly landed and crossed the broad expanse of white rugged beach, and the pong of rubbish hit her. She held her breath and looked around for it. And she found it! It was lying and blowing all along the roads. Papers, empty beer cans, organic refuse of all sorts, drunken louts…

The Rebellion was supposed to have replanted and repopulated this place? Well, it looked as though repopulation was still going on! She inserted herself between Shawney and a scene she seriously hoped he hadn't spotted. Honestly, in plain view of the main street! And as for the plants – there were weeds everywhere, and a sort of unique tangled island jungle. If these trees were all younger than sixty years, they were fast-growing stuff! Paean wondered if there was genetic tampering involved.

She and Shawn trudged after the older sailors down the main road. To the left, some run-down shops, some ramshackle houses a gust of wind could blow over, and in the background, the sea. To the right, more pubs and ramshackle houses; overgrown gardens with more half-passed-out parties going on; and in the background, the mountain. She peered up at it.

Those slopes looked wild. Really wild. The jungle looked untouched. No ugly dwellings breaking it. She prodded Shawney.

"Tomorrow," she said and motioned. He agreed enthusiastically.

"Federi said," he started.

Paean studied him. Nothing further came out.

"What?"

"No womanising," laughed Shawn. "No drinking alone! No – och, he was so full of rules, it was weird."

Paean shrugged. "Wonder what's eating him."

"Make me some coffee, my friend."

Jon Marsden stood in the doorway to the galley. Federi moved automatically to the coffee machine and created an espresso for his friend.

"How's the programming going?"

"Frustrating, Federi. Not much coming out of it. Feels as though I'm missing a whole key for the information. Feels as though there's actual data missing."

"And the box from the Angelfish?"

"Yes," said Marsden. "She didn't know that much more than us, but basically she suspected things. A rift in the Rebellion."

Federi nodded, thinking about the sanguine blonde Angelina who wasn't ever going to grace the world with her laughter and crude jokes anymore. One more friend down. They were all doomed anyway.

"But the core issue…"

Marsden sighed. "They're all beating about the bush. Wish I could get close enough to see what bush it is. Had some glimpses of some really poisonous words, but that's all."

"Worrying," said Federi, sticking the coffee into his friend's hand. He glanced out of the portside porthole.

Marsden followed his glance to the green shores. "Going ashore, my friend?"

"We'll see," said the Tzigan with a frown. "Not today."

The sun had disappeared behind the volcano. A long shadow hung over the beach; further out though the sunlight was still dancing on the blue waves. Paean stared at the sea.

She and Shawn had watched the loading of potatoes and coffee until they were blue with boredom; they had hurried up and waited around the shops in the main street until there were no shops left to wait around. She had bought her little brother an ice cream, a childhood dream from Molly Street; he had bought her a two-piece swimsuit in turquoise and blue with an illegally bright pink stripe across and a sarong to match.

"Come," said Shawn. Paean followed him away from the wooden quay where goods were packed onto the Stormrider, and along the white sandy beach.

The sea levels had been much higher than today; but first, they had been lower. Corners and edges of broken buildings stuck out of the sand; once Paean slipped and scrambled a bit as the sand rolled away under her feet into a buried room. It was a strange feeling to walk on this sunken town; she thought of Herculaneum and Pompey, cities buried in volcanic outbursts. There was an eerie sense of time to these ruined structures.

"Look," Shawney called from further up. "Tracks!"

She hurried up and joined him. She had to laugh.

"Yes. Human tracks." She followed the trail with her eyes, right to the edge of the undergrowth. "Signs of human habitation, too!"

"Visitation," corrected Shawn. She understood. In his creative mind he was currently on another planet.

She went closer to that heap of old rags and beer cans. That was odd! Was that a label? She picked up one of the dirty rags and looked closely, and let it go with a scream.

Stuck to the piece of clothing was a single, dried-out human finger.

16

High Stakes

The room was full of smoke, curling up to the low ceiling where it billowed and twirled around itself.

There was a dance floor, but nobody really knew why. People didn't dance in a crummy joint such as this, in Atuona. Canned music from the previous two decades thumped out of an archaic speaker system which was luckily so old that the din of conversation drowned it out.

Wolf had been in this pub before. The Dirty Dog. Today he was teaching Rhine Gold the ropes; the young German needed to learn how to make a bit of money on the side, being a pirate. They'd had a go at this before, in Dublin Port; but the Unicate had been a serious hindrance, closing pubs at ten and chasing the patrons home with penalties. For those who only got off from their shift at eight, until ten was not really enough time to get drunk enough for this game.

Plymouth had been a dead loss. They had only gone as far as coffee houses. Captain had been too nervous at the point, having to find a way through Panama. Well, Wolf hoped that they wouldn't have to go that way again in a long time.

But Atuona now – that was the real place to teach someone how to be a complete pirate! Here there were no rules. You could stay in the pub all night, and they didn't mind, because people did anyway. Plenty of opportunity to make good money.

Wolf himself had learnt from the best – Federi and Marsden. There was always a new trick to be learnt from the gypsy. Then again, the First Mate knew the rules of the game so well he had taught Wolf how to stay within them and still win, reliably, almost every time. And to watch out for Tzigan tricks.

Federi had elected to stay aboard tonight; Marsden was elsewhere altogether, with the Captain, conducting some political business. But

Wolf was good at this by now. He needed no more help.

He raised his voice over the general din, placing his playing cards face-up on the round table with the filthy red-chequered table cloth.

"Gotcha," he grinned smugly. "Again!"

Paean drifted into the galley.

"What's for supper?"

There was Ronan, drunk as a lord, trying to teach Federi, equally far gone, how to play the bagpipes. They were hanging more than sitting around the Ironwood Table and making the most awful racket. Federi caved in with laughter every time he tried to get a noise out of the infernal instrument.

"Tortured duck," Ronan shouted. "Do the Tortured Duck again!"

Federi produced something that wasn't quite a note.

Ronan shook his head. "That was the flatulent elephant."

"It *was* the tortured duck," argued Federi, swigging directly from the bottle of rum and handing it to Ronan, who followed suit. "Or possibly the Squashed Python."

"Ronan!" shouted Paean, dismayed. "Federi! You guys are totally drunk! I can't believe you guys! What kind of example are you setting for Shawn?"

Federi stared at her for a few seconds, left eyebrow raised. "Hey! You're back aboard!"

"Get off of yer high horse, Pae," said Ronan amiably, holding the bottle for her. "Come on, get your chainsaw and join the Ceilidh!"

Paean turned on her heels, disgusted. Drunkenness ashore, drunkenness aboard – wait! They were breaching Captain's rules!

"You're breaking Captain's rules, drinking like that!" she shouted at them. By now Ronan had unpacked his concertina that he had bought in Plymouth and was trying to compete with the rude noises Federi got out of the bagpipes.

" 's what the stuff is for, little luv," replied the gypsy. Paean wasn't quite sure if he was referring to the rules or the rum. "Was the shore fun?"

"No! That's a stinky place!"

Federi grinned. Paean turned tail and ran off in search of Shawn. She had to warn him to stay out of the galley! She felt badly let down by

Ronan. And as for Federi – well… This was a lesson she seemed to have to learn repeatedly. He was just a rotten old Tzigan! A rotten young Tzigan, rather. No less rotten.

"Haha," said Ronan. "Great show, Federi! Sorry, man, she gets like that sometimes!"

Federi stared after the little redhead, scowling. That had been an overreaction!

"You'll have to focus now, Federi," scolded Ronan. "Can't let Sherman win this bet!"

Shawn trundled into the galley, his curiosity peaked by Paean's ominous warning.

"What are you guys doing?"

"Shh," said Federi, grinning. "It's a secret."

"Yip, we've made a bet," said Ronan. Federi glared at him. Donegal, he thought, learn the definition of 'secret'!

"Och, let me in on it," begged Shawn.

"Alright. We're betting whether Paean can be made to climb into the Crow's Nest," grinned Ronan. Federi listened up. This was not a bet he was aware of having made!

"Pigs might fly," replied Shawn caustically.

"Pirates must face their fears," said Federi, frowning. "Shawn, help yourself to food, it's all over there!"

There was a buffet of scrumptious-smelling food prepared, keeping warm on the stove. Shawn wondered why the Romany considered himself a lousy cook.

"Everyone eats as they come in tonight," said Federi.

"Except Paean," grinned Ronan.

"Except Paean, it turns out," agreed Federi. " 's not my fault," he said in answer to Shawn's accusing stare. "She took one look at the food and turned tail."

"Actually she was looking at you," laughed Ronan.

Federi smiled and shook his head. "Wonder how much of the crew is actually coming back aboard at all tonight."

Ronan nodded sagely, grinning.

"They want to drink all night?" asked Shawn. "Or are they out looking for predators?"

"Actually…" started Ronan.

"Dead right," said Federi, pan-faced. "They drink all night. Grown-ups sometimes do that. And play cards." He refrained from telling the two Donegal brothers that, despite of what Ronan was thinking and broadly grinning about, that was actually exactly what they were doing – and cleaning the local populace out of cash on the way.

Because looking for predators was prohibited by the Captain's rules.

"Did you not want to go ashore too, Federi?" asked Shawn. "Drink all night too?"

"Ha!" Federi's eyes rolled skywards. "And look for predators! No, thanks! I can drink right here if I want to! No need to go ashore for that!" He laughed.

Paean dug herself into her bunk, making a wall with her pillow. She didn't want to go and play along with the Ceilidh. She didn't want to study. She didn't want to see her brother! She was deeply disgusted.

Atuona had come as a shock. You carried images of tropical island paradises in your impressionable teen heart, and then, when you arrived at the place, it turned out to be a worse dump than downtown Dublin. And with unknown nasties running wild!

And then you returned to the safety of the ship and found that the rot had spread - that people you'd thought of as decent, Ronan and Federi, were just bums on the inside as well. Wolf had turned out to be an uncouth ruffian, despite his education. Rhine Gold had this arrogant way about him. Rushka was remote. She didn't associate at all, whether by choice or by orders. And Federi – well, he was really just a gyppo loser. And pulling her brother down into it!

Paean had grown up a bit today.

She got up. Blast them all. She padded along the passage until she found Ailyss in her cabin. She hung around that cabin for a while, trying to have a chat with Ailyss without talking too much. This was complex. Eventually the older girl lent her a spy novel and sent her back to bed. Paean was not going to be picky about this. She read until she fell asleep.

In the Dirty Dog, the atmosphere was getting a bit prickly.

"He cheats," said the man called Cairns, who claimed to be a scientist but ran a pawn shop down-town. He pointed a finger at Wolf.

"He doesn't cheat," said Wolf. "His name is Wolf Svendsson, and Wolf Svendsson is honest! I've won this, fair and square, now hand over your chips and let's get on with the game!"

Rhine Gold grinned.

"I know about you pirates," said Cairns. "Call yourself honest! Ha!" He added a few slippery expletives.

"Tell them, Rhine Gold," challenged Wolf.

"Nah – he's honest, guys. Well, most of the time!"

"Thanks!" Wolf frowned. "I think."

After the Donegal brothers had eaten, they moved the Ceilidh out onto the deck. It was cooler here. Glorious stars spangled the skies. Now and then vague noises carried over from the land above the surf. Land was noisy! Ronan and Shawn played their tunes; Federi studied the stars and listened, and worried. He didn't have a very good feeling about Wolf and Rhine Gold out gambling alone.

Rushka appeared soundlessly on the deck and chose a spot nearby Ronan, who was oblivious to her. Federi greeted her with a smile and a wink; a greeting she returned. Och! So the Princess was thawing under the Donegal magic, thought Federi.

"I declare this round invalid," said Cairns loudly. His friend, Ethel Sloan, agreed heartily. It was the third round of five that they declared invalid.

"On what grounds?" asked Wolf. Poker was poker, damn them! He had played decently; if they simply declared each round they did not win as invalid, that was as good as cheating!

"On the grounds that you've been taught this game by a gypsy, and there's no telling what tricks you use to get the good cards!"

"Who taught me the game is irrelevant," said Wolf. "The rules are simple enough! Not my fault that *you* don't know how to bluff! But I play it honestly!"

"Yes, sure – like the Tzigan!" laughed Sloan. "That pathological long-finger!"

"Radomir Lascek's little assassin," added Cairns, raising his voice.

A silence descended. Heads turned. The golden oldies hammering out of the ancient DJ-system were suddenly audible again.

Wolf felt the stares of the whole patronage of the Dirty Dog on him.

"Take that back, you damned dirty dog," he said dangerously, getting to his feet. "Take it back now!"

"It's true!" laughed Cairns. "You're denying it? What else are you denying?"

Shut this loudmouth up right now, thought Wolf. His fist slipped. He had a long arm, a fairly hairy one. On the end of it sat a solid piece of machinery, honed by working with heavy equipment, sails, drives, spanners and computers every day. And a fair amount of flying the Solar Wind before tropical storms. This piece connected with Cairn's jaw, all the way across the table. The man was flung backwards and his chair overturned, the rough cement floor dealing his skull a second blow from the other side. Cairns' loud mouth had effectively been shut up.

The pseudo-scientist tried getting up. Wolf was already towering over him, fists up. He had knocked over the table to get to the ruffian faster. Cairns was no midget himself. Rhine Gold moved his chair back a bit to be out of the fray.

A knife flashed. Wolf saw it in time and twisted the other guy's hand back on itself. With a scream, Cairns dropped the knife. Wolf kicked it out of reach.

"Take back what you said!" he challenged.

Cairns kicked Wolf's knees out under him. They both went down in a wrestle, dealing kicks and punches, each trying to get a better grip on the other. Cairns' arm got Wolf around the neck in a single Nelson. Wolf was too angry to understand the implications: The other could technically break his neck. But the young engineer was thinking with his crocodile brain; his head jerked back reflexively and caught Cairns sharply on the nose. With a scream Cairns let go. Wolf used this respite to turn about and grip his collar, winding up his fist for the next good one. He was faster, stronger and bigger. Cairns would have to yield any second now.

Cairns reached behind himself and found a beer bottle. His hand closed around it and he smashed it on the ground. Wolf didn't miss the point this time. His opponent was armed now, he held a jagged-edged bottle-neck in his hand.

For the stink in Atuona! This guy was actually trying to kill him! Wolf pushed him over again and kneeled on his hand, prizing the shard free and flinging it away. Thugs, all of them! He loved a good punch-up; but this man was fighting dirty. Clearly an experienced heavy. He'd believe him the archaeologist when he saw him digging up finds!

Now would be the right moment to pick the guy up by his collar and his belt and throw him head-first out of the pub. But Wolf had a score to settle, and once he was angry, he didn't give up until he got what he wanted.

"You've still got to take it back!" he shouted, his fist loaded and poised. "Take it back about Federi!"

On the deck of the Solar Wind the gypsy listened up.

"Quiet!" he hushed the two Donegal brothers. They paused in their music.

"Pub brawl," said Federi. They strained to hear over the sound of the surf.

The voices from the pub became louder and louder. Two crystallized out of the rest, shouting at each other with passion, interlaced with angry screams.

"Blood will flow any moment now," predicted Federi. Sure enough, just then a shot cracked. They listened in fascination. A second shot echoed across to them; followed by a scream.

"Rhine Gold," said Federi, getting to his feet in a swift movement. "We'll have to wake up the Doctor. She'll have to stitch."

"How on Earth did he hear that?" Ronan asked incredulously. "How could he tell it's one of ours?"

"He just knows. Got this gypsy radar," replied Rushka from the shadows and clammed up again.

Wolf stared up at his opponent, confused. He had lost his footing and gone down; an ideal opportunity for Cairns to pitch right in and descend on him, except he didn't. He had scurried back a few paces. There was a wrestling knot around Sloan. Rhine Gold screamed; but nobody was attacking him. He was staring at Wolf in horror. Man, did the guy have a voice! If he didn't make it as a pirate, he could still become a town crier, thought Wolf.

A third shot cracked, and this time the nuclear engineer heard it consciously. That was the one that went wide, of everything and everyone, because the gun was already halfway out of Ethel Sloan's grip. Something warm dripped on Wolf's hand. The bullet, he thought illogically and glanced down. No, wrong. Just plain old blood.

"You're shot," said Rhine Gold, pale as a blank screen.

Pain registered. Wolf glanced at his knee. He grinned. "Oh bum!"

All he could think of this moment was Doc Judith's angry face.

Federi knocked on Doc Judith's cabin door, the two Donegal brothers in tow.

"Doc, they're bringing in one of ours. Bin in a brawl."

"Who?"

"Not sure yet." He had heard Rhine Gold scream. But that didn't mean that Rhine Gold was the injured one!

Doc Judith could guess. Whom did she have to suture up after every darned pub fight? For once the doctor was fed up with stitching brawling pirates.

"Get the Captain to jolly well forbid that Wolf to set foot ashore! – And tell Paean to patch him, she needs the practice," she said curtly, and closed her cabin door in their faces.

Federi glanced at Shawn, then at Ronan. What now?

"Wake her up," said the older brother.

They woke Paean up by pounding loudly on her cabin door. She opened the door, wearing ducky pyjamas and a sour frown.

"There's a problem, little songbird," Federi began. He lapsed into puzzled silence seeing her expression.

"You rats are sober!" she shot.

Federi's eyebrows reached for the sky. "Is that a problem? Want us drunk, rather?"

Shawn exploded into laughter.

"Why did you and Ronan make me think you were drunk, Federi?" Paean asked accusingly.

"It was worth the look on your face, lil sister," grinned Ronan. "I told

Federi you'd be shocked; he wouldn't believe it; so we made a bet."

"You made a bet!" Paean sounded almost more disgusted than before. In fact she felt embarrassed and was covering it with temper.

"Sorry, Paean," smiled Federi, amused. He didn't even realize how piratical he looked as he considered. Pigs might fly? His gutsy little green pirate had been made a fool of. Her brothers clearly enjoyed this. In honesty Federi hadn't believed Ronan that she'd overreact like that. What if he showed them some flying pigs tonight? It would certainly boost Paean. He owed it to her.

Was there time? The shore party would have to get the injured sailor back to the Lawnmower, and then it would take a few minutes to cross from the shore to where the Solar Wind lay anchored... Yes, there was time to fly some pigs and win a quick bet!

She was eyeing him with suspicion.

"Go put on your green scarf, quick."

Paean rushed inside her cabin and tied the scarf around her head.

"Stick to the rules, man!" warned Ronan, picking up on what the gypsy had in mind. "You're not allowed to tell her the bet until you've won or given up! Telling her is giving up."

"I always stick to the rules," lied Federi. Paean appeared, green scarf and all.

Federi grinned. Lime-green scarf on red hair... Oh, that compulsion for teasing people!

"Ah, good. Pirate Paean. Now follow me."

Paean followed Federi and her brothers onto the deck. She was still fuming; they had tricked her! A bet! Well, at least it was better than her brother and her friend genuinely turning into drunken losers!

Federi moved ahead and into the rigging. Paean stopped. Ha! Gotcha! He was out to expose her fear of heights! The rat!

"Come on now," called the gypsy.

She stared at the wonky structure, the way it swayed slowly with the rise and fall of the swells and laughed cynically. "Kidding!"

"Paean, come up! Can only see it from up here."

"*Nyet!*" said Paean. "Your left foot!"

The entertainer climbed back down.

"You've never been up there, have you!"

"Surprise," Shawn said softly behind her.

"No," said Paean decisively, drawing herself up to her full, not very tall height with dignity and folding her arms. "And I'm not going to start now! Not every sailor needs to turn into a Great Ape!"

"Alright, look here," said Federi quietly, taking her by the wrist and leading her away from her brothers. "Thing is," he started.

She stared into those dark hypnotic eyes. "You guys can quit making fun of me right now," she suggested tightly. "What's the point anyway?"

"Not making fun of you, Paean," said the Tzigan. He smiled mischievously. "There's something I want to tell you," he added under his breath. "Away from *that* infantile lot!"

Seconds passed. Paean weighed it up. Freezing hells! To hear his secret, she had to go up there! The gypsy's stare was still locked with hers. Ronan was making loud coughing noises in the background. What was this?

Well, hell with Ro as well! She'd show them! To the speechless amazement of her two brothers, Paean climbed after Federi into the rigging, clinging as it swayed gently with the waves. It wasn't so bad after all. Her eyes narrowed as she looked up determinedly and slowly clambered all the way into the Crow's Nest.

Federi was waiting for her with a unique grin of elation.

"I knew it! Knew you had it in you!" He was beaming. She grinned back at him, catching her breath. It had been interesting going up. She wasn't going to think about going down yet. She gripped the rim of the Crow's Nest and looked at the stars. They were tangibly close from up here.

"We did it wrong," said the gypsy, alarmed. "Oh hell! Federi forgot about lifelines! Little luv, never ever come up here without a line!"

"Okay," said Paean. "Promise. Say, what was that you wanted to tell me?"

"Aw," said Federi with a skew grin, "can't tell you!"

"Hey!" This wasn't right! "Out with it! Fair's fair! I've already paid the price!"

Federi sighed loudly and rolled his eyes.

"Made a bet with your brothers that I'd get you to climb up here," he

215

admitted.

"Aargh! I knew it! You pirate!" She attacked him, pummelling him with her small, bony fists. Federi laughed and caught her by the wrists.

"Hey, look! Look up! Aren't the stars beautiful from up here?"

She wrestled with him, trying to get him to release her. Eventually she gave up and laughed too.

Federi reached up and stretched and picked a star out of the night sky and presented it to her. She gasped. In his hand lay a tiny silver thing on a fishhook.

"What's that?"

"The other half. Don't let Ronan destroy that one too!"

She picked the little transmitter up out of his hand. "What do I do with it?"

"I don't know. Keep it. Put it on your scarf." He smiled.

"Aw, Federi!" She grinned and attached the little piece of equipment without a function to her lime-green scarf. "You're a hopeless case! All this to win a rotten old bet? You guys woke me up for this? I'll get you all back when you're not watching!"

"Actually that's not it." The Romany got serious again. "Look out there."

A droning hum carried over across the waves. It had been there before, but Paean only noticed it now.

"The Lawnmower's coming back?"

"There was a fight," said Federi. "We heard shots. They're bringing someone in. Wolf or Rhine Gold. I hope it's not too serious."

Paean whistled through her teeth. "Sheer!" She looked up at Federi, scared.

"You're the paramedic," he said. "I'll help you. We're going to patch the injured one up. If it's critical, we wake up Doc Judith. But if it's not that bad, we'll cope by ourselves, see?"

Going down the rigging was an adventure in its own right. Grip by grip, Paean felt her way back down. The Lawnmower was already being moored alongside when she finally stood on the deck again, all her muscles quivering.

"Was that Paean up there in the Crow's Nest?" asked Rhine Gold as they lifted Wolf aboard. The nuclear engineer's face was twisted into a brave grin.

"Trick o' the light," said Shawn. Rhine Gold and Ronan supported Wolf to the infirmary.

Paean ran ahead to prepare things. She washed her hands and straightened one of the two bunks, the left one on the prow-side wall. The three strapping young sailors pushed in through the door, Wolf hobbling between the other two. She stared at him, horrified. He looked like hell. She backed away and gave the others space to help him onto that bunk.

Half his face was drenched in blood; all of it was contorted and white with pain. Rhine Gold and Ronan stepped back; Federi chased them out of the infirmary, giving them orders for something or other. Paean bent over her patient to figure out what was going on. She got a close-up look at those sea-green eyes and her stare locked with his.

This was not the moment to chew him out for drinking and stinking. She filled a bowl with lukewarm water and rinsed the blood off his cheek with gauze so she could see where the damage was. She was burning to ask what had happened; but darned if she'd make small-talk with this one!

Wolf was equally speechless. He watched her as she worked. Didn't it worry her that all that water and blood was seeping into the pillow? Hadn't she noticed his knee? The major source of blood and mess and pain?

"Be brave now," she bit out through clenched teeth and dabbed some iodine tincture on his cheek. She looked at Federi, who was supervising.

"Looks like a bullet has scraped him there," said the Romany. He approved of the minimal talking policy. "But I'd take a look at that knee, little songbird."

"Uh-huh," said Paean. "I'll stitch up the cheek, that looks easier, then it's done and then I can focus on the knee."

"If you're going to stitch you may want anaesthetic," said Federi. He indicated the drawer. She found the right stuff and injected Wolf's cheek. Federi handed her a mask and gloves, which she compliantly put on. He opened a sterile pack of instruments for her. She nodded her thanks and picked the suturing needle, threading it.

217

Wolf watched with wide eyes, a feeling of unreality descending over him. His cheek was being stitched up in perfect silence by this young kid here – and no lecturing, resonating, scolding Doc Judith!

Rhine Gold stuck his head through the door.

"Captain and Marsden back aboard, Federi."

"Good."

"How's it going in here?"

"You!" Paean put her suturing needle down and glared at Rhine Gold. "Drunk, stinky lout! Go and *breathe* your sticky breath on some other victim! Push off!"

Rhine Gold fled.

"Honestly," huffed Paean and returned to her suturing. Wolf's eyes went one notch wider.

"That was unnecessary," said Federi quietly.

"Was it?" retorted Paean. Federi lapsed into worried silence.

She finished the cheek and sealed it off with a generous helping of frightening red iodine ointment and a big white bandage. Then she turned her attention to Wolf's knee.

"I'll need scissors," she said vaguely. The next moment they were placed into her hand. She nodded acknowledgement and cut Wolf's jeans open from the bottom end. Wolf made a movement to object.

"The hell are you going to take your pants off," snapped Paean. "Keep still!" She cut the jeans away all the way past the knee. Then she looked at the mess.

"Oh my God." She squeezed her eyes shut for a second and shook her head. "Wolf, it's going to be general anaesthetic. Not doing this under local. Too deep."

"What the hell is going on there, actually?" asked Wolf, straining to sound friendly.

"A bloody mess," retorted Paean. She took off gloves and mask and charged off to the upper crew deck. Federi shrugged. He had no idea what the little wildcard had in mind.

Several minutes later she was back, a half-empty bottle of rum and a glass in her hands. She poured a bit of rum into the glass and fished a vial out of her moonbag. This she cracked open and tipped its powdered contents into the glass.

"Drink," she ordered and handed the whole affair to Wolf.

"What is it?" he asked suspiciously.

"Anaesthetic."

He downed it. The pain faded out, swept out of him by an overwhelming wave of tiredness. He glanced at Federi, and at little Paean…

"Done!" Paean looked up and straightened out. It was long past midnight. Shawn had come in some while back, to keep them company. Even though he didn't say anything, his presence was reassuring.

They'd had to dose Wolf a second time when he started coming to in the middle of the operation. It had lasted longer than three and a half hours.

Paean glanced at the discarded cotton wool and the bowl with bloody water. And suddenly she slipped to the floor.

"Flying pigs!" Federi shot to his feet. "What now?" He checked the little redhead's vital signs. Shawn bent over her too.

"I think she can't handle blood," the youngest Donegal commented.

"She's timed it well," said Federi approvingly. He checked on the still unconscious Wolf, then picked Paean up off the floor like a child and carried her down the passage to her cabin. He tucked her into her bunk.

"Brave little songbird," he muttered as he closed the door.

"That she is," agreed her proud little brother. "Totally brave."

17

Savage Wolf

Sherman Dougherty looked up from the console screen. Pale purple dawn was fading in over the lagoon. His eyes were twitching from too much console work.

Radomir Lascek had just arrived on the bridge.

"How's it going here?"

"Same," said Sherman despondently. "Captain, Jon and I have been hacking at this thing for days now. I'm ready to throw in the towel! I'm positive there's some more information we need, in order to decrypt that capsule."

Radomir Lascek nodded. He'd almost dared to hope that his brilliant information genii would manage. But deep down he had known from the first, when Marsden had been unable to crack the code right away.

"We'll put it on ice," he suggested. "Carry on at Prime Oil. Maybe Vincent has learnt a trick we don't know yet."

Sherman shrugged. "I suspect we'd have to break into the headquarters of the Unicate to find the answer to that one!"

"Anything more out of the log of the Angelfish?"

Sherman shook his head. "She didn't know much. The informant wasn't going to endanger her by telling her too much."

"Fat help that was," sighed Lascek. "Both died anyway."

They both lapsed into thoughtful silence for a minute.

"Gomez and Gina?" prodded Sherman eventually.

Radomir Lascek grinned.

"I've committed matrimony on those two. Was interesting. Just as she was about to tell him 'I do', couple of shots cracked. Put her off her track. She said 'I think so' instead."

Sherman chuckled. "Was she a pretty bride?"

"As pretty as they get in their Stab uniforms," replied Lascek. "Was an emergency wedding."

"Is she…"

"No, they're deserting together. Guess what they want to call their craft."

Sherman shook his head.

"The Black Star," said Radomir Lascek with a grin. "And I asked them – I've always wondered –what does the T in T-craft stand for."

"What does it?"

"Terminator," said Radomir Lascek, and he and Sherman doubled over with laughter.

Shawn and Federi were in diving gear, ready to go explore the reefs in the lagoon. Federi instructed Shawn on the correct way of wearing the mask, and primed him on several details of diving. The kid was fast on the uptake.

Wolf came through the hatch, hanging onto the rail of the steps, looking like a bomb blast zone.

"Going diving?" he asked.

"You can't come," said Federi shortly with a glance at Wolf's bandaged knee. "Go ask Ronan for bagpipe lessons if you're bored!"

Wolf spat onto the deck. It sizzled. "I'm not bored," he said. "Just asking!"

"No spitting," said Federi automatically. "Or else you'll…" er. He couldn't force Wolf in his current state to scrub the deck! Chancer!

"Hey!" complained Shawn. "I'll have to clean that!"

Federi studied the savage Wolf. An enormous white gauze strip had been pasted over the sutures on his cheek, where the second bullet had grazed him. If he but knew it, the seam underneath looked like those poor chicken carcasses that had been through Paean's hands. His right knee was thickly bandaged. It had been shattered by the first shot.

How on Earth was that sailor managing to walk on that?

"Get back into Sick Bay," ordered Federi. He let himself fall overboard backwards. It was a long drop down. As he surfaced, he saw that Shawn was getting ready to copy the movement.

"Don't, Shawn," yelled Federi, spitting out his mouthpiece. "Stay right

221

where you are!" He shimmied up the rungs and climbed back aboard. "That move is just for old pros," he explained. "It'll knock your breath out. Come with me."

Shawn grudgingly followed Federi down the rungs.

"And I'm a show-off, but I'm not old!" cautioned the Romany with a grin.

"I didn't say anything!"

"You were thinking it very loudly."

Wolf went in search of Paean, working his way along the storm rails that lined all the corridors. His knee felt as though a swarm of termites had made its nest there and was eating it from inside. It made the throbbing pain in his cheek nearly a pleasure.

Why the hell had that guy Cairns tried to kill him? Since he had come to at dawn from the pain, he'd been lying wondering about this. A knife, a Nelson, a broken bottle? And then Sloan with his gun, aiming at his leg – oy, possibly at some other features, thought Wolf uneasily; and then at his head? That had been attempted murder! For what? Winning in poker?

It was Paean who had stitched him up; maybe she could tell him what was going on! Today she was wearing her shocking-green scarf again. It made her easy to find. He spotted her on the upper crew deck, miles away in the galley, stacking plates. He hailed her. She gifted him a defiant glare and trotted up.

"What have you done to my knee?"

"I rescued your leg," replied Paean curtly. "Maybe I should have amputated." She peered at his face with her baby-blue eyes. He wasn't a good face-reader. He couldn't tell what she was thinking. "Get thee back to the infirmary! I'll give you a painkiller."

Unfriendly wench. He wondered what had happened to the little blue-eyed wonder who had come seeking him out in the machine room, half infatuated with him. Or had he misread that? Freaking rabbits, but he could do without more hostility today!

She made him drag his wounded leg all the way back to the infirmary, just so she could dig in the drawers there. The stuff she produced eventually was folded precariously in bits of paper; it presented as a grainy white powder.

"What's that?" asked Wolf.

"Painkiller," she snapped.

He eyed it with suspicion. "Your own concoction?"

"No, it's a pharmaceutical recipe."

Wolf swallowed the powder, shaking himself with revulsion. "It's acid!"

"Salicylic acid," Paean said. "Purified from willow bark powder."

Willow flying bark! "It doesn't do anything!" At least, he hoped it wouldn't! Not the kind of thing he suspected it might. Like that darned wonder bug in rum, yesterday! He vaguely recalled coming to in the middle of surgery, whimpering like a baby and begging for another dosage.

This kid was dangerous! She should come with a label, with a skull-and-crossbones and a cautionary note saying "toxic teen".

"You'll have to wait five minutes," said Paean impatiently. "Honestly! I don't think you ought to be walking on that yet! The wound is too fresh. Give it some time to heal."

"I'm a man, not a whimpering little girl," growled Wolf. "There's things I've got to take care of!"

Whoops. Wrong wording. He saw how she charged up her fist, then changed her mind. Why? Because it would pop some stitches, no doubt.

"Well, big strong man, then how about, you come into the galley and I'll make you some coffee," smiled Paean, suddenly sweet as sugar. He stared at her with caution. Hells, coffee sounded good, but that quick about-turn? He limped and hobbled and crawled after her to the galley, wishing he could get his hands on a crutch. Or a stick. Whatever.

"Gunshots," said Marsden. "Well-aimed too, by the looks. Concerning!"

"According to Rhine Gold, that wasn't all," Rushka reported. "A knife, a broken glass bottle. At some point the guy had Wolf's head in a breakneck grip. That was attempted murder, no less!"

Jon Marsden frowned. He knew they ought to investigate this! Cairns? He had never heard that name in Atuona before! Nor, Ethyl Sloan! And Atuona was not that large.

"Think they're in any way connected with that Sancho?" he asked.

"Not impossible," said Rushka. "We ought to investigate!"

"*We* do nothing, Rushka! I'll look into it with Federi tonight! *You* stay well away. Understood?"

"Captain's daughter and less of a say than the cleaner," grumbled Rushka.

"Who, precisely, is the cleaner on this ship?" asked Marsden, nonplussed.

Rushka grinned. "All of us?"

Jon Marsden turned back to his programming. Rushka briefly touched his shoulder in greeting as she got up and left him alone so he could get on with it.

Sherman had thrown in the towel. That stood to reason. But he'd be absolutely blasted and doomed if he'd give an inch! He'd wrench this forsaken capsule's secrets from its innards with his bare hands!

There was a tentative knock, and Paean stuck her head onto the bridge. "Sir?"

"How can I help you, Miss Donegal?" asked Jon Marsden.

She seemed uncertain. Guilty, somehow. "Need some help. Need to carry Wolf back to the infirmary. He's fallen asleep in the galley. I told him not to walk on that leg yet. It must have exhausted him."

Jon Marsden gave the little green pirate a long, searching look.

"Your buddy Federi would probably be proud of you," he muttered. "Go round up Rhine Gold and your brother, Paean. We'll get that pesky patient of yours put back in bed."

There he lay, large, helpless and passed-out. Paean gazed at her patient, usually so full of rubbish. His bearded face, relaxed. It made him look somehow vulnerable. He couldn't be very much older than Ronan. Hard to connect this heap of senseless meat here with the insulting lout he was when awake!

She sighed and started unravelling the bandage around his knee. Rhine Gold and Ronan watched; Marsden had returned to his programming.

"I wouldn't open that, if I were you," advised Ronan. "We still want to go ashore today!"

"I've got to!" retorted Paean. She took a look at the wound.

Eyeballs on sticks! His walkabout had popped several stitches! Blood

224

was seeping unceasingly out of the wound. Paean reached for the needle and thread and patiently redid the burst sutures. She only hoped all the internal stitching was still in place. Well, if it wasn't, he'd have hell to pay!

"We need someone on guard with a hammer," she said angrily. "He's to stay in bed at least a week."

"How about tying him down?" suggested Ronan.

Paean looked at her brother and Rhine Gold and thought about Atuona. She had been on the open sea so long. It was enough to drive a girl mad. Despite the horrid condition of the town she would like to go ashore too, hike up into the mountainside a bit, feel solid ground under her feet, see some lush green tropical jungle. But not alone! She had a feeling that as long as they went in groups and provoked nobody, they'd be alright.

"By the way, sis, that scarf – most becoming!" teased Ronan.

"Well, I might as well accept an award when I'm presented with one," said Paean with dignity.

"One can spot you sea miles away. Just don't wear it in an attack," quipped Ronan.

Atuona. She wondered. Was it a great risk to leave him aboard and go ashore? She knew the answer. Was it worth staying aboard and keeping him company? Giving it another shot at friendship? Having herself chewed out another time for talking too much? No, thanks! She snorted.

"A regular beacon," Ronan continued to tease her. "If you climb into the rigging, you can be a lighthouse."

"Not climbing up there again," muttered Paean. It had been terrifying enough.

"I'll have to make Federi another bet then, won't I?" grinned Ronan. Paean gifted him a scathing look.

Rhine Gold was grinning as well.

Atuona.

"What exactly are your plans today?" asked Paean.

"Just going to pad about the town a bit," said Ronan.

"Care to go climbing up into the mountains?"

Rhine Gold looked very impressed by that idea. Ronan nodded.

"Sounds like fun. If you come along, we won't need torches."

"I've been told there are old cannibal altars and archaeological digs up there," said Paean. "I'd like to see some." Though where they should have come from, if the island had supposedly been submerged...

Whoa. It was *Samoa* that had been submerged! No wonder the jungle here looked older than sixty years! It was!

"Don't worry Pae," joked Ronan. "I think cannibals don't eat their greens..."

Only their browns, she thought with a shudder. But that could have been anything. Predators. They'd have to be careful.

"But Doc is in town too, so it's only me to look after this horrible fellow here..."

"Did she tell you to stay aboard and baby-sit him?" asked Ronan.

"Not exactly, but – I just know it'll come down on my head if I don't." She had a bad conscience. Mr Marsden had not been impressed with her Valeriensis trick.

Ronan shook his head pityingly.

"Come, sis," he said. "Finish tucking the big hairy baby in and then let's have a brainstorm."

Sherman Dougherty entered the bridge. Jon Marsden looked up from the console.

"I think perhaps you ought to check on things in the galley, Jon," said Sherman quietly. "Looks like the three hags from Hamlet gathered around the cauldron there!"

Jon Marsden shot to his feet.

"Thanks for the warning, Sherman," he said. "It's that Paean again, right?"

"And her brother, and young Reinhold Schatz."

"Pesky Donegals!"

Marsden made his way to the galley.

"What's happening here?"

"She's brewing a potion," said Ronan with a huge grin before Paean could caution him in any way.

Marsden planted himself in front of Paean.

"You had better tell me all about it," he invited.

Paean explained her idea of distilling the valeriensis protein back from the live bacterium. This way she could dose it a lot more accurately, for instance to put it into a drip. She had intended to add the decoction to a bottle of rum and put it next to Wolf's bunk, with a message for quick recovery. It would keep him so drowsy, he'd not get in the mood for getting up.

There were three bottles of steaming decoction standing on the shelf; she had been on the point of filling the rest into the fourth.

"You honestly believe he'll self-dose?" asked Marsden. "I'll take these. You're getting more dangerous, Paean!"

"But sir, how must I keep the man from getting up? He won't listen to me! And his leg won't heal if he hops about on it!"

Marsden looked again. There was a quaver in her voice and a stressed little fold between her eyebrows. That bad?

Paean sniffed. "It looks terrible! Sir, I can't tell you how many fragments I tried putting back together yesterday! Like a Chinese puzzle!"

"Can't really sit there with a hammer," said Marsden thoughtfully.

"Oh no, please don't," said Paean quickly. "It was way too much work…" She petered off uncertainly as he couldn't keep a straight face.

"But I wonder why he won't stay put," added Marsden thoughtfully. "There's something to that! See there, Paean, if he won't listen to the orders of his paramedic, he must listen to mine!"

Paean looked relieved. "You'd do that for me?"

"Of course," smiled Marsden. "Can't have pirates limping about! We'll end up with a Long John Silver situation. What time will he wake up?"

"Twelve thirty about," said Paean, clapping her hand over her mouth.

He laughed. "You'll have to learn to cover your tracks better, little green pirate! Well, from about quarter past I'll be at his bedside, and as he opens his eyes, I'll give him his medicine. That should buy you – how much longer?"

"Three hours," muttered Paean contritely, hanging her head. "Sir, we can't dose him continuously for the next six weeks!"

"We shouldn't have to," said Marsden. "Isn't there a cast in the infirmary?"

"Couldn't find one," said Paean.

"Alright. There's a medical supplier in Atuona. Organize a cast, Doc Judith's got an account there. Be back by three. What rum is this?"

"Just a bottle from the supplies," said Paean. "Ronan selected it – he said the other type is too expensive."

"Does Federi know you're plundering his supplies?"

"I was going to tell him," said Paean sheepishly. "He'll understand!"

"Do so. It's nasty when things go missing!" Marsden took the bottle of rum. "Go ashore, kids. Have fun. Just be back on time. I'll take it from here." He moved off to the infirmary, worrying. That girl was headed for trouble in an unstoppable straight line, and no mistake!

Finally they could go ashore. They found the medical supplies shop and bought a clip-on cast for Wolf's leg. Then they walked up into the sweltering hills.

Paean had been right. Up here it was still a paradise. They walked on what seemed to be a well-worn path until it disappeared, then simply followed their noses. The forest was quiet. Even the birds seemed to be holding siesta. When they came to a small stream, they all drank from the cold water, then rinsed the sweat off their faces.

"I wonder how Marsden's doing," worried Paean.

Wolf peered through heavy eyelids. His head was throbbing worse than his knee. He wondered for a second who had hit him over the skull with a blunt weapon and thrown him off his chair. Then he realized that everything was yellow. This was not the galley. He was back in Sick Bay. He groaned.

"Hey sailor! Your little girlfriend sent this to console you!"

Jonathan Marsden was on the chair next to his bunk, holding up a bottle of rum. Wolf groaned louder. Last thing he needed now!

Things started to make sense. The little red fox had given him coffee. It had been laced! With her horrible wonder bug! The thought made his head want to split with toxic ache. Her sugary smile suddenly made sense! If he got his hands around her scrawny little neck!

"She doesn't want you getting too bored in the six weeks you've got to stay in here," added the First Mate.

Six weeks! Wolf sat up.

"I've got to get back!"

"Back where, Wolf?"

"To work, sir! There's stuff I've got to take care of!"

"Paean says, six weeks," Marsden repeated.

Wolf's hackles rose. "I don't have to listen to that half-baked little bully! I'm getting up!"

"Not so fast, mate," said Marsden. "She's right. Your knee won't heal if you get up."

"She's got no clue, with respect, sir!" growled the young engineer. "I've got to get on with things!"

If he could just grab this knee of his and wring the pain out of it with both hands, like a drenched towel!

Jon Marsden was looking at him strangely.

"Wolf, what's going on in the machine room?"

"Nothing, sir, absolutely nothing! The drives are all functional and the torpedoes are okay, and the computer system is up to date, and the nuclear stuff – sir, I only think Ailyss is too green to cope alone. Dr Jake is ashore."

"Ailyss," repeated Marsden, studying him. "Has she been behaving?"

"Yes, sir." Wolf went silent.

"Then there's nothing to worry about," said Jon Marsden and poured them each half a cup of rum. "Drink to your health, Wolf!"

"But sir…"

"That's an order," said Marsden cheerfully and handed him his cup. Wolf obediently downed the rum and fell back down that slippery abyss he had just managed to struggle out of.

Paean, Rhine Gold and Ronan returned from their island excursion just as Federi and Shawn came back from the diving, Shawn's eyes full of "hey-shoo-wow".

"You must see it, sis," he said. "It's incredible down there!"

"You should see the sacrificial cannibal sites," she replied.

Marsden appeared from below deck. "You should see Wolf," he reminded Paean.

"Oh, right, Wolf," said Paean with a heavy sigh. "Is he at least still asleep?"

"Like a baby," replied Marsden with a wink.

Paean went down to the yellow infirmary. Wolf was still passed out.

229

Sleeping, he looked like a much nicer person. There were fine laughter lines detectible around his closed eyes. She smiled. There had to be a nice guy lurking in there somewhere! Perhaps with a bit of coaxing he would emerge? But the yellow hue of the room did make him look jaundiced. Or maybe it was just punishment for his drinking spree yesterday.

She put the cast on his leg with help from Rhine Gold. Ronan had gone for a swim. She wanted to go swimming too. The island had been very hot. But once again, she wasn't going to go alone. There were sharks, according to Shawn.

She put the pile of books she'd got for Wolf in an antique shop, on his bedside table.

"Why do you go to all that trouble for him?" asked Rhine Gold.

She studied the blond giant and wondered if she should take him along when she went to swim. Probably a good idea. The buddy system: Feed the shark your buddy.

"Because he'll be in here for a while, Reinhold. I would imagine if it were me lying there, I'd go crazy without something to read. I'd hope someone would bring me some books."

"I wonder if he can even read," muttered Rhine Gold unkindly. "Brute like him! If it were me, would you go to the same trouble?"

Paean looked up at him, surprised. "Of course," she said, then laughed. "I'd probably go to a lot *more* trouble for you!"

"Why?" smiled Rhine Gold.

"Because I like you." She gazed down at her patient, sighing. Green eyes, laughter lines… Let's be realistic here, Paean! Brute like him… "This one's not a particularly nice person."

Wolf opened his eyes a tiny slit.

Across from him, on the other bunk, sat a quiet little presence, so quiet he might not have seen her if she hadn't been looking straight at him with her huge eyes. A wild animal, come close.

His head was still throbbing with chemical overload and his knee was transmitting pulses of leaden ache. But somehow the need for water overrode all.

"Wolf," said Ailyss quietly. "Are you thirsty?"

230

He groaned something. She could force him to drink anything right now, just not rum or green bug.

The dark-haired phantom girl slipped from her spot without disturbing a molecule of air. She took a metal beaker out of the cabinet, rinsed it under the tap, filled it and gave it to him.

Water! Pure, clean desalinated ship water! That was the moment Wolf fell in love with her.

18

Donegal Magic

"Going somewhere?"

Paean turned around to see the gypsy's black eyes following her and Shawn from his shady corner in the storage space at the Solar Wind's prow. Paean and Shawn had backpacks and were now only waiting for Ronan and Rhine Gold. It was still early. They wanted to go out before the day heated up too much.

"We're going up into the hills again this morning," said Paean.

"I know you don't like Atuona," added Shawn. "Or I'd have asked you to come along."

"Into the hills?" said Federi.

His left eyebrow went up. There were things in those hills. He wouldn't want the kids to go alone. A tropical jungle was not a Dublin green! It worried him that the three teens had gone by themselves yesterday, when he'd been diving. They could have got lost, or worse.

He didn't want to bust their little party, but somehow he had to find an excuse to go along and supervise.

"Well, would you like to join us?" asked Paean.

The gypsy grinned. Little mind-reader! "Wouldn't I just be in the way?"

"You? Never!" exclaimed the little green pirate.

"You sure it's not a strictly-kids-only outing?"

Paean growled.

Federi pocketed the thing he'd been carving and stood up. He stretched. "Well, then I'm ready." He eyed Paean approvingly. "By the way, girl, becoming scarf."

She laughed.

"Don't you need to pack anything?" she asked. "To take along?"

"Pack? Pack what? Is this a weight-lifting exercise?"

Paean laughed. Federi winked at her. "So what all are you kids relocating across the paradise island?"

"A bit of water, some towels, some lunch," said Paean. "Not much really!"

"The island has water," said Federi. "Towels?"

"Going swimming," said Paean.

"It's so hot," replied the Romany. "Think you'll need towels?"

"Well – to sit on," explained Paean, beginning to get the distinct impression that she was being ridiculed.

"Perfectly good grass for that," replied Federi. "And *lunch*?"

Paean peered at him with narrowed eyes.

"Just some sandwiches," Shawn came to her rescue. He laughed. "But you're going to tell us, you'll just catch us a fish instead, or quickly snare a bunny, and then we'll have a genuine jungle-dinner?"

"Not actually," said Federi. "I thought, we have lunch on the ship, and then we go diving?"

"Oh, yay!" Now Paean was beaming.

Rhine Gold and Ronan appeared on the deck. This time, all of them were taking their swimming gear. Yesterday they had discovered several gorgeous rock pools with cold streams cascading into them. It would be a welcome change to the warm sea. And Paean was wearing her brand new swimsuit under her clothes. She wouldn't have to swim in shorts and shirts anymore as she had done so far.

"Nice scarf, sis," commented Ronan, once again. Was she going to wear it every day now? "Trying to scare the birds away?"

"By the way, Federi's joining us," said Paean.

"Oh no," groaned Ronan. "Two jingly scarecrows!"

It earned him a thoughtful gaze from the Romany.

Ten o'clock. Jon Marsden got up and stretched. Time for a break, time to check on everything. He turned and came face to face with Rushka.

"They're ashore," she stated flatly.

"Were you not allowed to go along?" asked Jon. "Thought Federi had cleared that with your father for you?"

"Och..." Rushka couldn't explain it. Now that she was allowed to, she suddenly didn't want to. Land wasn't all it was cracked up to be. And Atuona of all places! And a certain someone mustn't think she was tagging him! She hadn't exactly been *invited* along!

Marsden nodded sagely. He thought he understood.

"I don't like the way Paean frats with that Ailyss," commented Rushka.

"What -?" He frowned. This was an ugly little development!

"She borrowed a book from Ailyss," said Rushka. "Last night. A spy novel, ironically."

Marsden brooded. What could that mean?

"Donegal Trouble, Donegal Magic," he muttered. "We'll have to monitor that."

Did it relate in any way to Wolf's restlessness? He wondered. Perhaps closer supervision was required for their Irish spy? But how much closer could it get? Wolf and Dr Jake were monitoring her non-stop in the machine room, and she didn't exactly associate with anyone in her time off. Stuck in her cabin reading, most of her free time. Tough to supervise that, beyond watching the electronic eye. He glanced at the console screen, then paged through the options. The electronic eye showed Ailyss in the machine room, reading.

The mountaineering party was tramping up the blistering mountainside. Shawn scouted ahead, with his sibs unable to call him to order. He was like a runaway horse exploring the jungle. Around every bend in the path new things delighted him and caused him to break into a run to get there faster. Rhine Gold and Ronan had their hands full trying to catch up with him.

Paean was very soon fed up with chasing after Shawn. She settled back into a pace that suited her, and found her gypsy friend walking alongside her.

"He shouldn't run ahead like that," commented the Romany.

"Good exercise for Ro and for Reinhold," said Paean lightly, following the voices. Yesterday the jungle had been so jolly quiet, it was just as well that there was some noise happening now, further on. "Nothing can really happen to him, can it? I mean, they're right there…"

Federi peered at her. "What have you seen?"

She told him about what she and Shawn had found on the beach, two

234

days ago. He nodded thoughtfully.

"What does that?" asked Paean.

"Could be anything," replied Federi evasively. "Only tells you to be on guard!"

"But we'll be okay in a group?"

"Especially with Federi looking after you," he reassured her with a smile. "Don't worry, little sunbird."

"You know, night before last, when you made me climb into the rigging?"

"Hmm?" Federi bent a green branch of something out of their way.

"You manipulated me!"

"Hmm!" Federi grinned. "And it won us the bet!"

She paused. "Us?" What had she won?

"Well, you overcame your fear," said Federi. "That's a big win, believe me! You'll realize it in time, little pirate."

"Still! You manipulated me!"

"I had my reasons," said Federi lightly.

"Yes. Your rotten bet! How much did you pull out of my poor brother's pocket then?"

"Only one bottle of really cheap Chilean Real Jamaican, and the promise for instrumental lessons."

"Oh!" That effectively shut her up, because she hadn't even told him yet about the bottle of Chilean she had annexed from his store. The more she thought about it, the more she had to laugh.

"What's so funny suddenly?" asked Federi.

"I'm so sorry, Federi!" she giggled.

"Why? What have you done now? Spit it out!"

She told him about the plan they had cooked up for keeping Wolf in bed, and how in the end Marsden had been the one to confiscate the bottle of Chilean Real Jamaican and feed it to Wolf himself.

"That smarts," said Federi.

"Oh, I'm really sorry, Federi. I'll replace the bottle."

"That it had to be the bottle I had just won!"

"Well, I'd have picked a better quality rum…"

"For that lout Wolf Svendsson? That smarts even more! Why not a hammer?"

Paean cast the Romany a suspicious look. Was the idea of keeping Wolf subdued with a hammer a widespread one?

"It's ironic, though," she smiled. "You won that bottle from Ronan by manipulating me. But Ronan then manipulated the bottle back away, via me." She paused, taken aback. "Hey! Means I got manipulated twice! Anna bottle o' rum!"

Federi chuckled.

"But at least my brother had the last laugh," shot Paean.

"Never trust an Irishman," concluded the gypsy. "Besides, you're wrong. *You* get the last laugh! See? And Federi is laughing with you. Anyway, little luv, I didn't only manipulate you into climbing up there just to win a silly bet. I'm sure Ronan would have taught me some instruments anyway."

"So then, why did you?"

Federi laughed. "For the sports, I suppose," he said. "I like manipulating people."

Paean scowled. That was even worse!

"You guys! The lot of you!"

"The lot of us what?"

She didn't grace that with an answer.

"I'll be manipulating you again," he predicted darkly. "I manipulate everybody. It's in my nature. I'm just not quite sure yet when and about what."

Ronan and Rhine Gold were coming towards them. "Can't find Shawn."

"Should have given him a pink head-scarf," said Federi. "Alright, we'll search for him. You two go east and we go west. We meet here in twenty minutes. He can't have gone far."

Shawn was already at the rock pool. He had dived in and was now exploring all its crevices, not hearing anyone call him over the noise of the waterfall.

There was a cave behind the waterfall. He went in and considered it for a hidey-hole or a hiding spot for a treasure until he found unmistakable traces of recent human habitation. Empty bottles and signs of a campfire a bit further in the cave were a dead giveaway, and he nearly stumbled over

236

the sleeping form of a hobo.

Disappointment riddled Shawn. He'd have to come back again in about a hundred years and see if the place had been forgotten then. He nearly kicked the hobo, then thought better of it and looked at the man's hands. The fingers were all there, and the wrong colour anyway. Next to the hobo, something gleamed softly. Something small, metallic. Shawn picked it up. It had resembled a flat rock, at first. It was heavy. He was sure it had some electronic function. He looked for any openings or buttons on it and found none, just smooth surface. Well, he'd ask Marsden about it later on. Cradling it carefully to prevent it from getting wet, he made his way back out of the cave and put the object in amongst his clothes on the shore. Then he dived into the cool water again.

When he surfaced, Federi was towering over him.

"What are you doing, boy? Can't run away like that! You could have got seriously lost in this wilderness!"

Jonathan Marsden descended into the machine room.

"Hello, Ailyss."

The skinny brunette glanced up from her book.

"Hi, Mr Marsden."

"Everything ship-shape down here?"

"Perfect, Mr Marsden."

"Wolf sends his regards," said Jon Marsden and watched for the reaction.

Ailyss allowed him a tiny smile.

"My regards back," she replied. "Tell him from me to get well soon."

"He is concerned about the workload," added Jon Marsden, studying her intently.

That minute smile recurred.

"Mr Marsden, you can be assured that there's not much work down here," she said, lifting the book she was reading to show him. "We haven't had a Unicate attack since Lake Gatun."

Jon Marsden took a look around the machine room. All was fine. Not a single wire out of place; Dr Jake ran a very tidy operation.

"Do you like it on the ship?" he asked casually.

"It'll do," said Ailyss. "I prefer it without storms, sir."

Jonathan Marsden studied her a little while longer; she didn't try to look busy, she simply sat there and waited for him to say something.

"That'll be all, Ailyss," he ended up saying. "Keep up the good work."

"Thank you, Mr Marsden," replied Ailyss. The First Mate turned and left the machineroom.

If he didn't have any sense, he'd begin to think that Donegal Magic was the spy instead of Ailyss! The teen was highly volatile in her thinking and her actions, whereas this one had the potential of a solid, dependable crewmember. Although making conversation was like fly-fishing, with her.

Donegal Magic was currently stretched out on her towel, having had a lovely cold swim herself, watching her brothers and Rhine Gold play water polo with a beach ball they had acquired for next to nothing in Atuona. The gypsy was leaning against a shady tree close by, in swimming trunks too, carving away at something again. The day was heating up, but it was not yet sweltering. He had promised that later he'd take them diving. It was the only way to survive this tropical climate.

"What is our actual mission here in Atuona?"

"To enjoy ourselves," said Federi.

"Och, you're joking!" Paean hadn't been a pirate long, but still long enough to figure out that the shortcut from Panama to Hawaii didn't exactly run southwest over Atuona! After all that time pressure and scraping through near-lethal Panama!

"Quite serious. The Captain was quite clear on this, that while he is conducting his business, the young crowd are to enjoy themselves and stay out of trouble."

Paean smiled and half-closed her eyes. She had expected a snub for her nosiness. Instead she got this playful evasiveness. It tied in with the Thieves' Honour guy who'd plucked a star from the sky for her two nights ago as a reward for winning him a bet.

You took Federi the way he was, or you left it. There was nothing in between.

She stretched out in the warm tropical shade. Far, far away from cold rainy Dublin, from the mud of Molly Street and the terror of the Unicate. On a paradise island with her brothers and a couple of friends. If she were

238

a kitten, she'd be purring.

"You know how you want to frame some moments and hang them into a memory gallery?" she asked dreamily. "This is one of those moments."

Federi smiled too and kept on carving. He wished he could say the same. This place made him uneasy. A sense of something not right. Land always did; but this was more specific, somehow, sharper. This was really close by.

Paean looked up at him.

"What are all those vicious scars on your back and your chest?"

"And everywhere else all over me," completed Federi with a grin. "They are reminders."

"Reminders?"

"Of who I am."

She sat up. "What do you mean?"

"I'm the one that got away," said Federi.

Paean frowned. She didn't find that particularly funny.

"You're not about to tell me, are you," she said.

"You're right I'm not," smiled Federi. He scanned the undergrowth. Still nothing. He hoped it would last until they'd set sail again, north. With luck, Captain would be done negotiating and gathering new information by tomorrow this time.

When they returned to the ship it was past noon. Marsden informed Paean that her big baby had been crying for her for a while now. She cast her eyes skywards, sighed an abysmal sigh and trotted down to the infirmary.

"How long do I still have to lie here?" Wolf greeted her with unconcealed irritation.

"Good afternoon to you too," she replied. "You'll have to stay down until Doc decides you can get up. I can tell you it'll be at least three weeks, maybe six." She sat down by his bedside and reached for his pulse.

He yanked his arm away. Ye Gods, three weeks! Anything could happen in three weeks! He calculated frantically. Those were the three weeks within which the Solar Wind should reach Honolulu!

"Now, Wolf, I only wanted to check your pulse!"

"I don't need you holding my hand!" he snapped. "I'm not sick, Paean!" How on Earth was he going to turn things so he could find out if his suspicions in the engine room were correct or – hopefully – dead wrong?

Could he trust Marsden with this dilemma? But if he was wrong -

And if he was right? Was there a way to turn things still? He thought back to a wild spirit girl with huge eyes who had saved his life.

"Alright," said Paean with dignity, getting up. A nice guy lurking in there? Must have been a trick of the light! "Clearly I'm not needed here. If you have something constructive to say to me, you can call me again." She walked to the door, silently relieved that it had been such a short visit. She really wanted to go diving.

Wolf returned to reality. Whoa! There went the paramedic!

"Wait, Paean!"

She stopped, turned. Glared at Wolf.

"Thank you for the books," he muttered. "That was thoughtful. Sorry I'm so antisocial. Don't go yet."

Oh! This was a different tune! Paean smiled.

"You're welcome. You'd have done the same for me."

"I doubt it," said Wolf, suddenly grinning. "I'm not a particularly nice person, you know."

"Oh, I noticed," said Paean. "Okay, not particularly nice person, will you please let me check on your health now? If you'd rather have the Doc, I'll call her, but you know – I wouldn't like to bother her with easy stuff I can take over for her."

"It's okay, you don't need to worry her," said Wolf. "I'll be good."

Paean took his pulse and measured his temperature. "Let me have a look at that knee," she commanded.

Reluctantly Wolf allowed her to take the cast and then the bandage off, examine the sutures and swab the entire thing with disinfectant. He even tried to be brave about it, although she knew that the iodine tincture burnt like hell.

"What changed your mind?" asked Paean while she worked.

"My mind? What do you mean?"

"Well, that you decided you want me around after all!"

"I don't exactly –" Wolf stopped himself just in time. He didn't particularly care who the hell the paramedic was! As long as she got the job done! But telling her this might just result in her walking out of that door again. And then he'd have to call Doc instead, and then that overdue ruffle was definitely coming his way! So he agreed wholeheartedly with Paean about not bothering Doc Judith if they didn't absolutely have to. But then he'd have to count his words, be a bit political, not speak too frankly to the meddling little busybody... Oh heck, this was ticklish!

"Course I want you around, Paean, who wouldn't," he lied. "Actually I asked for you because – Paean, can I have one of your magic powders? You don't seem to mind giving a grown man painkillers! - OW!"

Wolf winced as she poured some tincture over his knee straight from her bottle. Little ruffian!

"Oh, I'm sorry!" exclaimed Paean. "Painkillers! Of course!" She put down the bottle and dug a home-powdered aspirin out of the drawer. Red iodine tincture stained the bed sheet where it dripped. This was ignored. "There you go, Wolf! Now why didn't you say you're in pain? I'm grouchy too when I'm hurting!"

"Usually I just wait it out," said Wolf, swallowing the powder down with a violent shudder. "Yuk!"

"You don't like yourself very much, do you?" Paean asked as she got back to work. As long as he did the talking, he couldn't accuse her of being a chatterbox!

"I get along with myself just fine, thank you," replied Wolf with a grin. "At least..."

"At least?" Paean put some really sticky disinfectant ointment on a fresh gauze patch and pasted it over the knee.

"Ouch! Well, ever since you've told that blond goodie two-shoes how nasty you think I am, I've been wondering a bit about the way I deal with kids. Ouch! Sheesh! Could you be gentler?!"

"Sorry," muttered Paean. "Thought you were tough." This conversation was beginning to worry her. "You heard all that?"

"Wasn't asleep," grinned Wolf. "Just half dead."

Paean's forehead furrowed. "You heard that! That means – oh no!" She stared at him in dismay. "Did it hurt very much when I dug out the bullet?"

"What?"

241

"After you were shot. I took about four hours all in all digging out the bullet and stitching you up. Looked up and it was two ay em. Could you feel anything?"

"Not a thing," said Wolf. "Except for my waking up in the middle of it. Your forsaken green bug works really well, Paean. I just woke up with a sore knee yesterday morning."

"Good."

Wolf turned his eyes skywards. "Now what have I done to deserve that?"

"Och, stop being such a big baby," she scolded him. "I thought you were the toughest of the lot of us! I never knew pirates were such sissies!"

That stung! Wolf snapped his mouth shut and resolved to bear all torture without a peep. But then he just had to add something.

"Putting that stuff in my coffee just so you could go ashore – now that wasn't nice, Paean!"

"Wolf, you won't heal walking around. You were being stupid. I'm a practical person."

"I can see that," he grinned, pointing to her green scarf.

"That was an award," she said with dignity. "For becoming a real pirate." She clipped the cast closed again. "And if *you* were a real pirate, Mr. Nuclear Engineer, you'd understand there's no point in losing your leg if it can be saved."

"Oh." Sheesh! Did she mean that? Losing his leg? Wolf swallowed hard as the implications began to trickle in. "Paean – is it that bad?"

Paean sat back, sighing. Anxiety was written clearly in her ice-blue eyes. "Worse. So how old exactly are you, Mr Oh-so-grown-up?"

"Twenty-two," replied Wolf.

"That jolly well explains it," said Paean angrily.

"Explains what?"

"Why you have to put me down for being younger all the time," said Paean. "You're only just grown up by the skin of your teeth. You're still trying to convince yourself. Tell me, Wolf! Why on Earth did you get yourself shot that night? How idiotic is that?"

Wolf gasped. What had he said that had upset her this time?

"Grown-up is as grown-up does, Svendsson! What the hell was going through your mind?" she scolded. "Can't you steer clear of trouble when you see it? Cor! I've seen so many unnecessary pub brawls in Dublin. It's always some drunken, stupid hothead who starts it off, riling some other drunken stupid hothead. Next thing it's punches and knives and sometimes pistol shots. And then the darned Unicate descends like a flock of vultures and closes the place, and the little Donegal sibs had better clear out before they get caught. I lost my chromonica that way!"

Wolf stared at Paean, speechless. He'd never thought that she would have been exposed to anything of that sort! He had been under the impression that she had been sheltered up to the point of boarding the Solar Wind.

"I'm that tired of guys getting motherless and then punching each other up," she added heatedly. "But Wolf, you're a nuclear engineer! I'd have said you're too intelligent for that kind of stuff!"

"Someone was insulting one of the guys here aboard," Wolf defended himself. He felt strangely moved. This girl actually cared about him! Nobody had ever called him too intelligent, too high-class for anything before! Rough Wolf! "I wouldn't stand for it. Regardless if what they say is true. He might be a cold-blooded assassin and a pathological long-finger, but nobody speaks badly of my friends and shipmates!"

Paean paused. She stared at Wolf, a lop-sided smile slowly spreading over her face.

"I already like you a lot more," she said. She caught herself and quit gazing at him. "Still blooming stupid to get your knee wrecked like that. Are you feeling braver now?"

"Why?"

"Because," said Paean and ripped the tape off his cheek in a swift movement. Quite a bit of beard came with it. Wolf roared.

"Not brave," said Paean sadly and shook her head. She noted with a frown that she had actually torn two of the sutures in the process. Not so clever!

"Pirate!" snapped Wolf. "Why did you do that?"

"Because," said Paean and swabbed the stitch wound with some tincture. Boy, had she sewn a nasty seam! "Now hold still, you big hairy baby!"

"You bloodthirsty harpy," gasped Wolf, tears streaming from his eyes. That blasted tincture stung like hell!

243

"You've got a lot to learn," she told him sagely.

Oh yes, thought Wolf. Most importantly, that you don't insult your paramedic when in a compromised position. Revenge, in her case, seemed to be an involuntary reflex.

"Hmm," she added, frowning. "So do I, actually. I have to learn how to suture a straight seam. I'm really sorry, Wolf. I have no choice. I'll have to undo this whole cheek wound and get it sterile again. It's gruesome."

"Will it hurt?"

"Well now," said Paean pensively. "That depends. Do you want me to give you some coffee first or would you prefer to tough it out?"

"Whatever," growled Wolf, trying not to grin because grinning hurt. "Just fix it nicely this time, will you, little Paean?"

She prepared him some valeriensis. He downed it stoically and passed out. He was a brave man after all. And she had been right. There was a nice guy somewhere in there. She had seen him shimmer through. She got to work undoing the sutures.

19

Three-toes

Marsden and Federi beached the Lawnmower in the spot Paean had described, with the sunken buildings in the sand. They got out and found the Donegal sibs' footprints. The tide had come up quite high last night; on the other hand it was the only set of prints, as nobody else walked here. This stretch of beach was dangerous. You could fall into a broken building and get stuck or break a limb. The Donegals had been lucky. Federi resolved not to let those two out of his sight again.

He shot a brief glance at the sky, which was sporting a fine layer of haze through which the noonday sun was beating down. It was muggy. Storm brewing? Not yet, he thought. Perhaps tonight.

"I think we found it," said Marsden, indicating the place where the two siblings' footprints milled about a bit and turned back. Federi peered into the undergrowth. He saw the pile of clothes and picked up the top one. As Paean had said, a finger was stuck to it, so dried out that even the ants were leaving it alone.

He crouched down and dug in the heap. Odd! The clothes were still good! There were some other remains, but not many. Nothing larger than that finger. All dried, desiccated.

The clothes, all in browns and military greens except where they were stained with dry blood, said that this couldn't have happened more than a few days ago. The human remains spoke of weeks. It didn't rhyme.

"Did she say, old rags?" asked Marsden quizzically, lifting a label up for Federi to read. It said 'Axil'. A very expensive designer of outdoor and mountaineering gear! This had been no beach bum!

"Shall we take them along? Exhibit A?" asked Marsden.

"Do you have a morbid fascination with such forensic stuff?" replied Federi with a shudder. They filched through the clothes, but besides those few human bits there was absolutely nothing, no identification, no metal parts, not even bones. This worried Federi.

"A tourist maybe?" he surmised.

"To Hiva Oa?" Marsden asked back, sceptical.

"Look, either whatever did this was intelligent and took everything, or Atuona has picked him clean over time," said the Romany. "But I don't exactly see tracks of Atuona," he added, falcon eyebrows furrowed. "And they wouldn't have left the clothes!"

"Here," said Marsden, indicating. Federi went over to where the First Mate was pointing at the ground. Strange, three-toed animal imprints. Long toes, centrally anchored. Like a bird's. Or perhaps a reptile's.

These prints couldn't be older than two, maybe three days, thought Federi. They still looked comparatively crisp. And there hadn't been any rain. One rain and they were gone. A bit of wind, some small wildlife, insects, lizards, and they would fade, too!

Federi searched and found more of the same prints, leading away from the crime scene. He beckoned to Marsden, and the First Mate followed, keeping a few steps behind, giving the gypsy space.

"Four-legged," said Federi. "See there, Jon?"

Marsden moved closer to look. He couldn't tell!

"The gait," explained Federi. "And there's a really obvious clue!" He pointed to one of the prints and looked expectantly at Marsden. The First Mate narrowed his eyes, crouched down, peered at the print...

"Aw, come now, Jon, can't tell me you're not seeing it," prompted Federi.

Marsden straightened out. "Sorry, Federi. Not spotting it."

Federi went down himself and indicated.

"Look there! It had something stuck to its hind foot! Bit of twig or something. See? There it is – and there it's not – and there it is again! That one's the front paw." He examined a tree trunk where the tracks overlaid and came directly up to the tree. He could practically see the animal rubbing up against the bark. And if he was lucky today... "Pay dirt!" He picked a small translucent flake of something off the bark. There were more. Now that he knew what he was looking for... he looked at the microchip-sized flake. Two-square millimetres. "Reptilian, I think."

"A shedding four-legged reptile with three toes? Not a Komodo dragon?"

"Dragons are five-toed," Federi pointed out. "And last time I looked they didn't eat rich folk. Not that many three-toed animals on Planet Earth! Weird!" He shook his head. "Jon, honestly, I'm mystified. I'd have to look in Sherman's files for a match. 's not exactly Romania, this," he added with a grin. "Maybe the islands have a few unique animals..."

"Well, we know now that there are dangerous predators running around," said Marsden. "Let's keep a close eye on our troublesome little ones!"

"What I'm doing, my friend, what I'm doing!" Federi followed the track further. He had been lucky in the past, sometimes, finding the animal he had been looking for. These tracks were not that fresh, they had only remained undisturbed, but you never knew where they'd take you.

In fact, they took him only a bit further on, through a few more twists of undergrowth. Then, where they ought to have been clearest, they stopped. There were no other tracks to indicate anything happening. The ground was sandy here, with a light crust where it had been dampened from the last rain, and where there were still tracks, they were sharp and pristine. The animal had cracked the virgin crust where it had walked.

Federi frowned and searched, and studied the trees. There were a few branches and leaves higher up that looked singed, and the moss was dry in patches and partially blackened. And no further indication what had happened to the three-toe.

"What?" asked Marsden, reading Federi's face. "Something wrong?"

"Something darned wrong, anna bottle," growled the gypsy. "She vanished! Think it was a she."

"What makes you think that?"

"Walked with a slink," said Federi. "Swung her bum a bit."

Federi read tracks three-dimensionally, his gypsy radar doing a lot of the work, looking at the psychic trail the animal had left in time. He could practically see how she had slunk along, but he couldn't get a proper fix on her shape – and here he was stumped, gypsy radar and all. He couldn't imagine what had happened.

"But look here, Jon! End of tracks. Whoosh. Gone. Thin air. *Rien, nada, gar keins!*"

Spontaneous combustion? Why were there singed bits up in the trees, right over where the thing had gone onto its hind legs, reared up – it was not close enough to any trees to have leaped and climbed its way further, and anyway, he'd see tracks up there then! Scrapes perhaps, some torn leaves and brutalized twigs where the animal had scrabbled up… the tracks would also have told him! The imprints would be deeper where the creature might have leaped, and they'd have dug into the sand in a telltale pattern. He'd be able to tell where she had jumped! There were physical dynamics involved in a jump!

Federi stared helplessly at Marsden. He felt as though the real problem was that he had walked into a paradigm trap in his own mind. There was a basic assumption he was making that was incorrect.

"Unicate," said Marsden helpfully. "They have been tampering with virus – why not with reptiles?"

They exchanged a grin and both shook their heads.

"Just kidding," sighed Marsden.

"I'll work on it," promised Federi. "Come, pal. There's nothing more we can do here at this point."

They went back to the shore, boarded the Lawnmower and returned to the Solar Wind.

Paean was in the yellow room, absorbed in bits of skin, beard, small capillaries and black self-dissolving thread. Which actually looked like more beard. She contemplated fleetingly whether she simply ought to pluck out Wolf's beard hair and use it for suturing thread.

Rhine Gold's head popped around the door.

"Hi Paean. You in here again?"

"Yip," she said, focusing on her job.

"You spend a lot of time in here," said Rhine Gold grudgingly.

Paean turned and looked at him scathingly until he shrivelled and backed out of the room.

Some time later, Ronan stuck his head through the door.

"Coming diving, sis?"

"Och, please wait for me," she begged. "This cheek is a mess, Ro, I'm battling – and the knee – well, we'll just have to see. I'm still going to be a while."

248

Ronan gazed at the comatose Wolf. "Dead meat again, is he?"

"Please tell them to wait for me," Paean implored. "I really want to go diving!"

"Okay, sis. I'll tell them."

"I'm very nearly done," panicked Paean when she could once again feel a stare resting on her neck. "Please don't go diving without me! But I've got to finish up here!"

"Well," said Federi, taking a chair, "they can't go diving without the instructor. I've come to let you know. Take all the time you want. Can I watch?"

"Do you love the sight of blood and messy wounds?" asked Paean.

"Nothing better," said Federi with a contented smile. He wondered to himself what the others were doing leaving her to cope alone. She who passed out from the sight of blood. "Explain to me what you're doing!"

So Paean tried to explain what she was doing as she worked. Her explanations turned into a cryptic, semi-coherent monologue after a while, with Paean so focused on the job she didn't even notice she wasn't talking in full sentences anymore.

"So now here I've got to....." she murmured. "See, here it has..." She felt around on the table, not taking her eyes off the wound. "I need..." Federi placed the tincture in her hand. "Thanks, nurse," she mumbled.

Suddenly she sat bolt upright and frowned at Federi.

"Why did he call you a cold-blooded assassin?"

"Probably because I'm so good at shooting down filthy pirates," said Federi. "Though I'm sure this wasn't supposed to reach my ears!"

"Oh!" said Paean, taken aback. "I'm sorry. Of course not!"

"Did he get injured defending my reputation?" asked Federi with a little smile.

"Sounds like it!"

"The silly boy! And here I am, working so hard on becoming notorious!"

Paean grinned. Yes! A silly boy! Indeed! She returned to her wound technology.

"He's a good guy, that Wolf," added Federi.

"You know, I wouldn't have agreed with you yesterday."

"But now you do," smiled Federi.

"If the tables had been turned," said Paean, "would you have stood up for him like that?"

"That's a good question," replied Federi, watching how she sutured. "I doubt the tables would have been turned though. Federi doesn't get himself into such situations in the first place."

Uh-huh. That stood to reason. On the grown-up scale, Federi rated several notches higher than Wolf Svendsson. Paean suspected that she herself rated higher than the engineer!

She stared at the gypsy once more, her thoughts coursing.

"Gee, Federi. I really don't know about that knee. It looks terrible. I'm very worried."

"Isn't it time to turn it over to the doctor?" suggested the gypsy.

"But she said…" Paean trailed off. She had in fact forgotten that there was a doctor on the ship! She had been the one responsible for nursing Mother, for six long months; in charge of finding out what to do next, and then getting it done. Her brothers had helped, but she had definitely been the driving force behind it! That kind of awful responsibility was so familiar, she had slipped into it without realizing it.

Federi read her expression. Poor little songbird!

"That was just that night, Paean. Doc has to stitch up pirates after every pub brawl. No wonder she's sick of it. People get hit and cut with broken bottles, beer cans, jack knives. Mostly clean cuts, although sometimes there is a bit of disinfecting."

"And you help her," completed Paean. It was obvious from the veteran way in which Federi knew his way around the infirmary and the procedures.

"Well, little luv, somebody has to!"

"Why don't *you* stitch?" she asked, putting down the suturing needle. "You'd do it better!"

"I'm not a medic," Federi protested. "I don't stitch. Only assist."

Paean frowned thoughtfully and retook the procedure. "But if you're the one who helps her patch them, after every pub fight… that means that your reminders are not from drunken punch-em-ups?"

Federi blinked. "Huh?"

"It means, you're not normally the one being patched!"

"Heaven forbid!" laughed the Romany. "I told you Federi doesn't get himself into such scrapes!"

"So you don't hit the pub every time the ship lands?"

Federi shook his head, amused. "Do I look it? Anna bottle of rum!" He paused. "Aha. I get it. Federi's silly little pet cliché. 's a good pet. Never mind." He glanced at Paean's work-in-progress. "Done?"

"Nearly."

"I'd suspect Doc Judith would like to know about a messy bullet wound like this one, though. We should tell her."

Paean looked scared. "Have I done wrong, not calling her?"

Federi frowned. Actually, if someone had done wrong, it was himself! It had not been his first concern. Atuona kept on worrying him. A sense of foreboding that made it difficult to focus on anything. Ever since their trip into the mountains it had got worse. Today's finds still had to be consolidated, looked up... Something was definitely wrong! The sooner they could turn their backs on this place, the better.

"Not at all, Paean. You were doing as you were told. I'm just saying, maybe it's time she had a look at this."

"Should I call her now?"

"No. Just finish up. Bring her with you next time."

Wolf opened his eyes to the empty sick yellow of the infirmary. His cheek felt stiff. There was something to be said for the old procedure, where the man used to wake up before his wound, giving him time to come to his senses! He had to admit though that it itched less; it had been driving him mad before. Now it only pained.

His leg was another story. That felt as though it ought not belong to him. It had assumed a whole separate personality, and that personality was dying on the battlefield. He whimpered, and caught himself in horror. This was not good. Visions of himself with only one leg hovered on the edge of his awareness. He groaned, this time at the implications. How the hell would he get his job done? How was he to fly the Solar Wind before the storm? Captain would put him ashore!

He reached for his book and found no strength in his arm. His hand fell short and flopped limply back onto the bunk.

251

"Oh bum," he mouthed and closed his eyes again. He was going to die.

Jon Marsden was on another mission. He was going through the Sherman files, trying to make sense of those large three-toed prints.

Before the Unicate take-over, there had been a lot of strange things going on. Sherman had ghost stories that dealt with genetic engineering of people into animal shapes. From a logical aspect this made no sense at all; those attempts had been abortive. But it wasn't impossible that they had managed to clone something that was larger, stronger and more intelligent than its ancestor. Take a little lizard for example...

That was exactly where the problem came in. Three-toed reptiles?

What if Federi was wrong with his assumption and they were actually dealing with a bird? But – a four-legged bird? Marsden was prepared to stand trial on Federi's theory of the four legs. Nobody could read tracks the way the Tzigan could!

And the Tzigan had been stumped. Jon Marsden sighed impatiently and gave the hacking at Anya Miller's capsule another go.

Shawn was right with his hey-shoo-wow. The reef was magnificent.

It was a weird feeling diving in bathwater! Green sunlight filtered down in a wavering curtain, illuminating corals and anemones in the richest colours. Ronan was filming with Federi's (probably stolen) underwater camera.

In a crevice in the rock sat a spotted eel, mouth open, waiting for things to swim into it. Good luck to him, thought Paean. A bit further a couple of rays came slowly flopping by, weird flying blankets of the oceans. And then three reef sharks came inspecting who was diving in their reef. The sharks gaped at the humans and the humans gaped at the sharks.

Paean looked around for Shawn. There he was, beckoning her from a bit further on. She hurried and caught up with him. He led her on, around another coral outcrop, up over the top of the reef. There, completely hidden in a rocky enclave, open only to the top –

Wow! She gaped, eyes wide. There was an entire ship resting on the rocks.

The two Donegal Troubles circled the wreck. It was a metal hull, mostly intact except for the rust that was beginning to eat its way into the steel from around the seams. Shawn pointed to two large round holes in the ship's flank. Paean wondered if he meant that it had been torpedoed down.

They swam into the bridge through the open door, the thick glass of the windshield still intact. Shawn fumbled with the console a bit and extracted a chip. Paean showed him a thumbs-up. He was getting good at looting. She looked around and spotted the wooden drinks cabinet, the swollen and warped doors still hanging in their rusted hinges. On a whim she forced them open. Inside she found several bottles with different alcoholic contents, amongst them some very old Irish Whisky and some equally ancient Scottish Brandy. And lo and behold, some genuine Jamaican Rum.

That it had to be the bottle he had just won! Paean smiled. She was going to replace Federi's rum! She ignored the half-full bottles and stashed three unopened ones in her diver's pouch. Shawn was casting her some very questioning glances.

Behind the bottles there was a rust-free safety lock. Some other metal, maybe silver or titanium. She tugged at it. It held firm. Amazing, really. She motioned Shawn over. But even together they couldn't get that old safe opened.

They left the bridge and drifted down the spiral staircase, into the upper deck. There was a lot of luxury. This was passenger liner. In the cabins, prizing open some swollen and cracked wooden drawers, Paean found treasure. Jewellery, old coins. Shawn cracked open wooden cupboard doors. Clothes and shoes, in a state of beginning decay. He shook his head. What was the point in looting these?

Paean got uneasy after a while. They ought to get back with the others. She beckoned to Shawn, and together they cleared out of the wreck and out over the top of the coral and back to where they had left the others.

A form came swimming towards them at a rate. It turned into Federi. Ronan and Rhine Gold were following at a small distance. The Romany gestured them frantically to surface.

They surfaced slowly, observing procedure, and followed him back to the ship and up the rope ladder. Federi ripped his mask off.

"Get dressed," he snapped. "And then, Shawn and Paean Donegal, I expect to see you in my galley."

20

Treasure

The two Donegal Troubles stood in shell-shocked silence as Federi let rip. They had never yet seen him angry. Shawn thought he looked like a wild man, with his eyes shooting sparks of fury and the rage radiating off him in waves. Paean stood paralysed, watching in horror how her gentle friend transformed into something nuclear. He had reason, she knew. It didn't help that she had realized too late that they should have told him where they were going.

They had breached the first rule of diving and got separated from the instructor. They had dived right out of his sight and disappeared for a long time. They were his responsibility; if something happened to them or they went missing, the consequences were huge. Federi took the opportunity to ruffle Shawn for running away during the excursion earlier that morning. He doomed both Donegals to the scrubbing of pots, decks and heads until Hawaii.

At some point during Federi's tirade, Jon Marsden came into the galley to check what was going on. Instantly, Federi was casual, wearing an easy smile.

"Just making us all some coffee after that dive," he lied amiably.

Marsden said nothing and left again. The Donegals had it coming! They were troublemakers. He didn't envy his friend this task, nor could he take it upon himself. It had to do with respect. Marsden had foreseen this kind of thing happening.

After the First Mate left the galley, the smile dropped back off Federi's face. All the fight suddenly drained out of him.

"Shawn," he said gloomily, "Paean. I expected better from you both. If anything had happened to either of you..." He frowned darkly and stared out of the starboard porthole at the aquamarine day outside.

"Sorry, Federi," said Shawn contritely. He felt guilty. He had led the treasure hunt; Paean had only followed. In any case he took looking after his sister very seriously.

Paean bolted from the galley.

"Was I too harsh?" asked the Romany uncertainly, his gaze following the bouncy little livewire. "You two needed to hear it!"

A few moments later, Paean was back, clutching her diver's pouch to her, and her green scarf. She sat down, put the pouch on the Ironwood table, wound the scarf around her wet hair gypsy-style, and extracted a still-dripping bottle from the pouch. She handed it to Federi, who stared at it in amazement.

"Where on earth did you get that?" He turned the gift over and over in his hands. "2015 Jamaican Rum! *20 - 15 -!*" he read again, just be sure. "Looks genuine! Hundred years old? Cor!" He looked sharply at Paean. "What on earth have you found down there?"

Paean upended the treasure from her pouch on the Ironwood table.

"You found a shipwreck, didn't you?" asked Federi. He picked up the various items, examining them closely. Rings and chains, and earrings, and fancy cufflinks, in solid gold, studded with genuine stones. His Kalderash fingertips with their hereditary touch for riches detected high-carat diamonds, rubies, pearls. And a few stones he didn't recognize at all, which bothered him. Had there been new discoveries of precious stones on Planet Earth? Were there stones that had been known before the sixties, of which nothing was catalogued? Were these perhaps manufactured? But they had a natural feel to them. His mind backed away from thinking about it. One paradigm trap was enough for one day.

The styles of the jewellery varied, but the most recent had to be at least beginning of last century. He looked for items in the elaborate Hectagonite style of the twenties, but found none.

"Metal hull?" he asked Shawn, his artistic fingers still sifting through the small pile of jewellery. Shawn nodded enthusiastically.

Federi whistled softly through his teeth and pushed the whole pile back towards Paean.

"You have it, Federi," she said spontaneously.

"But *dulciuri*, this is a fortune! You have no idea what you've got your hands on! I'm amazed you found one that hasn't been plundered!" He gazed from her to Shawn. No wonder they had forgotten all the rules over the excitement! And an un-plundered shipwreck, this close to land? There was a mystery there, no mistake! "This meeting had better be taken to my cabin," he suggested. "This place is too noisy." He got up.

Paean pocketed her treasure again, seeing that Federi simply left it on the table. She grabbed her coffee mug and followed him and Shawn to the gypsy's cabin.

The Donegal sibs entered the cabin with a sense of awe. The door was always closed, so neither of them had ever had a glimpse into it before.

Most cabins on the ship were fairly frugal, functional. This one was the opposite. It looked like a magical forest of treasures. There were gems, wind chimes and sun catchers suspended from the ceiling as far as the eye could roam, all moving gently with the ship's rolling on the waves. Across the porthole hung a huge dream-catcher with gems woven into it. Woodcarvings were mounted all along the walls, similar to those carvings in the boardroom and infirmary. The carvings were of ships in storms, wrecks in reefs, sharks, islands and bloody battles on the sea. Paean marvelled at the way they all seemed so alive. There was one that depicted a sunset over the sea, where the artist had transformed the colours and grain of the wood into red and golden sunset glow.

The gypsy closed the door behind them.

"When this door closes," he explained, "everything spoken in here is confidential. Is this understood?"

Both Donegal siblings nodded. Paean looked worried. No secrets from the Captain, coursed through her head. The very first message that had been imprinted on the Donegals when they were tried for their fugitive state.

"I'll put Ronan in the picture," promised Federi. "I know. Donegals keep no secrets from each other."

Paean felt partially relieved. What about the Captain?

"Now, Paean," the Romany instructed. "First thing. Never offer Federi your treasure. He'll take it!"

"But I want you to have it! You love treasure!"

He smiled. She had misunderstood. Picking the enemy's ship clean of electronics and weaponry wasn't about treasure.

"Listen, little songbird, it was difficult enough saying no the first time!

Don't push it! Now, second thing, both of you. Why do you go exploring a shipwreck and not tell Federi about it?"

"Because he'd want to take all the treasure for himself?" hazarded Shawn, following logic.

"No!" Federi laughed. "I mean, of course he would! Well observed, Donegal! But that wasn't the point. Why did you leave me out?"

"We got so excited, I suppose," said Paean contritely. "We couldn't think of anything else!"

Federi smiled sadly. They were still children, regardless. He shouldn't lose sight of that. Little Paean, so nearly of legal adult status… Of course children and young teens broke the rules at times! In their case, it hadn't been rebellion but simple thoughtlessness.

"Did you at least have fun?" he asked with a wink.

Now the details came pouring out. Shawn and Paean fell over each other recalling all the things they had seen and found on the shipwreck. Shawn laid his electronic findings on the table, Paean the rest of her treasure, small items looted from the passenger cabins.

"These are interesting," said Federi, picking up the electronics. "Should we give them to Captain so he can try to make sense of them?"

Shawn shook his head.

"Don't want to tell anybody."

"We have to tell Captain," said Federi. "There isn't a thing on this ship that ought to be a secret from Captain."

Shawn nodded reluctantly. Paean frowned, confused. Hadn't Federi just said about his cabin…

"Except what is spoken in this cabin," added Federi, smiling at her and shaking his head. "So let's take a vote. We tell him?"

Paean looked at Shawn. Either way round it felt wrong to her. She decided to grill Federi about it a little later, get to the bottom of all this. Got my own secrets, he had once told her.

Shawn didn't seem to have a problem with the concept.

"It's your shipwreck," said Paean to her brother. "You found it. You decide."

"I suppose we'd better tell him," sighed Shawn. He also preferred not having secrets from Captain Lascek.

Federi nodded approvingly.

257

"Good that you decided that," he said. "I couldn't have kept you two in my cabin indefinitely. The others would have started wondering where you are!"

Paean laughed.

"Now, next time," Federi said, "call me. I want to be there. Anyway those old ships can be dangerous, there have been cases of divers getting stuck in there. What's the very first rule of diving, Shawn?"

"Never dive alone," said Shawn.

"Now," said Federi. "I'm going back in there. Are you two coming with me or do I have to go alone?"

Not much later they were circling the wreck a second time.

Federi trailed a hand along the hull. Metal, certainly; some or other alloy. There was iron in it, or it wouldn't have started rusting along the edges. The visor window of the bridge looked like volcaniplex glass. He couldn't be sure. He'd have to look that up in Sherman's files, too. He went through the bridge more thoroughly and extracted a lot of electronic circuitry out of the console. It looked well preserved; maybe they would be able to get it running, and find out more.

He started methodically searching the entire ship.

The presence of the shipwreck worried him. He knew from Sherman's ship files that in those days, liners already had satellite-tracking systems. No luxury liner like this one would have sunk and remained un-looted. He had also spotted the holes in the hull. They didn't look like torpedo damage to him. Everything on the ship looked too well preserved for a hundred years of lukewarm saltwater! The actual items were all congruent with that time frame; their state of decay, not.

Federi found the galley and unearthed boxes upon boxes of more rum, whiskey and brandy. There was wine and beer too; it would be interesting to see what they had done chemically in a hundred years. The thing to do, he thought, was to bring the Stormrider, and lower crates and fill them with whatever, and take them up to the boat.

There was a system to his plundering. He knew what to look for and where to search. Next he investigated the cabins, Paean and Shawn following closely behind. The Donegal sibs hadn't even looted half of the cabins on the passenger deck. They hadn't been to the lower crew deck at all. Now the three of them swam through the spooky, dark decks, having switched their headlamps on. There was nothing much here. Federi refused to touch the money found in some of these drawers, shaking his head violently when Paean wanted to take some. He'd have to explain to them about the curse of stealing a dead man's last wages.

Deeper they went, down through another hatch, into the bilges. Here, in the pitch-dark storage area, only relieved by their torch beams, the real treasure awaited. Old wooden crates full of stuff, transported for those passengers who were emigrating. Furniture, ruined books, some paintings. Federi led them through the entire place, picking out things here and there to show them. There were a number of paintings that had been sealed so tightly in plastic that they weren't damaged at all.

And there in the dark, too, lay a clue towards the solution of the puzzle. No skeletons? Here they were, an easy fifteen of them, with the chains still around their hands and feet. Their clothes, that should have mouldered off them an age ago, were still intact. Their skeletons had been picked clean though by the fish; one could see in places where the clothes had been torn at and shredded.

Fifteen of them. By their attire, the crew and the Captain. If Federi hadn't been wearing his mouthpiece he would have whistled through his teeth.

He signalled to the sibs to go to the surface and followed them, observing their surfacing procedure. They were good kids. Doing very well.

"We'll have to get help," he said when they were finally at the surface. "Got to bring the Stormrider. There's simply too much here. And to leave it to some other pirates to loot…"

They both agreed; it didn't bear thinking about.

Back on the ship, Shawn beckoned Paean to follow him. In the cabin that he shared with Ronan, behind a closed door, he showed her what he had taken off the hobo in the cave. Paean examined it closely. It was some sort of device, that was clear. Heavy, smooth, metallic. No seams or buttons on it whatsoever; still, it had that electronic feel to it.

"Where did you get this?"

"Behind the waterfall where we swam. There was a cave, and in the cave there was a drunk hobo lying sleeping, and it had fallen out of his hand."

"You stole it off a drunken hobo?"

"Face it, sis, he's probably stolen it himself."

"Shawn!" Paean frowned terribly. "Looting an ancient shipwreck is one thing. But stealing stuff off people? You're now learning the wrong stuff from your gypsy friend!"

"Paean! He's your friend too!"

"Course he is. Doesn't mean I condone stealing! Could be the hobo had it given to him by some rich tourist whom he helped in some way. You never know these things! You're returning this to its owner, tomorrow first thing! Early. And Shawn, I'm going with you, and I think it's a good idea to tell at least one adult on this ship where we are going. Technically we ought to tell the Captain."

"In practice it's enough if we tell Federi," said Shawn. "Although he won't understand."

"He will, Shawn. He's got his principles too."

Dusk was already settling over Atuona when the divers returned to the Solar Wind in the Stormrider. Rhine Gold, Ronan and Rushka had helped Federi and the younger Donegals loot the cruiser. Jon Marsden had insisted on staying aboard. He was responsible for the Solar Wind in the Captain's absence. Still between the six of them, the salvage team had managed to get quite a bit of treasure loaded onto the motorboat.

Paean went to shower off the salt and headed to her cabin. She was only going to lie down for a moment before checking on all the things she needed to check on. And Wolf! She stared at the plastered-over camera in the corner of her cabin. Nobody had removed the plaster. She wondered idly if there were cameras at all in Federi's cabin, or if that privilege was reserved for new crew.

All the images of the day came back to her. It had been an enormously full day. It could easily have fitted into four or five days without losing lustre. She had learnt a lot. The mystery of the Solar Wind was deepening. Loyalty to the point of getting yourself shot! And ancient white scars crisscrossing all over Federi's sun-bronzed hide. Wind chimes. The one that got away? What on Earth was that supposed to mean? And Rushka, always hiding. And Atuona! A chewed-off finger. Skeletons in the bilges of the wreck, chained forever to their doom. The Dead Man's Wage. Anna bottle, specifically, of rum! She smiled and didn't realize that she had already wandered off into dreamland.

"I don't have to like it," Federi confided in his friend Marsden. "Want to get away from the island. Got this feeling. There's something very nasty wrong here."

"Think the wreck is a set-up?" asked Marsden lightly.

"That wreck is an incredible *baksheesh* for the Donegals," said Federi. "Course we can't just abandon it!"

"But you ignore your hunches at your peril," Marsden reminded him. "Think it has anything to do with our vanishing lizard?"

Federi grimaced. "That one," he said. "Can't just assume that a whole bunch of vanishing lizards ate the passengers and tied up the crew and sunk the liner and then disappeared! Sheesh! Haven't had time yet to look in Sherman's files!"

"I've been looking," said Marsden.

Federi nodded. His friend need say no more. Marsden found what he searched for, or it wasn't there. Federi knew that the First Mate would in any case go back into the files again and search again, true to his obsessive character. He himself would still dig too, he thought. In keeping with his own compulsive nature! Always the suspicion that there was some more treasure he or others had overlooked.

"So, the two incidents are not related," summarized Marsden.

"My friend, how often did we land here before?"

"Many times!"

"And how often have we gone diving?"

"Plenty!"

"And we've never seen this wreck before?"

Marsden nodded grimly.

"What's it look like with the negotiations?" asked Federi. "Bin so busy keeping the young crew out of scrapes, I forget to update myself."

"As you know," replied Marsden, "Doc and Sherman and Dr Jake are still ashore with Captain. How they are doing I'm not sure, but cast-off is scheduled for tomorrow noon."

261

"Tomorrow noon," repeated Federi. So there was enough time to organize the systematic recovery of the treasure tomorrow morning. He glanced through the volcaniplex windshield of the bridge. Outside dusk was settling over the lagoon like an exhausted grey haze. Supper, then check on everyone…

Marsden was saying something.

"Sorry, Jon?"

"Captain says Benita's being difficult. She's got all sorts of ifs and buts. She's holding up the works."

"That's strange," said Federi. "Always seen her as a sensible, down-to-Earth person!"

"Might have something to do with Angelina," replied Marsden. "I'll tell you, that's going to send a ripple through the Rebellion! Blasted Sancho! If Captain hadn't killed him, I would have!"

"And me," agreed the gypsy. "Hell's rockets!"

"Not so convinced anymore that we're right about Ailyss," added Marsden. "Beginning to think Paean Donegal is the agent, Federi."

The Romany frowned. Hells' jingles! He knew for a fact that little Paean couldn't be the agent! He was the one who'd talked Captain into hiring those three! What was going on now? He'd have to investigate, he decided. He sighed.

Talk about overload! Vanishing lizards, killed tourists – on Hiva Oa! Sunken treasure ships that weren't supposed to be there, with fifteen skeletons in the bilges – and quietly, in the background, intrigues on the ship! He was the self-appointed guardian, the ghost of the Solar Wind; there wasn't anything on the ship that wasn't his responsibility.

Sometimes the whole darned thing felt like a puppet theatre, with him the puppeteer and all the puppets dancing out of line, and him having to unravel all the tangles. His mind ticked over and he withdrew to the galley.

Wolf lowered the novel he was reading. It took special skill to read such a weathered book; the print on the silica-imbued paper was so faded by now, and the paper component of the page so yellowed, a lot of it was a guessing game. Especially in the deepening dusk. But it kept his mind off the pain…

He peered at the dark-haired girl who had appeared in the infirmary.

"Hey, Wolf," said Ailyss.

"Hey, Ailyss!"

"How's the knee?"

"Painful."

Without a word she left. Wolf stared after her, uncertain what to make of this encounter. But a few seconds later she was back with a small turquoise pill and a glass of water. She held both out to him. Wolf took them warily.

"What's that?"

"Codeine."

"Where do you get those?" he asked, swallowing the pill down.

"Drug store," said Ailyss with a shrug. "I use them periodically."

Wolf grinned. "I see."

"All's fine in the machine room," added Ailyss. She sat down on the second bunk. "Nuclear drives nuking away happily to themselves, everything else quiet."

"Thanks," smiled Wolf. Heck, that was thoughtful of her!

She peered at the novel he was still holding. "Can you read that?"

"Contrary to appearances," said Wolf with a half-grin that favoured his injured cheek, "I am in fact literate!"

Ailyss laughed. Wolf half-smiled. She was gorgeous.

"I've got some that are in better condition," she told him. "Want to borrow them?"

"Would like to, thanks."

"When you're done with these, can I read them?"

"Sure!"

They spent a few more loaded moments saying nothing.

"Just wanted to check in on you," said Ailyss eventually.

"Thanks," said Wolf once again.

"Paean's a good kid," said Ailyss out of context.

"Yup!"

"Don't give her so much uphill!"

Wolf narrowed his eyes at her. "Did she send you to give me that message?"

"Don't be ridiculous! She's asleep in her cabin, in ducky pyjamas, just thought you'd like to know."

"Ducky pyjamas!" Wolf smiled again with the left-hand side of his face. "Now there's an entertaining thought!"

"I'll leave you to that thought," said Ailyss, got up and left without a sound.

"Ducky pyjamas," repeated Wolf to himself, shaking his head.

21

Traitor

Early the next morning Shawn and Paean went to find Federi. He was in the Crow's Nest experimenting softly on a tin whistle he'd borrowed from Ronan. No real tunes. Birdcalls and the likes.

"Morning, Federi," they called up to him.

"Morning, you two."

"Come down," called Paean. "We want to talk to you!"

Federi got a sly smile.

"If you want me, come up!"

Shawn clambered up in a couple of seconds.

"You too," Federi told Paean. She groaned.

"Do I really have to?"

"And you're calling Wolf a big baby?" laughed Federi.

"Manipulator!" fumed Paean and slowly inched her way into the rigging and then eventually into the Crow's Nest. "Shawn, you could have told Federi yourself!"

"But I'm not the one who wants to do this," objected Shawn. "It wouldn't be logical for me to make this easy for you!"

"Little monster!"

"Hey, hey. What's going on here?" asked Federi. "Do the Donegals ever quarrel?"

"Not as a rule," said Paean. "Federi, no offence, but this is your fault. Somehow Shawn got the idea that stealing is cool."

Federi frowned. "What?"

"He's taken something off a drunk guy he found in a cave."

Shawn showed Federi his "find". The Tzigan stared at it with wide eyes.

"That cave by the rock pools where we had a swim yesterday?"

"Yup," said Shawn happily. "So now we're going to return it, and

265

we'll be back in time to help with the treasure. Just wanted to tell you so you know where we are."

Federi held out his hand. Shawn gave him the little item, and Federi turned it over and over, staring at it from all angles. Then his hand closed tightly around it and it vanished into his pocket.

"You're not taking anything back," he warned. "You got no idea what this is."

"But we want to give it back to the man!" protested Paean. "It's his! I can understand about *your* stealing, Federi, you're a Free Gypsy, but not Shawn. He's got no reason to learn that habit!"

Federi glared at her.

"My bad habits are *my* bad habits," he said softly, tightly controlled rage edging his voice. "They got nothing to do with my Kalderash roots! Leave my people out of it! The Romanian Tzigany do *not* steal! They stick to the wild parts! And the *gadje* have their fair share of thieves too! Bigger thieves and worse ethics!"

"That's why we want to return it," retorted Paean angrily. "There's no way my brother is turning into one of those!"

"Paean, you and Shawn are not going anywhere! Nowhere, do you read me? In fact, I believe the galley's floor needs a scrub!"

Paean stared at Federi in disbelief. "Why are you doing this?"

"Both of you are still in disgrace! Bout diving off without telling me! Now go wash the deck! Scoot!"

Marsden was up too. He was surprised when Federi sought him out in his cabin.

"Got something here," said the Romany. "Have a look."

Marsden looked at the item and whistled through his teeth.

"This is it," said Federi.

The First Mate nodded thoughtfully as Federi relayed the story to him.

"And Paean tried to return it, you say?" he pointed out with a significantly raised eyebrow.

Federi rolled his eyes. "She's just ignorant, Jon! She had no cooking clue what she held in her hands there! If she were an agent, I doubt she'd have come to me with this!"

"There's that," agreed Jon Marsden, wondering why he detected anger in his friend's voice.

The galley's floor wasn't the end of the world. Scrubbing it could be accomplished in a few minutes, if one knew the shortcuts. Paean had figured out all the shortcuts to scrubbing floors back in Dublin and shared them with her brothers. Shawn and Paean got busy.

"I think I'll tell the Captain about this one," said Paean through her teeth. "This can't be right!"

Just then Marsden popped into the galley.

"Federi told me I could find you here, Paean. Your patient needs you."

Paean nodded, not even realizing how surly she looked that moment. Marsden smiled at her.

"Paean, trust me, your friend knows what he's doing. You're an honest girl for wanting to return that piece. But it would be extremely dangerous for you and your brother to go back. That's all I'll say now."

This made Paean feel somewhat better, although to her, the whole thing reeked. She flung her floor cloth into the bucket and went looking for Doc Judith.

Guilt niggled at her about Wolf. Yesterday in the excitement of the treasure, all of them had completely forgotten that they wanted to ask the Doc to have a look at the savage Wolf. In fact they had so forgotten about him, she wondered if anyone had bothered to bring him supper! Poor Wolf! She resolved to take her role as nurse much more seriously.

"In the first place," Doc Judith greeted her as she entered the infirmary, "how long were the two of you going to keep me in the dark?"

Paean stared at her, taken aback. What did she mean?

"Medicine is not a game, Paean Donegal," scolded the Doc. "I'll pull that Federi's skin over his ears too for only telling me now! Hell knows! I thought, a couple of cuts and bruises, like this lout is prone to get whenever he sets foot in a pub. But bullets, and shattered kneecaps! I'd have thought you'd call me right away!"

"We were scared," admitted Paean.

"Scared! Of me?" The Doc paused. That stood to reason, actually. Paean had just experienced Doc Judith's sternest side. "And you, Wolf Svendsson! You ought to have called for me!"

"Was scared too," grinned Wolf.

"If you lose a leg, Captain will put you ashore, you know it!" snapped the Doc.

Wolf went silent. And pale. Paean thought that there were unhealthy red fever spots in his cheeks.

The Doc had a close-up look at Wolf's cheek and praised Paean for a job well done. Despite its gruesome condition yesterday, thanks to her intervention it looked much better today. It would heal straight and clean now. Paean warily accepted the praise. Wolf gave her a lopsided smile, trying to avoid using the injured cheek. A conspirator's smile. They were on the same side against a formidable foe: The angry Doc.

The knee was a different story. As the Doc removed first the cast and then the bandaging, the smell hit. Paean's stomach turned. She glanced at the wound and squeezed her eyes shut, sitting down on the other bunk.

"Urgh!"

"Got to operate that right away," said the Doc. "See, Paean, these red lines travelling up – Paean?"

"Just a seccie," said Paean, breathing slowly.

"You've got a co-ex," said the Doc, frowning at her assistant.

"Just queasy," said Paean.

"A co-ex is a memory short-cut to some dramatic event in your past," explained the Doc. "Paean, you can't study medicine if you can't handle blood. Get over it!"

"I know," said Paean. She was beginning to feel a bit better. "Working on it!"

"Here," said Doc Judith and filled a glass with water and stuck it in Paean's hand. "Drink!"

Paean sipped obediently. Her stomach relaxed. She opened her eyes. Wolf was staring at her wide-eyed.

"Did you observe sterile procedures when you operated?" asked the Doc.

"I used gloves," said Paean. "And I used new scalpel blades and the rest of the tools were from the sterile drawer. Federi opened a new pack for me."

"Did you wear a mask?"

"I did," said Paean.

"And was there anyone helping you?"

"Federi and Shawn."

"Were they wearing masks and gloves?"

Paean thought back. "Federi was. Shawn wasn't. But he didn't touch anything!"

"That defeats the object," said the Doc. "Did you sterilize the air with ethanol spray the way I showed you?"

"Forgot," said Paean sheepishly.

"Well, that explains it!" exclaimed Doc Judith. "There you have your reason for the wound sepsis!"

Paean grimaced. "Gods, Wolf, I'm sorry! Made a mess!"

"Relax, Paean," said Wolf. "It's going to be alright. You did what you could. 's probably my fault for walking around the first morning!"

"You walked on this?!" exclaimed the doctor. "Why?"

"I was being a pinhead," admitted Wolf.

"You certainly were, mister! *That* explains it! You're risking losing this leg! What a mess!"

Paean shrivelled smaller and smaller.

"You should have woken me up that night, Paean!" scolded the Doc. "And you – pinhead! I only hope you've learnt to respect doctor's orders, even if they come from our natural healer!"

Paean looked ready to cry.

"Only hope we can rescue that leg," added the Doc.

"I'll live." Wolf gave Paean a comforting half-grin.

"Paean, please prepare your anaesthetic for me," said the Doc. "This can't wait. I'm going in right away."

Paean hopped to it. She put some Valeriensis decoction into some rum for Wolf, as he didn't seem to mind it as much that way. As Wolf's consciousness slipped away, he briefly reached for her hand and gave it a squeeze. Paean heaved a shuddering sigh that was on its way to turning into a sob.

"Oh no!" The Doc nailed her with a scathing glare. "You're not going to cry! There's no time!"

Paean obediently swallowed back her tears and got on with putting on sterile gloves and a mask.

The treasure team was waiting for Federi to give them instructions. Eventually Ronan extracted Shawn from the galley.

"Where's Federi?" he questioned him.

"No cooking clue!"

So Shawn led the way. They started loading the remaining contents of the sunken vessel onto the Stormrider. The going was slower than yesterday. Today there were only four of them: Himself, Ronan, Rhine Gold and Rushka. Shawn thought she looked fascinating with her long red hair streaming around her head like seaweed.

Around noon Rushka called them together on the Stormrider. The sea was rather choppy now; clouds were conspiring above them.

"Guys, I've got a message from the Captain. The senior crew is back aboard. We should come; Captain wants to raise anchor."

"We're not done yet," objected Shawn.

Rushka nailed him with a stare from her rather interesting green eyes. Then, unexpectedly, she smiled.

"Shawn, your treasure is important. But the stuff the seniors have been discussing takes precedence. Far, far more important!"

"How do you know?" challenged Shawn.

"Because I'm an officer," said Rushka. "Come now, crew! Let's get back aboard!"

"There you are!" Radomir Lascek greeted the diving team. He, Dr Jake and Ailyss helped unload the treasure into the storage deck of the Solar Wind. Lascek took Rushka aside.

"Where are Federi and Jon?"

"I don't know, Captain. They didn't come with us!"

Radomir Lascek stared at his daughter in dismay. He'd assumed that Federi and Marsden were naturally looting with the others! In which case, where were they? This put a square spanner in his works!

"Nobody informed me! Who would know where they are?"

"It was only me and Sherman and the diving team aboard this morning," said Rushka. "And Doc, I think. Maybe she knows."

She ran off to find Doc Judith. Radomir Lascek paged his veteran.

"They went off to the island this morning, Captain. Dr Jake took them, in the Stormrider. He's waiting for their signal to pick them up again."

"Did they say when they'd be back?"

"No, Captain. But they are aware that the cast-off was scheduled for now."

Radomir Lascek sighed. His First Mate was reliable. But even the most reliable person might get delayed sometimes. Who knew what strange mission they were pursuing! Marsden had touched on that all was not quite as it seemed on the island.

Well, the cast-off wasn't written in stone. The Solar Wind could wait a little. Two hours wouldn't make the critical difference.

"Got to get the ship into deeper water," he commented as the Solar Wind pitched hazardously towards the rocks. "They'll be safe from the storm on land. We'll submerge. We can pick them up when this squall is over."

Slowly the beautiful Zephyr unfurled her sails and moved out of the rocky, churning bay, into much deeper waters. Sherman was taking over the duty of First Mate for the time, checking on everything. Once she was out behind the breakers, he heaved a sigh of relief.

"Haven't done First Mating in a while," he declared. "It's a hard job! Wouldn't want to do it every day!"

The two men approached the place with caution.

"Here," said Marsden and indicated the ground.

"Blast me," replied Federi. A three-toed footprint! Only one. He searched, but couldn't find any more. He studied the trees but couldn't find any scorch marks either. Maybe those burnt bits on the beach had nothing to do with the tracks. "Well done, buddy," he said. "We'll make a tracker of you yet!"

"So old Three-Toes was here," said Marsden.

Federi eyed the waterfall behind the rock pools. He had been to that little cave before! He wondered…

"In there," he said softly, indicating. "That's where he picked it up!"

They approached the cave quietly, staying hidden as far as they could. Whatever might be in there could be intelligent. Shawn had been incredibly lucky not to be eaten just like that poor guy on the beach! Federi iced, thinking about it.

"I'll go in first," he said. "You cover me out here!"

271

Marsden nodded.   Federi readied his semiautomatic handgun and inched into the cave.

It was as Shawn had described. There were empty bottles, rubbish, a dead fire site. A bit further on was the sleeping hobo. The Romany took one look at him. Poisoned. Just to confirm, he knelt down, looking more closely. He was right. The man was dead. Black rings had formed under his nail beds and his face and body were puffed up ready to explode by now.

Federi frowned. Shawn had spoken of a sleeping hobo. He doubted that the kid was so dense that he'd have missed those signs! They were blatant. But maybe – yes, that had to be it: Shawn had been here a very short time after the man had died, or perhaps even before! This was a very fresh case, days fresher than the one on the beach. And yet they were connected, by vice of a three-toed print...

As children, back in Romania, they had carved weird shapes out of wood to make "alien footprints", he remembered. Perhaps this was such a trick. But then he ought to have picked up the footprints of the trickster. Unless the latter was an experienced tracker himself of course and knew how to cover. A completely wayward little theory; but the only real logical explanation he could think of at this point. He still felt that he was wrong. There was that wall, that paradigm trap in his mind. And besides, why would anyone waste time playing such silly games when a murder was involved – rather than just simply disappear and leave no evidence?

Which still left the mystery of where all the bones of the other casualty had gone. It all made less sense the longer he picked at it.

A small unusual sound over the rush of the waterfall triggered Federi's finely tuned senses. The three-toed predator? He got up and flowed into the shadows in one sleek, swift movement. Federi was well honed at becoming invisible, even to wild animals.

"Don't move," said a low voice by his ear. He felt the barrel of a gun poking into his neck. Slowly Federi raised his hands, dropping his gun. Urgh! Someone else had experience being invisible too!

Paean and the Doc came up from below deck. Both of them looked pretty worn down now. The operation had lasted several hours. Wolf had started coming to at one point, at which the Doc had rigged a drip with

272

standard issue anaesthetic and put Paean in charge of all that, including his vital signs. Paean had worried every nerve in her body raw. She was one heap of overanxious jitters right now.

"That was a nasty one! Usually Federi would have assisted," said Doc Judith. "He's an old hand with that. Wonder where he is!"

Federi! Paean's teeth gnashed. Her other urgent mission had just come burning back to her!

She spotted the Captain emerging from the bridge and zoomed in on him.

"Captain, I need to discuss something."

The Captain gave her a considering gaze. She looked upset.

"Alright, young lady," said Captain Lascek, motioning her onto the bridge.

Paean looked nervous. She hadn't been face to face with the Captain like this ever since the Panama incident.

"So make it short," he prompted.

"Captain, I just thought – Federi said, nothing happening on this ship should be kept secret from you."

This didn't sound promising. "Go on," said the Captain with a frown.

Suddenly all of this didn't seem such a good idea anymore. Hadn't Federi said once that people who spilt each other's secrets didn't deserve friends? She looked uncertainly at the Captain.

"Go on," Lascek urged a second time.

Oh, in for a penny…

"Captain, I feel that this morning something happened that wasn't right."

She came out with the entire story, with Shawn running ahead and getting separated from them, finding the cave behind the waterfall and stealing the device from the sleeping hobo; her insisting that he return it; them informing Federi and him confiscating the item and dooming them to wash the floor.

"And then I had to assist Doc with fixing up Wolf's knee, so I didn't get a chance to talk to you before now, sir."

Captain Lascek's frown deepened. He started pacing up and down.

Paean felt miserable. Oh, Federi! She had betrayed his friendship! She should have kept her big trap shut!

"Please, Captain, don't be mad with him," she put in. "It's only in his nature, he can't help the way he is, just – I don't want Shawn turning into a thief!"

Captain Lascek stopped pacing and fixed her with a steel-blue stare.

"This is a lot more serious than me getting angry, little Paean,", he said. "Federi and Marsden could be in serious danger. Could you identify the item? There's a chance he's left it in his cabin."

When the Captain and Paean entered Federi's cabin, she felt even more like a traitor. The Captain however seemed little worried about the details of the ornate realm; he went straight to the squat carved chest of drawers and opened them one by one. Federi's clothes and personal belongings were in there, neatly organized; there weren't many, but all were colourful and decorated with "treasure" all over. Two of the four drawers were devoted exclusively to treasure. Not so neat. Jumbled heaps. In one of them, amongst a lot of Shawn and Federi's electronic pickings from the shipwreck and probably from the Hun, Paean instantly spotted the device. She picked it up and handed it to the Captain.

Lascek's features darkened to match the storm outside.

22

Old Leather

Federi's blindfold had been removed. This did not alleviate anything as it was pitch dark where he lay tied up, dumped unceremoniously on the floor. There was water; Federi lay in a puddle of it. He knew exactly where he was anyway: He had been in the bilges of ships often enough.

He had been stripped of all weapons – that was, all weapons they could find. This didn't leave him many options. His captors had spoken very little beyond pushing him on, marching him and Marsden all the way across the island. By the position of the sun blasting in their necks Federi had known that they were going west. He had turned back once, blindfold and all, to confirm the position of the morning sun and had received another bruise for it. One bruise. Not a bad price for such information.

He and Marsden had tried to exchange a few words but immediately felt the barrels of guns being rammed into their ribs.

They had walked over a jetty and onto a ship. There was no way Federi could ever mistake those sensations for anything else. This meant that there had to be a sheltered harbour on the far side of Hiva Oa. This was very interesting. The harbour had not existed a year ago, when Federi was here last; also, Atuona's beach tower hadn't exactly advertised its existence.

"Take care, buddy," had been Federi's parting words to Marsden, which had cost him another bruise to his ribcage; and then they had shoved him roughly down the hatch and he had tumbled all the way down the wooden stepladder into the dark, to where he lay now, in a puddle of cool seawater sloshing around him. Someone had forcefully ripped off his blindfold, the decorations of his scarf catching in it and almost tearing his scalp from his head.

"Stupid jingly paradise-bird," the man had commented, throwing

Federi's treasure-laden scarf on the ground next to him. Federi had received a parting kick, then the man had left, throwing one backward glance at him out of a sparsely bearded face. As he climbed out of the hatch, silhouetted against the dim light of the lower deck, Federi sized him up. He wasn't too tall; possibly as short as the gypsy himself. Long straggly hair. His cheekbones were crassly high-set. And he was armed to the teeth, it appeared. Pirate or terrorist, had been Federi's assessment; possibly both. Oh hell, there would be some target practice again some time soon!

Federi wondered how Marsden fared. They were keeping the two of them separate, so he could hope that Marsden was somewhat more comfortable. On the other hand it was possible that they were torturing Marsden to extract information. It would have been Shawn and Paean instead. Federi shuddered at the thought.

His ribcage was aching from the fall; but he had rolled, instinctively, the way he had learnt before he could even remember. Had it been Shawn, the boy might have broken his neck. His left side on which he had landed was beginning to feel numb. He wormed his way out of the shifting puddle as best he could, looking for higher ground. Didn't these terrorists ever pump their bilges out? It felt as though a suction pump had been fastened to his head, sucking his consciousness away. Federi fought the whirlpool; he had to stay alert, his captors might return any moment.

Fancy Shawn finding the missing part! How did the vanishing lizard tie into that?

The ship began to roll a bit. Federi realized that she was moving. This was bad news! Where were he and Marsden being abducted to?

In any case it wasn't part of his greater plan to drown in a puddle of stinking water in the bottom of a Rebel ship! The Romany moved in his bonds and smiled a vicious little smile. It glinted. Alright! Siesta was over! Tying Federi down was a moot thing. Federi was the one who got away. Consistently.

Shawn and Paean sat together in the deserted galley. Shawn was stressing over the device he'd picked off the hobo. It was dark outside; Captain had decided to submerge the Solar Wind to protect her rigging. Shawn felt guilty. He should have told the Captain straight away about

276

the device instead of trying to play treasure.

Paean listened to her little brother with half an ear. Her mind was on Federi – her friend whom she had betrayed. Where was he? Were he and the First Mate only sitting in Atuona in a stinky pub waiting out the rain? Or had they got stuck somehow?

She had an impression of him caught in a dark place. Alone. He was not exactly afraid or hurt; but he was in trouble. Aw, Federi! She'd had no idea how serious this thing with the darned device was until she'd seen the Captain react.

Ronan joined them in the galley, and Rhine Gold wasn't far behind. Shawn updated them.

"This is bad, very bad," said Ronan. "What about Federi and Marsden? What do you think has happened? Think they've come to grief? Does the Captain have a plan?"

"If he does, he isna telling us," said Shawn.

"I can't see how he can have a plan, if we have no idea what happened to the two," added Paean.

"What is that device anyway?" asked Rhine Gold.

Paean shrugged. She had no clue. All she knew was that it was important, probably to the Unicate and the Rebellion too. Captain hadn't been too elaborate in his explanations.

"I suppose the logical thing is go ashore and find that cave," suggested Rhine Gold. "Take it from there!"

Paean frowned. She wasn't going to argue with the logical Hamburger. Only somehow it felt to her as though doing that would be the worst mistake of them all.

Old Sherman looked into the galley. "Paean, Wolf wants you," he said with a deep frown. Paean looked at him and shot to her feet.

"I'm on my way," she said.

"Him again," mumbled Rhine Gold. Paean's back straightened out all of a sudden. She glared at Rhine Gold from a dizzying height – for her.

"Listen, Reinhold. You have no idea what kind of pain the man is going through. He can use every friend he can get right now, and then some. Why don't *you* pay him a visit?"

"Sorry, Paean! Didn't know you were so touchy about this."

Ronan rose to his sister's side. "She's right, you know, Rhine Gold.

277

She'd do no less for any of us. Kindly get off her case with your petty jealousy."

Rhine Gold stared at the two Donegals, speechless for the moment, a high colour creeping into his face from the tip of his beard to the tips of his ears.

"Thanks, Ro. Later, Whine Gold," said Paean curtly and spun on her heel, marching off to the infirmary.

Shawn came galloping after. "Wait up, sis, I'm coming with you!"

"You're a darling, Shawn!"

Federi sat rubbing his sore joints to restore circulation. Once he could feel his fingertips again, he felt about for his scarf and found it.

"Aw, to hell they all sailed on their motorized yacht!" he cursed, wringing the water out of it. He inspected the decorations by touch and found them still complete, with only one little earring having torn off. That one had luckily been only an ordinary bead anyway. An emerald or a topaz, he couldn't quite remember. He tied the scarf around his head again. It was damp and horrible. He made a few attempts at standing up.

The vessel was moving without any engine noise, so she was probably running electrically on stored up solar power. The roll of the ship had increased dramatically. Federi could smell and feel that there was a storm going on outside; the storm that had been brewing all morning. He wondered if he had passed out there for a second, experiencing a time lapse.

They were definitely out of the harbour now. No ship rolled this badly in a sheltered bay! He moved around the bilges a bit, finding crates of cargo, more water and some very lively rats. Oh well, at least there wasn't much risk of starving in case they forgot him down here. This polite society really didn't take very good care of their vessel! It would be no surprise at all when she sank.

He wedged himself between some crates and settled into waiting out the storm. Before that abated, there wasn't much hope for putting his plan into action. In case someone came in, he pulled his stiletto blade out of his sleeve where the sheath had been sown into the material right along the seam.

He wondered if the Solar Wind's crew had managed to load all the treasure from the shipwreck before the storm hit. And how a hundred-year-old shipwreck had suddenly appeared on a coral reef they had been over probably twenty times in the past. It was creepy.

His mind moved back to this morning and little Paean chewing him out for Shawn learning to steal. Blaming the Tzigany... like *gadje* had done since the dawn of time. He shook his head sadly. She was very young. She couldn't know. He would have to educate her a little. And where Shawn was concerned... he rolled his eyes. He supposed she had a point. He'd better change his thieving ways a bit. He wondered if Marsden had managed to decrypt – aw hell, Marsden was caught, just like him! He seriously hoped that little Paean had the sense to tell Captain about the capsule.

The data capsule Shawn had picked off that man was the second half to Anya Miller's capsule. He was willing to bet his head on that! A picture began to emerge. Anya reporting in panic about the capsule gone from her ship. The other half, without which decryption was not possible, being rushed to safety by the Unicate. To Hawaii – or Hong Kong, or Perth... who knew. Two Unicate agents meeting on Hiva Oa for the transfer of the capsule. The Rebellion cottoning on... sending a vanishing lizard to eat the contact on the beach... no. The Rebellion coming sniffing around the cave, where the second man had already received the capsule and was lying dying from poisoning... The exploding lizard eating the Rebellion...

Aargh! Federi shook his head. He resolved to leave the combining to Jon and Captain. Hells, he hoped they weren't actually torturing Marsden! If they did, if they managed to pry the location of the data capsule out of him, then it was doom for the Solar Wind!

He sat and listened to the ship, and after a while he slipped into a half-tranced doze.

Radomir Lascek was feverishly decrypting the contents of the data capsule. Sherman and Dr Jake were there with him, decoding too and copying the data over into ship files. He was delighted finally to have his hands on the information. The actual information that was coming out of the capsule was hair-raising. He'd have to rethink; re-plan. His original plans were never going to pan out now! He needed something larger, and fast!

He was also deeply concerned about the fate of his two sailors. Right now he was trawling for clues, indications of where to start looking to rescue the two – if they were still alive.

Paean, with Shawn on her heels, arrived in the infirmary and stared in alarm. Wolf looked terrible. His eyes were bright and shiny; his cheeks had dark spots of high fever in them while the rest of his face was white as a sheet. He stretched out a hand as she came in, and tried to tell her something. His mouth was so dry that she couldn't understand what he was saying.

"Water!" she exclaimed. "Ye Powers, you poor fellow!" She charged over to the tap and grabbed the nearest receptacle – an empty metal beaker – and filled it. "There, drink that!"

Wolf tried taking the cup; it slipped out of his grasp and spilt on the floor. Paean picked it up and refilled it, and sat down on the edge of the bunk with it. Her hand went automatically to his forehead. He was burning up! She tried to cover her fright.

"Can you sit up?"

Wolf tried sitting up. Paean tried supporting him with her arm around his back. She had done this so often for Mother... except that it didn't want to work, because Wolf was solid and muscular! Mother had weighed nothing, in the end. Literally faded away. Paean could have lifted her and carried her about, except that she had bruised at the lightest touch. And then the fever...

"Are you alright, Pae?" asked Shawn.

She sniffed. "Grab those pillows from the other bunk and stuff them in his back, Shawney! Got to get liquids into this old piece of furniture here."

Shawn obeyed. Paean hoisted Wolf up a little, with his own added efforts, and Shawn quickly placed the pillows. Paean held the beaker with water for Wolf while he drank thirstily.

"There! If we can just get enough liquids into you..." She put the empty beaker down and injected Wolf with a potent painkiller. Heavy guns. She sat down again and put her hand on his forehead and kept it there, as it seemed to have a soothing effect on him. On her. On them both.

"Don't let me die," muttered Wolf.

"Shawn!" Paean's voice struck panic pitch as she turned to her little brother. "Please run and get the Doc. This is very bad!"

Shawn scooted off, breaking the speed limit. He was glad that the Solar Wind was submerged, because he had tried running in a storm before when she hadn't been.

Paean measured Wolf's temperature. Dangerously high. Ye Gods, the Fever!

"Wolf," she begged, stroking his limp black hair out of his face, "hang in there! Don't die! Don't do this to me!"

She refilled the beaker and fed him some more water. This would never be enough.

"You'll be fine," she told him resolutely, then she hunted for something that could be used as a long, flexible straw. "You're young and strong and you can beat this! Least it's not a darned Unicate virus!" Only a situation Paean has landed you in, she thought, gnashing her teeth. There were several sterile tubes in a drawer, the type that was used for IV drips. She could use one of these tubes as a straw for Wolf, and she'd also ask Doc to put up a drip for him.

Wolf moaned, and she turned around just in time to see his eyes flip back and him starting to thrash about. Fever convulsions! She watched with wide frightened eyes.

Shawn entered the yellow Sick Bay with Doc Judith.

"Oh no," said Doc Judith, assessing the situation. "This will never do! Paean, give him a bit of your green wonder bug! Don't want him pulling stitches!"

Paean loaded some of her decoction into a syringe and handed it to the Doc. She and Shawn hung onto Wolf's arm while Doc Judith injected the sedative into his vein. The stress went out of Wolf's face and he went limp.

"Oh, hell," said Paean. Her throat ached from fighting down tears. She didn't dare to cry in the presence of the Doc though. "Doc, I think he's dehydrated and must get a drip right away. He's running a high fever. I've given him this," and she showed the Doc the painkiller she had given him.

"Wound sepsis can be very dangerous," said Dr Judith, sealing and discarding the syringe. "You did right calling me! Careful there for his kidneys and liver. If a patient's dehydrated and you give him chemical drugs, there's always a risk. Let's get that drip going." She showed Paean how to insert the needle of the drip; then Paean secured it and the IV line with a long plaster strip. Soon the saline was flowing. "Paean, how did Wolf get that dehydrated anyway?"

"I don't know," whispered Paean. "We were all so busy…"

Shawn moved quietly to the door and escaped.

"You immobilize the man in the infirmary, fail to tell the doctor and then leave him to his fate?" challenged the doctor.

Paean swallowed back her tears. She didn't deserve to cry about this. If he died…

A heart monitor and thermometer were connected to Wolf, displaying his vital signs on the screen and also as audible blips, a different frequency from the submarine radar blips.

"See now," soothed the Doc. "You can see that his heart rate is strong, and his brain activity is good. Probably dreaming."

Paean sniffed. "Should I check on the knee?"

"No. We only just closed it up. We'll have a look at it first thing tomorrow morning." She added more antibiotic into the IV drip. "Now you relax," she instructed Paean. "He should be alright. But I want you to stay here, and if anything turns for the worse, call me immediately."

She threw the patient a doubtful glance. There was something niggling at her. She excused herself.

Paean burst into tears the second the Doc was out of the infirmary. The Fever! She dreaded fever with a grey, primal terror born out of experience. She glanced down at her hands and thought of that perfect, still moment yesterday, by the rock pool.

While she had hung images in her memory gallery, Wolf had been lying here thirsty and hungry with nobody giving a rip! She hadn't even given it half a thought!

That peaceful moment! It had been an illusion anyway, she realized. Federi had been uneasy. Not visibly, but she had sensed it. He had been right! The awful little device came from that spot! And probably that was where Federi had gone back.

A sleeping hobo in a cave?

What if Federi didn't come back? What if he had been... What if his and Marsden's poor bodies got left there, next to that dead man, and the Solar Wind set sail because Captain couldn't find them?

She had to take Captain to that spot! Then again, what if that was exactly what they were waiting for – whoever they were? What if it was a trap?

Her hands stroked the hair of the dying young engineer. How could she have forgotten to bring him water? The saline drip was rigged now, that was good, but what if the heavy painkiller she had given him finished off his liver? All the tears streaming down her face wouldn't bring him back!

Someone who betrays his friends, doesn't deserve friends, Federi had said. By her act of betrayal, had she forfeit her right on friendship in total? Was she to lose them both in one single night, irreversibly, to death?

Shawn peered into the infirmary with a mug of coffee for his sister. He studied the scene that presented there. She had fallen asleep on the chair next to the bunk, her head on Wolf's chest, both her hands clinging to his left hand. And she was still crying in her sleep.

"Oy," said Shawn and put her mug down. He made himself comfortable on the opposite infirmary bunk and grabbed a book. He'd better keep watch while little sister got some shuteye. Just as well Wolf was valeriensed out.

Federi!
The Romany lifted his head.
Remember who you are, Federi!

"Katya?"
There was nothing.
Remember who I am? Hells, Katya, sometimes you tax me!
He was wedged between his crates on the Rebel ship. His eyes were shut; his dreaming mind was seeing things as they were, in a grey dream-

light. It was a state of awareness he loved. It didn't happen often; but when it did, sometimes he could visit with his sister's spirit, and sometimes he could see the future clearly, and sometimes...

"Federi?"

A frightened little red-haired child-woman stood before him, slightly luminescent in the grey light.

Whoa! This was bad news!

"Paean? Are you okay? What happened? Don't tell me you and Shawn followed us?"

"Federi – I'm sorry..."

The little phantom burst into tears.

Federi felt like crying too. *He* was sorry. More sorry than her! If he hadn't talked Captain into hiring her, she might still be alive. If he had coached her better, told her more! If he had made sure she understood the dangers of being a Lascekian pirate...

"So how many of the crew did the Rebellion get?" he asked.

"What?"

"How many were killed?"

"No," said the little mockingbird. "Nobody. We're on the ship. Federi, I'm sorry! I don't want my friends to die! I betrayed you! I'm sorry!"

"What?" His eyebrows shot up. Marsden's ominous warning surfaced briefly in his mind, like an enemy submarine. Like a shark fin. "Little luv, whatever you've done, we can fix it! Just tell the Captain everything, and then wait for Federi!"

At least she was alive, he thought with a huge surge of relief. Everything else was fixable.

"I've already done, Federi! I've told him about that little device Shawn stole. Captain fished it right out of your cabin, Federi..." She dissolved in sobs. "I'm so sorry I betrayed your friendship!"

"What?" Thinking logically in dream space wasn't always an easy thing.

"I spilt your secret to Captain," repeated Paean miserably.

"Okay, let me get this straight. Your betrayal is that you've told Captain about the data capsule? You little genius! They need that capsule! It's Marsden's missing puzzle piece! Was going to give it to

284

him anyway! So he found it?"

Paean nodded.

The little superstar! "Stop crying, sweetheart! You did right! I'm proud of you!" He wondered. She was in dream space too; how much would she remember when she woke up? "Little luv, can you give them a message from Federi?"

She sniffed. "I'll try, Federi. You're not angry?"

"No, hell! Listen up, *dulciuri*. Tell Captain this. There's a secret Rebellion port on the west side of Hiva Oa. They've captured us, their ship is moving, I don't know where. He must keep the Solar Wind submerged and wait for my signal! He must not search for us on land, under no circumstances! Can you remember that?"

"A secret port," repeated Paean. "On the west side of the island. He must submerge and wait for your signal. Not search for you."

"Right," said Federi. "If we're not back by midnight, he must go. On with his plan."

"Abandon you?"

"Yes. By then we're dead."

Aw! Some things were not so clever to say to this little phantom.

"Please stop crying," begged Federi. "Course we'll survive this! I'm the one who gets away!"

"Promise?" sobbed Paean.

"Absolute promise!" He reached out for her hand and gave it a squeeze. "Not Thieves' Honour. Guarantee. From Federi."

"Okay."

"Now go," he nudged her. "Go give Captain the message before you forget."

"I will," promised Paean. "*Kathal,* Federi! Come back intact."

She faded out. Federi sighed and shook himself out of dream space and into the darkness of the bilges.

Her crying over him more than made up for her thoughtless remark about the Tzigany earlier. She had been so real, he had actually managed to reach out and touch her! He hoped she'd remember.

Time to get on with his plan.

Paean came to with a jolt.

285

"Are you alright?" asked Shawn. He handed her the mug of coffee.

Paean stared at him, trying to organize her thoughts. She was to give the Captain a message. What was it? Abandon Federi! No! Wrong! She trailed back over her dream.

Dr Jake opened the door to the stairwell.

"Paean?"

On the bridge were the Captain, Doc Judith, Dr Jake and Sherman. Dr Judith looked sharply at Paean.

"Is Wolf in trouble?" the doctor asked, worried.

"Wolf's looking better, Doc. Shawn's keeping watch. It's only a moment. I have to speak to Captain," said Paean. "It's urgent."

Captain Lascek got up from his programming.

"Carry on, all of you," he said to the three officers. "I'll be back in a moment." He turned to Paean, his thoughts clearly still stuck in the computer. "Is this important?"

"Very, Captain, or I wouldn't bother you with it," said Paean earnestly.

"Alright, to the boardroom."

When they were in the boardroom a few seconds later, Captain Lascek turned to Paean.

"Make it quick."

"Captain, I've made mental contact with Federi."

Captain Lascek's brows furrowed.

"What's this nonsense?"

"The device," said Paean. "It's a data capsule. Federi thinks it's Marsden's missing puzzle piece. Whatever that means."

Lascek's brows flew up.

"How do you know all this?"

"Federi just told me! Captain, there's apparently a secret Rebellion port on the west side of Hiva Oa. They've taken him captive, he's sitting in the bilges of a ship, he says the ship is moving but he doesn't know where to." She paused, frowned, worked on recalling the rest. The Captain was nailing her with his cold blue eyes. Federi, help me out here... "Captain, he says, wait for his signal and keep the Solar Wind submerged. If they're not back by midnight..." She shook her head. No way was she relaying that bit of message!

A disbelieving smile spread over Radomir Lascek's face. Jon Marsden had voiced his suspicion that perhaps they were suspecting the wrong girl of being a spy. Up until this point he had almost begun to believe Jon.

But this…

"What's the rest?" he prompted. "What did Federi say?"

"No, Captain, nothing. We mustn't look for them on land, they're not there and it's dangerous."

"What about midnight?"

The girl shook her head, looking frantic. She was in fact withholding information. Radomir Lascek knew now. She was telling the truth. Somehow her voodoo gift of lucid dreaming or whatever had connected with Federi's gypsy radar. Because…

"He said I should set sail and carry on without them if he hadn't managed by midnight," he completed. "Right?" That was Federi! Hundred percent!

The Irish redhead was shaking her head, tears streaming.

"Paean," said Radomir Lascek, placing a calming hand on her shoulder and bending down to level with her eyes, "look at me! Do you believe for a second that I'd abandon Federi and Jon Marsden? I'll shoot the Rebellion *and* the Unicate to shrapnel before I do that!"

Paean smiled and wiped over her face with her sleeve. Radomir Lascek straightened out.

"West of Hiva Oa, you say?"

"Just the port, Captain. He doesn't know where the ship is by now."

"Well then, let's follow his trail of voodoo," said Lascek optimistically. "Go to sleep, Paean. Let someone else take over Wolf's vital signs! We'll get this sorted."

23

Bloodshed

Federi shook his head and smiled. *Kathal!*

It was comforting to believe that he had somehow reached Paean. But in fact he was still as alone as before and had to act upon that certainty. Plan A was still Plan A. If Marsden was still alive, he had to find him and free him. He had to kill the entire crew and make contact with the Solar Wind, and as he got back aboard his home ship, he had to sink this vessel. The latter shouldn't prove too much of a challenge, he thought acerbically.

The storm was slowing down, by the sounds of it, though the sea was still very high. He sheathed the Stiletto and got up, his body aching all over. He began to search once again. In the dark he stepped on something and picked it up. A self-satisfied grin spread across his face. They had lost his spring-loaded pocket knife! Or perhaps it had fallen out of his pocket when he had tumbled down the stairs.

Well, he was very happy to have it back! It had special memories for him. His first knife. He mainly used it for woodcarving these days, keeping the blade honed on a bit of leather. Still a very sharp, strong knife. He opened the solid blade, and with it he removed the pins from the lid of one of the cargo boxes and levered the crate open. It didn't take much leverage – the lid was of lesser quality wood and came apart. Damp damage, he could feel. The moment he could get his fingers in, he prized it open.

Under a silica gel blanket, beautiful guns greeted him. He fumbled with a bead on one of his several rings and gave it a twist. Soft chemical light spilled from it. He took a closer look at his find in the crate. Brand new semi-automatic and automatic weapons. He armed himself, not to the teeth, but enough that he could get by. A bit deeper under the guns he found ammunition. He checked for damp here too; but the Rebellion were no complete idiots, they had packed silica gel blankets around the ammunition too. He loaded the two guns he had taken, slinging extra belts of rounds around himself. Then he moved on.

The guns and ammunition were merely a backup – Plan B, in case he was discovered or cornered. He wasn't keen on shooting his way out of a group of terrorists; he didn't have a bullet-proof vest, so he'd have to rely on speed and accuracy alone. Plan A involved stealth. A lot of stealth.

He found the ship's desalination system. With a little smile he examined all the ornaments on his scarf and then detached one. It happened to be a minute blue glass vial, so small it could be mistaken for another elaborate bead. He cracked it open over the desalination plant.

"Sweet dreams," he murmured. "Thanks, little green pirate!"

The tiny chemical light was working itself out now. He used its last few moments to move up the stepladder to the lower deck. He stopped and listened for sounds at the hatch. There was nothing happening overhead. They all seemed to be on the top deck. Warily he lifted the hatch – those geniuses had been so sure of having him tied, they hadn't even bothered locking it! He smiled. It was useful at times to be taken for several rats short of a full cargo deck. His slight build and his garish sense of style helped this impression along. Nobody was in sight. It was quite dark, although to his eyes, having been in almost complete darkness so long, the dim lighting was lots. With a swift movement he slipped out of the hatch and melted into the shadows of the passageway.

A man came walking by. Federi was waiting inside an empty cabin with bated breath. Quietly he crept in behind the man, and slashed his carotid artery with a swift flash of his stiletto before the surprised victim could utter a sound. Quickly, professionally. Minimal blood; no noise; hardly any time lapse at all. He dragged the man into the cabin, thinking of the vanishing lizard. A predator, that was what he was.

Rubbish! A murderer, in human terms. Yes, this was a war; yes, it was him or them. Excuses, all. Federi closed the cabin door and slipped back into the passageway, looking and listening for the next victim. Wolf was right to call him a cold-blooded assassin. He felt moved suddenly that the bright young nuclear engineer would get himself shot in the knee for him. How did scum like him deserve friends like Wolf?

The Solar Wind surfaced just enough for the Captain to have a good look at the west side of Hiva Oa. Lights; ships. Rebellion-style schooners, by the patterns of light.

Captain Radomir Lascek whistled through his teeth, satisfied.

"I'll be -! The girl was right! There is a harbour!"

"So we can count on the rest too?" asked Sherman Dougherty.

"I would," said Radomir Lascek. "I certainly would."

Federi had quietly killed and sneaked his way all the way to the bridge. Here, just on the other side of the door, two low voices were speaking in Spanish. He tried to listen in, but couldn't make out a word. They were speaking too softly.

"*¿Café?*" said the one suddenly.

"*Si, por favor.*"

Federi melted into the dark corner below the stepladder. He had a choice: Let the coffee do the trick, or do the trick himself. When it came do doing tricks, Federi would rather not trust the coffee. Another dead weight slipped quietly to the floor.

Interesting, thought Federi. The Rebellion was traditionally South American. What were English-speaking people like Sloan and Cairns doing among them? What was going on?

Suddenly he wished that he were better informed. He knew that Jon Marsden accompanied the Captain to many of his secret meetings with diverse contacts; he himself usually elected to stay aboard the ship and guard over Rushka and the crew. He hadn't exactly been invited to come along that often, either. Like now, typically. Perhaps if he'd gone with Captain and Jon to meet Benita D'Araujo even once, he'd know the answer to his question now.

Regardless, it came to the same thing at this moment.

"*¿Este usted, Juan?*" asked the other man without turning around as Federi opened the door to the bridge.

"No," said Federi softly. "It's me, your angel of death."

"The signal!" shouted Lascek. He jumped to his feet. "Dr Judith, go get Paean! She's got to see this!"

Paean stumbled onto the bridge thirty seconds later, still very confused from sleeping. She bent over the monitor they were motioning to. It took

290

her a moment to read. Her heart skipped a beat.

"It's Federi! He made it!" she shouted. "I knew it! Didn't I tell you?" She grinned triumphantly at the officers.

"You did well, Paean," said Dr Judith, and Dr Jake clapped his hand on her shoulder approvingly.

Paean fixed her gaze on the screen again.

"Solar Wind come in," it read.

"Solar Wind coming in," Dr Jake had typed.

"This is Federi. Aboard the Rebel Schooner RS 6923. Haven't found Marsden yet. Sending our satellite signal. Am free. Situation precarious, all crew not yet dead. Say hi to Paean. Hope you guys listened to her."

All eyes were fixed on Paean.

"What?" she asked, suddenly self-conscious. The Captain motioned her out of the way as Federi activated the satellite signal of the RS vessel to be sent to the Solar Wind.

Federi had stopped all the engines. He had set the signal to continue sending, so that the Solar Wind could track them easily.

He glanced at the dead Rebel. Young man caught in the crossfire. And at his own hands. Blood had sprayed everywhere, over the console, over his shirt... he'd have to clean the Stiletto, too...

"Sorry, man! Blast, life's short! Sorry about Juan too."

He couldn't start thinking like this right now! He hadn't yet finished the job! Federi took a deep breath and left the bridge in search of Marsden.

The little green bug had started working. People had been getting themselves something to drink. Similar to Captain's rules, the Rebellion had a policy that forbade the Rebels the use of alcohol while on duty, so coffee was the favoured beverage. Federi only had half as many Rebels to execute. For now, he left the sleeping ones in peace.

Suddenly a commotion arose from the direction of the bridge. Federi crept closer to the control room again and waited. Somebody had found the body on the floor beneath the stepladder. Seconds later, another outcry came from the bridge itself. They had found the second dead man. He hadn't bothered hiding either of them. He wanted to know when people discovered that their bridge had been usurped.

Federi waited in the shadows beneath the stepladder for the finder to come charging down; then he lost no time terminating him as well. He abhorred that kind of noise. It had a way of following him into his dreams.

In one of the cabins Federi found Marsden. He was not alone; the slant-eyed terrorist who had shoved Federi down the stairs was with him, extracting pain. Sloan. Same guy who had shot at Wolf. And who had waited for him in the cave...

Marsden's tired eyes fleetingly found the gypsy; then he quickly looked away again.

Such a lot of blood, Federi suddenly felt queasy. His eyes narrowed. His friend had how many minutes left to live?

"Still not talking, pirate?" asked the slant-eyed one and prepared to carve another shallow but painful gash in Marsden's triceps. Federi silently walked up to him, swiftly put his arms around the man's head and broke his neck. The Stiletto was too darned good for this kind of scum. He stood staring at the man's twisted shape on the grey cabin flooring, and at Marsden, and waited for the red haze to clear from before his eyes. Sloan. Scum. Like Federi. Slightly different race; but all the other variables were the same.

"Federi," rasped the First Mate.

The Romany pulled the door closed and bolted it, and freed Marsden from his bonds.

"Hey Jon, how are you doing?" He stared at the damage. Marsden looked perforated. Blood was seeping out everywhere, and already the bunk on which he was lying was drenched in it. Cor, was he going to have reminders! At least, Federi hoped so. He shook himself and got focused.

"You sure took your time freeing me!" muttered Marsden with a weak grin. "If I don't get into Paean's gentle care quickly, there won't be much left to tell!"

"Poor lil' Paean," sighed Federi, rolling his eyes skywards. He ripped up a bed sheet from one of the four military-style stack bunks and started to make tourniquets and pressure bandages. "Got no rum on me, pal. Don't know how I'll get the stuff disinfected. Right now all I can do is try

292

to stop you from running out."

Marsden grinned. "They're leeches, my friend. I didn't know I had that much blood inside me!"

"Seven litres," said Federi, "Of which, if you lose four, you're dead. Seen any vanishing lizards?"

Marsden rolled his eyes. Federi took that as a no.

"The Solar Wind is coming for us, Jon. I've sent a signal. Hang in there."

"I've never asked you this, my friend," said Marsden dreamily. "But I'd like to know before I go. I've always just known you as Federi. Is that your first name or your surname, and what is your other name?"

"You're not going anywhere, Jon," said Federi firmly. "I've got Captain's Orders for you to wait for the Solar Wind. He needs you to decode the data in that capsule."

"Oh," said Marsden. "Okay, I'll wait. Would have thought that Radomir…" He sighed and passed out.

"And it's only Federi," said Federi quietly. "There's luckily only one of me."

He took the key to the cabin with him when he went to "clean up". Curse those Rebels! If Jon Marsden didn't survive this! The compassion for the slain Rebels died in Federi. By now the only crewmembers that hadn't already been executed were the ones that had been knocked out by the Valeriensis. He had briefly considered leaving all the sleeping dogs lie; now he changed his mind and executed them instead, with his stiletto. One small, professional incision per rebel, at the base of the throat. A hair on Jonathan Marsden's head was worth more than all these rats together!

Federi was as thorough as with the shipwreck the day before, starting on one end and going through the entire ship, cabin by cabin, leaving nothing out. Eventually he returned to the unconscious Marsden. Except for the rats in the bilges, the two of them were now the only ones alive. Were they? He checked Jon Marsden's pulse in his throat just to make sure. It was weak and hard to find, but still there. Blood was still coursing through his veins. The tourniquets were doing their work.

"Now we wait, my friend," Federi said. "Hells! Just hang in there! Should have come for you first, before sending the signal!" But he knew that that would have been a death trap. The enemy would have found the dead terrorist and Marsden freed; they would have sounded alarm, and there would have been a lot more blood shed. His. The signal would never have been sent.

It felt to Paean as though she had only just got back to sleep. Ronan was shaking her awake again. She groaned.

"Sorry, sis. Dr Judith needs your help."

"Tellem to carry on without me," she mumbled. "They're nice an big now…" She lapsed back into dreams. Shawn was really old enough to organize his own kiddies' party now!

"Pae, Doc Judith is calling for you!"

The relative actuality of the ship listed into Paean's mind. "Wha?"

"Doc Judith wants you in the infirmary, sis!"

Oh, the Doc. Medical studies. Yes, it was probably time she got up…

"I'm there," said Paean drowsily, turned over and slept on.

A few minutes later Ronan was shaking her again.

"Are you up, sis? Dr Judith is waiting."

"Hmm?" muttered Paean. "Why's it so dark?" She was exhausted and certainly not awake.

"Och, Paean! I know it's tough, but you've got to get up. Doc needs you. Federi and Marsden are back!"

The ship rocked. Paean rolled out of her bunk and landed with a thump on the floor.

"Ouch," she declared. "I think I'm awake now."

It was a waste. Half a minute later, stumbling into the infirmary, she passed right out again. Too much blood.

Doc Judith treated her with a glass of cold water in her face. There was no time for this kind of thing now.

"Is Mr Marsden – alive?" she muttered as her senses returned to her.

"Barely," said the Doc.

"Sorry, Doc. For blacking out."

"Don't worry. We'll need to do a transfusion. I've sent Shawn to get a type printout of everyone aboard, and it seems Ronan's the closest match."

Ronan had settled himself on the only chair in the small cabin. "Tap away," he grinned. He presented his arm for the doctor to insert the IV needle; it would be a direct, person to person transfer this time, as there was no time to lose. Another IV drip with saline was already installed in Marsden's other arm.

Federi sat at the end of Marsden's bunk, looking grey with exhaustion. Paean shot him a tentative look from under hooded eyelids. He lifted a tired eyebrow.

"How are you doing?" she asked shyly.

"I hate those tropical squalls," muttered Federi, giving her a lopsided grin. "But I managed to find Ronan's tin whistle again. Took some doing."

"Hang onto it a bit longer, Federi," said Ronan generously. "You've only just started learning."

"Thanks, shipmate," replied the gypsy cook. He looked like a wizened old leprechaun to Paean, all of a sudden. Not old, but tired, so tired…

Wolf surfaced.

"Got to get up and check – Hey," he said, looking around in bewildered amazement. "A party!"

"Aargh," groaned Federi, getting up. "A party!" He escaped.

"Here I am, Captain."

"Federi!" Lascek clapped his hand on the Romany's shoulder. "Man, am I glad to see you!"

"You already said that, Captain," grinned Federi.

"Well, I still mean it!" Lascek shook his head. "That could have gone wrong! Next time, tell me! It might have been the wiser idea to gather everyone and set sail as fast as we could!"

"What's in the capsule?" asked Federi, glancing at the console. "Was it worth it?"

"Never," said the Captain. "Unicate strategies until the next century won't be worth your and Jon's lives!"

"A man was murdered back in that cave," said Federi. "Wonder who, and which side he belonged to, and why he had that capsule." He hesitated.

Radomir Lascek was overtired too. He would not have missed it under usual circumstances.

"Well, you've avenged him, right?" he asked. Federi rolled his eyes. "Go catch some sleep," ordered the Captain.

"Ghosts," muttered Federi. He took himself off to the galley. Coffee first. He wanted to stay awake enough tonight to have a say in his own dreams. In fact, if he had a choice, he'd rather not fall asleep at all.

Hours later Paean stumbled into the galley. She found Federi sleeping with his head on his arms at the big black Ironwood table. The attempts of making himself a cup of coffee were standing on the working surface at the coffee station. Despite its rubberised bottom the cup had slipped right up to where the raised rim stopped it from falling off. There was no rim stopping Federi from sliding off the table. But Paean suspected that he had developed a special kind of seafarer's glue that stuck him into place. She had experience herself by now. It was called subconsciously clinging to the mattress. Or whatever. She left Federi's coffee in peace and got coffee for herself.

Doc Judith had been happy to see Wolf's condition improved, though he was far from recovered. She had given him the task of watching over Marsden's vital signs. Ailyss had been called in to help too. She was to watch over both patients and call the doctor if necessary. Paean had noticed how relief had spread across Wolf's stressed face on seeing Ailyss. It had her wondering.

"I hate seeing grown men immobilized like that," said Paean to herself, settling down by the table waiting for the water to boil. She studied Federi's black hair that had fallen in strands across his face. And his headscarf, that seriously needed a wash. It had been immersed in muddy water and had dried by now. And his sleeves, his shirt – drying blood. The gypsy was a mess. She shook her head. "Yodiho and a bottle of. Whatever! Valeriensis!"

"Ha," mumbled the recumbent form of Federi. "You should have seen them on the Rebel Schooner! They were far more immobilizeder!"

Paean peered at his eyes under all that hair. They were still shut.

"Shall I make you your coffee now?" she asked.

"That'll be nice," muttered Federi without moving. "You and Shawn did a good job with the deck. How many stitches for Marsden?"

"Two hundred and sixteen," said Paean, smiling. "Just about four times as many as Wolf – but then I did Wolf's over about four times, so I suppose they're even."

"Wolf nearly died there, earlier, didn't he?"

"Who told you?"

"You were broadcasting it," said Federi. His black eyes were open now, gazing at her. "You were stretched very thin when you visitated – er – spectred – whatever one calls it –"

"Gods, Federi! He had the Fever!"

"You sound like someone from the Middle Ages," smiled Federi.

"You've no idea!"

"Aw, little luv!" Federi straightened out and reached for her hand. Poor little hummingbird! "I think I know. But on the Solar Wind we've got medicines, and we've got Doc. Can't tell you how many times she's pulled us out of death's clutches."

"She's brilliant," said Paean.

"You're not alone anymore, Paean," said Federi soothingly. "You don't have to do it alone. You're really only the assistant. Wolf is Doc's responsibility."

Paean smiled, relieved.

"Seems like both of us had a friend to keep alive," said Federi. "Was touch and go for Marsden there, too! Wanted to keep my tabs on him, but you saw…"

Yes, Paean had seen. Federi got crowded out.

"Is he still critical?" he asked.

"Doc's got him stabilized. They tapped Ronan quite a bit, he may need something potent later on… Marsden will be fine. It's Doc who stitched him, not some bleeding amateur."

"And they're clean cuts," replied Federi. "Easier than that patella. Lots of ammo on that ship," he said dreamily, "Anyone looting?"

"I think, everybody," said Paean. "Sherman's on the bridge. Of the Solar Wind. Ronan's sleeping and Ailyss is watching the patients."

"*Shukar*," commented Federi.

It was good to make light conversation. Good to touch sides and know tangibly that he had come back, he had survived. He had kept his promise.

Now that the danger was over, it worried her that she had been able to access the Romany telepathically. It worried her even more that everyone knew about it.

"Hope it doesn't upset Shawn too much," said Federi with a wink.

"What? What would upset him?"

"All the dead terrorists…"

Paean finished preparing coffee. She handed Federi his mug. Dead terrorists. A heap of poor chained skeletons in the bilges of a sunken cruise liner. A chewed-off finger, a dead hobo in a cave. What a place!

She didn't know the half of it, thought Federi. An ancient sunken cruiser that *hadn't been there last time round!* A vanishing lizard! At least, they suspected it might only be one, but for all they knew… A *politically active* vanishing lizard, to boot!

"You look wiped out," she commented.

"May I return the compliment," Federi smiled.

"Are you hurt?"

"Not so I'd notice," said the gypsy. "They kicked old Federi about a bit, that's all. And after that, they got hurt. Not me."

"Aw, Federi… you still angry with me?"

"Angry? Why?" He frowned, mystified. He'd never been angry! Not that he could recall.

"I betrayed our friendship! I told the Captain about the data capsule and all that!"

"You were being sensible," said Federi. "You've probably saved Captain from walking into the same trap. Was hoping you'd tell him! Glad to have you for a telepathic ally! Makes things a lot easier!" He grinned.

"So we're still friends?"

"Course!" Federi smiled broadly, shaking his head. "Silly girl!"

"And…" she hesitated. He raised an eyebrow at her. "You're not angry about what I said earlier?"

"About the Tzigany?" Aha! So he was!

Federi smiled and shook his head. "No, little luv. Got to educate you a bit, that's all. You didn't know, you come from a –" he sighed. "A *gadjo* family. Didn't want to say it that way. The *gadje* have all sorts of preconceived ideas about gypsies." He rolled his eyes. "Too tired to go into that now, see."

"I'm sorry," said Paean contritely. He grinned at her and sipped his coffee.

" 's fine."

There was something Shawn had said. And the Captain.

"Tell me about that stiletto?"

"What stiletto?" asked Federi innocently.

"The one you were holding there in the…" Doubts assaulted her. What if she had only dreamt the whole thing? "I thought I saw…" She went silent.

Federi smiled thoughtfully.

"That's the thing," he said. "The fine line between illusion and dreams and psychic impressions. And wishful thinking. They really are all the same. And nobody believes us anyway. So how would we ever really know?"

"But was it real?" she wanted to know.

Federi smiled at her, left eyebrow arched. She suddenly understood that he had answered her question before she asked it. She blinked. Mind games!

Wishful thinking?! Hey!

"You killed them all single-handedly?"

"Both hands, little hummingbird. Never try stunts in a life-and-death situation. Oh, and your green bug helped."

"But how did you do it?" she asked, incredulous.

"You who pass out at the sight of blood," he warned her, "do you really want to hear it?"

She nodded.

"One by one," he said, "quietly, from behind." He squeezed his eyes shut for a second. The worst one of the nightmares he was waiting for tonight was the one in which his body went around breaking the necks of all his friends and shipmates and his mind looked on helplessly, unable to bring the demon under control. Worse than all the ghosts of all the guys he'd had to terminate today. "I'm a coward, sweetheart," he added, getting up. "Come, Paean. I need some fresh air. Let's get on deck and watch those men at work. And one boy."

They watched the men move the cargo from the Rebel Schooner onto the Solar Wind under the pre-dawn stars. The wind was still quite fresh, the sea quite high after the storm. Federi took out Ronan's pennywhistle and blew a wistful Romanian tune. Paean picked up the tune after two repeats and started humming a second voice, so softly she was almost keeping it to herself.

Memory gallery, thought Federi. This was one of life's undeserved treasures. Life itself was undeserved, in his case. He ought to have died years upon years ago, back in Romania. What he had turned into in his struggle to survive could hardly be called human. The sweeter this jewel of a moment, with his homesick tune elaborated on in pristine harmonies by this little songbird, this precious little redhead...

Minutes later both her brothers were there, instruments and all, turning the magical bubble into a Donegal Ceilidh.

"I think we declare Federi an honorary Donegal," suggested Shawn. His sibs agreed, delighted.

Federi smiled sadly. Another undeserved treasure.

Darling Katya...

Your brother is in trouble. You know I've got this streak. It comes out every time I have to pull a stunt like today. And you know whose bloodlines those are! Been my survival for many years. Now suddenly I wish it weren't there!

Didn't worry the little pirate though. Federi goes and kills a whole ship full of people, and the next thing these Donegals declare me an honorary brother of theirs! Have they no concept?

In which way are killings okay but stealing is not? How on Earth does the little alien's mind work? And drinking! Hells, one shouldn't touch alcohol! Quite glad for Wolf that he was out cold that night, he wouldn't have heard the end of it! She probably chewed him out while Federi wasn't there to protect him, the little terror! Doesn't she get it? Men drink! Pirates steal! And her Federi is a murderer.

Must say, being adopted by the Donegals works better than that St John's Wort!

Katya, my values used to be clear-cut. Federi used to have no conscience. And only one drive: Revenge. Now I'm trying to be honourable! When did this happen, that people started liking me? And now that they do, I can suddenly see what I am: A coward full of excuses. What's there to like?

All this deep stuff! Wish it would just let me go! Not cut out for philosophy. Driving me nuts.

Kathal – and that's another good question! Well, kathal, my sister

Your **Federi**

Hey, hey! Brand new diary!

Ailyss suggested I keep one. Got me the book in Atuona. And the pen too! Maybe she thinks I'll talk less if I write more…

Aargh, land madness! I'm only so glad we're back at sea. We've all had a bash at it! Wolf got himself shot. Ro has gone morose, wonder what's eating him. Rushka has gone weird, opens her long hair everywhere now, good luck to her with all the tangles. Shawney running away like that, and stealing that gadget and dumping Federi and Marsden so deep in trouble they could have died. And myself – boy, all I can say is I'm glad we're back at sea, much more of that land and I'd have gone crazy. Back here on the deep blue, thank goodness we're all just normal crewmembers again, shipmates, team mates, friends… it was getting too awkward for words! Loaded, I'll tell you!

Wolf is over the worst. Sheesh, that could have gone wrong. But Federi is right, Doc Judith knows what she's doing, and Federi has promised me to help me check on Wolf around every corner. Wolf is a nice guy after all, I knew it. But not Rhine Gold! Hell, that Reinhold is a rat! He was in the same pub as Wolf, and he told me all about it, someone called Federi some ugly stuff and Rhine Gold feels it's actually deserved! So he sat there looking on while Wolf stood up and defended Federi's reputation! And now he's on his high horse calling Wolf a hot-tempered lout and being smug-faced about being so sensible! Well, I hope Federi lets him peel potatoes until they come out of his ears! (Or anagram of same.)

Cut Ronan's hair today, Shawn wants his long like most of the crew. I wanted to cut my own a bit too, it gets tangled in the wind now, and there's Federi suddenly and borrows the scissors and forgets to return them! Tzigan trick! When I demanded them back, he told me very seriously that there's a moratorium on women with short hair on this ship! Ordered me as my superior to leave my hair alone and let it grow! Cor! But an order is an order. Didn't know there's a sort-of reverse, anti-military dress code going on the Solar Wind! Hey, the only ones who have short hair are actually the Captain, Marsden and Ronan! I think all the others are competing with Rushka. Wonder if Federi's forced Rushka to grow her hair too! Wonder if it's a Rom thing... Going to grill Federi a bit about the Tzigany. Want to know more; not going to step into that particular hole again! Hurting him is like... torturing a wild animal. Totally unfair.

Noticed something about Federi. When he doesn't know what to say to you, he'll make you coffee. So to get him to make coffee, you go into the galley and start a conversation and let it dry up. Shawn & I will test it again tomorrow morning.

Kathal.
Paean D.

24

Rodriguez

The Solar Wind ploughed onward through the blue Pacific, towards Hawaii. Paean stood on the raised jibs deck, leaning on the rail by the bowsprit, at the figurehead. She had seen it now, from the motorboat, in Atuona: There were indeed two electronic eyes mounted into the Mermaid's face. Black eyes. And they were capable of moving, changing their angle. She had not imagined it! And it was a mermaid. Carved by Federi. Intentionally vague. You could only see it from a certain angle. He had explained to her that he didn't enjoy carving compounding so much. It wasn't alive in the same way that wood was.

She peered at the horizon behind them to starboard, in the southeast, just where the end-of-afternoon fog started. At the faint light of that other ship. That ship that had been visible now several nights in a row.

Ailyss was on her stomach, on her bunk, reading, her left foot up in the air. These novels Paean had selected for Wolf were not bad at all; some space action thrillers, one murder mystery, one historical adventure... well, in a way they were all historical, being novels of course.

She became aware of being watched. She lifted her head, glanced at the door...

"Oh," she said.

"Ailyss," Federi greeted her, entering the cabin, pulling the second bunk down out of the wall and sitting down on it cross-legged. He folded his hands and regarded her.

The brunette stared at him. What did he want?

"You've visited Wolf in the infirmary various times," Federi came to the point.

"Yes," said Ailyss.

"Why?"

"He's my colleague," said Ailyss.

"In that case, why do you feed him drugs?"

"*What?!*"

"We have video footage," said Federi, "the night before Marsden and I got captured, you fed Wolf drugs."

Ailyss frowned. "Federi, nothing personal, but have you been drinking?"

"That same night," continued Federi, "I brought him his supper. He was so spaced out, he could hardly eat. He was only halfway coherent. And the next day he got really, really sick. What does that tell me?"

"That he had jolly wound sepsis?" shot Ailyss. "Yes, I remember now! Hells! I gave him a codeine, he was in pain! And his medical team had just simply abandoned him!"

"Let me see," demanded Federi.

Ailyss got off her bunk with a sigh. She opened the top drawer of her chest and reached inside, and pulled out a small bag of sugar-coated blue-green tablets. Federi reached for them.

"Whoa," said Ailyss with a smile. "Who says *you're* not an addict?"

Federi snatched her hand, bag and all, and held it in a firm clasp, holding her glare captive too. They sized each other up for several endless seconds. Then suddenly Ailyss yielded.

"Go on, have a look," she said, handing over the Spiffy bag.

Federi tipped several of the small pills into his palm. He examined them, found the minute bar code imprinted in black on each. He nodded and tipped them back into their bag.

"For headaches, I presume?"

"Dysmenorrhoea," said Ailyss unflinchingly. If the damned character was nosy enough to want to see her painkillers, he might as well know what they were for – and knock himself out on that knowledge.

"Bit potent for that, *nu?*" probed Federi.

"Hah! What do you know?" shot Ailyss, annoyed. "When last have *you* had your period?"

Federi handed them back. "I'm sorry," he said.

"Why am I under suspicion, if I may ask?" pushed Ailyss, surprised at his apology.

"*Everyone's* under suspicion," said the Romany darkly.

305

"Yes, but yet you did not go to Paean and ask her to prove that those horrible aspirin powders she feeds him are not in actuality purified cocaine," she retorted.

"How would you know that I didn't? Maybe I did," said Federi, his left eyebrow arched. Codeine was an opiate! It certainly explained why Wolf had been dazed that night! But the painkillers were legitimate, and they did indeed look exactly like what she had given Wolf.

"You didn't ask her," smiled Ailyss. "And you didn't examine Rhine Gold either, after that pub brawl, for possible connections to the Rebellion."

"You're clued in," commented Federi.

"I'm just not completely blind, deaf and dumb," shot Ailyss.

Federi got up and stretched, from the tip of his sun-browned fingers to his white deck-sneakers. Ailyss summed him up. His sharp-cut features were undecipherable, laugh-lines not quite managing to balance out the warning in his black eyes. Shifty eyes, she thought. His purple decorated headscarf and Eastern European style waistcoat with the beads and embroidery, the ancient jeans and the flared sleeves of his shirt said gypsy, entertainer, harmless. His empty hands, stretching their artistic knuckles to the sky, said unarmed, peaceful. The gaudy getup didn't fool her, never had. The man was extremely dangerous.

She had her impression confirmed the next second. Federi smiled, that special glinty smile meant to convey a threat. Shark-tooth.

"Neither," he said softly, "am I. Ailyss, you seem to have a soft spot for Paean. Hang onto that. She's a good kid. It might become your lifeline, one day!"

Ailyss stared speechlessly at him as he left the cabin, her heart beating in her throat. She tried to return to the novel and found she couldn't. Her entire body was shaking.

Paean turned. Here came the Sunshine Gypsy!

"Hey, little mockingbird." Federi joined her at the rail. "Happy?"

"Very," she smiled.

"Still want to jump ship at Hawaii?"

"No! Huh? Why?" Hawaii. She had forgotten about their plan to get off there! She'd have to call a sibs meeting and discuss it. For her, it didn't seem like a good option anymore.

She gestured at the light point on the south-eastern horizon. "What's that ship there?"

"Ha," said Federi. "Cuban Coastal Guard!"

"Ah," said Paean, "bounty hunters again? *Cuban Coastal* guard?!"

"Yup," grinned the gypsy. "Thought that would tickle you!"

"Are you saying they followed us all the way from *Cuba* ?"

"That's what I'm saying," smiled Federi.

"We shouldn't run then," said Paean. "We should wait for them and board them and loot them!"

Federi laughed. "Little pirate!"

"Why? They want to turn us over to the Unicate! For cash! Who's the pirate in that?"

"We are," said Federi. "We still are. They are the system guys. We're the lawbreakers. Has nothing to do with who kills more people."

There had to be something wrong with that!

"You were going to explain about Marsden's missing puzzle piece," said Paean.

"I was?"

"You said you'd explain later."

"I did."

"Well, now's later!"

"I meant the other later," grinned Federi. "Later, later."

"You pirate!"

"Thank you."

"You're not going to, are you."

Federi shook his head. Thieves' honour!

"I will too, little luv," he said. "But at this point it's still classified, unfortunately."

"So then why did you tell me in the first place?"

"Sweet thing, I had to ask you to tell them that so they'd take you seriously about the rest! There was no time to explain. Captain already knew. Trust me, he figured it out the moment he decrypted that stuff."

Paean said nothing and listened to the snatches of music that carried down from the Crow's Nest. Good enough to bear a crucial message, good enough to patch people, and to be solid crew on the pirate ship – but not good enough to be let in on what Captain planned for all of them for their future!

Federi frowned too as he peered at that Cuban. They were decrypting the information, this he knew – but what it was, that was another story! They didn't exactly inform him! *That* classified. Ha! Good enough to get the darned information to them… He grinned.

Shawn was trying Irish settings for Romanian tunes on his ocarina. Paean grimaced. He ought to try some Scandinavian tunes, damn him! Why not some Aleutian ones?

"He's good," said Federi appreciatively.

"I know," replied Paean. "Just too glad to be back at sea."

"You or he?" probed Federi.

"Both of us," said Paean with feeling. "Say, what about Rushka?"

"What about Rushka?"

"Does she know Captain's plans?"

"You bet. Guess what: She's his daughter."

"And you're in on his plans," said Paean.

His *plans*. Yes. "I'm an officer," said Federi. Said like that, it sounded strange. He frowned and repeated it to himself a few times, in his mind. Almost like saying he was *poliția!*

"And Ronan knows, too!"

"Yup," said Federi. He wasn't prepared for this onslaught.

"He's not an officer," said Paean.

"Nope," replied Federi, eyes round and innocent.

"So when will you tell me?"

Federi smiled, reached out and ruffled her hair. "Where's your scarf?"

"When will you tell me?"

"When you've learnt to keep a confidence, little sunbird."

That stung! Federi watched her face and wished he could take back his words. He saw Ronan making his way towards them.

"Come join me later in the galley, little luv?" he asked.

"Kay," said Paean listlessly. It was probably an order anyway!

"Got to go." Federi clasped her wrist for a second.

"*Kathal*, Federi," she said as he moved off. She saw him hesitate for a second before he carried on.

"Hey, sis!"

"Hey, Ro."

"What's with the gypsy?" asked Ronan.

"Nothing, why?" Paean pulled her fluorescent green scarf out of her pocket and tied it around her head. Was high time anyway; the wind was freshening up. Her curls were getting out of hand.

Rushka appeared on Paean's other side. The Irish girl braced herself for the Captain's order she was about to receive. Instead Rushka pulled her cap off her head and shook her glorious hair back. She leaned on the rail and stared out at the horizon.

Federi glanced back at the small group of teens as he climbed up into the rigging. With his binoculars he peered at the solitary light on the horizon, following the Solar Wind. Its satellite signal showed in translucent white letters in the lens, picked up by the binoculars' electronics. Id CSUCG8997390221 – CS Silver Bullet. Federi had to smile. Hunting pirates or hunting werewolves?

One solitary coastal guard. No threat. The sense of foreboding hit him hard, a faceful of undiluted black doom. Blast, that couldn't be! The last time he'd had such a vile feeling had been before Lake Gatun. A feeling of can't-escape; another net closing on the Solar Wind.

He grimaced. Perhaps he ought to include more fresh greens in the menu. His guts should feel better then.

All good and well though, making light of these feelings – they had all made light of their fears of the Unicate, back in Romania. Been happy Tzigany instead of morose gloom-diggers. Until the day the Unicate was suddenly there, with their dogs…

The Captain and Marsden were also watching the teens; gazing out from the bridge at the three.

"Amazing," said Marsden. "What a beauty Rushka has become! Can you believe she's already grown up?"

"She's not," growled Lascek. "She's just tall for her age."

Marsden smiled. That hardly applied at age nineteen!

"And she's not supposed to fraternize with the new crew," added Lascek sourly.

"But Radomir, surely you can't forbid her to –"

309

"I can forbid whoever whatever on my ship," retorted the Captain.

"I could think of a worse match than Ronan Donegal," remarked Marsden.

"Whom?"

"Just about everyone on the Solar Wind," laughed Marsden. "Ronan is not a pirate!"

"You're right," said the Captain thoughtfully. "But *match* ? She's hopelessly to young for us to be thinking in those lines!"

"Uh-huh," smiled Marsden. "So what are we going to do with our little tag?"

"That Salvatore Rodriguez?" Lascek lightened up. "Wonder what he's trying!"

"Waiting to corner us in a dark and lonely alley on the Pacific," said Marsden. "Overwhelm us with his crew of five."

Lascek laughed. "I missed you on the bridge these past few days, old friend!" He hit a button on the console. "Shawn Donegal! Come to the bridge!"

A few seconds later the twelve-year-old stood on the bridge.

"That ship you've been tracking," said Lascek.

"She's still following us, Captain," said Shawn breathlessly.

"I know. What would you suggest we do with her?"

"Captain, Paean feels we should turn around and board and loot her."

"Ha," said Lascek. "Plunder, hack, slash and mutilate?"

"I don't know," said Shawn. "Maybe, put them all to sleep with the little green bug in the water tank."

"You told her who they are?" asked Lascek.

"No, Captain, but she seems to think that's what ships are for! Captain, their captain will turn us in at Hawaii!"

"Hmm. You've got a point, they will alert the Unicate," said Lascek. "But I don't agree that we have to be pirates about this. What does Shawn suggest?"

"Invite them for a cup of tea," grinned Shawn. "Worked for Gomez!"

"Sounds like a good idea," said Lascek. "Do we have the time, Jon?"

"I think we can spare an hour or two," smiled the First Mate.

Radomir Lascek punched a sequence into the console and relayed an order to Dr Jake. The engines stalled and the sails furled. The Solar Wind

310

lay waiting.

The gypsy beckoned to Paean from the Crow's Nest. Obediently she tied on a lifeline and climbed up, clenching her teeth. The sails of the Solar Wind were furled. She wondered how the sailors coped climbing up there when the sails were open. And it stayed scary.

Oh well! In for a penny…

"Look," said Federi when she stood in the Crow's Nest next to him. He gestured at the sky and sea as though he owned them. Paean grimaced. He could feel her stress; but she was mastering that fear of heights nicely. It was the third time she was up here. He was proud of her.

Of course he had an ulterior motive for calling her up here. It made him feel better. Her sunshine flooded out the horrible sense of doom. Like the sun that was drenching the ship and sails and sea and crew and everything in its golden-and-red beams.

"If you love treasure," she muttered, "this is like being inside a ruby."

"A garnet," he corrected with a smile. "Have a look down there!"

She glanced at the deck and giggled. To the left of the Mermaid's Head, Ronan. To the right, Rushka. Both studiously ignoring each other, with a Paean-shaped hole between them.

"Thought that would amuse you," grinned the gypsy. "That's dynamics. Watch those two the next few days!" He peered critically at her, then he reached out and removed that awful lime-green scarf from her head with a swift movement.

She flew around and stared at him, fuming. "Hey!"

"That's a horrible bandana, little luv!"

"*You* gave it to me!"

He grinned. Guilty as charged. He studied her intently. For a moment he thought he could see the masses of flaming hair billowing around her incensed face, the way it should have been. It was a trick of the light. The sun was catching the red in her short curls and lighting it up like fire. Memory gallery. He should capture it in a woodcarving.

And suddenly he had a vision of the red flames turning into splashes of blood, and her face a black hole. He caught his breath. What was this? How few days, or perhaps hours, did she have left to live? Did it tie in with that other awful hunch? He should keep her close. If she stuck with

311

Federi, he could protect her.

Those blue eyes were stretching in worry. Aw, it was no good that she should pick up on all that morose stuff. Federi grinned briefly and pulled out of his pocket, with the same prestidigitation as the first time, another scarf. A turquoise one. Much more her colour! He tied it into her hair.

"Stole it for you in Atuona," he said. "Wanted to get that colour in Plymouth, but they didn't have. They're too British, they just don't understand…"

Paean smiled uncertainly.

"Thanks, Federi. Actually you shouldn't steal stuff for me…"

"You don't want it?" he asked, shocked.

"No, I do, it's lovely… Federi, why do you?"

"Steal?" Aw hell, they had been through that! "Sorry, little bird. Ancient habit. Had to learn the streets, the hard way. You're right, girl, Federi should lay off the thieving, it's unnecessary now. Look!" He put his hand back on her shoulder and pointed. "There's that coastal guard now. Watch the sports!"

The Solar Wind was now in shouting distance from the Silver Bullet, a fast-moving Barracuda, solar-driven with back-up fuel-cell drives. The coastal guard ship veered towards them.

"This is Captain Rodriguez of the Silver Bullet," came the announcement over the ship intercom. "State your identity and purpose!"

"Captain Rodriguez, as you know I am Captain Lascek of the pirate vessel Solar Wind. You've been following me so long, I feel we are friends. I would like to invite you for a cup of coffee."

There was a shocked silence.

"I'll lace it with genuine 2015 Jamaican Rum," added Captain Lascek.

More muffled silence followed as a furious discussion broke out aboard the Silver Bullet, and someone kept their hand clapped over the microphone.

"The rum is the real thing, taken from a shipwreck only this week," advertised Lascek.

More furry silence. Then the voice of Captain Rodriguez.

"If this is a trap, Captain Lascek, you'll have to think of a better one!"

"This is no trap, Captain Rodriguez. You may even come armed if it gives you emotional security. I only want to have the opportunity to meet my honourable opponent."

More restrained sounds failed to come through clearly.

"There are scones too," added Lascek. "I have an excellent cook."

"I'll bring my First Mate," said Rodriguez.

"Feel free," said Lascek. "But I'm not trading."

"The man is dangerous," said Pedro Romero, the First Mate.

"The man is funny," said Little Cloud Navarro, the Hispanic ship engineer, pan-faced.

"The man," said the Captain, "is a pirate and not to be trusted. Still, what can happen? We go in fully armed." He engaged the intercom again.

"Captain Lascek, I'm coming in with three of my men. We are fully armed. One wrong move on your side –"

"I know, I know," sighed Captain Lascek. "And you'll give us a hangover until Monday and fry our electronic equipment. Point taken. We'll be good."

Captain Rodriguez and his First Mate, ship engineer and medic all came aboard. The only one left behind was the technician, who was rather grumpy about being left out.

"How many still on your ship?" asked Federi as the Cuban Coastal Guard climbed aboard. Paean was still inching her way down from the Crow's Nest, jaws clenched. Down was worse than up, but she had known that.

"One."

"Why not attach your ship, and then he can also join us and not miss out!"

Captain Rodriguez thought this was a good idea, so Rhine Gold, Ronan, Federi and Shawn quickly organized the mooring of the Silver Bullet to the Solar Wind.

It turned into quite a party. Out here on the open sea, who cared if the bounty hunter took a bit longer roping in the prey, and had some fun in the process? Who cared, for that matter, if they chose to party through the night, dancing to Rodriguez's Spanish guitar, accompanied by the Solar Wind's band, and emptying bottle after bottle of priceless 2015 Jamaican rum (and later, when nobody cared, bottle after bottle of real cheap 2116 Chilean Real Jamaican Hangover Rum)? Who cared if they stayed so late that eventually they slept right on the deck of the pirate vessel, under tropical stars, wherever they passed out?

Sherman Dougherty peered out from the bridge onto the deck, where Paean was playing one tireless jig after another at the Cubans.

"She's good," he commented.

"Better than many," agreed Jonathan Marsden next to him. "And so darned young."

Sherman glanced at the First Mate in surprise. There had been a very odd undertone in that remark!

"Jon, what do you mean?"

"We still don't know what the Unicate is hunting them for," Marsden pointed out. "We have this story of their mother being executed. But Sherman, seriously now. Even if that is true. You know the Unicate. If they have it in for people, do they let them get away?"

Sherman nodded thoughtfully. "What you're saying…"

"What I'm saying," completed Marsden, "is I'm not saying anything. You know, we're assuming that Ailyss is an agent, right?"

"Come now, Jon," said Sherman. "I think this is an established fact?"

"Because Federi dislikes her? What if she's a decoy?"

Sherman frowned.

"All I'm saying," said Jon Marsden, "is that it strikes me as odd that they got away. Unicate doesn't let people escape like that – especially three inexperienced youths! Right?"

"Right," echoed Sherman with a scowl.

"Unless it's for a purpose," added Jon Marsden.

Sherman whistled softly through his teeth.

Late that night Federi went around the deck tying lifelines on the passed-out Cubans. They had literally fallen asleep wherever they fell over from drinking. Jonathan Marsden wandered out onto the deck and peered up through the rigging at the star-strewn sky.

"Man, do I have square eyes!"

"Making progress?"

314

"Yup. Federi, that was a brilliant coup. Next meeting you'll be hearing all about it. Don't really want to discuss it in the open."

"Course not!" Classified, thought Federi.

Marsden smiled. "So your little green pirate has a new scarf?"

"Your eyes can't be all that square then, Jon, can they?" laughed Federi. "Cor! The poor girl! I couldn't do it to her any longer! Everyone teases her!"

"Only serves to bring out her own witty replies," said Jon with a smile. "And you've taught her the rigging!"

"Still think she's the agent?" asked Federi with a raised eyebrow.

"We shall see, my friend," replied Marsden.

Federi nodded. Jon would indeed see! "What are we going to do with all this dead meat if a squall comes up?"

"Stash them in the storage deck."

"Can't submerge then," said Federi.

"Couldn't submerge before the Solar Wind was submersible," said Marsden. "Come, Federi! She's weathered a lot of storms." He frowned at the gypsy. "Why, are you picking up a squall on its way?"

Federi shook his head, worried. "Jon, I can't say exactly what I'm picking up! Hells! Didn't see poor Wolf's injury coming either. And that proved life-threatening! And back there in Atuona? Walked right into their trap! Can you buy that? Here Federi's supposed to keep the Solar Wind safe, and my radar's acting like a rank beginner! Can't understand what's going on."

"Non-specific feeling of doom?" asked Jon Marsden.

"More or less."

"Interspersed with completely unrelated concerns about little green pirates?"

Federi laughed brightly. "Honestly, Jon! Should I steal you a green scarf too?"

"So we can share a telepathic connection too? What's on that scarf?"

"You know," said Federi, "that telepathic contact we had. Simple. Paean was stretched; she feared for our lives; she reached out. Might have reached to you first in fact, except that you keep your radar switched off!"

"Federi, not everyone has a gypsy radar!"

"Correction, Jon. Everyone has one! Some dare to use it!"

315

"How can you say that?"

"Ever watched animals communicate?"

"Oh," said Marsden. "Like cats? Loudly caterwauling all night through?"

Federi laughed brightly. "What's with you, Jon? Is it the prospect of Prime Oil in a few more days?"

"Could be that," grinned Marsden. "Could be that!"

"I'll stay up," said Federi. "Not taking the risk of these drunken louts here drowning by accident."

"Call me when you need me to take over," said Marsden. "I don't mind the graveyard shift. Going to get some shut-eye now."

"Thanks, old bud." Federi resolved that his friend would get a complete night's sleep. Marsden was not yet recovered from being bled within an inch of his life. And Federi was not yet ready to trust his cabin to keep the ghosts out. Maybe he should make a few more totems to hang into the dream-catcher. And hang up a few more chimes to invite more good spirits. Aargh! Rampant superstition all of it, anna bottle! He sighed. Even deliberately being a pirate didn't help. Ghosts were in your head. There was no keeping them out, annabottle.

Ailyss snuck into the infirmary. Wolf lowered the book he was reading. She nodded at him. He nodded back, a question in his eyes.

"Mind if I sit here a bit and read?" asked Ailyss.

"Sure," said Wolf, watching her as she settled on the bunk Marsden had only vacated today, pulling her legs in under her. She leaned back against the wall and lifted her novel.

Wolf continued to watch her for a little while, then returned to his own book. It was a book on herb lore. You got to the point where you couldn't stomach another cliché from the bygone century, and then it was time to read something more substantial. Except that he knew all his own manuals off by heart, so asking Paean once again had resulted in something, if not particularly interesting, then at least off-the-wall. He suspected she didn't own much beyond this and her music, which he honestly didn't know how to read.

Ailyss waited until the engineer was engrossed in his reading again before her glance darted to all the electronic equipment. Somewhere in there, a camera was hidden. Hell's bells, but this bunch of pirates was paranoid! And that Federi – while she had known that the clown getup was a façade hiding a dangerous criminal, she hadn't actually realized how closely he was watching her!

Well, *his* secret was out of the bag, she thought. Nobody slaughtered their way through the entire crew of a ship without having some very special attributes!

She felt safer here, in the company of her colleague. Wolf was enough of a friend to Federi to take a bullet in his kneecap for him. She doubted the gypsy would slit her throat in front of the nuclear engineer! She'd be staying in plain sight a lot for now. If she always stayed somewhere in the picture, they'd get used to her presence.

Federi was doing his late-night round of the ship. Only the senior crew was actually aware of these little routines. He peered into the infirmary.

Wolf lowered his book.

"Hello, Federi!"

"Hey, Wolf," replied the Romany, indicating Ailyss. "Company?"

"Sort-of," grinned Wolf. The Irish brunette had fallen asleep over her book, her black hair draped over the pea-green cover of the bunk. Federi studied her for a moment. Her closed eyes were sunken and moving about, in dream sleep. She looked haunted. He knew that he had scared her badly today. He had done it on purpose.

Marsden was wrong. The very fact that Ailyss had sought refuge here in Sick Bay, where her strong, injured colleague could protect her…

There were goose bumps on her pale, skinny calves where they stuck out of her black ski-pants.

"Poor thing," said Federi and shook his head. He opened the top compartment of the infirmary's narrow built-in cupboard behind the door and pulled out a spare blanket, spreading it over her. He turned back to Wolf. The young man was following his movements.

"Why did you do that for her?" asked Wolf quizzically. "You don't like her!"

"Doesn't mean she must catch a cold," said Federi logically. "Keep her safe in here, see, Wolf? Maybe…" He trailed off, shaking his head again. It was always a tough one, waiting for a cookie to crumble. Maybe it wouldn't crumble, this time. Maybe there was no cookie. Maybe they *were* wrong.

Maybe the moon was a silver dollar.

25
Flamenco

Dawn was seeping through the two large portholes of the galley. Paean hung in the doorway.

"Hey, Federi!"

"Hey, little sunbird," smiled the gypsy.

Paean watched him prepare breakfast. He wandered over to the coffee machine and reached for the coffee grounds. He paused, shot her a glance, grinned.

"Why don't you make your own coffee," he laughed. "Minx!"

Paean stood rooted to her spot, grinning too. He had nailed her!

Nevertheless he made her a mug of fresh, steaming coffee and handed it to her, smiling and shaking his head.

" 's a gesture of appreciation, you know," he informed her.

"How did you know?" She smiled and sipped her coffee. Lots of milk, the way she liked it. He preheated the milk for her. She never managed to make her own coffee that nice. "Actually, Federi, there's something I've been wanting to ask you…"

Just then Jon Marsden peered into the galley. "Paean? Wolf is calling you."

Paean put her coffee down and ran. Federi gazed after her. Poor girl!

"She's quick to jump when Wolf calls," remarked Marsden, watching her disappear down the passage.

"She knows what happens if she doesn't," said Federi. He peered sharply at his friend. What precisely had gone down that Jon suspected Paean like that? And that he had acquitted Ailyss of being a secret agent for the Unicate?

Shortly after, Paean wrapped up her daily inspection of Wolf's wounds. They were healing; mostly the man needed a bath. He was right.

You couldn't keep a good pirate down. And hope to breathe in his vicinity.

She glanced at him and smiled.

"Your friends have been scarce, *nu?*" she prodded.

"Except Paean," replied the young engineer with a bearded smile. "Talks my ears off my head! And Ailyss checks in. And Federi. But Rhine Gold and Ronan – not really."

"S'pose they're working really hard," said Paean thoughtfully. "I love the way the men get to do the kitchen work on this ship! Had to wrestle my brothers down and force them to help, back in Molly Street!"

Wolf grinned at this concept. "Different rules apply. Here, it's the directionless and the under-qualified who get to do the menial tasks."

The directionless and the under-qualified -?! That stung!

"You're talking about my little brother, and Federi," said Paean acidly. "And I do my fair bit of scrubbing decks, too! Under-qualified! I wonder if *you'd* have got right what Federi did there on that Rebel ship."

Wolf stared at her. What? Hundred percent reversed tack?

"Finishing off the entire crew single-handedly," added Paean through her teeth. "Wolf, you've got backbone standing up for your friend. But *that* is style!"

"Ah," Wolf smiled hopelessly, flopping back onto his pillow. "Hero craft! Can't compete with that, nope!"

Radomir Lascek was pacing, watching the deck from the bridge. Shawn and Federi were passing out plates with hangover breakfast to the hung-over Coastal Guard of Cuba.

It had been fun last night, with the Donegals keeping the Ceilidh going so loudly that the Cubans had been fully occupied. It had given him and Jon Marsden time to dig deeper into that load of information on the two capsules. Right under the Unicate's nose; the way he loved best!

Sometimes he wondered if the Solar Wind had a guardian angel that led the diverse crew members in the right direction, to play things like the two halves of the Unicate plans into his hands. If he started believing in that, he'd also have to accept that it came with a responsibility attached – the duty to change the course of events and prevent the Unicate from carrying out what they were intending.

But today now – that posed a problem. How were they going to keep decrypting? He had to find a way either to throw Rodriguez back off the ship, or to keep him occupied. Throwing him out might just cancel what they had achieved yesterday. But how to keep him off the bridge?

A soft knock on the door interrupted his calculations. Paean Donegal appeared on the bridge, wearing a scarf of a different colour. Remotely better than the previous one. She teamed the loud turquoise tastefully with a cheap white T-shirt and her daily jeans. It would be alright, though Lascek, recovering from his fright. The girl did have colour sense of sorts. The sailors wouldn't be incapacitated by migraines.

"Captain, I only want to ask for clearance – is it okay if I ask Captain Rodriguez to teach Wolf flamenco?"

Radomir Lascek smiled broadly. Yes, he'd have to accept the responsibility. There were definitely paranormal forces involved in the events on his ship!

A short while later, the captain from the Cuban Coastal Guard, Salvatore Rodriguez, stood in the infirmary's doorway with his guitar. Wolf raised a hand in greeting.

"Er…" What did one say to a visiting captain with a Spanish guitar, anyway?

"What happened to your knee, *hombre?*" asked Rodriguez, settling himself on the second infirmary bunk and tuning up. He still stank of drinking party; alcohol and cigars. Wolf saw how Paean melted towards the door. He grinned at her. 'Thanks!' he mouthed at her before she disappeared from the doorway. She winked and gave him a thumbs-up.

"Pistol shot," Wolf replied to Rodriguez's question.

"*Carramba!* Pistol shot!"

"Yes, sir."

"And you got that wound -?"

"Pub brawl, sir."

The Cuban was temporarily speechless. Wolf glanced at his guitar.

"Oh. Well, your girlfriend tells me you would like to learn some Spanish Guitar?"

"Please, sir. I'd love to." Girlfriend, thought Wolf with an ironic little smile.

"Muy bien!" The hung-over Coastal Guard Captain sat down and started demonstrating flamenco for the wounded pirate.

"Federi?"

The Romany glanced up from his woodcarving. It was cooler here in the jib stowage. The morning was sweltering. A matter of time...

The redhead found herself a spot on the floor between the boxes. She sat down cross-legged, close to him, observing him.

"You were going to ask me something, earlier," prompted Federi.

"Yes. Why are there two such distinct groups on the Solar Wind? Half of the crew is young and newly hired and the others are old salts."

The gypsy laughed. "So now you're calling Federi old?"

"Not you!" she exclaimed. "You're young! You're almost one of the young group! Just wish you were still a wee bit younger, because –" There she got stuck and gazed at him, confused.

That eyebrow arched. "So that I didn't have to wish so hard that you were a bit older?"

She stared at him with wild eyes.

"Meet me halfways," suggested Federi. "You speed up and I slow down. When we're both twenty..." He grinned broadly and touched her hand. "Just playing with your mind, *dulciuri!* What do you think of this?"

She looked closely at the string puppet he was carving. "That's Shawn!"

Federi dug in his pocket and pulled out another. Paean laughed.

"The Captain! Federi, are you making a puppet theatre out of our crew?"

"Got bored with carving ship scenes. Needed a new challenge."

Paean hesitated, puzzled. "Evading my question!" she shot.

"Right." He sighed. "Not a nice story. Really want to hear it?"

Paean nodded.

"This is classified," said Federi, leaning back against the crate and staring out over the ocean to port. Bummer, he was going to spill confidential stuff to her. He shook his head and sighed again.

"Okay," said Paean. "It's okay. I won't dig. Don't want you getting trouble, Federi."

Nimic! It was enough. He *was* going to tell her! "Little luv," said Federi, meeting Paean's eyes. "The Solar Wind's entangled in a huge political plot. We were doing our own thing, keeping out of people's faces and surviving, and then Captain stumbled across something, and suddenly here we're in the middle of it all. Unicate's been hunting for us since. Two years ago they led the Solar Wind into a trap. Tried to murder us all. We fought our way out of it. Cost us dearly. Unicate fights dirty. They sniped a few of us right off our ship as we were negotiating her out of the English Channel. You think Wolf's injury is bad. You haven't yet seen a friend next to you be shot down and go overboard and you can't do a thing... They hid an assassin aboard who went around slitting throats until Federi got her – cor! I hate killing girls!" He glanced down at his hands. He'd have to do it again, in the near future. He knew. "I had to, little luv! She managed to put poison in our drinking water and two good friends died horribly and another just barely made it. Jon Marsden."

She was staring at him with her worried blue eyes. "Poor Mr Marsden," she said.

"They fired at the Solar Wind and damaged her. Very nearly sank her." Federi patted the deck. "We patched like crazy, but couldn't get the leaks fixed. Crossed the whole Atlantic like that! Landed at Hamilton so deep in water, she was nearly a mermaid castle. Arrived there on wind power alone, everything had cut out from the water. Tensioning those lines without the hydraulics – that's a lot, promise you! Had the sails half furled, wouldn't have managed otherwise. We'd stopped bailing. Doesn't help on a ship this size! Sherman was steering. Federi and Rushka were controlling the sails manually. What a team! And Dr Jake and Captain and Wolf –"

He noted her surprised stare and smiled. "Yes, the furry beast was already aboard, little luv. Was his first brush with what it means to work for Radomir Lascek. They were down there in diving suits, trying to patch still. Sweetness, you have no idea!" Federi shook his head with a cynical smile. "And Jono, lying half dead on the floor on the bridge, with Doc trying to revive him. Because the bridge and the outer deck was all that wasn't yet flooded. That was all who were left. We lost three quarters of our crew that time." He gazed moodily at her freckles, recalling the friends he had lost. "Little hummingbird, you should jump ship as soon as

323

you can."

"Why?"

That surprise was so genuine! " 's a bad deal, the Solar Wind. You end up seeing your friends die. You know, when you've sailed around the world with some people for a few years, they become your family."

"I know, Federi," said Paean. "Doesn't take years."

"So that's the story," said Federi. "After that we floated around the Pacific for a while building contacts and doing target practice on terrorist vessels. We needed a few more crew members, so we hired you lot when we found you."

"Only two years later?" asked Paean.

" 's not so easy, screening new crew," said Federi. "Can't tell you how long it took Captain to want to risk hiring anybody. After that poison episode. And then we had to throw spies off the Solar Wind every time. We got one aboard right now. Least she's not hurting anyone!"

"Are you sure she's not just an unhappy young woman with baggage?" asked Paean, glancing at where Ailyss was standing at the rail, reading a novel. "I catch her sometimes, staring out at the sea and looking terribly sad."

"We shall see," said Federi with a sigh. He picked himself up from the deck. "Come on, little mockingbird. Help me get more food stuffed into that crew of ours." He gave her a hand up.

"Looks like you were right," Marsden said casually from the doorway. The gypsy looked up from the fish he was gutting for lunch. He was alone in the galley. Doc had called Paean away.

"My friend, I'm always right. What about, this time, specifically?"

"Look outside."

Federi glanced through the porthole.

Oh yes, he was aware of the darkening outside, the erratic gusts blowing in. He'd have to close the portholes soon, though he himself loved the wind. But you never knew when Captain decided to submerge. And while he enjoyed diving…

Shawn had quizzed him about those portholes. Why they were manual in this day and age. Well, Captain used technology but that didn't mean he was in love with it! And every electronic system occasionally had a glitch; an open porthole under water meant the end of the Solar Wind. Some things should certainly *not* be left to electronics! But an electronic checking system was in place, as a back-up.

"It's a big one," Marsden added. "Captain is ordering all the crew on deck, so we can fly her."

"Ha," said Federi. "Time for lunch first?"

"No, sorry."

With a sigh, Federi got up, wrapped the fish in silver paper and stuck it in one of the drawers in the freezer. He washed his hands and moved aimlessly over to the coffee machine.

"Not for me, thanks," Marsden forestalled him. Federi drew up his eyebrows, puzzled.

"Right!" He closed and bolted both portholes. "Captain wants us on deck. Jon, I hope *you're* not part of the flying team today?"

"No, he's forbidden me," replied the First Mate with a grin. "Bummer. Feels stupid, being *weak!* I was really looking forward to teaching Donegal and Schatz the ropes."

"Going to miss your sour expressions when I sing," Federi grinned back.

"I'll be there," replied Marsden. "Only in a supervisory capacity."

"Oh, good!"

Drunk coastal guards were tottering across the deck as the ship rolled. Federi cursed quietly. He shouldn't have dosed them with more rum, earlier. Marsden curtly ordered the Cubans below deck, and the two men worked together to set up handhold lines and tense them, and release the staysail so it could furl away. The sails flapped loudly in the turbulences like oversized albatross wings. Federi peered up into them and back down to where the Silver Bullet was moored.

"That's a bad idea," he said, pointing.

"Captain's already thought of it," Marsden pacified. "See there."

Old Sherman and Paean were boarding the Silver Bullet. Federi frowned. It was wrong! Paean was supposed to keep close, so he could protect her...

"Why them?"

"Who else?" asked Marsden, putting on a fluorescent survival rainskin.

"Captain decided that I'm not healed enough. If I were, I'd be flying instead. Sherman has more years of bridge experience than the rest of us put together!"

"There's that," said Federi. Still it struck him as a bad idea. You ignored a hunch at your peril! "Sherman was born with the millennium," he said moodily. "If something happens to him, medically?"

"See Paean?" asked Marsden.

It didn't help. A vision of her red hair turned to blood...

"There's of course one thing," said Marsden thoughtfully. "If she's the agent, I only hope Sherman will cope. Can't say I feel too easy about this."

Federi scowled. Aw Jon, he thought angrily, shut up for once!

Paean and Old Sherman climbed over onto the Silver Bullet, and Rhine Gold cast off the heavy lines mooring them to the Solar Wind's cleats, and released and stowed the buffers. Immediately the Silver Bullet was swept to one side by the wash of the Solar Wind, and left astern. The sea was choppy. White crests rode the waves, which had turned grey-green with the clouds piling up.

Sherman and Paean looked around on the vessel. It wasn't a very large ship. Thirty-footer, designed as though it had been adapted from a fishing boat. The insides were frugal, everything in Unicate-grey. Compounding came in any colour one wanted it to; a very versatile material. Of all those potential colours, the Unicate found steel-grey the most appropriate for their military! Probably to boost their morale, thought Paean. She couldn't imagine why Ronan had ever considered the navy for a career!

At least the Silver Bullet was clean and not leaky. Well maintained, as a Unicate ship should be. Paean assumed that Rodriguez made more liberal use of the shower on his own ship than on the Solar Wind.

"Funny name, actually, the Silver Bullet," she said.

"Och, aye," agreed Sherman. "Shows you it wasn't Rodriguez who named her but the Unicate shipyard. He'd have picked something Spanish, now wouldn't he? But coastal guards tend to get names like that. The Executioner. The Sword of Justice. Excalibur. The Long Arm."

Paean laughed. "The Long-finger?"

They returned to the bridge. Sherman's hands played over the console.

"Easy," he stated. And then he turned and nailed the redhead with a sharp glare. "Paean Donegal, now you tell me where you got your subversive education."

She blinked. What had she done to upset her old countryman?

"Mrs Flanagan," she said. "You'd love her, Sherman. Next time we're in Dublin I'll introduce you."

Shawn climbed into the Crow's Nest.

"Hey, Federi!" he called from up there, activating his wrist-com. "See there! That's so weird!"

Federi glanced up, and over to where the youngest Donegal was pointing. Something was wrong with the shape and colour of the sea. He climbed up into the rigging and was only halfway when the Solar Wind lifted onto a crest and he got a clear view. Waves breaking in the middle of the ocean! Ay!! There was a huge submerged reef, and they were heading towards it!

"Captain!" Federi hooked his elbow around one of the stays and activated his wrist-com. "Captain! There's a reef! Veer to starboard! Repeat, veer to starboard! There's a reef off port, we're driving straight at it!"

He heard the Captain swear juicily in Hungarian. The Solar Wind turned, heeling heavily to starboard before the sails sheeted out to accommodate the move from close-hauled to a reach. The mast described an arc, and Shawn slipped. He caught onto the rim of the Crow's Nest. Federi moved up the rest of the rigging with the lightning-fast reflex of a wall-lizard. He grabbed onto the boy and the Crow's Nest and levered himself into the structure, pulling Shawn down to the floor of the box.

"Lifeline!" he snapped. "Donegal, never ever climb up here without a lifeline!"

Shawn looked rattled for once.

"Yes, Federi. Sorry."

"*Never* forget it again! Understood? Or I'll forbid you to come up here!"

Shawn nodded, contrite. Federi grabbed one of the several lifelines that were installed permanently up here, and clipped it around Shawn's middle. "Life vest," he snapped, and pulled a thin orange piece of cloth out of one of his pockets. He handed it to Shawn, who opened it and looked at it.

"Put it on!"

Shawn pulled the filmy vestment over his head and stuck his arms into the sleeves. It covered him like a rain skin, with a hood over his head and everything. It was too big. "Life vest?" he asked, puzzled, stuffing it in past the lifeline around his middle, so he could pull it down to its full length. It came down to his knees, with a stretch. This was a dress!

"Life vest," insisted Federi. "Stop stretching it, Shawn! It will get as big as you make it! If you do go overboard, its inside combines chemically with saltwater to create a kind of floating board. It won't get in your way, don't worry. And it lights up."

"Explodes?" asked Shawn, amused.

"Cut it," snapped Federi. Oy! The entertainer was not into fun right now, was he!

"Thanks." Shawn peered down at the deck and saw how the other sailors were also putting on similar garments.

"Look after it," warned Federi.

"Okay."

"Right," growled Federi. "Next!" He activated his wrist-com again. "Captain, what's with the reef? Why were we heading towards it?"

"The radar is gone," came the reply. "Federi, Shawn Donegal, stay up there. I need you both as lookouts."

"Yes, Captain." The *radar* was gone? How -?

Rodriguez approached the bridge. Federi saw him exchange words with the Captain. The Cuban didn't look too happy about his ship being navigated by someone else. Well, too bad, Rodriguez, thought Federi. You mess with pirates at your peril! He watched as Marsden and Rushka completed the task of tensioning handhold lines and how Rhine Gold helped them secure the main and foresail. He became aware of Shawn Donegal staring at him intently, holding something out to him.

"Lifeline for you too, Federi," the twelve-year-old said.

"Oh!" There was no getting out of it. The gypsy detested being tied up. He gingerly took the line from Shawn and fastened it around himself. "Thanks."

"And a life vest?"

"You're wearing mine," said Federi. "Keep it on, anna bottle! Federi can swim!"

In any case he shouldn't be watching the procedures aboard. He was up here to look out for danger from the sea! He hung onto the mast as the rigging swung. Changing tack to get back on course now that they were past the reef. Wet spray shot up all the way from the prow wave and showered them. The Solar Wind dipped steeply into a trough. These were big waves. But then, a storm caused big waves. Federi hadn't lied. He hated these tropical squalls.

Down on the deck another sailor was clinging on for dear life. Ailyss had pocketed her novel and was holding the rail with both hands now, trying to deal with the roller-coaster of the rough seas. She had conquered most of her seasickness over the past weeks; but she hoped that her stomach was steady enough by now to hold up through another storm.

It was fascinating being amongst them all for a change. Her decision to stay in plain sight had been a good one. In the first place, that terrifying gypsy couldn't creep up on her unobserved and break her neck from behind, as he had done to many on that Rebellion Schooner. Secondly she was learning a lot about the way the ship and crew operated. But it had its drawbacks too. She was actually beginning to like some of them. That was not part of the plan.

Marsden placed his hand on her shoulder.

"Feeling up to this storm?" he enquired.

"So far so good, sir!"

"Great. You take that position over there, between Rhine Gold and Ronan."

"Thank you, sir!"

She fought her way across the lurching deck, clinging onto the handhold lines, and took her position between the two indicated. Ronan Donegal, her compatriot, who was at heart not a pirate and had been shocked at his predicament; and Reinhold Schatz, who was straight and honest and intended to jump ship at Hawaii anyway. No, she didn't mind being placed between these two. They could be relied on, to an extent.

She almost liked Marsden. He was a likeable fellow. But even so, the feeling niggled that there was more to the First Mate than met the eye. He'd not be First Mate on a pirate ship otherwise!

"Rhine Gold," instructed Marsden, "take the speedbar sheet. When the kite rises, wait for Rushka's instructions. Remember that Captain's orders overrule Rushka's."

"Yes, sir!"

On the other side of the deck, Captain Rodriguez had positioned himself in the spot opposite Ailyss, picking up the starboard brake sheet and looking pensively at it.

"Rodriguez," challenged Marsden, turning to the coast guard captain. "Are you with us? Ready for some sports?"

"You guys are *locos,*" commented Rodriguez with a grin. "I like it!"

Federi peered over the sea, back to where the Silver Bullet was barely visible any longer. Drifting away, with the little hummingbird on it! For a second he had the impression of a sunlit dream that had graced his life for a while, vanishing into the distance. Snuffed out. Gone.

He shook his head.

"They'll be alright," said Shawn.

"Hope so," muttered Federi. He studied the team on the deck that was getting set up for flying. Ronan and Rhine Gold, with Ailyss between them. Who meant nothing. He didn't think she could be relied on to do anything beyond fight her own seasickness. At least he hoped that. Rushka. Rodriguez, for mercy's sake! And Dr Jake! That meant that the jolly drives were unattended!

No, there was Marsden moving off below deck. Federi activated his wrist-com.

"Buddy, where are you headed?"

"Machine room, Federi. Our radar's been sabotaged! Dr Jake says the receptors to the sensors have been damaged."

Federi cursed, in Romanian. And then in Spanish, for added impetus. And rounded it off in Southern Free.

"We knew she'd try something, sometime," Marsden placated.

"Ha! So now it wasn't Paean?"

"We can't really say, Federi. She gets into the machine room too. Although I suspect that she'd have poisoned the water instead. With something GM."

Federi snorted. "And if it was the Cuban?"

"Rodriguez?"

"Not impossible, *nu?* "

"*Nu,*" agreed Marsden. "*Nu* indeed."

"Check on the nuclear drives too, Jon," said Federi. "Doesn't feel easy, with a bomb in the making under our bums."

Jon grunted acknowledgement. The kite sail went up past the Crow's Nest and popped open with an explosive crack. It rattled the gypsy. He looked again at the flying team and let fly a curse.

"Oh, for the sake of vanishing lizards!" The whole blasted team slipping about on the deck was green! There was not one experienced hand amongst them! He pushed the code for the ship com, activating the powerful speakers that clung to the mast like fungal growth. "Guys, wrap your flying sheets around your hands twice the way I showed you! Hang in there! Wind's going to steady out now!" The Solar Wind failed to achieve the necessary lift. The reason lay ahead. He fingered another sequence on his com. "Captain, veer to port – rocks ahead!"

"Well done, Federi," came Captain's response. "Keep your eye on the sea!"

They shouldn't be attempting to fly this, thought the Tzigan with a frown. Too many rocks! "Captain, I'd rather be down there with the flyers."

"Stay in the Crow's Nest, Federi. Need you as a lookout. It's crucial."

Federi gazed down once more with misgivings. Shawn plucked his sleeve.

"What's that?"

"Urgh," said the gypsy, staring at it. It was a rogue wave. Some way off starboard. "Captain, rogue wave to starboard," he muttered into his wrist-com, his eyes fixed upon the monster.

"*WHAT?!*" came the Captain's response. "Freezing hells! I see her!" The Solar Wind turned to face the monstrosity. Federi gripped the rail of the Crow's Nest and hung on, watching the monster lumbering ponderously towards the Solar Wind and her crew. He knew that Captain was going to try getting over the top – the safest course, seeing that she hadn't finished building and was not yet at tipping point.

Not a terribly big rogue, if he compared it to the data. Forty-footer or so. But terrible enough. In a few seconds the sailors would be washed off the deck like so many matchsticks. The Solar Wind would almost certainly capsize, with the bottom of the wave lifting her keel clear. With the rigging closed she'd have a chance of righting herself, but with the rigging fully open like it was... their hope lay in the masts breaking off; but if that caught any of the sailors, with their feet under the straps...

Federi's mind raced ahead, flashing him survival images. The thing would be to duck down into the Crow's Nest with Shawn, hoping that the collision with the water wouldn't kill them; and then to free Shawn first, and after that, go diving for the others, cutting them free of their lifelines... diving into the ship to free Marsden and Doc... and Wolf... and those idiots of the Coastal guard -

Shawn screamed, next to him. The wave doubled in height, suddenly. Its crest tipped and crashed down in a foaming whitecap.

That wasn't something Captain could nip over any longer!

"Captain," started Federi, his eyes fixed on that wave. The kite sail was hauled back in. The rigging swung. Captain had already understood. The Solar Wind was turning. They would try to outrun the wave.

This was taking too long! The wave was gushing and foaming like mad. And then, abruptly, it flattened out. White foamy suds laced the dark-green water. Turbulences boiled around them.

"Captain, veer to port!" Federi screamed into his wrist-com. There was a bleeding huge reef underneath! And the rogue was a lot flatter now, but she had picked rocks off it. Missiles. The Solar Wind swung. And pitched. And tilted. Spray shot up to them. The Solar Wind bobbed and danced upon the unpredictable currents and waves. White foam on green soufflé water. Reefs and shoals everywhere. The Solar Wind positioned herself nose-first at the rogue a second time; there wasn't any time left for anything beyond that. The massive force of water pushed at the ship and lifted her high. Federi clung to the Crow's Nest rim and muttered an old gypsy blessing on the buoyancy of compounding.

"What happened?" asked Shawn, white with fright. "Why was this thing suddenly so huge? – Wow, look at that trough!"

"Submerged reef," said Federi. "That built it up but broke some of the force. Then it flattened a bit as it got back to deep water."

The Solar Wind skidded sideways down the mountain of water as it moved on. It was a single, a loner. No wicked sisters following it. They returned to their previous course.

The kite sail was hauled back to fold automatically into the launching catapult and shot up past them again, noisily snapping open over their heads. Federi glanced at the deck. Aargh! He ought to be down there! Ronan slipped and righted himself. Ailyss hung onto her flying sheet with one hand and the handholds with the other as instructed, looking miserable. She had a port brake sheet. The leading one. Blast! Was Jon suicidal? Ronan was doubling up behind her with a second port brake sheet. The less important leach one. Ah. Interesting. But to put the inexperienced Donegal into the position of correcting her mistakes?

Rhine Gold, at the port speedbar sheet, had at least flown one and a half storms by now, if you counted in that dead loss there after Panama. But to put him in charge of a speedbar? There was nobody else, realized Federi. Dr Jake, who hadn't flown more than two or three storms yet because usually he was in the machine room, was doubling up for Rodriguez on the starboard side.

Rushka? She was highly experienced, in the sense that she had flown many storms; but she had never yet taken a full position. They had always conspired to double up behind her so she'd be shielded. Today there was nobody to double up for her. She was positioned centrally, at the controller, and all the remaining speedbar sheets had been linked into that.

What a team! It was sink or...

"Sing, Federi," shouted Shawn Donegal.

Federi shook his head, staring down at the foamy waves that splashed over the deck, feeling cold inside. So they had an ace helmsman, the best on all of Earth's oceans. But the sailors? And what about the Silver Bullet? Would the coastal guard's vessel make it through these rocks?

"Captain," Federi gasped into his wrist-com, "this is a bad idea. Let's get through this on drives, *nu?* Let's get out of the rocks, please?"

Radomir Lascek laughed. The mad Magyar coming through.

"Captain, listen," shouted Federi, panicky. "The whole flying team is green!"

"Rushka's done it before, Federi, and Rhine Gold," said Lascek calmly. "They can instruct the others!"

"Just look at them, Captain! Hell, no, don't look at them, veer to starboard! Aargh!"

The Solar Wind veered. Radomir Lascek emerged from the bridge. He shouted an order, and Dr Jake put down his flying line and took over the helm.

"Captain, that's even worse!" yelled Federi. He watched how waves washed around the sailors' knees; how the pitching of the ship threw the greenies off-balance and left them clinging to the handhold lines. Rushka had her hands full with that controller. The kite went down. He wasn't even aware that he was shaking his head.

Lightning streaked across, cutting a raggedy pattern. The Solar Wind never got hit by lightning; compounding was a poor conductor, an unattractive target for the searching finger of electricity. But it didn't do much to alleviate Federi's primal fear. He was Tzigan. Tzigany lived in the open. They had respect for electric weather. So far, only wind and mayhem. It would get worse. Visibility was going to go bang. The clouds were so low, and so heavy, they were about to pop.

"Captain," begged Federi, "get back on the bridge instantly! Let's call it a day, blast it! Let's just do this on drive power!"

"Tzigan!" the Captain's voice came thundering over his com. "Hold your tongue! I'll have no insubordination!"

Ailyss was suspended between the flying rope and the handhold lines, swinging with the ship, beginning to feel green around the face. She had her reservations about being able to "fly" this ship. She knew from a refresher course she had taken before embarking about the vectors that operated at the wind speeds of a tropical storm. She doubted that humans, capable of lifting maybe, at most, a hundred kilograms, could control anything that got buffeted by such blasts.

She glanced at her hands, her knuckles white from clinging to the ropes. The nails were chewed to the quick. A habit she had better snap out of. She had thought that she was out of it, but what with recent developments she had found last night, after reading two chapters in her novel without taking anything in, that there was not a single nail that had escaped. That was when she had sought out the safety of the infirmary, with its cameras and Wolf.

As she followed the arc of the kite sail back to the top, her gaze stopped compulsively at the rigging, where the Death Threat was hanging on in the Crow's Nest. Corrupting the little Donegal boy! Her eyes met Federi's and she caught his scowl. Oh yes, she knew! She was under observation!

Fat help it would be for them all. She was going down with the ship. With or without her mission accomplished, she couldn't see how they could survive this storm.

Radomir Lascek stepped out onto the deck.

"Hoy!" his voice boomed across, above the storm. "Flyers!"

He stared at them all, hands on hips. The sailors calmed down. To her surprise, Ailyss felt the fear ebbing out of her. The Captain moved forward, in amongst them.

"Right, you mangy lot!" announced Radomir Lascek. "This is how you do it."

He took the position right ahead of Rushka, slipping both boots in under toe-straps, and acquiring two speedbar sheets from his daughter. He clipped two lifelines on, one to a handhold line on each side. He wrapped both speedbar sheets around his left hand, grabbed the winch lines in his right and turned to give Dr Jake a signal. The wind steadied. Dr Jake's steering smoothed. The Solar Wind's uncontrolled rolling and pitching calmed.

Ailyss stared at the Pirate Captain, stunned. It was just as though he held the controls of the ship, the sea, the storm and the internal workings of the whole crew in his large, powerful hands!

The kite sail soared upwards, and then she suddenly stopped. There was a jolt. The huge parafoil pulled the Solar Wind from the crest of a wave, right out of the water.

Shawn emitted a gleeful whoop. "Federi, we're doing ski-jumps!"

The Tzigan shook his head with a smile. "No. We're on hydrofoils. Watch."

"What are hydrofoils?"

"Just observe," said Federi. "I'll explain later. Watch the sea, lots of shoals here!"

335

Radomir Lascek instructed the flyers as he handled the speedbar sheets. And then the kite steadied out and Ailyss understood about the flying. The sails rounded out and got filled to capacity with new untamed wind. The ship pulled ahead at a speed she had never yet witnessed, skimming along the crests. It felt like flying alright! The Solar Wind seemed to have lifted right out of the water, apparently gliding along on her keel, surfing over the waves. She caught her breath. In all her years of secret service she had never heard or read of anything like this. Was she dreaming?

Her eyes were glued to that kite sail and she was responding almost intuitively to it, loving every moment. Catching the wind was like lassoing a swarm of wild Pegasus, one at a time; each added its own force to the ship before escaping. The sea still rocked and splashed; but much less, as the deck was so much higher above sea level! And the Captain's calm persona was protecting them all from the elements. For an odd moment Ailyss wondered what it would be like to be one of them. Really be a pirate. Follow this man's leadership! Oh, it was tempting. Scruples aside, on a ship like his, with a Captain like him, what could possibly go wrong? He was capable of defying gravity itself!

What an illusion! She shook herself back to reality. Always on the wrong side of the law? What could go right?

Pirates, they all were reckless pirates. Criminals! Her glance dashed to the terror in the Crow's Nest. Her days were numbered, that was clear. The number was One.

Federi ground his teeth even as Shawn yelled in delight. Flying before the storm was a game to be played in the open sea, not in between coral reefs and sandbanks! And with a green team! They should all get below deck. He would stay in the Crow's Nest, this he understood – without radar, visual was the only reliable way of getting through the rocks. But there was no reason to endanger the others. What had got into Captain? Was he trying to show Rodriguez what a daredevil he could be? Or perhaps driving the point home that the Cuban shouldn't try to mess with the Solar Wind, because he stood no chance?

A fat splash hit Shawn's face.

"Hey!" the boy shouted and peered up at the clouds. "No spitting on the Solar Wind!"

"Here comes the rain," said Federi. He counted seconds. One… two… three… four… five… six…

The downpour washed in over the Solar Wind. Six degrees darker and badly impaired sight.

"Funny how fast things can turn at sea," commented Shawn, his wet locks plastered to his face. "Federi, sing! Go on!"

"Cor, Shawn. Blasted ship is out of control. Nothing that singing's going to fix this time," said Federi, hanging onto the mast as the ship swung once more in response to the surf. The boy lost his balance; Federi's hand shot out and grabbed his arm, steadying him.

Down on the deck people slipped and scrambled. Blast, Dr Jake at the helm – the nuclear scientist hardly ever had bridge duty as his job in the machine room took so much time! And Marsden, checking on the drives! Would he know what to do? Would he know how to balance the flying with the right amount of nuclear blasts to correct bad angles and help keep the ship's nose turned the right way? Would he be able to read the screens fast enough, would his exsanguinated reflexes be enough to take over Dr Jake's crucial role in the flying phenomenon – the part nobody ever knew about unless they took the time to have midnight conversations with the silent scientist? He didn't have time, blast it! He was trying to fix the radar. So they were flying without their support system! And the most experienced flyer up in the Crow's Nest!

Sherman, the centenarian, steering the Silver Bullet! Had they even done a round of the ship before taking the bridge? Were there not perhaps more Coast Guards hidden aboard that Barracuda?

What specifically was that feeling of disaster trying to tell him? Why was his radar so blasted vague? Like everything else on this forsaken pirate vessel?

26

Betrayal

"There's something wrong with the Solar Wind's radar," stated Sherman. "Did you see that? She nearly ran onto those rocks!"

Paean felt grey dread creeping over her.

"Then we've got to get back aboard and warn them, Sherman!"

"Captain will have noticed by now," replied Sherman, pointing. "See? There are two in the Crow's Nest."

Paean narrowed her eyes and peered. One of the two figures was glowing with a faint orange light. "Shawn and Federi, I'm sure. Sherman, will they be okay? I don't like this! Let's get back aboard!"

"Captain has navigated many storms," replied Sherman. "In any case visuals are safer to navigate by, through such heads. What I don't understand is why he wants to fly this one! Through the reefs?"

"Sherman, let's go back," begged Paean. "That's my brothers on that ship!"

"We can't anyway, Paean," replied Sherman Dougherty. "Look, there she pulls away!"

The Silver Bullet's engines were going full throttle; but there was no way to catch up to the Solar Wind now. It was hard enough to keep sight of her past the huge swells. Paean scowled. It was wrong! Things were upside down on the Solar Wind, she could sense it.

"How does a ship's radar get damaged anyway?" she asked.

"In the Solar Wind's case," replied old Sherman, "sabotage."

Paean gasped. "What!"

"There's a spy aboard," mentioned Sherman.

"I don't buy it," said Paean. "They say she's a spy. But she hasn't done anything! Anyway why should she sabotage the ship she's on herself? If we sink, she dies with us!"

"Oh, aye, that's the question," said Sherman, looking strangely at her.

"Panic, perhaps?"

"But why should she panic?"

"If she had the mission to sabotage the Solar Wind all along," said Sherman, "and we're drawing near to Hawaii now, which is maybe where she meets with her superiors... she'd have to do it soon, or her mission would have failed."

"But she would go down with the ship," objected Paean. "Still doesn't make sense."

"Perhaps that is better than what awaits her if she fails her mission?"

"I don't know," said Paean doubtfully. "Sherman, what if all of you are wrong about her? What if she's not a spy? What if the radar got stuck some other way? Remember the Crow's Nest got stuck after Lake Gatun! Maybe this is damage from that battle too! Calling someone a spy – that's a pretty serious accusation! She's a nice girl! Just quiet-like."

"Or maybe she's had word..." speculated Sherman, on his own track. He activated the intercom.

"Sherman?"

The centenarian swore. Paean peered at the console. She couldn't really see what he was doing.

"Trying to get a warning through to Captain," muttered Sherman Dougherty.

"Why?"

"She's getting picked up," said Sherman with a long glance at Paean. She went quiet. This was bad. Maybe Ailyss was indeed a spy. Then what? Sherman was hammering the console. "They're not responding!"

The Solar Wind was not visible any longer either. She had disappeared in the veils of rain, in the huge waves ahead. Paean suddenly felt utterly deserted. If the Solar Wind didn't come through this storm...

"If Ailyss is getting picked up, she'll have alerted the Unicate where we are," she said with a frown. Cor! Another thought struck her. A vision. Sheer! What if... She whistled through her teeth. "Sherman, is this the fastest we can go?"

"Why?"

She squeezed her eyes shut. Sometimes life was so darned inevitable... She only hoped she'd be as brave as Federi, in another few seconds.

"What's that ship on the radar?" asked Sherman, zooming in. "RS 6338! And another. RS 6872. And..." He shook his head. "Paean, don't look now, but we're surrounded by Rebellion!"

Ailyss' hair was plastered in wet tangles through her face. She glanced fearfully at the way white lines of spray crawled along the tops of the waves, wind whipping up manes for the wild horses. A swathe of rain blanked out everything around her, thundering; then it thinned again. She shifted her eyes to the Crow's Nest, in the vain hope that maybe the menace had been blown away by the most recent gust of wind; to her surprise the mast and deck lights blinked on. The Solar Wind's dusk sensors had self-activated.

She had liked the sensation of flying at first; but by now her arms felt as though they were going to fall off and her whole body was battered from balancing against such nasty angles all the time. The knowledge that she was helping a pirate escape the law, didn't make it easier. And looking up all the time at that weird kite sail – her neck would be so stiff tomorrow! If it was still in one piece. Was there a tomorrow?

She focused on the sleek, synthetic rope in her hands, her legs and back straining against the precarious angle at which the ship was hanging in its descent into a trough. The deck of the Solar Wind was treacherous. The sweet-water from the swathes of rain was leeching the salt out of it. This reduced the stickiness of the non-slip coating; even with a foot in a toe-strap the Irish brunette had to work hard to stay on her feet. The ship skimmed down into the next trough, and then a massive wave gushed across the deck.

Ailyss let go of her flying line, yielding it to the wind, and grabbed at the handhold. Captain could tame his wild Pegasus alone! She had had enough!

In releasing her winch line to grab the handhold she gave it a jerk which released the winch lock. The abandoned sheet had been operating on half-pulled-in position for a manoeuvre of the kite and was therefore under strain, and it shot through the winch. The loose end, coiled at Ailyss' feet, whipped across viciously to wrap round Rhine Gold's legs

340

where he stood to the side and slightly forward of her position, pulled him off his feet, and dragged him towards the winch, while the speedbar sheet he had been paying out started dragging him uncontrollably as well. Ailyss saw it and squeezed her eyes shut. It was gruesome. Best to remember that they were all going down together, after all.

Federi watched from the Crow's Nest and gasped. Why hadn't the automatic safety override kicked in? Rhine Gold would get injured!

"Let go the lines, everyone," he shouted over the ship com. "Rhine Gold, let go!"

All except Captain Lascek dropped their lines instinctively. Rhine Gold would have had a hand taken off by the winch if he had not, but fortunately the brake line reached full sheeted-out position just before his legs reached Ailyss' winch. Lascek was ripped off his feet. Something wrong with the override on that side, too! Federi frowned. Could it be the dratted little saboteur had tampered with more than the radar? How suicidal was that girl?

"Captain, let go the line, you'll get hurt!" yelled Federi. Captain really ought to listen to him. He was the experienced flyer. Captain was usually on the bridge steering during a storm, as he should be now! Radomir Lascek was dragged all the way across the deck, helped along by another breaker surging over the ship. The rain silenced Federi as he watched in horror.

Captain Lascek fought to get back on his feet without abandoning his line. Ailyss gaped at the sheer power, the dogged will. Man against the elements? Captain was the master, this was clear! He reared up, forcing the deck to steady under his boots. Once more the Solar Wind quit bucking like a young horse and levelled out. As though there were a connection between the Captain and his ship; as though she were alive. Incredible!

"Everyone, take up your lines again," the Captain commanded, back on his feet. He cast Federi a murderous look. "Tzigan, stop interfering! Men, and ladies, continue!"

The ship plummeted into the depths of a trough. Ailyss was thrown off her feet. Rhine Gold caught her. She glared at him. If she'd known about all this, she would never, never have volunteered for the Solar Wind!

"Veer to port, Dr Jake!" yelled Federi over the ship com. "Rocks to starboard! – And that's not interfering, worthy Captain, yodiho!" he muttered under his breath, wiping the rain out of his eyes for a second. The downpour played a nasty trick on him and slackened for that crucial moment. The ship broadcast his angry comment.

"Gypsy, I'm warning you," said Lascek irately. Dr Jake steered clear of the rocks. He cut it much too fine and the ship danced on turbulences for a moment. The Crow's Nest jittered and jolted. The Solar Wind lost her height and dropped back to sea level with a splash, and instantly a band of curious waves investigated the deck.

Federi clenched his jaws shut. He was only trying to prevent people from getting injured, anna bottle! He peered into the shrouds of rain, through the twanging ropes. The Silver Bullet was not visible anymore, vanished behind mountains of waves. Lights were not enough to penetrate this soup of rain and spray. Lightning bolts riddled the ocean behind them. He stared hard at the grey sea, listening intently. What was that he had heard?

"Federi, what's wrong?"
Federi's eyes stopped at Shawn's puzzled face without his brain registering it.
"Nothing we can change right now," he said darkly. Blast! The little songbird should have jumped ship in Atuona!

Another wave gushed around Ailyss' knees. She stared at it and hung onto the lines, terrified. In her mind she was trying to recall what she had learnt about storms and ships. Modern ships were built to withstand thirty metre and larger waves. The boat, yes, she thought. Not the blasted crew! They weren't supposed to hang out on deck as though this were one huge party! She peered at Ronan Donegal who was crowing with delight. Her stomach was lurching along with the ship, and here her nutty countryman was having fun!

"You're enjoying this, aren't you?" asked Rhine Gold.
"Loving it," grinned Ronan. "It's what I've been dreaming of."

"You'll make a good sailor, Ronan!" said the Hamburger.

Radomir Lascek bestowed an approving gaze on the young sailor. The Captain's daughter glanced at him as well, before she returned her full attention to the parafoil and the flying console. She played the controls with an experienced hand as the Solar Wind was coaxed to lift and fly once more, her feet hooked under the deck hooks, her knees slightly bent for better balance. Rushka had been dreaming of flying too; dreams, at night, and daydreams by day. Ever since her father had got overprotective of her, her life had turned into a long, sorry stretch of so-so and lah-di-dah. This storm was exactly what she had been longing for; and being given the central position surpassed her wildest hopes.

"This is the point at which we all sing a shanty," crowed Ronan. "On a good ship wet, when it rains and snows…"

"Go away!" – "Stop that!" – "Honestly!" – "Go back to kindergarten!"

"Hey, guys, where's your sense of sports?" grinned Ronan. From the ship com came a muttered comment about singing lessons. "By the way we need some more people. Paean, won't you go below deck and – where's Paean?"

"On the Silver Bullet," Rhine Gold reminded him.

"Oh. Drat! Hope she's okay."

"The Silver Bullet is a motorboat," said Salvatore Rodriguez. "Much easier to navigate in a storm, but not nearly as fast as this of course."

"Oh, good. Only hope she can escape Sherman's ghost stories."

"Not much hope there, Ro," grinned Rhine Gold.

Ailyss hoped that poor little Paean would escape more than just the ghost stories of the old pirate. A breaker washed her feet out under her just as the Solar Wind achieved lift-off again. This time, however, Rhine Gold was prepared and caught her before the surf could drag her any further. Their eyes met for a moment. Tango, she thought. He looked wild, with his golden curls streaming rivulets of water on her. Rain stung Ailyss' face too. She freed herself.

"Stop that!" said Rhine Gold, surprised. "You're messing up the operations! You're doing it on purpose!"

"No," said Ailyss. Her eyes darted up to the Crow's Nest and locked with Federi's black stare. She got another faceful of rain for it.

343

Rhine Gold had glanced back at her from staring at his section of kite just long enough to see her. "You're scared of Federi!" he stated, even more baffled.

"No," repeated Ailyss. Scared didn't begin to describe it. If she didn't drown in this storm, the gypsy would kill her tonight. She wondered if he garrotted people.

Federi beckoned Shawn closer.

"This has gone far enough," he shouted through the rain. "Did you see what Ailyss is doing? Go down there, ask Captain if you can escort Ailyss below deck and rouse some of Rodriguez's men. It's better to have drunken sailors doing as they're told than have a saboteur doing her damnedest to sink us!"

"Okay," said Shawn.

"But it's your idea, understood?" said the Tzigan. "I have nothing to do with it. You saw." His hand flicked the Captain away in an insolent gesture. "He's on his own station. Can't hear Federi at all today."

Shawn nodded. "I'll tell Captain I'm seasick. And Ailyss too."

"She is," agreed Federi. He was amazed at the gumption of the spy, to carry through with her nuisances despite feeling very obviously green. Gumption? Or perhaps desperation?

"Just Shawn, be very careful when you climb down. Stick to the rules. Keep reattaching your lifeline securely the way I showed you. At all times. If something happens to you, I think Captain will sink this ship personally."

"Okay," said Shawn doubtfully. "I'll be careful." He started his descent. He had monkeyed up and down here often enough; he was completely secure with his footing no matter how the Solar Wind swayed. Still, he obeyed Federi's directives about the lifeline.

"Tzigan, what are you planning now?" the Captain's voice boomed over the speakers. Federi activated his com.

"Nothing, Captain. The boy wanted to get down. Can't say I blame him."

Shawn climbed down to the deck. He clung to the mast in a theatrical show for a second or two, then staggered over to the Captain, grabbing

344

onto all nearby sailors for support. Ronan watched in concern, and caught a wink. Oh, the little scoundrel!

"Captain, permission to go below deck," Shawn groaned, grimacing. And genuinely slipped on a bit of treacherous deck as the Solar Wind abruptly pointed her nose down into a trough. Radomir Lascek's hand shot out and caught him by the left shoulder; Rodriguez's by the right. The two Captains exchanged a glance.

"*Hombre*," said Rodriguez, "this child has no business learning to be a pirate! Let me take him into port so he can lead an honest life!"

"*Amigo,*" replied Lascek with a smile, "the Unicate orphanages are no place for a bright boy like him! With me he has a future!" He turned and directed his piercing gaze at Shawn. The boy swallowed. "Go below deck, Donegal!"

"Captain, please, I think Ailyss isn't feeling well either," added Shawn mournfully.

"You're right, young Donegal. Take her below, and then the two of you keep watch over Wolf in the infirmary."

"Yessir."

Shawn gestured to Ailyss, and she followed him down the hatch and below deck. One audacious wave followed them inside, splashing around them down the steps. Shawn pulled the hatch closed, Federi's comment echoing in his head. Some things should *not* be left to electronics!

Instantly there was quiet. The storm raged on – outside. Shawn led Ailyss along the undulating passage past the boardroom, where the four crew members of the Silver Bullet were sitting, not quite sober, yet not drunk enough to be oblivious to the storm outside and the fact that the Solar Wind was riding it. There was evidence oozing around the blue carpet, changing its direction with each tilt of the ship. Shawn peered at it and felt genuinely queasy. He'd have to mop that up!

Would these hung-over hoodlums do? They'd just jolly have to! Shawn Donegal straightened out.

"Your Captain needs you on deck," he instructed the men. "Right away."

They took themselves out of the boardroom and headed for the hatch.

"And close the blasted hatch behind you," Shawn yelled after them.

"We're taking the begging ocean aboard!" For a moment he felt a surge of uncharacteristic rage at these guys. They were grown men, for the wet in blankets! They shouldn't be hanging there drunk and sorry while boys and women braved the roaring sea! He shook a fist after their retreating backs.

Ailyss glared at him.

"You're not seasick," she snapped.

"Neither are you," replied Shawn, shaking his head. "Ailyss, why are you trying to sink this ship? You'll die with us!"

She paused and studied him pensively.

"Shawn, just stick close to me. I'll rescue you. You're innocent."

"But so is my brother! And all the others too!"

"The others!" She spat on the floor. Shawn looked at her with wide eyes.

"You like Paean," he stated.

"Paean's not aboard, luckily," replied Ailyss. "There's a chance she'll get away."

"And Federi? Don't you like Federi? He's been nice to you!"

"Federi?" Ailyss shuddered. "The man's a psycho! Doesn't he freak you?"

"No," said Shawn. He didn't think Federi was insane. Silly and a clown, yes, but that was deliberate. And an accurate shot, like Shawn Donegal, and a calm head in a crisis.

"But aren't you worried he'll turn and slit your throat one fine day? If the mood takes him?" asked Ailyss.

Shawn shook his head. "You misunderstand him. You do him wrong."

"Don't think so," said Ailyss cynically.

"And Wolf?"

"Wolf," smiled Ailyss. "Shawn, you little innocent! Wolf's a juvenile delinquent! He comes from a correctional school! This is a ship full of human garbage! No loss to humanity!"

"Why do you hate us all so much, Ailyss?"

"Hate?" Ailyss stopped and stared at him, frowning. She shook her head, grabbing onto the rail lining the passage as the rear of the ship lifted steeply once again. "I don't actually, Shawn. I don't hate *you* at all. You

346

remind me of my little brother."

"You have a little brother!"

"His name is Keenan. He's got the same round eyes as you have." She suddenly stopped talking. Her eyes became sheltered again.

"Where's Keenan?" asked Shawn.

"Don't ask!"

"Are you all that's left of your family, Ailyss? Are you orphans too?"

"Be quiet," she snapped.

"Your little brother is in a bad place, isn't he?"

"Shawn, shut up!"

"Ailyss, is there anything I can do to help you get your brother back?" asked Shawn. "I'm sure Captain will want to give him shelter on the Solar Wind too!"

"Shawney, you're naïve. Radomir Lascek is a crook. Don't you get it? Sinking the Solar Wind's the only way I can save my little brother!"

Ailyss saw Shawn's rattled expression and knew that she had told him too much. He was a pirate. There was no rescuing him. Too late – and he was only twelve! Poor little Paean – her brothers would have to go down with the ship.

"Ailyss," said Shawn, "we'll help you. We Donegals. Just Ronan and Federi and I. We can do it! Tell me where we must find your little brother and we'll go and pull him out of the very hands of the Rebel terrorists if we have to."

"Ironically that's exactly where he is," retorted Ailyss. "How are you proposing to do this?"

"Federi will have a plan," said Shawn confidently. "He always does. Will you trust me?"

"I trust nobody," said Ailyss.

"Telling me that, you've already shown trust," Shawn pointed out.

"Och, quit your mind games, little Donegal!"

"I'm an orphan too," said Shawn. "If you sink our ship, you kill my brother and sister, and then I've no family left in the world. Come, we have orders to look after Wolf."

"Oh, Shawn?"

He looked up at her with his eyes round.

"A single word of this, to anyone," she warned and drew her finger

347

across her throat.

"Roger," said Shawn. "I'll stay mum." A promise to a psychopath didn't count, he thought to himself. Hell with her.

Federi had redirected his wrist-com to the bridge, navigating for Dr Jake and not bothering with the flying team any longer. Let Captain figure it out! If a sailor went overboard, there was still time to furl the sails and launch a rescue mission! If someone lost a hand – he shook his wet mane and wiped the rain back out of his face. A vivid imagination wasn't always a blessing. But the hell would he allow Captain to put a guy ashore who had been disabled because of Radomir Lascek's stubborn lack of foresight!

Foresight – that was what he was, thought Federi acidly. A gust of wind tore at his scarf; a swarm of stinging raindrops whipped across his back. *He* was the Captain's radar to the future. Ailyss – or perhaps that Rodriguez, who knew – had sabotaged the ship's spatial radar; Captain was sabotaging his own time radar! Blast, but that made no difference! Federi would continue functioning.

There it was again, carried on the wind, clearer this time – Federi and Ronan, Crow's Nest to deck, exchanged troubled glances. Both had sensed it at the same time: Paean's panicked cry for help.

"Captain, we need to slow down and wait for the Silver Bullet," called Federi on the ship com. Ronan shot him a thankful look.

"Federi, butt out," Lascek snapped into his wrist-com. "You've messed with the works quite enough!"

"To hell with it, Captain!" the Romany reared up, the wind whipping the ends of his ridiculous bandana into his face along with his own black tangles. "I'm not messing! I'm telling you! We've got to wait for them!"

"One more word from you, gypsy..." warned Lascek. "Rhine Gold! Pick up that slack! The hydraulics don't know what to do!"

"Captain," shouted Federi, boiling over, "if you don't stop the Solar Wind immediately so we can wait for them –"

The Captain fiddled with his wrist-com.

"I'll get out of the Crow's Nest and go looking for them myself, and you can navigate by touch, anna bottle," completed Federi and realized that the ship com had been switched off. He threw back his head and yelled with rage. And tested his wrist-com. He had access to the bridge and to most of the sailors; not to Captain though. Rats on the old tyrant!

What the hell was wrong with Captain? He expected to wake up from this nightmare any second now. Except that he knew that it was no dream. A clown? A fool! The flipside of being the Jester was that in life-and-death situations you stood alone, because nobody took you seriously. He started whistling a mournful Romany tune through his teeth over the wind, trawling desperately for possibilities in the dark depths of his mind.

Ronan was saying something, in all probability imploring the Captain to stop and wait. Federi watched the exchange and read from the body language how Ronan was snubbed too.

"Doomed," he muttered. "We're doomed. Our Captain's lost his mind. We're a dead crew walking." A sunken Rebel Schooner full of dead terrorists loomed briefly out of the veils of rain to port, shadowing them. Juan on the bridge. A trick of the light. For Federi's eyes only. Making sure they would meet again in hell!

Rushka was now confronting her father. Federi could practically read from their lips what was being said. Lascek snapped at his daughter. She backed down.

Federi felt like screaming. He could feel Paean's fear like a tangible presence and knew beyond a shadow of a doubt that something had happened to the Silver Bullet. If only he could to come down from the Crow's Nest, stop this flying nonsense for a moment, speak to his Captain eyeball to eyeball... but he couldn't do that without endangering the whole ship. If only this accursed storm would abate soon!

Ailyss sat in the infirmary, curled up small on the empty bunk with the pea-green blanket, wedged into the corner between the wall and the equipment at the head of the bunk. Shawn was sprawled on the single narrow chair that was usually hiding in the corner, having plonked it in the middle between the two bunks, riding it as the ship rocked. He was telling Wolf in excited detail about the detaching of the Silver Bullet and the flying of the Solar Wind, and the way he and Federi had been navigating the ship by sight. The heavy rolling of the ship enhanced the feel of drama in his tale. Ailyss deliberately refused to think about those sailors on the deck, in the rain and surf. They were pirates. They had cast their lot.

Suddenly Shawn paused and listened. "Paean's in trouble!"

"How do you know?" asked Wolf.

"Telepathic link," said Shawn. If they laughed, he'd point out the telepathic contact they *all* knew Paean had established that time with Federi.

"There's nothing we can do," said Wolf. "Not in this storm."

Ailyss sat listening. Against her better judgment she was drawn into the young pirate's wild account, even though she had been there. This was a tale nothing short of heroism! Shawn had also picked up on Captain's amazing ability to stabilize wind, weather and the sailing ship. Wolf was nodding with an appreciative grin and adding, "yes, he does that!"

But the ship's radar, broken… She countered the long, searching looks Wolf bestowed on her with sadness. Too late she realized how much she had come to like her rough-cut colleague, the one she had referred to minutes ago as a juvenile delinquent. Wolf was not actually rough in daily life. He was quiet and intelligent, and always kind to her, and he kept things to himself. The way he had stood up for his scaly, undeserving shipmate – that loyalty, that backbone – she could appreciate it. And she had begun to find his company comforting.

She liked too many of them. It was too bad. It wasn't her first mission. She closed her eyes and felt the ship roll and tilt around her. It would not be long now.

Federi had lost track of time. The swaying of the rigging, the flapping and bunching of the sails, the quivering of the lines and the wet wind around his ears had put him into a trance. He was eyes and ears only, calling out rocks and danger zones to Dr Jake over the com and shutting his mind to everything else. After a while it felt to him as though clinging to the rim of the Crow's Nest with fingers numb from the pelting rain, and pushing the com's button was all he knew how to do. As though Federi was only a part of the Crow's Nest.

When the wind suddenly stopped, it came as a surprise. The Solar Wind moved out under the heavy rain and into a calm, light patch, only faint drizzle…

"Dr Jake, veer to port, bright weather to starboard," shouted Federi and stopped, stumped. What had he said there? He felt as though he had awakened from a dream. His entire psyche felt blanked out.

There had been things in that dream. Wild passages through Lake Gatun. Flights out of Stab nests in the Atlantic. A crazy episode of towing Unicate military. And towing, and towing again. The Solar Wind, a towing service. Dark bits too. A man eaten by a vanishing lizard, for a Unicate capsule. Having to slaughter his way out of a ship. That darned capsule was bothering him! What the hell was in it?

And through it, the sound of laughter, light and carefree, as though there were another side to the world, one that was pure innocent sunshine… the sound of her terrified screams, and her panicked little calls, and then her silence…

"Federi, I want to see you on the bridge," the Captain's voice cut authoritatively out of his com. Ha! So now the blasted com was good enough again?

"Yessir." He flung his wrist-com into the Crow's Nest, stripped off his lifeline and climbed down from the drenched rigging. There was a fire burning in his gut. If they had murdered Paean, and he had been unable to prevent it because of Captain's doggedness…

Captain Rodriguez clapped Captain Lascek on the shoulder.

"That was marvellous, Capitano, *estupendo!* I'm exhausted!"

"It was a good one," agreed Lascek. He gestured toward the bridge. Federi obeyed, his hands twitching. "Please excuse me, Captain Rodriguez."

"I'll round up my men," said Rodriguez. He turned away.

Federi's fists clenched and unclenched as he stood waiting on the bridge. There was only one thing he could do now. And it had nothing whatever to do with Captain! He had drowned out Paean's screams for help. She was silent now. That silence was terrible.

The Captain was messing him around wasting time. He was lagging behind on the deck, complimenting Rushka, Ronan, Rhine Gold, and the Cubans on a job well done. He entered the bridge and thanked Dr Jake

351

and sent him back down to the machine room to Marsden, to check on the repairs.

He ignored Federi completely until they were alone on the bridge. Then he turned and stared at the Romany for a good thirty seconds in silence.

Get it over with, thought Federi, his fingers and toes tingling. Move, blast you! I've got a mission!

"Tzigan, what were you thinking? Giving me uphill while another Captain is visiting?"

Was this a real question? "I'm sorry, Captain. I was only -"

"Who gives the orders on a ship?"

Ah. Not a real question. "The Captain, sir."

"So what were you doing giving orders? Contradicting me? Staging a mutiny in a crisis?"

"A mutiny?!" That was too much! "Blast it, Captain, get off my back! I have no time for your little issues now! You've wasted enough of my time! Got to get to Sherman and Paean!"

Lascek's mouth hung open. *"Little issues -?"*

Blast. That had come out wrong! Federi counted. One... two...

Radomir Lascek's Hungarian temper exploded. Federi stood struck into silence as the Captain let rip, about good-for-nothing Tzigany and their lack of discipline, and the way a ship had one clear command line, and if he didn't like it, he could get off! Lascek took a breath.

"Thanks, Captain, that's exactly what I was about to –"

Federi's words went under in the next bomb blast. Hells, Captain was taking long! And there was no defending yourself when Lascek was in such a mood. Walk out, thought Federi, apologize later. But, being Federi, he just had to try once more the correct way.

"I'm sorry, Captain," he said. "I never meant –"

"To hell with what you meant! Can't you submit to authority at all?"

Federi shut his mouth. There was a remote chance that Paean was still alive. And here was Captain, wasting time on an ego trip. Federi decided to give it another thirty seconds, then he'd walk away, and to hell with the future! What future was there anyway? He'd stand trial on this if he had to, damn the Captain! No, on the contrary: He'd simply not come back.

"An answer, gypsy."

Federi smiled viciously. "Permission to speak, Captain?"

"Now don't get snotty with me! What do you do while aboard this ship?"

Federi bit back his retort. Snotty! "Obey your command, Captain," he said with insolent patience.

"Exactly. May you but never forget that again! Now get on with your job!"

"Thank you, Captain." It had taken less than thirty seconds.

Federi turned and left the bridge.

27

Federi

There was absolutely no wind; only this otherworldly fine drizzle. Low-flying clouds, Paean had called it once, and Irish Fresh Air. The sense of unreality kept lingering on the fringes of Federi's awareness as his hands worked the holdings of the Stormrider loose in the drizzling rain and released the catch on the Mother Ship. The electric winches lowered the motorboat onto the rolling water. The Stormrider bobbed on the agitated sea. The Tzigan cast a suspicious eye at the strange colour of the clouds up there before climbing over the Solar Wind's rail and slipping down a lifeline into the Stormrider. Pure luck, that.

"Now we're on our own, you realize," he commented, glaring at the Stormrider's screens. "Captain will think this is mutiny." He keyed in the security sequence on the console, and the electric outboard drive whizzed into life. He glanced uncertainly back at the ship. It didn't sit well, abandoning them to Ailyss' devices right now! But there was no choice.

"I don't care," said Ronan Donegal. "My first loyalty is to my family. My job comes second."

"Good man, Donegal!" Federi nodded approvingly. The boy had his priorities straight! His hand moved to the gear lever.

Rushka took a flying leap off the Solar Wind towards the lifeboat. She landed in the sea close by and surfaced in the high waves, a bit winded. Federi steered the boat closer to her and Ronan helped her aboard.

"Thank you," she gasped. "Why are you running away?"

"We're only going to rescue my sister," said Ronan bitterly. Federi turned and pulled the gear lever. The Stormrider shot forward soundlessly. Federi whistled his relief through his teeth. We're on our way, little songbird, and Sherman! Here we come!

"My father can be a very harsh man at times," said Rushka. "And also he has sometimes been known to make mistakes." She looked knowingly at Federi.

"Oh well," said Federi with a shrug, sounding more cheerful than he felt. "Your father is a good man, Rushka. Don't break him down. You know we'll all sail to hell for him. He'll come round. Don't worry about it, Princess, I sure don't." He bent over the display panel, testing all the functions as the boat put ocean between them and the Solar Wind. That blasted spy had at least not thought of disabling the Stormrider's radar! All was fully operational.

"Now we follow her signals," said Federi, turning, and understood that he was suddenly alone on the boat. Oh, sure, there was this bubble behind him, with the two pretty teens in it having discovered each other's eye colour. Not really part of reality though. Merely a spectre.

"Aw, hell, Princess," cursed Federi, adding a juicy expression in Romani. They weren't even aware of being spoken to! The fine prickling of accelerated drizzle didn't even seem to bother them. He had considered pulling the roof over; now he wasn't going to.

This certainly complicated matters! A psychic signal always came through clearer to next of kin – why he had taken Ronan along in the first place! He wished he could have taken Shawn instead. But this mission was far too dangerous for the boy.

He peered uneasily at the clouds. They were green, and very high up. They were trying to tell him something! This was no ordinary tropical storm! And what about this weird calm moat in the middle of it… where the violence should be at its worst?

Radomir Lascek watched from the rail as the three took off in the lifeboat. He was beside himself with anger. Mutiny, on the Solar Wind! And that Donegal laying his filthy hands on Rushka! But that his daughter had deserted him –

"There goes the Royal Couple," said Marsden quietly behind him. The Captain turned. Jon Marsden was smiling.

"I'll skin him alive!" growled Lascek. "The brat!"

"I don't believe he really knew what hit him there," laughed Marsden. "Radomir, that was Rushka's doing, not Ronan's!"

"Insubordination nonetheless," thundered Lascek. "Damn them! Mutiny! Desertion!"

"They'll be back," said Marsden. "I believe they're only checking on the Silver Bullet. Captain, the radar is irreparable, unfortunately. We'll have to wait until we're at Prime."

"I was going to put that Donegal in charge of Ailyss," said the Captain crossly. "She needs supervision! Svendsson was doing a fine job until he got himself shot!"

"There're plenty of others," Marsden placated him. "I wouldn't cross your daughter on this. You might lose her."

"Hells, Marsden, whose side are you on?" Lascek peered into the miserable drizzle. Ronan Donegal was a hormonal teenager. He could possibly be forgiven, provided he hadn't already dishonoured Rushka! But Federi! He had organized it all! Rushka eloping! He was a tough, unpredictable gypsy with not a shred of conscience or loyalty. Lascek found it hard to understand now how he could ever have allowed him aboard. The Romany had been following only his own agenda at all times, never worrying about the rules. A rotten, ruthless Tzigan.

Lascek got a nasty grin. Well, if Federi ever set foot aboard the Solar Wind again, he would pay for this.

The Solar Wind's sails were closed; she lay rolling on the high surf. Radomir Lascek gestured at the sea, and the sky. "What the heck do you make of this storm, Jon?"

"Hurricane," said Jon. Their eyes met and they both shook their heads. They had been in hurricanes before, and there was only one course of action. Submerge.

This was no hurricane.

"The Eye," said Jon, but as Lascek started shaking his head, the First Mate continued, "should have bright skies and no precipitation at all. This is not an Eye. Ergo, it can't be a hurricane."

"Wasn't a blasted hurricane when I looked on the charts," replied the Captain. He fingered a sequence on the console, and a satellite picture jumped to view. "There, you see? No hurricane. Ordinary storm. I'd never make this bunch fly a hurricane! I'm not off my mind!"

"When was this?" asked Jon Marsden.

"This is now!"

Marsden shook his head and zoomed in until the microscopic date and time in the bottom corner became visible. "That was ten this morning,

Captain."

Lascek leaned forward into the screen as though his eyes couldn't process what he saw there. "What! But…"

Jon Marsden's fingers flashed across the console, tried various options. He straightened out with a disbelieving smile on his face.

"She's done more than the radar," he said.

"That explains why we were off-course earlier!" snapped Lascek. "How we landed in those blasted shoals I wanted to skirt!"

Marsden nodded sagely.

"And Federi had a feeling of this turning into a huge storm?" pushed Lascek. "The blasted mutineer!"

"What happened back there?" asked Marsden, as puzzled with Federi's desertion as with his Captain's stranger decisions this morning. Lascek told him the sequence of events, barely containing his rage.

Marsden got thoughtful. "I disagree that Federi committed mutiny. He's probably only worried about our people on the Silver Bullet."

"He's an unpredictable Tzigan," snapped Lascek.

"No, Radomir. Federi is one of your most loyal friends and shipmates. He has never done anything like this before. Think it may be a nervous breakdown?"

"A breakdown?" Lascek laughed aloud. "He's not a little old lady, Jon!" The Captain paused and considered. Then again, Federi did have an insane streak. He was tough-minded enough to clean up a whole schooner's terrorist crew alone. But such killings generally caught him afterwards. Radomir Lascek had been waiting for the gypsy to disappear from sight, withdraw into his cabin, be antisocial; it hadn't happened. Yes, perhaps Marsden was right. Possibly the gypsy had gone off his rocker this time.

Lascek sighed. While it was good to have found an alternative reason for the desertion of the Romany, it wasn't much better. How was he going to cope with a lunatic aboard? He shrugged impatiently. Federi had never yet been normal. So far they'd coped with him just fine. The man only needed a bit firmer command structure, basta. And where Ailyss was concerned – Lascek was suddenly certain that Ronan wouldn't have coped with her anyway. The boy was too blue-eyed. Neither would Wolf, for that matter. Lascek scowled into the unusually light rain.

"That out there," he said, pointing, "is an Eye in the making."

"Then we've got to get out of here," said Marsden, "before the transformation is complete."

"Can't," replied Lascek heavily. "Not with the Stormrider and the Silver Bullet still out there!"

Federi had lied when he had made light of Lascek's mood to the Captain's daughter. In truth his loyal heart was breaking. He steered into the shifting veils of drizzle, waiting for that signal.

The surreal sense clung, just under the surface, as though they had drifted into the Alb World. It was quiet; the only sounds the splash of the prow wave, the nearly inaudible electric buzz of the engine, the whisper of the rain on the sea, and the subdued, unintelligible soft talk going on behind him. Blast, but Rushka couldn't have picked a worse moment, politically.

Federi found himself smiling on her behalf. Lucky little Rushka. Och! Hells, was he selfish! Sure, Captain would be livid. His revered, deified Captain who thought nothing of calling him a mutineer. Who was he, Federi, to take away a few moments of pure happiness from Rushka? And from Ronan? It was only borrowed anyway! Who knew what they would find on the Silver Bullet? Who knew how badly the two would need each other in the nearest future?

Och! Captain could be livid all he liked. And if Captain got it into his head to fly the second half of the storm too – then he'd have to find another victim to send up there. Fact – he was now in a position where he couldn't fly. Not enough crew. Federi laughed voicelessly.

Where to now, Tzigan?

He had been following the direction in which he sensed Paean. But now he was listening to another signal coming in. Ye Gods, Juan! Steering the phantom ship, chasing Federi. It wasn't a phantom ship at all. It was a projection. There were at least six of them, or he could call himself gypsy no longer!

He had sunk a Rebellion Schooner. The Rebellion was a solid organ. He couldn't hope to get away with that. The Rebellion, Lords of the Pacific, were closing the net on the Solar Wind just like the Unicate had done on the civilized hemisphere. Earth only had two hemispheres! Where could they escape? And he, Federi, had brought it down on their heads! Yes, he deserved every kind of insult the Captain could heap on him.

It was hopelessly too late. He could try to rescue the little sunbird, try to salvage the Solar Wind's crew one more time. In the big picture, he was only buying time. Two, three more weeks perhaps. Panic framed his dark eyes.

He glanced back over his shoulder at the beautiful young couple. He had to send them both back and work this one alone. Just as well. Stealth was his best modus. His middle name. Time for action.

"Now, you two," he said, turning. *"Atenţie!"* He was ignored. He raised his voice. "I said, *Atenţie!"*

Now he did have their *atenţie*.

"Federi's going to jump. Take the boat back to the Solar Wind as fast as you can make her go. Tell the Captain of the Rebel Fleet hunting us, Ronan. Rushka, you back him up, *capîche?"*

"Rebel fleet -?" Ronan's eyes widened.

"I'm going to rescue your sister, and Sherman," said Federi. "Don't be heroes, you hear? Don't the hell come after me. They'll shoot you kids to bits! Go straight back to the Solar Wind, come hell or high water. *Hai shala?"*

"Understood," said Rushka. "Be careful, Federi!"

He glinted her a grin.

"Tell the Captain," said Federi, tying a rope around his middle in frantic haste and opening a little red glass bead from his scarf, pouring the contents over the other end of the rope. His fingers were trembling as he worked. "I'll return to the Solar Wind when I'm done with my mission. Dead or alive. Federi's no renegade."

He kept the radar screen in the corner of his eye. If the fleet registered, they'd have to run like hell. A gust of rain blew over them. His gypsy radar's fuse cut out. He glanced at the surrounding shoals. Regardless. He couldn't wait any longer.

"Rushka, take her back to the Solar Wind right now! Start turning!"

"Federi, you don't have a life vest! You gave yours to Shawn!"

"Just turn! Don't argue!"

"Take one from the boat," she urged.

He shook his head. "Life vest would get me killed this time."

Rushka cocked her head and gazed at him, worried.

"Princess," implored Federi, "I know your father can't trust me. But Federi knows what he's doing! Can you?"

She went wordlessly to the controls and performed a beautiful U-turn. Federi double-checked the boat's course, latched the Stormrider's signal onto the Solar Wind's ship com and jumped into the treacherous waves. The boat sped away, back to the Mother Ship.

Federi waited.

Shawn climbed back into the Crow's Nest when he realized his brother was missing; he was looking out for Ronan. He had also heard the distress calls from Paean, something about which he was completely helpless. But he understood that Federi and Ronan had gone to rescue her, so hopefully that would be alright.

"Hey, hey, what's this?" he asked, picking up Federi's abandoned wrist-com. "Can't be mine, I'm wearing mine. Got to be Federi's!" He tested it out by calling Federi on his com. The other com transmitted his voice.

Shawn put Federi's com on his other wrist and watched as his brother and Rushka re-emerged out of the renewed rain.

"There they come," he yelled. But where was Federi? And Sherman, and Paean?

Shawn stared at the under-crewed boat, and at the wrist-com and at the sea, with white crests riding the high peaks again. Still pretty rough, and the rain picking up again. The clouds were darkening once more. Federi's life vest shone like a beacon on him.

"Uh-oh," he commented.

Rhine Gold helped Ronan stabilize the Stormrider and get her locked back safely into her hold.

"Need to speak to the Captain," said Ronan urgently.

"On the bridge," said Rhine Gold.

Ronan ran.

"Captain! There's a fleet of Rebel ships hunting the Solar Wind!"

"How many?" asked the Captain, alarmed.

"Don't really know."

"Where's Rushka?"

"Right here, Captain," said his daughter.

"I'll speak to you later, young lady," warned Lascek. "Ronan, where the hell's the gypsy?"

"Sir, he asked me to tell you – he's not betraying you, Captain. He jumped off. He's trying to rescue Paean and Sherman."

"Uh-huh," said the Captain with irony. "Do you believe him?"

Ronan's back straightened and he frowned angrily. "Implicitly, sir. He says he'll be coming back to the Solar Wind when he's freed Paean and Sherman. Asked me to relay to you that Federi is no renegade; in those words."

Lascek shook his head. Confirmation of Marsden's theory! "The crazy loon. And he believes he can do it alone?"

"So it seems, Captain." Ronan's chin lifted defiantly. He also believed Federi could do it!

The Captain stared at Marsden. The First Mate stared at Ronan.

"You are meaning to say Federi jumped onto the Rebel Schooners?" asked Jonathan Marsden. "How did you get away? Are you now leading them straight to us?"

"No, sir. There wasn't a ship in sight yet when he jumped overboard. Not even on the radar."

"He just jumped overboard? Into the sea? What if he's wrong?" Marsden was worried. "What if there aren't any ships?"

Ronan looked troubled. This was a possibility that hadn't even crossed his mind, so sure had Federi been of the fleet.

"Then he's all alone out there," he realized. "But the Silver Bullet should pick him up."

"Son, the ocean is no freeway," said Radomir Lascek. "If he made a mistake with the direction, even by half a degree, he'll be lost at sea."

"There were lots of heads," said Ronan.

"Even worse!" Lascek activated his com. "Federi, come in. Don't move. Stay where you are. We're picking you up."

"Captain, this is Shawn," came the reply, two octaves too high. "Federi left his wrist-com in the Crow's Nest, must have lost it in the storm."

The Captain switched off his com. He stared at Ronan, dumbfounded.

"He's jolly taken off his com! He's out there without a com! The faithless vagabond!" Radomir Lascek started pacing like a caged tiger. "What the hell do we do now?"

"Captain," said Rushka with horror in her voice, "he gave his life vest to Shawn. He's out there without a float!"

Marsden sat down with his head in his hands.

"No vest, no com! We'd better start praying, my friend," he said softly. "Let's hope that this isn't the day Federi's instincts have let him down."

"Either way," growled Lascek. "Lousy deal either way!"

Rodriguez had organized his by now comparatively sober, rain-washed rabble of men and approached the bridge.

"Captain, we must get back onto our own ship."

Lascek nodded, applying a bland expression. Federi's lunacy was none of the Cuban's business. "I understand. You need to get ahead to Hawaii so you can alert the Unicate that we're coming, otherwise you can't go back to your job in Cuba."

Rodriguez laughed, sounding embarrassed. Captain Lascek knew exactly what was going through his mind. It was a lot of cash. But Rodriguez was battling his own ethics – he had enjoyed the association with the Solar Wind. Then again, who knew if the Cuban knew about the capsules? Unlikely, thought Lascek. A mere Coastal Guard.

Lascek grinned. "No problem, *amigo*. She should be right behind us. Then we can give you a fair run for your money! Shall we make a bet on it, old pirate? They'll never catch the Solar Wind in Hawaii!"

"If they do, it's your life," said Rodriguez.

"And if they don't, you're an outlaw," laughed Lascek. "Welcome to the pirate life, Rodriguez!"

He was not going to share any wild theories about Rebel fleets! Radomir Lascek resolved to wait it out. He'd await the arrival of the Silver Bullet and then fish his marooned gypsy out of the raging main, however long that took. He had a bad conscience about it. He'd find him somehow. The position where the Stormrider had turned, should still be

362

in the memory of the console. And then he'd give the man some of Paean's green wonder bug and have him sleep it off – whatever it was.

The Solar Wind lay waiting for the Silver Bullet, rocking on the rough seas, painted grey by the heavy rain.

Federi had been waiting so long, floating in the churning water, his purple, flared shirt billowing in the restless waves around him, he had begun to wonder if his radar had lost its accuracy.

Now they came looming out of the downpour. One, two of them; three, and more. He looked at the end of his rope; his little chemical had done its trick, the end had become a swollen and sticky glob on contact with the seawater. His hand had very nearly gone numb holding the darned rope, preventing it from sticking to anything in the meantime. He was positioned perfectly. The Schooners were bearing down on him directly. The chances that they'd spot him were miniscule, he knew. His purple scarf acted as camouflage in this dark weather; and with only the top of his head sticking out of the water, they'd have a hard time spotting him in the rocking waves even without rain obscuring the matter. Their instruments wouldn't pick him up either; he was not wearing anything that gave off any electronic signals. And on their radar he was but a shark…

For a tense moment he thought his positioning was too perfect and he'd be run over. In the mood for a keelhauling? Hah! But the prow wave of the nearest ship, the dangerous one, lifted him out of the way. He smacked the end of his rope as high up against the hull as he could and hoped that the glue had attached properly. It was supposed to bond instantly. Well, this would be the test, wouldn't it? He began to inch up the rope.

It was easier to be led into the bilges of a Rebellion Schooner blindfolded and tackle the ship from within than try to get to that single, open porthole! Federi suddenly had a lot more appreciation for geckos, and for spiders. They could climb up smooth walls. Then again their walls weren't wet and rocking insanely! He added drops of glue to the rope as he went, to secure it against the ship's hull, because he'd go through a porthole otherwise – unintentionally. A grand dramatic entrance in a shower of glass wasn't exactly what he had in mind.

As he climbed higher he detached the rope underneath him from the hull again, pouring solvent from a flat flask out of his pocket, over it. And then he hung on for a moment, assessing the situation. There was one open porthole, but it was towards the stern of the ship. And it was open only by a small fraction. Probably a little used cabin, because the ship was moving through a rainstorm. A storeroom or something.

Federi cast a quick glance overhead, where rain was cascading down again in a nearly solid entity. Wet was wet, he thought, shaking his black Tzigan mane back in bravado. The sea temperature had dropped significantly while he was in it; now the waves splashing over him were even colder. Bad waves, punishing his back and tugging him, trying to wash him off the ship's side – the ship rolled, trying to buck him off like a hostile horse. Federi bared his teeth and laughed. Oh no, they weren't going to get rid of this flea that easily! And his magic glue was coming through in spades. But those waves – they were trying to tell him something too! Unnaturally cold for the subtropics; almost as though they came from really deep down... He only seriously hoped that Captain wouldn't try to fly the second half too! He hoped that by now, someone had calmed Radomir Lascek down enough for him to listen to reason, to Ronan and Rushka. Because if Captain did, in *this* wind, with *these* waves, in *these* temperatures, the whole crew would die from exposure...

How was he going to get to that porthole? He wasn't, he decided. He was going to do his two-rope monkey trick instead. He unwound the other end of the rope from his middle and added a drop of glue from another tiny vial from his scarf. He held it out for the rain to swell it a bit and launched it, up as far as it would go. It stuck. He took hold of it, tested it; and poured solvent on his first rope end. He sunk the flask back in his pocket, detached the first rope end, climbed up to the second, and repeated the whole procedure. It was faster to inch up and over the rail than to reach that porthole! Hell knew he had little enough time!

Through the torrents of rain, Federi slid over the rail and slithered straight across the deck as the ship pitched. He grabbed onto a cleat as it passed, and raised his eyes fearfully to the bridge. The lights were on; the ship's potent searchlights were beaming paths into the pelting rain, but they hadn't spotted him. It had been too fast. He realized that the rope was still in his hand, and stuck it onto the deck, and glued his way to the door that led to the stairwell, up to the bridge and down into the crew decks, on the side of the bridge house. It was locked. He overrode the security codes with his decoder, a tiny piece of really crooked equipment no larger than a credit card, which he'd stolen off a cat burglar in Italy, years ago. The door unlocked. Federi slipped in and pulled it to, and crouched in the shadowed passage, savouring the silence and the absence of wet.

Now. Strategy. This ship was a part of a flotilla of six. If it fell behind, the others would suspect foul play. He'd have to leave the helmsman and the navigator alive for now. He moved down into the decks.

The storm outside was raging on. Federi listened closely. Was he on the right ship? He had expected that his radar would put him in the way of the Silver Bullet, not one of the Schooners! But there was a reason; there was always a reason. His radar was not in the habit of failing him!

He iced. It *had* failed him, in Atuona! It had led him right into the hands of the enemy, into a position where, to survive, he had to initiate an action against the Rebellion – and bring down doom on the Solar Wind! Maybe Federi was used up? Maybe his radar was finished?

Where were they all? He sneaked along the passageway, opening cabins, looking into rooms, wishing he had more insight into the workings of the Rebellion.

There had been about twenty on that Schooner at Hiva Oa. Was that a normal sized crew? If that single schooner had been part of the greater Rebellion fleet, probably. Two would be on the bridge, navigating the storm. The rest?

They were closing the net on the Solar Wind, it occurred to him. They'd be in the bilges, getting armed.

Soundlessly he opened another cabin door, and his heart stuck in his throat. For a moment it looked like dark blood, by the dim light that filtered through the porthole. But it was indeed only her curls spilling around her white, still face. She was lying on the floor, tied into an O, with her hands and feet knotted together behind her back; and her eyes were shut. Was he too late? The way her anguished psychic cries for help had become softer and then faded into silence… Had Federi let her die?

Old Sherman was lying next to her, tied up in a similar fashion; he was alive. His eyes were open. There was nobody guarding them.

Federi locked the door behind himself, crouched down and felt for Paean's pulse at her throat. He sat down from the sheer rush of relief. Her skin was warm; her pulse, good and strong. She was only unconscious. He would not be bringing back a lifeless little body to the Solar Wind! He turned and cut Sherman's ties.

"Federi," whispered the old sailor. "You're a blessing! I'm not even going to ask! You can tell me the story later. I see you're not done yet!"

"Haven't found any of them yet," confirmed Federi.

"Paean's only unconscious," said Sherman, reading the stress in the Romany's eyes.

"Did they hurt her?"

"No. Not me either," added the centenarian, smiling at Federi's apologetic face.

"Why is she unconscious?"

"She gave backchat. Started asking pointy questions. I'm impressed with your little green pirate! She has mettle! They knocked her over the head. But they checked her vital signs, Federi, and she's breathing..."

"How long has she been out cold?" He sliced through her bonds. Her limp little body collapsed into a convoluted heap. Sherman sat up and rubbed his sore joints. Federi straightened Paean's limbs out on the floor, and gently lifted her head to release the torsion on her neck.

"Not long – fifteen minutes maybe," estimated Sherman.

"Fifteen minutes, Gods!" Federi ran his fingers through those soft red locks, untangling them a bit. She had been wearing her new scarf; it had fallen to the floor though. He could feel the significant bump on her scalp where they had "knocked" her. She'd be sore for days! He was upset. They hadn't hurt her? They had bashed her lights out! That was not hurting her?

"Where are they, Sherman?"

"From what I gather, they're at their various posts. They've seen that the girl and the old man are no threat," Sherman Dougherty added with a grin. "So they've been leaving us unguarded at times."

Federi glanced down at Paean and saw that her eyes were open, and she was gazing at him. He withdrew his hand from her hair, electrified.

"Ah, good, she's awake," he said. "I'm going now. Keep this door locked until I give the signal, okay?"

366

"Sure!" said Sherman. Paean gave the gypsy a slightly dazed smile.

Federi slipped out to continue his round. He closed the door behind himself and stared into the surprised face of a clean-shaved Latino.

"Sorry, José," he said. The Stiletto appeared in a whirr out of his sleeve. The Rebel went down in a shocked heap spraying arterial blood, his gun only halfway out of its holster. Federi supported his fall. He didn't want to make noise. He registered at the back of his mind how Sherman bolted the cabin door from the inside.

Rats! That had been self-defence! Blood everywhere! Federi dragged the dead man into the cabin across and closed the door. He took out his solvent and shook some over the mess, and spread it a bit with his sneaker. It was still a mess, but now it was the wrong colour. They wouldn't see it as fast.

Aw hell! How was he going to get the little sunbeam past this and spare her the sight? There was no way round it. He shook his head ironically. This time she wouldn't fail to see what scum he was.

28
Wrecks

Outside, the storm roared. The ship tilted and rolled. Paean sat on the compounding cabin floor, holding her head. It really hurt. The pitching didn't make it better. She ought to be sensible and take one of her own willow bark powders. If she only had any in her moonbag!

A knock on the cabin door; a hushed call. "Paean! Sherman! It's me!"

Sherman opened the door. Federi slipped back into the cabin and closed and bolted it. There was blood on his shirt.

"You're still not done, I gather," said Sherman.

Federi shook his head. "Done to an extent. Out of darts. Paean, do you have any of your little green bug on you by any chance?"

Paean dug wordlessly in her moonbag and handed him a vial.

"Great. Thanks!"

"You're only putting them under?" asked Sherman, surprised. "And if they come to?"

"No," said Federi sadly. "Don't know if that will buy enough time. Don't want them turning on us when we need it least."

Sherman nodded. A wise, strategic decision – and a terrible one.

Federi glanced at him, then at Paean – her eyes wide, anxious; his, regretful. Poor little sunshine. She was about to learn a few nasty truths. Tangibly.

"Lock yourselves in again and wait for me," he instructed. "*Kathal.*" He left, and waited outside the cabin door until he heard Sherman bolting it again, and continued on his way.

Federi had morphed into something that was not entirely human. His senses were deadly and sharpened like those of a wild animal; his thinking, reduced to strategy and stalking. His emotions, momentarily switched off, traded in for instinctual reflexes. His identity, his sense of self, merged into the surrounds. The Survivor.

It was a matter of speed. The plan of action, implemented so far, had been to shoot darts, hide the victims and finish them off with the Stiletto if there was time. There were quite a few who had escaped the Stiletto so far, as he carried on too quickly. He had to get them all before someone found a dead victim and sounded alarm. Twelve were already down. But he hadn't been on the lower crew deck yet, and not in the machine room either.

In his head he kept count. Seven had been killed, five only put under. He'd have to go back and finish the job, but first he had to be dead certain that nothing else moved on this ship.

And the two on the bridge – they'd be last. He was going to substitute them with Paean and Sherman, under instructions to keep the ship in the exact same pattern as it was, in formation with the flotilla.

Ailyss sat in the Solar Wind's infirmary, curled up on the second bunk hugging her knees to her, following Captain's orders to keep Wolf company. High stress drew its lines all around her green eyes.

The Solar Wind had not sunk. Despite being without a radar and riding a storm, through reefs and heads and shallows, she had not sunk. Captain Radomir Lascek, with his huge mystic power over the ship, the sea and the raw elements, had tamed the situation and brought them through it in one piece. And now –

They would find her aboard still, if she didn't jump off the ship through a porthole or something. For that, she had to find the place from where to do it. The bathrooms perhaps? Or the galley. But if she did too early, she would be lost at sea. And if she waited too late, she'd go down with the ship. And that would be good and well, she thought. But then, who'd look after little Keenan?

There was the off-chance that she'd be executed even before the Solar Wind was trapped. Could they trace the sabotage back to her? Would little Shawn Donegal keep his trap shut? It had all failed. Her entire tack had failed. And now it was her little brother's life.

Shawn's offer of the Donegals and Federi helping her cut at her. She knew if someone was capable of such a feat, it would be the gypsy.

Would he be prepared to do it? If Shawn and Paean worked on him, perhaps. If he knew what else she had done, certainly not.

She had set things irreversibly in motion, sending the Rebels the signals by which they could trace the Solar Wind. It wouldn't be long now; the Solar Wind would be torpedoed down and then she'd have her brother back – if only for a short while. Ailyss had not much hope for tender mercy from the Rebels. But even if she survived – if the Unicate ever got hold of her, after her association with the Rebellion... She shuddered.

Wolf was watching her thoughtfully.

"You are quite a one for secrets," he stated.

She glared at him.

"Don't worry, I'm not going to ask," said Wolf. "Only know, Ailyss, no matter what is working on your mind, count me a friend."

Ailyss laughed shortly. "What do you know!"

Oh, he was a nice guy, despite the correctional schooling written all over him and his unpolished ways. If she'd only been a technician, she'd have fancied him. There was no space for such friends in the life of an agent, though. Couldn't afford such attachments. He was going down with the rest of the crew. Oh, hell!

She shook her head. Wolf looked hurt. Well, he'd be more than hurt in another hour or so! He'd be dead! That pesky knee that little Paean had made such a mess of, would never give him trouble again! Ailyss sighed.

And would Paean get away? There was no chance! They had already found her, had already overtaken the Silver Bullet, by Ailyss' calculations. Poor Paean! Some help the damned gypsy was when his little friend needed him most!

The only chance the Solar Wind had now was to flee – to run like the wind before the storm, and head straight to Hawaii, to the harbour. How they'd get away from the military there was an open question, but by now she thought that Radomir Lascek might, somehow. And the Unicate would take great delight in shooting the Rebel Fleet to shrapnel, and with it, Keenan...

But the Solar Wind wasn't running. She lay stationary, lifted and tossed by the storm and stabilized by directional bursts from the various drives in the machine room. Waiting for the Silver Bullet! There was no getting away.

Ailyss lifted her head very slightly. Something subtle reached her fine-tunes senses. Immediately the confirmation came in Shawney's scream, carrying down to them over the com. The dance had begun.

"Captain, ships astern," yelled Shawn, his voice panicky. He counted. "Sir, there's six of them! And – the Silver Bullet."

"Donegal! Are you still in the Crow's Nest?" Lascek shouted back, shocked.

"Yes, sir! I never got an order to get down!"

Lascek stared at Marsden. The waves were huge now, and the visibility near to nothing. He'd ordered all the flyers below deck a while back. But his lookout... To keep track of this crazy crew...

Captain Rodriguez stared at Lascek.

"Is your radar out of order?" he asked.

"We have had a little trouble with it," said Lascek through his teeth. He punched at the ship com. "Shawn, stay up there and watch for more rocks. Ronan Donegal, get up there with your brother! Tie extra lifelines! Both of you! Put on a life vest again! Blast, in this gale! Dr Jake, get the drives ready. Marsden, take the helm. Schatz, get the crew armed. Hang it, where's that Tzigan when you need him!"

Rodriguez' eyes flew open. Lascek grinned mirthlessly at him. He watched as it hit the Cuban that they had been navigated through all sorts of reefs by visuals only.

"Lascek, old animal," said Rodriguez, shaking the Captain's hand. "You can count me and my men as allies! Rebellion is always the enemy to Cuba."

Lascek shook the Cuban's hand, wondering how long this pact would last and at which inopportune moment it would be broken. It was great to have Rodriguez' declaration; but that didn't mean that he'd give the Spanish men any firepower! Their own weapons had been carefully disabled by Federi last night when he had checked all the lifelines.

He didn't feel easy about leaving both Donegal brothers outside in the Crow's Nest. But submerging was not an option without the radar. In fact, navigation was impossible without a radar, unless he had a lookout.

Ailyss had known what she was doing. He only hoped that the weather would lighten soon.

The Solar Wind's internal intercom sounded.

"Captain, it's Sherman. Don't shoot at the foremost Rebel Schooner, that's us."

A yell of delight sounded from the Crow's Nest. Rodriguez found himself and his men cheering too.

"Are you free, Sherman, or are you hostages?" asked Lascek.

"Free, Captain! Our Federi came along on his white charger. Just in time! Was getting terribly bored!"

The Captain laughed. Our Federi! Our Federi deserved a medal! The genius!

"Sherman, I read you! We'll open fire on the others. Give me a signal to show me which ship you're on."

Sherman flashed the mast light twice.

The Solar Wind launched a torpedo at each of the two ships flanking Sherman's. Then she had to flee.

Sherman opened the Schooner's engines at full throttle and set off after the Solar Wind. The enemy Schooners opened the chase.

Paean was hanging onto the Schooner's helm for dear life. She had never actually done the steering of a ship yet and found that it wasn't all that easy in such rough seas. Federi was somewhere below deck; she assumed he was still "cleaning up".

Poor Federi! What a totally dirty job description! Hero craft, Wolf had called it. Well, Wolf had no idea! She had seen the fixated blood on the compounding deck just outside their cabin door. And the drag tracks. Oh hey, if that didn't get to him! And the worried, hooded glances he cast her, as though she ought to be spitting on him now!

A small boy emerged on the bridge. He couldn't be older than ten or eleven. Paean glanced at him. He looked frightened. Dark shadows ringed his eyes. His face was gaunt.

"The scary man with the knife said I must go to the bridge and look for the red-haired lady," he said. "He says you're friends with my sister."

"Who is your sister?" asked Paean, keeping a sharp lookout for rocks. She'd have very sore arms after this one, she knew. The helm was a smallish wheel that swivelled in three dimensions, relaying her movements electronically; but the tension cramps in her arms and hands were analogue. But she'd rather die than let on to Sherman Dougherty! Hero craft.

"Her name's Ailyss Quinlan. I'm Keenan."

"Ailyss!" exclaimed Sherman, shocked. "You're Ailyss' little brother?"

"Yes, sir."

"Come, sit here," said Sherman, pointing to the console chair next to him. "Ailyss is aboard the Solar Wind. She'll be very happy to see you!" He engaged the intercom. "Solar Wind, come in. This is Sherman. Captain, we have Ailyss' little brother with us. He is unharmed."

The Captain stared at Marsden. "Ailyss has a brother!"

"I'll call her," said Marsden.

"*Nem*, Marsden. I'll get her myself. Want to see her face."

Marsden took the bridge as the Captain walked off at a rate, down below the deck, and into the infirmary.

"Ailyss, your brother wants to speak to you. Get to the bridge."

All colour drained out of Ailyss' face.

"Yes, Captain!" She stood up without a further word and rushed out of the infirmary. Wolf's despondent gaze followed her. He had been right! Radomir Lascek followed Ailyss. He didn't want to miss the exchange between the Quinlan sibs!

"There you go," Sherman said to Keenan, handing over his wrist-com. "Talk to your sister, Keenan."

The wrist-coms and the internal communication system of the Solar Wind, unlike her official ship-to-ship com, didn't function on radio waves. They were extremely limited-range devices, so that the rest of the world couldn't accidentally pick up the conversations of the Solar Wind and locate her by it. It was luck that she was in range.

"Hi, Ailyss," said Keenan.

"Keenan! Are you alright? Did they hurt you?"

"No. Only, they didn't give me any food and told me they'll kill you when you come aboard."

Ailyss looked at the Captain in shock. He glared at her.

"Ailyss?" the pleading voice of the little boy came out of the com, verging on tears. "They can't, can they? You won't let them kill you, right? Please?"

A foreign voice crackled over the Solar Wind's ship-to-ship radio intercom in Spanish.

"This is Commander Peras from the Rebellion. Radomir Lascek, give yourself up. You are outnumbered."

Lascek didn't bother replying. He locked two more torpedoes onto the enemy ships. The devices never got released, though. Something stuck.

"This is your doing too?" he asked Ailyss. She shook her head, terrified.

"We'll have to use what is around us," said Lascek. "Can't get close enough to fire with the drives. By then they'll have sunk us." He punched another sequence into the console. The sails unfurled again.

Jon Marsden looked up in surprise, realizing what his Captain intended.

"Captain – that would-be hurricane out there -?"

"Men back to positions," shouted Lascek. "We'll fly her again!" He grinned at Marsden. "It's only a would-be. Its bluff is up."

The First Mate frowned, but said nothing. Those waves out there were still enormous. The wind was vicious. It was a risk having the two Donegal brothers up in the Crow's Nest, no matter how many lifelines they tied on. But to chase the whole crew back outside…

Rodriguez organized his four sailors back into the posts they had occupied the first time the ship had flown. Marsden understood. Complete command, was what Captain was after. He was testing the Cubans, and his own crew after that show of defiance from Federi. And it was after all not quite a hurricane.

"We won't come out where we meant to come out," commented Lascek quietly to his First Mate. "Wind is pushing south here. Can't tack in a storm. But it's worth it, I think?" He motioned to those Rebellion ships out there. "We're in the rocks, Jon. They break a lot of the force of the wind. Waves not as high as they'd like to be. It will be fine."

Marsden nodded and resumed his place behind the console. Captain didn't have any choice, if he thought about it carefully. His alternatives

374

had been sabotaged. Rushka and Rhine Gold went back to their posts too. Ailyss moved to join them.

"You stay on the bridge!" Lascek snapped at her. He placed a heavy hand on her shoulder, fixing her with a penetrating stare. "Your game's up, Ailyss Quinlan! I want you to see what Radomir Lascek does when his technician betrays him and delivers him into the hands of an enemy fleet!"

Ailyss looked down. She couldn't hold that steely stare. She had lost, she knew this. She also knew suddenly that he was right and she was wrong. That hand on her shoulder steadied her milling thoughts just as his solid grip had steadied the Solar Wind. They quietened down. All was becoming clear. The entire damned Unicate was wrong! The Rebellion, even worse! Radomir Lascek was the only honourable soul out there.

"Sorry, Captain," she muttered. "I'm so sorry!" If she'd only trusted her own instincts and abandoned her mission earlier! But her brother... "I know, I'm dead – but you won't harm Keenan, will you, Captain?"

"We don't harm innocents, damn you, girl," exploded Lascek. He turned away, back to Marsden, and pointed at the sea ahead. "We're a day and a half outside Prime, would you say?"

"Yes, Captain."

"I know this area," said Lascek loudly, activating the ship com so the Cubans could hear. "What's the name of this volcanic system of reefs and shoals that popped up here in the nineties? The one that was an island atoll for about a week?"

"Canebo, I think," said Marsden. He smiled. "Oh, Radomir!"

"Incorrigible, you say?" grinned Lascek. He activated the com. "Any reefs yet, Donegals?" As though reefs were not what they had been navigating past for the last three hours!

Sherman saw from the bridge of the Rebel Schooner what Lascek was doing.

"Ah," he smiled. "Old sea-devil! He's leading them back into the rocks! Into Canebo! Doesn't anything scare that man?"

"Not more rocks," groaned Paean.

"These are too much for us," agreed Sherman. "I suggest we chart our own course, because we don't know this ship well and we might sink her.

We navigate around those rocks and meet up with the Solar Wind on the other side."

"Wish the storm would quit," she sighed.

"We're nearly out of it," placated Sherman. "But Radomir is deliberately leading them back into it! See that?"

"Why?"

"One Solar Wind against six Rebel ships? What else would you suggest?"

Ailyss hung onto the handholds, watching the Captain and Jon Marsden in action. Lascek had taken the helm; his First Mate was operating the console, and the Captain reached over every now and then to hammer a sequence into the keyboard himself, like a pianist in a duet. Marsden and the Captain seemed so tuned into each other, they appeared to share a consciousness.

She peered outside. Rain drenched the mostly Cuban flying team. Yet they responded like a finely tuned apparatus, obeying Rushka's commands brilliantly despite her being a young girl; she in turn complied instinctively with what her father demanded.

Ailyss lifted her gaze to the wild, rain-whipped sea beyond the deck. The heads and submerged reefs went on and on. The Solar Wind skimmed her way past on the right and then on the left at breakneck speed, and then on the right again, plummeting into troughs and ploughing up swells, and then skated on hydrofoils right over a shoal that was just too near the surface for the heavier Schooners, timing it perfectly with the erratic waves. Ronan Donegal shouted directions from the Crow's Nest to the bridge over the com, with Shawn piping up every so often, adding something in. Lascek responded to these directions intuitively, also taking into account – to Ailyss' surprise – several other readings the console showed, which weren't part of a normal ship console system! The Solar Wind gave constant data about the strength of waves and currents, the probability of submerged rocks as calculated by the behaviour of the water and its turbulences; the strength of the wind and the exact angle, and predictions of momentary currents and eddies and their vectors. Compared to this, radar seemed a crude, old-fashioned apparatus!

Radomir Lascek used it all, enhancing the stability of the ship with small bursts from various drives. Those in use had to be positioned at the very base of the keel. She herself ought to be in the machine room helping Dr Jake, she thought guiltily. He'd have his hands full! But the Captain had told her to stay right here where he could see her.

The Schooners couldn't get around the Solar Wind. In the first place she was faster; she could simply have outrun them. But this was not Lascek's plan. Dr Jake in the machine room and Marsden on the bridge exploded advancing torpedoes with nuclear bursts. Not that there was a whole lot of target for those torpedoes!

Ailyss watched, awed. She studied the men at work; Marsden with his suave, smooth appearance and manner, focus across his entire face. The Captain, smiling. Devils of light dancing in his steel-blue eyes. He was having fun! Ailyss could see that he loved the way his ship responded, the way he and his unlikely crew could sail her into near-impossibility, only to veer away from rocks and sandbanks at the last moment, watching with glee how another of the Schooners was drawn in by the tide and the currents, and dragged onto the rocks. Beached, wrecked.

She was amazed, and proud, and miserable. Proud to be on this ship and have the privilege of watching at such close range. Miserable, because she had picked the wrong side and doomed this extraordinary bunch of survivors. It had been wrong from the start. Unicate was a dicey employer; Rebellion, a terrible foe. Life was treacherous to begin with; working as a solitary agent had been her way of slinking past the most slippery bits. She was aware of Jon Marsden casting her searching glances; repeatedly she took a breath, meaning to throw herself at the Captain's feet and beg for his forgiveness, and every time she shrugged the urge off again. There was no point. Her life was forfeit. She didn't want mercy, only to be forgiven, but she doubted that she'd get that either.

She'd throw herself at the mercy of the gypsy, she decided. He was the most dangerous of the lot. He'd execute her, that was certain, but she'd implore him to take care of her brother. He had a soft spot for children. Keenan had done nothing wrong; he'd been caught in the crossfire. Federi looked after Shawn well enough.

The Solar Wind surfed over a huge swell, lifted high by the force of the wave, and glided into the trough. Behind her, the last of the Schooners that was still operational, cleared the same crest – almost. The wave had moved on. The Schooner came down on a sandbank, its keel hitting it with such a force that the whole ship cracked open like an egg. Radomir Lascek smiled broadly.

"Peras," he engaged the ship-to-ship intercom, "I won't ask you why you are hunting us. I know why. Understand one thing though. That war you're planning with the Unicate. It's not going to happen. That's a promise. I am Radomir Lascek, and I don't make empty promises."

A stream of juicy Spanish expressions poured out of the ship com. Radomir Lascek laughed, a loud, hearty laugh. The Solar Wind cleared the system of reefs and furled her sails, waiting for the Rebellion Schooner under Sherman Dougherty's command to finish rounding the rocks.

Radomir Lascek turned to Ailyss.

"Any comments, Miss Quinlan?"

"*War,* Captain?"

He smiled grimly. "You had the idea you were working for a noble organization?"

"Captain..." Ailyss sighed. "I know my life is forfeit. I'm only so sorry that I picked the wrong side!" She snapped her mouth shut. There hadn't been all that much freedom to pick, if she thought about it. If she looked closely, her whole career was really only a dance for survival.

"So am I, Ailyss Quinlan," said Radomir Lascek gravely. "So am I!"

Federi had finished his round of the Schooner. There had indeed been exactly twenty. Only Sherman, Paean and Ailyss' brother were now officially aboard. He considered for a moment doing the same on the neighbouring schooner. But it didn't really matter now. Captain would lead the other ships into a trap and finish them off, or simply outrun them. The head-start he needed, had been supplied. They would be alright now. Perhaps, for a little while, the Solar Wind would still have a future. A week, maybe two. After that...

Federi sat down on a crate. Of course *he* would get away again, he knew this. Federi always survived. Everyone else died, everyone he loved, and Federi lived. And Federi so richly deserved to die, this time! He had brought it down on all their heads! Federi, the low-life.

His radar had failed him, led him into this bloodbath. Federi was finished, used up. He couldn't do good for the Solar Wind anymore; only wreak havoc. It was as though against his will his past was catching up with him. And the past had no shape, you could not stab it in the heart. It was worse than ghosts. It would come and devour them all…

He examined his Stiletto, which he had rinsed carefully after finishing off his last victim. It was a beautiful blade, razor-sharp, so sharp he sometimes thought the edges blurred. His oldest friend.

His hands started playing with the smooth blade, and a small smile played in the corner of his mouth. There was always the real reason he carried this singing knife. Why not right now? It was a clean, pain-free way to die. Very fast, too. A nearly perfect death. Delete Federi, and you deleted his past!

He was quite curious.

The Schooner in Sherman's command emerged on the other side of a narrow gate of rocky heads, where the Solar Wind lay waiting. The sea over Canebo was green and foamy, lit up in reflection of the glorious sunset sky. The rain had blown over; the storm had moved on.

Paean glimpsed the beautiful scenery from the bridge of the Schooner. The sea never failed to leave her breathless with wonder. It took her back to the sunset yesterday, another perfect moment for her memory gallery. Peaceful, beautiful. Only twenty-four hours later, this: The system of reefs was graced with five ugly Rebellion Schooners and one Barracuda from Cuba. The sea was splashing up against them as though it had been doing so for centuries. Her skull hurt where the dratted Rebels had knocked her out. She wondered why Federi was taking so long.

Terrorists were crowded on the rocks where their ships had come to grief. Some were still bobbing around the insane waves in lifeboats trying to find landing spots. They were being watched by Radomir Lascek and Salvatore Rodriguez. Lascek knew that any moment now, Federi ought to appear on the deck of the Rebel Schooner and start taking them out with his long-range rifle. Cleaning up.

Captain Lascek waited. No Federi appeared. Perhaps he didn't have his rifle with him?

The Solar Wind drew up alongside the Rebellion ship. Grappling hooks shot across to the rail, pulling the Schooner closer.

"There you go," said Sherman Dougherty. "Come, Paean, Keenan! Let's get back aboard the Mother Ship! I'm sure both of you have some very impatient sibs waiting!"

"Sherman, you two go ahead," said Paean. "I'm just going to check on Federi."

"Certainly, lass," smiled the old sailor. "Just be careful. Come, Keenan! Let's meet your sister!"

Keenan allowed himself to be led off the bridge and across to the Solar Wind by Sherman.

What had Sherman meant, be careful? Maybe Federi had missed one or two of the terrorists? Maybe some of them would come to soon? Paean went in search of Federi, a loaded needle with Valeriensis hidden in her hand as self-defence. You never knew.

She descended the stairwell and found the captain and helmsman of the schooner under the stairs. Crumpled; dead. Blood seeping out of their necks. Paean heaved a shaky sigh. He hadn't just put them under, had he! She recalled the brief conversation he'd had with Sherman about not enough time.

She made her way along the deck, wondering if the other Schooner – on which she had never set foot – had looked as messy. There were incidents of blood everywhere. And bodies. He hadn't bothered hiding the last ones. Blood had splattered against walls and even the ceiling in some places. The further Paean searched, the more sinister the setup got. Her heart sank.

She could see from the way many of them had fallen and were lying that they had been anaesthetized first. But each and every one of those bore the same small, professional incision at the base of their throat. And a puddle of blood. In her mind she counted along as she made her way along the different decks. She found eighteen. Where was Federi?

Eventually she found the stairwell to the bilges. The machine room. It was dark except for the dim glow of dials and indicators, and the light falling in through the hatch. She descended down the steps, and froze. There was a solitary figure sitting on a crate in the dusk, its back to her. Sitting so still she only saw it now. It took her five breathless seconds to

380

figure out that it was Federi. And two more victims, sprawling in dark puddles, dead.

She peered at Federi's back. Was he breathing? She glanced back at his two last victims, and her throat constricted. She couldn't figure it out – how her gentle friend could be capable of this. It didn't make sense. She paused for several heartbeats, thinking hard about it, before she could force herself back into motion. Inside that still shape hunched on that crate lived a sweet, imaginative guy who carved puppets and hung jingles on his ceiling. A shy guy who made you coffee if you let the small-talk dry up. A man who had been a friend to her when she needed it most. No conditions whatsoever. Whoever else was in there with him, *that* Federi needed her right now. She walked up to him from behind and saw from a minute movement of his back straightening that he was alive, and aware of her.

"It's me," she said quietly and put her hand on his shoulder. He had his stiletto in his hand and was staring at it. The blade was clean, and shimmered softly in the semi-dark. "Come, Federi. We're moored to the Solar Wind!"

He turned slowly. She got a fright. Was that him in there, behind those eyes full of haunted shadows? Did he even recognize her?

"Aw, to hell with it," he said darkly. "Can't you leave a man alone when he wants to finish things?"

"Sorry, no," said Paean, feeling icy cold. "Not in general. Definitely not you." Her hand tightened around the syringe she had half forgotten about.

"Hand over," demanded Federi in a resigned voice, holding out his hand. She gave him the syringe, and it vanished into his pocket system. He turned away from her again.

" 's pointless," he said, studying the stiletto. "We're doomed anyway."

"Come, Federi." Paean gave his arm a tug. "I'll make you some coffee."

"Did you see them?" he asked with a cynical smile.

She nodded, her heart breaking. She didn't know how she was supposed to get him back up to the deck without him seeing all of that.

"All that blood," he muttered. "And what's the point? Some live, some die… in the end it's all just people. They only want to make a living and find a small spot in the sun. They eat and drink and piss just like the rest of us. In the end we all die. You should go, little songbird. They need you on the Solar Wind."

She stared at him speechlessly. She couldn't imagine what it must be like to be him, right now. How could she shine him a light onto the path to the future? Was there a future for him?

Federi avoided her eyes. "Little firebird, don't look at me like that! Go! You've got your whole life ahead of you."

"Forget it!" said Paean heatedly. "I'm not going back to the Solar Wind without you! Would be a bleak place! Please come now. Or they'll think we've deserted," she added. "Do you want *that* rumour spreading?"

"I could think of worse ones," smiled Federi. Paean peered at him critically. Still he didn't make any moves to get up.

"Fine," she said and sat down on the floor, leaning against the crate he was sitting on. Two could play that game. "That's okay. We can stay here if it makes you happier. And I know. I won't dig."

Suddenly the gypsy got angry. "And some people should have their jolly heads read. Calling Federi a mutineer! Ha! With bells on! True, I'm a piece of dirt, but not a deserter! – Hoy, and your brother's in for a tough time!"

"What – Shawney?"

"No. Ronan. He dares to date the Princess. Ha! Good luck! Poor Ronan!"

Paean was secretly pleased. Anger was a wonderful antidote for a suicidal mood. She made a mental note to brew some St John's Wort for Federi and – er – she supposed, tie him up and force it down his throat.

"Maybe you just need to talk to Captain," she said soothingly. "He's not worth losing your life over!"

"What?" Federi laughed bitterly. "*He's* not the reason! Cor, Paean," he added with another acrid laugh.

It had only been a little rile. A feeble attempt at misplaced humour. Aw, Federi! She sighed shakily. This was bad. Really bad. He'd done *this*... sacrificed his own soul, for her and Sherman, and Ailyss' little brother! For the whole Solar Wind, she realized. He'd rescued the ship from the Rebellion fleet. And it wasn't the first time. He'd done the same back at Hiva Oa. He didn't have a choice either time. If he'd left any of them alive, they would have come back and killed her and Sherman, and the little boy while Federi was putting others under with her green bug. It had been them or the Rebels. It was a war. And it was more than his loaded psyche could hold. She dashed angrily at something wet that was sneaking down her cheek.

It was like this. The Solar Wind only tried to stay alive; they didn't ask to be hunted and shot at and knocked over the head. But while Captain shot neat torpedoes at enemy ships from a distance, Federi got up close and watched how his enemies died under his knife, and saw how they were only human, too. Captain got the hero craft; Federi, the dirty work. She'd be suicidal too, anna bottle of cyanide!

"Are you justifying my misdeeds to yourself?" asked Federi softly, with a smile.

She swallowed.

"Well, it's true," she snapped, annoyed about the tearfulness of her voice. "You had to! It was us or them! Survival!"

"That's what they all say," he said, his despondent voice nearly a whisper.

Well, the heck was she going to let him see her cry! Her whistle could do the crying for her. Maybe it could untie the knot in her gentle friend's heart, too. Music was the vision of a better life, a better future. She subconsciously leaned back against him, searching for her pennywhistle in the depth of her pockets.

Federi picked up a handful of her soft red curls that were whirling out from under her turquoise scarf. Hair, not blood.

"Sweet," he said. The stiletto flashed, and a small lock stayed behind in his hand. "Paean, you lost this. Can I have it?"

She flew around. "What?! You cut off my hair! What did you do that for?"

"Black magic," said Federi with a dark grin. Interesting! His knife was content now. "Thanks, my little luv." He slipped the stiletto back into its sheath in his sleeve. Paean heaved a sigh of relief.

29

Ailyss

Radomir Lascek watched the tearful reunion of Ailyss and her brother, from the bridge. Jon Marsden next to him was staring at the scene too.

"Jon," said Lascek gravely, "what do we do with her?"

Jon Marsden didn't respond. Lascek knew that his First Mate didn't have an answer either.

The Law of the Pacific – Pirate Law – dealt swiftly with traitors. He didn't have to like it. Nevertheless from a practical angle too, there wasn't much else they could really do without risking the lives of everyone on the Solar Wind. Realistically, she had to die. Regardless of all high hopes he'd had for her. It was better than waiting for her to attempt murder on his crew once more.

But the little boy's voice haunted Radomir Lascek. "Ailyss, they can't, can they? You won't let them kill you, right? Please?"

If he executed her, how was he different from the Rebellion? He would be applying exactly the kind of bigotry he despised in them! But leaving her alive – was that even an option? What would she do next to endanger his crew?

"There's only one logical option," said Marsden, his voice sounding far-away. "And you won't like it, Captain."

"That is?" asked Radomir Lascek.

"Execute them both," said Marsden.

Lascek peered at his First Mate. Surely the man was joking? But Marsden's face was as impassive as though he were one of Federi's woodcarvings.

It was dark when Paean and Federi finally came across the gangway back to the Solar Wind. Radomir Lascek was waiting for them. He greeted Federi with a wry grin and a handshake.

"Tzigan! I wronged you, my friend. You were right. You saved the Solar Wind. Again."

Federi looked up at Lascek with a grin and a peculiar glint in his eye. One gypsy eyebrow was raised in irony.

" 's fine, Captain," he said. "Tzigan should sometimes stick to the rules."

"If you had, we'd all be dead," said Lascek. "Stay exactly as you are, Federi."

"*Nu,* Captain," retorted Federi, grinning. "*Niente!* I'll be brainlessly submissive ever after. 's what you ordered. You'll have to do all my thinking for me. And I want a written job description."

"Oh, for the love of spiky sea urchins, Tzigan! You've been given a brain for a purpose!"

"Haha," replied the Jester. "Too much work writing out job descriptions? Want to delegate it to Federi?"

"To Marsden," snapped Lascek. "Your handwriting is illegitimate. What? No! Nonsense! There shall be no written job descriptions on the pirate ship! You do as I tell you, *basta!"*

Federi was laughing. Radomir Lascek realized he'd just been talked around in a circle. He assessed the gypsy. Nervous breakdown? Jolly unlikely! And what was that allusion to rules? Which rules had been broken now? He wondered.

Paean made a beeline for the rigging and climbed via the handholds on the mast into the Crow's Nest. And that in the dark! Moments later, snatches of Irish tunes started floating down on the sea breeze. Lascek watched her with amazement, and some concern. What had gone down on that Schooner?

"Don't you want to fetch her down from there?" he suggested to Federi.

The response was silence. He turned to his Tzigan. The guy had vanished.

Hells! Sometimes the Solar Wind felt like a circus ship full of ghosts. And sometimes he wondered if he had ended in an asylum. As supervisor!

Ailyss turned to Marsden, who had followed the Captain down to the deck. Keenan was hanging onto her.

"Please, sir," she said.

The First Mate turned and nailed her with a hard glare. She flinched. She had never seen the courteous man look that angry.

"You know what, Ailyss, almost we had hoped we'd get to Hawaii without you doing anything of the sort," he said curtly. "Captain Radomir is no fool. He knew from the second you boarded that he was hiring a spy. Must have seen something special in you to take you on in any case."

This didn't help things along.

"I have to show you what else I've done, sir," said Ailyss. There was always a hope that Captain would be true to his word and keep her brother safe even after she was put ashore to be left to the Unicate. She knew in her deepest nuclear core that the ship was the only place Keenan would ever really be safe now. So the only way now was to play open cards. Well, as open as she could manage. It was a fine line. She'd have to be careful not to jeopardize things for Keenan.

"Just tell me," said Marsden.

"No, I have to show you this one, sir."

Ailyss led the computer technologist into the machine room and pulled something out behind the computer terminal. She placed it in Marsden's open palm.

"Got to destroy this, sir."

"My word," said Marsden with a smile. "Look at it! So small, so deadly!" Almost, he thought, like little Paean's green wonder bug. But that was not right. He had been wrong about Paean. Though she wreaked havoc, she was one of their own. This one... "Thanks for handing it over," said the First Mate. "Captain will be very interested in this! Are there any others?"

"No."

"Good!" Marsden turned Ailyss and Keenan over to Wolf in the infirmary and went to show the Captain the transmitter.

Rodriguez approached Lascek once again. "I don't want to intrude upon a tender moment, but I'm not quite clear now what my options are!"

Lascek summed him up. A piratical grin spread over his face. What

386

an interesting twist! The Barracuda lay wrecked upon the rocks. But there was a huge Rebellion Schooner that was, at this point, in the way... If Rodriguez arrived in Hawaii on a Rebellion ship, how would the Unicate react to that? Radomir Lascek couldn't resist such puzzles.

"Would you consider taking that Schooner?"

"Gladly," said Rodriguez. The course had been laid. There was no way he could return to Cuba without his Barracuda. The Unicate punished deserters efficiently and rather terminally; and losing a whole ship – well...

Dr Jake searched the Schooner for any further data capsules and chips. There was nothing. He took all he could off the ship computer. Marsden rewrote the Schooner's identity *in situ*. Rodriguez was unaware of all this. Radomir Lascek was keeping him in the boardroom with a cup of coffee, discussing his options. The obvious thing would be to sell the ship off and buy one of equal capacity that didn't have a Rebellion background. A good place to do this was the pirate port of Atuona. The most important question was about the bounty money. Radomir Lascek grinned and shrugged.

"It's a risk you take, as a bounty hunter," he said. "If you want bounty – there are lots of pirates on the Pacific!"

The Cuban took his men onto the Schooner. It was a beautiful ship, much larger and more elaborate than the little Barracuda he had been used to. This took being a captain to new dimensions. And she came fully provisioned and all!

Soon the Cuban Coastal Guard set off for new horizons.

"Urgh," said Little Cloud Navarro. "All these dead corpses aboard!"

"Ever seen a live corpse?" asked Romero.

"Never hope to."

Ronan and Rushka were celebrating their newly found romance in the dark jib stowage area at the Solar Wind's prow.

"There you are!" said Shawn brightly, shining a torch into the eyes of the blushing teen couple. "Listen, you two. Secret gathering in the Infirmary. Got a lady in distress."

"Go away!" growled Ronan.

"I think this is important," said Rushka. "Come, Ronan."

They followed the pesky twelve-year-old down to Sick Bay.

Radomir Lascek punched the dysfunctional radar. It made no difference. And it didn't solve his question about Ailyss either. What Marsden suggested was fiendish. But then Lascek wasn't even sure how serious his First Mate had been.

He himself was furious. According to Dr Jake, Ailyss was one of the most promising young nuclear technicians the scientist had ever worked with. And she knew how to program. At root level! A skill that betrayed just how good an agent she was. Unicate certainly didn't train just any spy to that level of insight. She would have been a brilliant addition to his crew – if the Lascekian magic had worked, which it hadn't. He had failed. He had been preoccupied. He ought to have given her more attention before she had reason to make her move.

The Rebellion had gone sour against the Solar Wind because of her!

"She should be made to walk the plank, keel-hauled and hung by her toes from the rigging," he growled. "The whole darned Rebellion on our tails! But her little brother…" And Radomir Lascek ought to be punished too, he thought bitterly, for rescuing someone who needed it, and then failing her.

Jonathan Marsden turned the transmitter over in his hand. What had Ailyss' unspoken message been, leading him to it? A cry for help! Why? Was she hoping to escape justice? Did she think he liked her any more or judged her any less harshly than the others for what she had done? He agreed with Captain Radomir – she deserved to be terminated.

"Won't go down very well," he said. "She's been one of us."

"If I'd found Federi to be a turncoat, I'd let him walk the plank," said Lascek grimly. "And no bones about it."

"You'd have a genuine mutiny on your hands then," advised Marsden. "And I can't even say I would pick your side. He's not a turncoat. Unwise and rash, sure, but not a turncoat."

"Yes, yes, Marsden, point taken. So what do we do with our little saboteur?"

"We interrogate her," said Marsden. "I'd like to know why, so suddenly."

"You're saying she acted out of character?" asked Lascek with surprise.

Marsden peered at him thoughtfully.

In the infirmary Rhine Gold, Wolf and Shawn were already interrogating Ailyss. Ronan and Rushka sat close together on the vacant bunk, holding hands and listening. Ailyss' little brother sat by her side on the same bunk and refused to budge. Shawn was seated cross-legged at the foot of Wolf's bed, having almost accidentally sat down on the man's recovering knee. Rhine Gold's tall frame occupied the only available chair. The cabin was rather small and seating limited; so the entire meeting had a feeling of a conspiracy to it. Which was what it was.

"You'd better spill it now, Ailyss," said Shawn. "This is the sympathetic crowd. We know you tried to kill us all. We want to know why."

Ailyss looked at them speechlessly.

"Captain will execute you, Ailyss," said Rushka. "You know he will. You must tell us what happened. Maybe we can change his mind."

Execute her? She had thought Captain would put her ashore for the Unicate to do their worst. There was always a chance on escape. But if he opted for the Law of the Pacific – she swallowed. Things were looking grim indeed. She glanced at her little brother who was clinging to her hand, pale as death. And the rest of Rushka's suggestion sank in. They were going to try *changing Captain's mind?*

"You'd do that for me?" And from *Rushka?* Ailyss was amazed.

"Of course," said Wolf. "Guys, can we have a vote? Who's going to help talk the Captain round?"

The young crowd was unanimous.

A few hours back she had deliberately thought of them all as delinquents, human garbage. She saw them differently now: A group of young survivors who cared about her. Good grief, with what did she deserve that? Who was the garbage?

"Guys," she sighed. "You don't understand. Surely Captain is justified to execute me. I definitely don't deserve you for friends."

Her little brother looked ready to cry.

She came out with her story. She was to meet with her original employers, who were Unicate, in Hawaii. The idea was to deliver as much

389

information about the Solar Wind as she could – such facts as that she could submerge, any soft spots she might have, her plan of action, of which Ailyss had gleaned nothing, and other items of interest, such as Paean's sleep bug. Unicate had employed her so they could finish the Solar Wind off once and for all. She was also to send a signal to prepare the harbour as they approached. It had so nearly worked in Port Hamilton! In Panama she hadn't stood a chance – Paean's bug had wiped her out before she'd had a gap to send any kind of signal. She smiled about this, thankful now that it had worked that way. It was one less charge against her.

But ever since the data capsule had gone missing on Hiva Oa and a Rebellion Schooner was sunk after capturing two Solar Wind pirates, the Rebellion also had it in for the Solar Wind. They wanted that capsule! Taking Paean and Sherman hostage had been a windfall for them, a lucky break. According to what Keenan had gathered, they had not hurt the captives so that they could bargain the data capsule back, if necessary by means of torture. And after that, they wanted Lascek out of the way, and no witnesses. Federi had shown no mercy on the Schooner; accordingly the Rebellion was going to show no mercy to Lascek and his crew.

Instead of paying Ailyss, they had kidnapped her brother right out of their apartment on Nuku Hiva, where he had stayed with their child carer. They had put pressure on Ailyss, threatening to kill her little brother, the only relative she had and whom she had practically raised alone ever since Mom and Da had died horribly.

She looked at Shawn in desperation. A wave splashed against the infirmary's dark porthole.

"We'll protect you," he promised. "We'd also kill to protect our families. Let's tell Federi! He's always the first with a good plan."

The others nodded approvingly. Ailyss shook her head sceptically. Federi? *He* wasn't going to protect her! He was going to kill her! Shawn scooted off to find him.

The Romany was in his cabin, cross-legged on his bunk, carefully wrapping thin gold wire around the middle of something small. It looked alive. Shawn came closer.

"Hey, a lock," he said when he recognized the small furry thing.

"Whose hair is this?"

"You can't tell?" asked Federi with a smile.

"Wow – it's Paean's! That's funny," said Shawn. "Didn't know she loses hair!"

"She's moulting," commented the gypsy. "You wanted me, Shawn?"

"Yip. Must help Ailyss get a plan."

Federi stopped his hands for a second. "Ailyss, huh. Yeah, I'll bet she needs all the help she can get now." He continued wrapping the wire. Then he reached for a small pair of pliers and twisted the ends around each other. He had looped a tiny metal nut into the gold wire, and now he dug in his treasure chest of drawers, extracting a long gold chain. He threaded the chain through the nut and hung the whole thing around his neck, hiding it under his clothes.

"You what – why have you – and why aren't you –" asked Shawn.

Federi waved his long fingers hypnotically.

"You didn't see anything," he said enigmatically.

"But why are you wearing Paean's hair?"

"Black magic," said Federi softly and grinned. When Shawn looked troubled, Federi laughed out loud. "Don't worry, my boy! I'd never hurt a hair on your sister's head!"

"Sure," said Shawn thoughtfully. "But you wouldn't help Keenan's sister, now would you?"

"Do you feel so strongly about it?"

"Captain will kill her! She tried to sink the Solar Wind! But he doesn't understand why!"

He didn't know what to make of the dark glare he received from the Romany. Suddenly he wasn't at all certain anymore that Federi was the right person to ask for help.

"Alright," sighed Federi. "Seeing that I'm the spokesperson for the younger crowd here – take me to your leader."

In the infirmary, the gypsy listened to the whole saga from Ailyss.

"Can't say I approve of having her aboard at all. I'd have thrown her off in Plymouth," he commented. Ailyss scowled, her green eyes narrowed like a cat's. She was more scared of him than of her prospects. She should be!

"Captain had his reasons," said Rhine Gold.

"Who knows what those are," said Federi darkly. "You know, Shawn, Ronan, I used to think I understood how the Captain's mind works. Must say today I've seen a side to him that I didn't know was there. I don't know if this is one that I can navigate, Shawn."

"But how do you feel about this, Federi? She must stay aboard, it's her only chance."

Federi studied the agent. He'd have said, her only chance were if Captain were silly enough to let her ashore. She was wily enough any day to escape the Unicate. *And* the Rebellion. Ha! Unless Captain delivered her directly into the hands of the Stabilizers, as he'd done with Miller. Almost, Federi felt sorry for the pale girl. But she would have sunk them all, anna bottle! His crew, his friends. Even Wolf who had a shine on her. Even Shawn who was only twelve! Why were they trying to protect her? He should blasted well hand her over to the authorities himself.

"I agree, the Unicate will not take kindly to all these details," he pointed out sarcastically. "Maybe they'll string her up. Like a puppet. Or maybe they'll just put her into a cage over the port and let her waste away." He saw the terrified eyes of the little boy and paused. It always hit the children! Keenan Quinlan, only eleven, having to witness his sister's death... And then? The Unicate was thorough. They wanted no witnesses. Keenan was next!

Damned! Not while he had a say in it! "I'm sorry. Keenan? Listen, boy. No harm shall come to you and your sister as long as Federi can do anything about it." Blast, Federi, he thought, you soft-bellied old pushover!

It seemed to comfort the little boy somewhat, although the Romany could see that the child didn't trust his word. It certainly brightened Shawn's mood a lot though. Federi realized that Shawn hadn't been all that certain of his case in the first place. Ailyss looked immensely surprised. Well hell, she should be! He was too! The gypsy glanced at her, a cryptic smile in the corner of his mouth.

"Lucky Ailyss," he said. "You still have your little brother!"

Ailyss nodded, and swallowed.

"We'll keep it that way," said Federi, turning to Keenan. "You've got to protect your sister, understood, Keenan?" He frowned. "You are starved! You'd better come with me to the galley, so I can give you some food!"

He led the way, Shawn following with Keenan who was still rather wary of the man with the blooded knife who had killed everybody aboard the Schooner.

Marsden came into the galley. He looked quite drained.

"You've been overdoing it a bit?" asked Federi, concerned. "You're not supposed to be hopping around like a mad thing!"

"I'm fine," insisted Marsden. "Make me some strong coffee, my friend." He narrowed his eyes. "You're looking better though," he said. "Not as stretched."

"Cor, old buddy," said Federi. "Then again we're not currently being hunted down by the Rebellion fleet, are we! 's a curse, that gypsy radar."

"It's a blessing," disagreed Marsden. "Without it we'd all be dead now."

"How much longer?" asked Federi. "Think about it! What's the point in executing Ailyss? Couple of weeks later it's all of us anyway!"

"There's that still," said Marsden with a sympathetic look at his friend. "Don't envy you, old pal!"

"What? Me?" The Tzigan laughed. "*Nu*, buddy, you're way off the mark. *I'm* not going to be cutting her down! Made a promise! The contrary!" He peered critically at Marsden. "You're with me there, aren't you."

"Hard to tell," replied the First Mate pan-faced. "Tell me about this new development?"

Federi told Marsden about the request from the younger group while he prepared the coffee.

"They're unanimous?" asked Marsden. Federi nodded. "Then I think, democratically they already have the majority."

Federi counted. "Easily." He grinned. Jon Marsden, their by-the-book-pirate! Democracy had been the rule on pirate ships of old. "Which way do you vote?"

"Difficult one," said Marsden. "I'm tempted to pick the humane way, but can we trust her to stick by the rules?"

"Don't know. We'll only find out in Hawaii, I guess."

"Or at the bottom of the sea," added Marsden darkly.

"This is her brother," said Federi, motioning to Keenan.

"Oh yes. In that case of course I vote we keep them both safe," said Marsden. "At least until they have new identities."

"They'll never really be safe outside Captain's realm," said the gypsy. He shook his head worriedly. Blast. Democracy had worked on the pirate ships of old. He guessed, even back then, it had been the democracy of the biggest gun. In this case, Captain was going to come to a conclusion – if he hadn't already. And all the democracy in the world wouldn't change his decision. On the Solar Wind, Captain's word was Law. It was the only way they survived. He didn't envy Captain for having to speak that verdict. Then again, who knew how the old pirate ticked! "Jon, I don't think I understand the Captain anymore."

"He had a lapse," said Marsden rationally. "Got to see it that way, buddy. Maybe he's also spread thin."

Ha! Spread thin! Federi smiled enigmatically and spread some peanut butter from Captain Ali's stocks onto a slice of toast, which he handed to Keenan. Shawn, always hungry, was the next in line. Marsden studied his friend who suddenly looked quite like the one that got away with it! What had he been up to? Well, the gypsy was an irrepressible optimist, that Jonathan Marsden knew. It was one of his best qualities. He always bounced back quickly.

"We could always keep her under lock and key," mused Marsden. "She'd be safe and unable to get into trouble that way."

"That's a bad solution," said Federi. "I know her type." He grinned. "They tend to escape."

"What would you suggest?"

"Jon, ol' buddy, she's made it difficult for us. If she'd connected even with one person here aboard to form a friendship, it would be easier. You can't expect loyalty from someone who has no ties."

"So what do we do?"

"We wait and see," said Federi. Maybe Captain was the one who needed to be chained up – only until a measure of reason had been established and Federi's promise was going to be kept.

"Actually," said Marsden thoughtfully, "she did connect."

"What? With whom?"

"Donegal Magic. Paean."

Federi bared his teeth. Was Jon still implying that Paean was a spy – even *after* Ailyss had been unmasked? Was he implying that they knew each other before boarding the Solar Wind – that they were from the same camp? Good grief, did his friend never pay attention at all? The Donegals had narrowly escaped the Unicate!

Even realistically – if you considered the possibility – which was absurd; then why should little Paean risk her own life and make doubly sure that the most dangerous sailor on the Solar Wind, the one who could cut down a whole enemy crew single-handedly, survived and didn't conveniently self-terminate? It wouldn't fit into her and Ailyss' agenda at all! His hand touched the place where that bit of hair was hidden under his shirt. Paean was innocent, *basta!*

"What makes you say that?" he asked warily.

"Lending her spy novels, apparently."

"Oh." Federi sighed. *That* was evidence? To incriminate Paean? "No, Jon, I'm aware of that one. It's a one-way street. She lends Paean novels to get her out of her hair."

"I see," said Marsden. "Poor little Donegal Magic!" He peered at his friend, waiting for a telltale reaction.

Federi glanced up. "What?" he asked, eyes wide.

"Federi," laughed Marsden, "forget it! You'll never manage the innocent look! Your eyes aren't blue enough!"

"Who, me? Innocent?" asked Federi, shocked.

Marsden glanced at the two young boys. "You're not going to tell me?"

"Tell you *what?*"

"What took so long on that Schooner?"

Federi laughed.

"Look, Jon," he said. "I know what you're thinking. Listen carefully now." His eyes darted to the boys. Darned right, explanations were due. Who knew what picture they'd build in their minds otherwise! "Paean's a very sensitive girl. All that blood, all those dead bodies got to her. I sat her down and made her play me a Ceilidh. On her tin whistle. *Isda!*"

Marsden nodded, his smile ironic. "Sure, Federi."

"Sure," agreed Federi, his mind returning inescapably to the bilges of the Schooner. The little mockingbird had given him his life back. She had indeed played a Ceilidh for him. She had sat there, leaning back against him, playing her heart out on her pennywhistle. *After* he had pirated her curl! How was that? He had listened, frozen; too scared he might chase the wild little sprite away. With her magical powers she had played the mottled sunlight back into his mottled soul; played him a vision of a future. A beach in the dusk, green waves, a ship that lay moored – not the Solar Wind though. A wild place; a place that existed nowhere on Earth. But now it existed in his mind. And she had run, indeed, as he had expected; *after* she had brought him safely back onto the ship!

Plan A was still Plan A – find a way for them all to survive, and urgently. And keep the little sunbird close, but without scaring her any further. He returned to the present, where Shawn and Jon Marsden were eyeing him with fascination, and Keenan was wolfing down his sandwiches.

"Focus on Ailyss," advised Federi, his silver eyetooth glinting.

Old Sherman, Dr Jake and Doc Judith all agreed once they understood the little boy was in the picture, that they had to protect the not-so-innocent along with the innocent.

"Have you spoken to Captain yet?"

Federi shook his head, his falcon eyebrows shooting up. Funny, he thought. They had all witnessed the way Captain had treated him. Yet they relied on him to be the spokesperson for the grown-up crowd too! Oh well. He supposed it came with the unwritten job description of being Federi.

Radomir Lascek looked up as his Tzigan arrived on the bridge, obedient as ever. Unreadable as usual.

"Are you rested, Federi?"

"I'm fine, Captain," replied Federi, eyebrows arched quizzically. "And otherwise I'm quite healthy too! Must say, every now and then I experience a bit of a zinging in my left ear..." He glanced down at his hands. "Haven't had any of that since I've somehow mislaid my com, though. Could have been that. Indeed." He grinned.

Radomir Lascek laughed. He had been forced to call the gypsy to the bridge on the ship com. "Good that I find you in health," he said. "Get your wrist-com back from Shawn, Tzigan! He kept it safe for you. And don't do that again! Now tell me. What must we do about Ailyss?"

Federi seated himself. He played with the buttons on the radar screen. It showed rocks and the like. "She that nearly sank the Solar Wind?" he asked with a shrug. Like magic, out came the stiletto. He inspected it, tested its edge. Played with it.

"Ailyss," repeated Captain Lascek, wondering if the innuendo with the blade was meant for him or Ailyss. With the gypsy, a statement was never just a statement. You had to listen carefully. Which he hadn't exactly been doing. But Federi had his attention now!

"Who has a little brother who has done nothing wrong but was nearly murdered by the Rebels?"

"The same."

"I had a sister once," said Federi dreamily. "Failed to rescue her."

"Federi, can one get a straight answer out of you?"

"Captain?"

"What do you suggest we do with Ailyss!"

"Little double agent," said Federi. "Scum. Not to be trusted."

"So what would you do?"

"Why are you asking me, Captain? In all respect, it's me, your gypsy turncoat speaking. Are you asking because you note a certain – should we say – symmetry?"

"Federi, why are you playing games with me?"

"Captain?"

"I'm asking for your ideas."

"Captain, I didn't know I had any."

Lascek shook his head. He was in fact near to stomping his foot.

"Federi, I have already apologized for this afternoon. What do you want me to do? Grovel?"

"That should be interesting," muttered Federi with a quirky little smile.

"What can I do to earn back your trust?"

"Ah," said Federi. "Trust. Loyalty. Friendship." He took one last loving look at his stiletto and then it vanished, sleight of hand.

"What happened to the impulsive, emotional Federi who was still aboard yesterday?" asked Captain Lascek. "Where's your heart, man?"

"That guy drowned out there today, Captain. He jumped off a lifeboat and nobody turned around to pick him up." He watched the Captain closely. "You know, the thing with my gypsy hunches: Voodoo all of it."

"Nonsense!" bellowed Lascek. "I don't know how you do it, but you've proved beyond doubt that you've got that gypsy radar!"

"And yet," smiled Federi. "Like all hocus-pocus. So accurate at times, and yet sometimes so completely off the mark."

"Now you're making up stories, Federi. I've never known your hunches to fail!"

"So you would *knowingly* have left Paean and Sherman to their fate? Who are you? What have you done with Captain Radomir?"

Lascek groaned. "I wronged you, Federi. I didn't listen to what you were trying to tell me. You actually had to desert in order to do what you had to."

"Oh, but I didn't," smiled Federi. "You told me to get on with my job, Captain. That's what I did."

Lascek stared at the Romany. Blast, the man was right! Again!

Federi got tired of the little game. Out came the stiletto again, and his artistic fingers twirled it into a dancing blur. He sighed.

"You only reminded me of my proper station in life," he said sadly. "Scum. Outcast of the outcasts. Tzigan without a tribe. Henchman. That's old Federi. Captain, do you really want another one like that aboard?"

Captain Lascek followed the blade of the stiletto, mesmerized.

"On the other hand, do you really want to throw her innocent little brother to the sharks?" The blade danced, whirled. "You could be an assassin yourself," said Federi thoughtfully. "Except that would be getting your hands dirty. Then again, sometimes you do. People respect you for it."

It danced and spun, reflecting the light back in all sorts of colours.

"Throw Ailyss off the ship and the Unicate tears her apart. Keep her aboard and she might tear us apart. What do you say, Captain?"

Lascek blinked his gaze away from the spinning blade.

"The difference is that you have a soft core," said the Captain. "That's why I had to rescue you. She is a cold fish."

"She's got a soft spot too," said Federi. "Her brother. That's why she started to sabotage us: Because they were threatening to kill her brother. Take that brother away from her and you have a cold little killing machine. Keep her brother close by and you have a mini-mom. Protect her brother and she'll be loyal. But – the Law of the Pacific demands a life, *ni?"*

Lascek sighed wearily.

"And once she's been executed, what do you do with her *innocent* little brother?" pushed the Tzigan. "Keep him on? On the ship that murdered his sister? Think he'll feel a shred of loyalty for us?"

"Loyalty," said Captain Lascek, relieved that the Romany had finally opened up. "That's the problem."

"Don't think that *I'll* terminate her, Captain," Federi added quickly. "Not a chance. You'll have to do the dirty work yourself. My quota of terminations for this month is used up." He grinned. "Better. Pay her to do it herself!"

Radomir Lascek gasped for air.

"Or am I on the wrong track?" asked the Tzigan, eyebrows raised innocently.

"The Law of the Pacific," said Lascek pensively. "Do we have to? She's a good nuclear technician, so Dr Jake informs me. Can't we come up with an alternative?"

"A *safe* alternative, Captain? Considering your *loyal* crew first?"

Lascek sighed. "She cracked, my friend. She's at a point where we could possibly influence her. Don't you think?"

An arched eyebrow for a response.

"Does it have to be death?" asked Lascek despondently. "Marsden pointed out that we'd have to execute them both."

This wiped the cynicism off the Romany's face. He looked shocked.

"Could we find a better solution, Federi?" pleaded the Captain.

"Putting her ashore comes to the same," said Federi. "Or worse. For us."

"I wasn't considering putting her ashore," said Lascek. "Nor marooning her and Keenan on a piece of plank in the Pacific."

"That's execution," agreed Federi. "Or a gamble. Girl's got resources."

Lascek nodded. "I was thinking, Federi – if we kept her on but tied her

399

down by emotional bonds? If her hormones are involved, she's more likely to be loyal."

Federi gazed at the dancing stiletto.

"Hormones. A boyfriend. Can't say I see much fault with that logic," he said. "Only, when her boyfriend dumps her, will she go on a Solar Wind rampage?"

"That's why she needs to have a boyfriend who won't dump her," said Lascek. "One who understands her perhaps, because he is… a lot like her?"

Federi looked sharply at the Captain. The spinning blade suddenly stood still.

"What exactly are you suggesting, Captain?"

"That you get involved with Ailyss. Why not? Could pull some Unicate information out of her too. Right, Federi? Shouldn't be too difficult – you are birds of a feather, aren't you?"

"What?!"

Federi's hand closed tightly over the stiletto's blade. A moment elapsed. Federi's black stare was locked with the Captain's. A hard stare with a psychopathic edge to it.

"Captain, in all respect, I can't believe I heard you say that! Are those your orders?"

"I thought it might be an assignment you'd enjoy," said Captain Lascek, taken aback. He hadn't expected such a violent refusal! What raw nerve had he touched there? Better to terminate an innocent than fake involvement? Or maybe it wasn't all that fake… "You can do with the emotional reinforcement too!"

"I'm better at slitting throats!" retorted Federi. "Can't believe you said that! There's a word for that!" With one last theatrical flare, the blade vanished. "Captain, 'scuse me, something's burning in the galley." He left.

Lascek looked pensively at the splashes of bright blood following the gypsy off the bridge.

30

Ailyss' Trial

Angry pennywhistle tunes splattered down from the Crow's Nest over the sound of the high surf. Ronan peered into the rigging. It was quite dark now; the deck lights and mast lights were on. The Solar Wind's sails were furled.

Paean had been up there, it seemed, for hours! But she needed to come down; they needed her voice. Captain had granted a huge concession – a trial for Ailyss. This was the result of Federi's negotiations.

"Come down, Pae! We need you on deck!" he called to her on his wrist-com.

The response was more disjointed snatches of tunes over the com. Medieval-sounding ones. Paean was in a bad frame, he could hear it.

"Pae, we need your voice," he tried again. "She's getting a trial! We're going to help her!"

"You and what army?" came the cynical reply, and more tunes crashed to the deck.

"You have to come down!" commanded Ronan. "Captain's orders!" The answer nearly wilted his ears. He seriously hoped that Captain had no way of hearing this conversation. "Och Pae!"

"She's stuck," said Federi behind him. "Let's get her down!"

"You go," replied Ronan. "She isn't listening to me."

"Come with me," ordered Federi. They climbed up the handholds on the mast, Federi somewhat more slowly than usual. He had a dishcloth wound tightly around his hand.

Paean looked at the two of them approaching and dug in her heels.

"You're wrong, Federi. I'm not stuck. I just don't want to be a part of the death sentence of a family member."

Federi looked at Ronan. "Maybe you're right, you'd best leave this to me."

Ronan obediently climbed down again. In any case his mind was not exactly on pulling up errant siblings. Federi had been nominated honorary Donegal; that made him an older brother, so he could take over this duty tonight.

Federi climbed into the Crow's Nest and found himself at the receiving end of an icy glare. And then she turned away and continued playing, ignoring him, her red hair backlit vaguely against the yellow glow coming from the deck lights. Anger was pulsing from her in blasts. And with it, heartbreak. Aw, little sunbird!

Federi sighed, and put on an easy smile. "Proud of you," he started.

"You can take your proud," she said scathingly, "and stick it..."

He shook his head. "She's getting a trial," he told her, studying her. "Law of the Pacific says Captain doesn't have to; her guilt is clear and she's also admitted to her sabotage. But Captain wants to hear us."

"Don't want any part in that!" snapped Paean. "Killing a family member! Federi, don't make me do this!"

He sighed. She had also been hoping for a silver-dollar moon and no cookie. Curse that Ailyss for breaking his little songbird's heart!

"And if we can stop her execution?" His teeth nearly blocked the words. Ailyss *deserved* execution, dammit! But, he supposed, there was the little brother, too. It always hit the children. And Captain's suggestion of killing them *both*...

"*You* want her dead," Paean observed accurately.

He shook his head. "Yes. I do. But her little brother needs her, Paean. We've *got* to keep her alive for his sake." A sly smile. "Captain has the same idea. I have a feeling he wants this trial as an excuse so he can let her live." Not quite a lie, he thought. Only something Captain had said, plus a little wishful thinking. "Somehow I think there won't be any execution tonight."

"*You're* going to kill her," said Paean.

"Ha! I'm not!" he exploded. "There's no flying way! Captain can do his bleeding -" He stopped himself short. The rest of his statement hung in the air between them. As though he'd spoken it.

Her eyebrows lifted, and her light eyes connected with his soul. "Least now you're truthful," she remarked, baring a corner tooth in an empty little smile. "Though I haven't much hope about that Law of the Pacific.

What the hell have you done to your hand?"

"Played with a knife," he grinned.

"Let me see it," demanded Paean.

"*Ni!* Don't want you falling out of the Crow's Nest!"

"That bad?"

He laughed. "No, Paean! Leave it!" And he stuck the hand, dirty dishcloth and all, into his pocket.

Paean shrugged and peered over the Crow's Nest's rim. The crew was gathering on the deck.

"We're going to hold the trial on the deck?" she asked. Federi followed her gaze. That was odd indeed!

There were quite a few crew on deck by now. Shawn had taken little Keenan under his wing. He was standing next to him, talking excitedly. Keenan was hanging close to his sister, who was quiet and sullen.

"She must be so scared," said Paean softly. "Poor Ailyss!"

Federi had to bite back a caustic remark about her sinking everyone – including Shawn and Ronan.

"Poor girl," added Paean. "I really hope we can sway Captain. She needs protection."

"She needs protection from Captain's scheming mastermind," muttered Federi sourly. "Don't we all, yodiho!"

She glanced at him in surprise, then turned her attention back to the deck. There were Doc, and Dr Jake and Marsden. The latter was heatedly discussing something with Sherman.

"Hay!" exclaimed Paean the next moment and left the Crow's Nest, shimmying down the rigging with the same agility Shawn usually displayed. "I'll be fried!" Federi heard her comment on her way down. He followed her, baffled. So it had taken Wolf hobbling onto the deck with a crutch, supported left and right by Ronan and Rhine Gold, to move her out of the Crow's Nest? Her angry voice chewing the injured engineer out carried up to where he was inching his way down. Blast that cut hand!

"What are you doing out here, Wolf?" exclaimed Paean. "Your knee! You're going to lose your leg!"

"Better than someone loses her life," replied Wolf seriously. "Sorry, Paean. Maybe more work for you later, I know."

"Oh, for the…" Paean couldn't think of a suitable curse. Sorry Paean? That was all? She watched speechlessly as Wolf hobbled over to Ailyss on his crutches. Well, she thought, revenge in the offing! She caught Ailyss' frightened gaze and revised that. Poor girl needed every ally she could get – even if that was One-legged Furbus!

Federi climbed down from the rigging slowly, carefully. Paean glanced back at him. She wondered whether all those reefs and shoals could maybe account for a bout of land madness amongst the crew. The Romany planted himself right behind her, with his left hand on her shoulder. His right hand in his pocket again.

"Promise you'll let me look at that hand later on?" she asked.

"Why? Want to read me my future?" teased Federi.

"No, anna bottle of – hey! You smell of – hey!!" she hissed, lowering her voice. "Federi, have you been drinking?"

" 's not contagious," he said with a smirk. "Don't tell Captain, will you?"

"Don't make it a habit," she growled. "Anna bottle of rum!"

"I hate trials," muttered Federi.

"Is that why?"

"What, the rum?"

She nodded.

"No. Little luv, you know I'm not a drunkard. Now let it go. Focus on Ailyss. She'll need your voice."

"Question, Captain," said Sherman Dougherty as the Captain came down from the bridge. "Why aren't we in the boardroom?"

"Because our radar is irreparable, at this point," said Lascek with irony. "I don't want surprises."

The crew of the Solar Wind found themselves places on the deck, some sitting, some standing. Ailyss' little brother was hanging onto his sister's hand, with Shawn by his side. Rushka stood tall and taciturn at the main mast, her hair tucked away, her face unreadable. A pillar of Law. Paean wondered how much she could count on the Captain's daughter backing them. Close to Rushka, Wolf had sat down on a box, flanked by Ronan and Rhine Gold, with his injured leg stretched out as straight as the cast allowed. Paean was watching him carefully. All hells, she had put too much work into that leg for him to lose it now!

404

Ailyss, on the point of being condemned to death. Wolf sacrificing his last chance on keeping his leg. Federi toying with suicide. She shuddered. Sometimes it felt to her as though it was all coming apart under her hands. She had to force herself out of this mental pattern. Where on Earth had that thought come from?

"Ailyss Quinlan," said the Captain. "You are charged with sabotage, treason and espionage. What have you to say for yourself?"

"Nothing, sir. Guilty as charged," said Ailyss brokenly. Paean's heart ached for the girl. Wasn't anyone going to do something about this? Give her the good news? She turned around to glance at Federi, her eyebrows raised in silent entreaty. His eyes were fixed on the accused.

"Ailyss Quinlan," continued the Captain, "according to the Law of the Pacific, your just punishment is to be hanged from the rigging."

Keenan emitted a scream, and suppressed it with both hands over his mouth. Paean gasped and turned around again to glare accusingly at Federi. Some trial! And he had said there would be no killing!

"Wait it out," he whispered.

Wait it out? Paean peered at Keenan, who was hanging onto Ailyss' hand as though this could stop his sister from being ripped away by death. The boy looked as though he'd fall over any moment now. Tears were streaming down his face. Paean clenched her jaw. Captain was torturing an innocent! And Federi was doing nothing about it! Federi had lied to her! She saw how Shawn put his hand on Keenan's shoulder, trying to console the little guy.

"Permission to speak, sir," said Wolf, struggling to his feet. He wasn't yet used to crutches. Rhine Gold and Ronan moved to his sides to help him stand on the rocking deck. Paean made an involuntary move towards him and felt the Romany's hand tweak her shoulder. She dashed Federi a glance – and saw the Abyss in his eyes. Oh hell!

"Speak up, Svendsson. And sit down!" commanded the Captain.

Obediently Wolf sat down again.

"Captain, Ailyss was under severe pressure. She was only trying to prevent the Rebellion from murdering her brother. Please, Captain, these are mitigating circumstances. The child is the only relative she has in the world. May I suggest that quite a few of us might have acted the same?"

"Indeed," said Lascek scornfully. "Would you, Svendsson? In which way does this absolve her from punishment?"

"Captain, I believe, with the threat to her brother gone, she won't have any reason to try anything like that again. She was acting under extreme duress. And also she failed, which proves that subconsciously she sabotaged her own actions."

Lascek nodded, scowling. "Anything further?"

"Captain, I work alongside Ailyss and she is a good and quiet colleague who never complains or gives any kind of trouble."

"In fact she never opens her mouth at all," Federi whispered behind Paean.

"She also does an excellent job," added Wolf. "She's quick, Captain. Highly intelligent."

He waited for Marsden to write all that down.

"That's why she was working for intelligence," muttered Federi.

"So on the whole, Captain," concluded Wolf, "she would be a real asset to keep aboard."

"As a mascot, dangling from the rigging," said Federi under his breath. Paean turned and shot him a withering glance. What was wrong with the man? There was that horrible darkness again…

"Point taken, Svendsson," said the Captain. "I also note that you've defied doctor's orders again. Did you clear it with the medic?"

"Captain, it's a matter of life and death." He peered over to Paean. She nodded resignedly.

"Don't worry, Wolf," she called across, rolling her eyes. "I need the practice anyway!"

The Captain frowned. "This is serious, Miss Donegal! Anyone else?"

"Yes, Captain." Ronan spoke up, flinching at the murderous look Lascek threw him. "I believe if we execute Ailyss, we rob Keenan of the only mother he knows. I can't imagine…" he trailed off. The loss of his own mother was still too raw.

"Captain, please, you can't do that to Keenan," pleaded Shawn. "Poor Keenan!"

"Permission to speak, Captain," Paean piped up. She had to clear her throat first. It took guts to confront the Captain right after being ruffled.

"You may speak, Miss Donegal."

406

"Captain," said Paean. "There isn't a single one of us who doesn't have some sort of troubled background. Och, okay, sorry, Reinhold." She glanced at the tall German who was looking stricken. He didn't qualify to be a pirate, in Paean's books?

"The rest of us are basically vermin," she said. "All of us somehow broken, the fallout of society. You've put us together and rescued each of us. You keep us safe and protect us, and we keep each other safe and protect each other. We are pirates. We break rules and laws. But we stick together. We on the Solar Wind are a family. I can't imagine executing one of my own family, no matter what they have done. Keenan wouldn't be the only one to lose Ailyss. It would be like executing my sister. Sir, if you are to condemn Ailyss to death, I'm afraid I can't be part of the Solar Wind family anymore either." Her voice had started shaking and she backed down. "That was all," she added softly.

"Well spoken," whispered Federi next to her ear. "But go easy on Rhine Gold!"

"Why? He's a hypocrite!"

"Miss Donegal," said the Captain gravely, "this is no child's play. Ailyss attempted to murder your whole Solar Wind family. The crime demands a life!"

"A life?" Paean's back straightened. "Captain, she didn't succeed! Nobody died!"

"This time, Paean Donegal."

"She won't try it again," said Paean heatedly. "I'll guarantee it!"

Federi's left hand tightened significantly on her shoulder.

"How do you propose to guarantee it, Miss Donegal?" asked the Captain scathingly. "Are you going to pledge your own life that she'll behave? If she tries something like that again, we execute you both?"

Drawn-out seconds. Paean narrowed her eyes at the Captain, trying to work out what he'd just said.

"There is such an option?" she asked. And saw her own little brother gasp, and her older brother half-rise to his feet.

"Don't do it!" Federi warned quietly, behind her.

"There is," said the Captain with an enigmatic smile, watching her. "In the Law of the Pacific, you can pledge your life for someone else's."

"Fine, then let's consider that a deal, Captain," said Paean. That grip on her shoulder got painful.

"Unless you are a minor," completed Radomir Lascek.

She felt more than heard Federi exhale behind her and saw how her two brothers came back to life again, too.

"Then again we are pirates," the Captain added with a malicious smile. "So to conclude, the Donegals and Mr Svendsson are agreed on letting Ailyss live. Anyone else?"

"Sir, I don't believe executing Ailyss is an option," said Rhine Gold emotively. "She's one of us! We can help her become a crewmember and escape her former employers." He took a deep breath. "Captain, it won't be necessary for Paean to pledge her life. We'll look after Ailyss. We won't allow her to get dangerous again! We'll supervise her."

"That's why you ought to go easy on the bloke," whispered Federi. She nodded. "And he peels a mean potato," added the gypsy cook quietly. Paean grinned.

"Uh-huh," said Lascek. "It's been recorded, Mr Schatz. And how do the older crewmembers feel?"

"Divided, Captain," said Sherman. "Doc and I feel that she should be put ashore in the next port. With her brother."

"And the others? They want the humane option?"

"Captain," said Sherman with a sigh, "that *is* the humane option. Dr Jake is withholding his opinion. He feels that we are losing a highly valuable nuclear technician, either way. As for Jonathan…"

"My concern is for your crew," said Marsden coolly. "Captain, you know where I stand."

Paean heard Federi draw a breath through his teeth. She glanced back at him. He looked angry.

"Captain," said Dr Jake hesitantly, "if there were a way of keeping her aboard *without* executing her… keeping her and Keenan safe from the Unicate and the Rebellion…"

"So they'll hunt the Solar Wind to get to Ailyss?" asked the Captain with a cryptic smile.

"Och, they're hunting the Solar Wind anyway!" The retort was out before Paean could stop herself. That hand on her shoulder tweaked her again. The Captain glared at her.

"She's a good technician," said Dr Jake. "Putting her ashore would be counterproductive. She might be forced into moving against us again. Besides, Captain, she knows nothing of your plans! There's no way she could have betrayed them to the Unicate because they weren't discussed in any way since before Hamburg! And she'll have scant incentive to leak anything now! She's not stupid! She knows which side her bread is buttered!"

"I hear you, Dr Jake," said the Captain. "And what do you say, Federi?"

"Nothing," said Federi, withdrawing his hand from Paean's shoulder and folding his arms. She glanced at him in disbelief.

"*Not* taking a stance?" asked Lascek, obviously surprised too.

"Captain, what would you have me say?" asked Federi with a smile. "I'm surprised you haven't hanged *me* from the rigging yet."

There was a shocked silence.

"Very well," said the Captain, a slow smile spreading across his face. "Thank you, Tzigan. Point taken. I'll be reviewing all of this. Meeting adjourned. Marsden, please come to the bridge."

The Captain and his First Mate departed to the bridge.

On the deck all sorts of commotion broke out.

"Why didn't you tell him everything?" Wolf shot at Ailyss. "You may have dug your own grave!"

Ailyss sat down. For the first time there were tears in her eyes. She was shaking her head.

"I had no idea you all liked me such a lot!" She looked up. "Specially you, Paean!" She was crying now. "It may have been pointless," she added, "but it meant a lot to me, believe me. Thanks, you all, for trying."

Paean put her arms around Ailyss. " 's not pointless!" she retorted. "We've changed his mind! 's only Mr Marsden who's being contrary. The rest all want you to live!"

Ailyss smiled at her through the tears and shook her head.

"Paean, he only wanted to know how much resistance he'll get," she explained. "The Law of the Pacific says I'm going to die. That's all there is to it."

"Then again we're pirates," said Paean.

"The Law of the Pacific is just a nice way of saying, the way it's done on a pirate ship," replied Ailyss.

Paean let go of her. "I'll make you coffee." She escaped.

"Little sister!" commented Ailyss softly after her. Fancy her finding the only loophole in the Pirate Law! But she doubted that Paean's magnanimous gesture was going to sway anything. Captain had said it: The girl was a minor.

Paean moved towards the hatch. And walked into a human barricade. Of one.

"I could strangle you myself," snarled Federi. "What the hell did you think you were doing, girl?"

"Rescuing my friend," she shot back.

The Tzigan put a hand on her shoulder – an unmistakable, *commanding* left hand with a definite grip, and directed her further towards the hatch.

"Let's make them coffee," he suggested.

And then Ronan was blocking their way. "Leave my sister alone!"

Federi's eyes widened in surprise and he let Paean go. She escaped down the hatch and below deck.

"Well, Donegal!" said Federi with amazement. "You do have backbone!"

"What the hell were you whispering at her throughout that whole trial?" demanded Ronan. "You put her up to this, didn't you?"

The Tzigan shook his head. "Not on your life, Donegal! That girl is precious! Captain should be careful!" He smiled bleakly. "But you heard the Captain too," he added. "She's a minor. She can't pledge."

" 'Then again we're pirates' ," quoted Ronan angrily. "And what the hell did you mean with your statement there – surprised he hasn't yet hanged *you?* "

"That," laughed Federi. "That was between Captain and me! He knew what I meant. Donegal, don't dig." He peered at the bridge. "He's still going to call me in, too."

"You'll tell him that this pledge thing is off?" Ronan's voice was wavering. Half angry still; half pleading. Federi realized that the young man had understood that he was an ally in this. Possibly the only ally who could turn things for silly, pig-headed Paean.

"Course," he reassured Ronan. "But understand another thing, Donegal."

Ronan waited, worried.

"You saw me take out those Sancho pirates," said Federi.

Ronan nodded.

"I'm a pretty accurate shot, would you say," added Federi.

Ronan nodded again, intimidated.

"How many bullets do you think I'd need for the Captain?" asked Federi.

"The crew is to hell," growled Lascek, glancing at the deck.

Marsden nodded gravely.

"Jon," added the Captain, "you didn't answer my question. Where *do* you stand?"

"Radomir," said Jon Marsden, "as I said. My concern is for your crew. I don't think staging this trial makes the decision any easier. I wouldn't have."

"It was important to hear them," said Lascek.

"Paean is prepared to stake her own life," Marsden pointed out. "What does that tell you about the Donegals? Where do her loyalties lie?"

"She's an emotional child, Jon," said Lascek. "Children can't pledge."

"Two months short of adult status?"

"Still," said the Pirate Captain. "So, Jon, what would your verdict be?"

"Captain, whatever you decide, I'll back you," said Jon. "I don't like executing the little boy, but if it has to be... Putting her ashore is not an option though."

"We're agreed on that," sighed Lascek.

"You are the Captain," said Jon. "Your word goes. It shall be my duty to prevent a mutiny or smooth over whatever happens after."

Radomir Lascek clapped his First Mate on the shoulder. "Thank you for that, Jon." He peered out at the deck. "Doesn't facilitate my decision in any way, but it's good to know that there is a future for the crew, afterwards."

Paean came back with coffee for Ailyss and also for Shawn. She peered uncertainly to where her older brother and Federi had taken their

411

debate – around the main mast, with the rest of the young crowd.

"Pae," said Shawn, "don't do that kind of thing again!"

"*Shukar,* little brother," she smiled and accepted his fierce hug. "I have no doubt that Ailyss will be good! Where I'm concerned there was no risk." She left him standing sipping his coffee and shaking his head at her. She had a few duties now. First things first.

"How's the knee, Wolf?"

"Holding up, thanks," grinned Wolf. She had learnt to recognize that grin. He was in pain.

"You're a brave man, and what you did here tonight was hero craft," said Paean firmly. "Now don't overdo it. You'll go back to the infirmary now."

"Just a little longer, Doctor?" begged Wolf.

Just a little longer could be the difference between him keeping or losing that leg! Oh for the love of furry animals! Hell with it. It was *his* leg after all. His choice.

"Fine," snapped Paean. "Under one condition."

"What condition?"

She smiled nastily. "I'll tell you later."

"Urgh! You drive a hard bargain!"

"Take it or leave it," said Paean lightly, turning away from him. She took a deep breath. And plunged right in.

"Come on, Federi," she ordered smartly. "Below deck. Let me look at your hand in the light."

Federi turned from his animated discussion with Ronan and regarded her, his eyebrows lifting in surprise at her snappy command.

"Right now?"

"Right now." Might as well get that ruffle over with!

Federi followed her below deck, mulling. He'd speak to Captain! There was no way. Ailyss wasn't worth a toenail clipping of this one! He was resolved that there would be no further killings; but if there had to be, he'd better choose who was going to survive. And speaking to this tempestuous young woman was pointless. She'd realize herself what she had done, once she'd slept on it.

Captain had said that minors couldn't pledge. He'd keep him to that.

Even if it meant... he rolled his eyes. Aargh! There was a way! Captain's vile suggestion. He nearly gagged.

In the spotlights of the yellow infirmary, Federi sat down on the empty bunk. The one with the pea-green blanket. He held out his dishcloth-wrapped hand.

The little Irish devil rammed her fists into her hips and glared at him.

"So what was the point in that whole bogus trial?"

Aw hell! She'd seen through it!

"Paean, this is a pirate ship," he started.

"Don't start that with me," she interrupted. "The Captain is King, his word is the Law, *et cetera*. I know! Why bother staging a trial?"

He shook his head, avoiding her eyes, which were glinting treacherously. "Sit down, little songbird!" He reached for her hand and pulled her towards the infirmary's chair. And met her gaze. She remained standing. "Listen, Paean. Captain's Law good and well. Federi hasn't yet said his say."

"Federi withheld his precious opinion, din't he now?" she snapped.

"Federi is better at influencing people one-on-one," he replied. "Going to talk to Captain in a second. When Jon is done delivering his absence of ideas."

That accusing glare was cutting at his heart.

"So then what will you suggest?" she pushed.

To hell with it. "There is a way, little luv." He grimaced. She'd have to understand that he was doing it for her. This was extremely complex. It was about buying time. There was always later.

"There's something you can do?"

He nodded. "There's a way," he repeated quietly. "Trust me."

The damp in her eyes condensed and trickled down her cheek as she smiled at him. He smiled too. Yes. This made the sacrifice worth it. This was one of these golden moments. He'd have to remind her, later. He really didn't have any choice.

Paean seated herself on the chair and took the makeshift wrapping off his right hand. Federi obediently held still, though she had the distinct impression that he was finding this whole exercise unnecessary. This

413

conference wasn't about the hand. The subject of the meeting was already resolved. She darted him a smile as she dashed those pesky tears away. She owed him. There really was some way he was going to prevent the execution.

The dishcloth was drenched in oxidized blood, and some clear liquid. Rum? She looked at the twin gashes across Federi's palm where his oldest friend, the Stiletto, had bitten him.

"Ye Gods!" Her gaze lifted to his dark eyes.

Federi got ready to stick out an arm to catch her before she collapsed on the floor, but she didn't. She was staring at him, trying to read the scenario from his mind. Seeing straight through him.

"This is deep! What happened again?"

"I told you. Played with a knife!"

Paean snatched the Stiletto out of its hiding place before he could stop her. "This one?"

Federi laughed. Little devil! He angled for that knife. She evaded him, snatched up some of his soft black, unruly hair and deftly sliced off a whole long strand, laughing loudly. Still with tears in it.

"What -? You little mischief!" Federi grinned and caught her by the wrist and wrestled the knife back from her. The strand of black hair vanished into her pocket.

"I'll have to put stitches in," she said, struggling to get serious again. "This is really bad. And look now! It's bleeding again! Och no, Federi! You shouldn't have wrestled me with this!"

Federi gaped at her. She was unbelievable!

"See, you do too much, and you don't take proper care of yourself," scolded Paean. "And you climbed into the rigging with this, too! What did you disinfect it with? Rum? That's what I smelt, isn't it. You haven't been drinking. And you tied it up with a dirty dishrag?"

Aw, at least she had brightened up! It had taken him sacrificing his personal values and a haircut, but after this afternoon he owed her his soul. He flashed her a grin.

"Just, please don't put me under with that GM bug of yours," he shot back, shuddering theatrically. "That thing gives me nightmares. I hate general anaesthetic. Always think I'm dying."

"Okay, I guess in your case some local would be enough," she shrugged. "Or would you prefer to tough it out without any?"

"No, I think I'd like some local," said Federi hurriedly, wondering what else was going to come his way.

Paean rummaged in the drawers until she found some local anaesthetic. "Never thought I'd be stitching *you* up in here! Why, Federi?"

"Why what, Paean?"

"Why did you try anyway?" She focused on drawing up the clear liquid into the syringe. She wasn't entirely sure if she had the calculation correct, but what the heck – a bit too much would only put his whole arm out of action. She wished she could put his left hand out of action too. Her shoulder still ached from his grip. Keep him distracted... keep him talking. Ha! Keep him immobilized! She scowled impatiently.

Federi looked thoroughly baffled. "What?"

"You toy with suicide, you make remarks like that one out there, you cut yourself like this... Why?"

"That remark?" Federi chuckled softly. "I was only reminding Captain of something. I once stood in Ailyss' shoes."

"You?" Paean laughed disbelievingly. "A saboteur? Do I detect a pattern again?" She poured some tincture over his hand and noticed with satisfaction that he hardly winced. "Give me a break! You come from a long line of professional liars. What else are you still going to tell me?"

"No, little sweetheart. Not a saboteur. And I'm telling you the truth. Federi is an assassin."

Paean took a step back in astonishment and stared at him. Assassin? That he was! Of course! Beyond the shadow of a doubt. Things fell into place.

Well, that explained a lot! Her heart ached. What had caused her gentle friend to pick such a horrible profession? How could she fix this one for Federi? She couldn't, she realized. Only take it from here, a day at a time... make him coffee... try to rehabilitate him... And Captain ruddy well exploited Federi's sinister skills! Who was the pirate?

"My assignment," added Federi with a half-smile, watching her closely, "was Radomir Lascek."

She gasped. "What! Not the Captain! The *Captain?*"

"The same," said Federi, smiling at her stricken face.

Oh hell! "Federi..."

He smiled.

"And then I got under his spell, just like everyone else here. How can one not revere him?"

"I know what you mean," muttered Paean. She prepared to inject the local anaesthetic. "Hold still now. This will hurt!" She glanced at his eyes, then she injected. "Federi," she said resolutely, "it changes nothing."

He smiled and shook his head.

"He's running a risk keeping me aboard," he said dreamily. "But he knows. I'm his most loyal sailor. Then again, that's why he doesn't trust me. You saw." He shook his head again. "You didn't see. You were on the Barracuda. Whatever. Point is, there's not a sailor on the Solar Wind who wouldn't lay down his life for Captain. I think, even our cold little Ailyss. Must have been a struggle for her, seeing all the good he does and still trying to carry out her mission."

"I s'pose," said Paean, beginning to suture. Right now Federi sounded confused and disoriented to her. She needed to give him direction. Hero worship could go too far! "Doesn't matter if Captain is a hypnotist though," she added through clenched teeth. "I'll not go along with murder, and neither will my brothers. And *basta*."

Federi sighed. Neither would he! Not that Captain's alternative was that much better…

31

Verdict

"Here I am, Captain." Federi found his comfort spot leaning against the drinks cabinet. He cast a glance at the radar screen. The same rocks as a half-hour ago. And the Solar Wind's sails were unfurled and catching the wind again. "Got to get this fixed, Captain!"

The ship was continuing its course. Enough time had been lost. Ronan on lookout duty. Without Rushka. She was guarding Ailyss.

"Federi," said Radomir Lascek, beaten. "I need you back aboard. This ship is harder to run without your unswerving loyalty."

Federi stared at him, shocked. Half an hour back he'd suggested to Ronan that there was always the option of taking Captain out if he endorsed Paean's madness. With the rifle. Add compulsive liar to that list, he thought.

And what had he told Paean, minutes later? That he was Captain's most loyal sailor! That, at least, was true to a point. Yet – what was loyalty amongst pirates? But what was loyalty to the Tzigan? His life! Did he ever have a choice?

"Captain, you've got that," he said emotionally. "You always had it. The day I fail to sail to hell for you, you can indeed hang me from the rigging." Sometimes he wished his Captain would do just that! Radomir Lascek was only trying to do what was best for all of them. There weren't going to be any further killings. Federi would see to it. *Basta*.

Radomir Lascek studied his gypsy thoughtfully. "I see you had your hand seen to," he commented.

"The deck was stacked, the dice were loaded," growled Federi, hoping the Captain wouldn't notice that his hair had also been slightly seen to. And his mind...

"She's a little bully, isn't she," laughed Radomir Lascek.

"Isn't she just! Anna bottle!" Federi frowned. "And a stubborn girl. And a silly minor who has no idea about anything."

"Absolutely," agreed Lascek. "So, about Ailyss?"

Federi heaved a sigh and rolled his eyes. From here there would be no turning back. He'd be doing it to protect Paean. He might end up executing Ailyss by accident. Or the Captain. No. No further killings.

"Captain, you know I'll ultimately obey any order you give me," he said through his teeth. "All hells!"

"I know," said Radomir Lascek, pouring two fingers of golden rum for Federi and some brandy for himself. Federi swirled the rum thoughtfully in its glass. He thought of dirty dishcloths and Paean. Her smile of thanks for his promise that Ailyss would live.

"I think," said Lascek, "you've made it patently clear that you wish no such involvement. I shall not ask it of you."

What? No! This was wrong! "Captain, I don't *like* the assignment, but if that's what it takes to stop her execution…"

"Federi?" Radomir Lascek scowled.

Federi cursed quietly.

"Captain, the Law of the Pacific doesn't apply to minors!"

"A minor is the reason we're in this pickle, Federi," the Captain pointed out. "Keenan. We have to adapt to that!"

"So what do we do?" Federi's left hand raked through his hair, moving the scarf. He stared at his bandaged right hand. And peered out to the deck. A solitary little figure was leaning against the rail at the bowsprit, watching the bridge. Unruly curls blowing about where they crawled out under the bandana.

How was he going to keep his promise now?

Radomir Lascek studied his Tzigan intently. There was a lot more boiling under the surface than the man was telling.

"Federi," he tried again, "all I'm asking is your honest opinion. What must we do with her? I don't want to decide without having heard you!"

Federi laughed mirthlessly. "Captain, my opinion? Necessarily it's that of a hypocrite!"

"I would like to hear it anyway," said the Captain. "It's the opinion of a very important hypocrite!"

"She tried to kill us all," said Federi. "If I were the Captain I'd have her strung up. I'd have strung *me* up, way back then!"

418

"I know," said Radomir Lascek. "And you nearly did, that day! Marsden had to talk you out of it and convince you that little Rushka needed you!"

"So then," said Federi, "Captain, that's maybe the insight you wanted into Ailyss' head at current! She's in the galley being mothered by the young crew. She doesn't deserve Paean's sacrifice, blast her!"

"You're right," agreed the Captain. "And I'm not about to allow a minor to pledge her life for a criminal!"

Federi blew a sigh of relief.

"But that takes us full circle," Lascek pointed out. "The crime demands a life. The Law of the Pacific…"

"When has Radomir Lascek ever bowed to the Law?" asked Federi angrily.

"When it made sense," said the Captain. "I'm not a rebel out of principle, Federi. I merely make my own choices. And in the case of Ailyss…"

"*My* life," said Federi, coming unstuck from the cabinet and gesturing towards the rigging with his glass. Rum flew across the console. He should have thought of it long ago! "You can execute *me* if she misbehaves. I'll blasted well see to it that she doesn't."

"*Your* life," said Lascek thoughtfully.

"Captain, there's another reason you want to keep her aboard," observed Federi, studying him intently.

Lascek sighed morosely. "It's not my style to execute someone I rescued from the Unicate. None of you would be alive today. Oh, sorry." He smiled bleakly. "Except Rhine Gold. And Jon is right too, if we execute her we'll have to put her little brother out too."

"Fiendish," commented Federi. "I won't stand for it, Captain. No more killings! *Basta!*"

Lascek studied him intently. And then he smiled. "It's good to have you back aboard, my friend."

"Captain, I never left."

"Federi, this whole law is backwards. To expect a captain to execute a good crewmember along with a bad egg…"

" 's a tough law," agreed Federi. "Tough being pirates."

"I don't think I can allow it," said Lascek. "She's too dangerous."

Federi put his glass down. "You're the Captain," he said. And waited for that nod that dismissed him.

The Solar Wind ploughed on through the night. Paean was in her favourite spot on the prow by the figurehead, gazing at the white spray of the prow wave.

"Hey, little luv!"

She peered at him. "So how did it go?"

Federi flashed her a smile.

"No problem," he said. "Never have a problem with the Captain!"

"Professional liar!"

"No," said Federi. "That's a principle. Never have a problem with the Captain."

"Ah!" Paean giggled softly. "I see." She peered across at the bridge. The night was nippy after that storm. "I see Mr Marsden's on the bridge with Captain again." She glanced back at the gypsy. "Think you made a difference?"

"Don't know. We should have results in a second. Where's Ailyss?"

"Being crowded in the galley," said Paean. "Don't think she's ever had so many friends before."

Federi smiled again. "Friends. What about you?"

"Just waiting for you," said Paean. Ailyss had enough people to look after her. The redhead smiled. "You got it right? That other way?"

Federi's smile dropped and he shook his head.

"Maybe, little luv. There are no guarantees. His word still goes. Keep your hopes up. Captain is a fair man." He bared his teeth. There was always a possibility of creating havoc on the ship at the moment of the verdict, and spiriting Ailyss away... *that* was the most counterproductive idea he'd had all evening! Why would he want to take action against the Solar Wind? For someone he didn't even like? No. He'd done what he could. All he could do now was wait for that cookie to crumble.

Paean squeezed his left hand briefly. "Thank you, Federi! Thanks for trying."

The Tzigan sighed. He certainly looked better than this afternoon. But she wasn't taking any chances yet. Federi, an assassin! She wondered how often he tried terminating himself! Oh hell, she'd better look after him!

Federi tugged at her scarf. "Thanks, little pirate. For waiting here for me."

"Och, Federi, any day! You know, it's funny," she said, "honour amongst thieves! I only understand now what you meant that time!"

"No, you don't," replied Federi, grinning. "Not by a long shot." He laughed. "Honour amongst thieves! Even the words are stolen!"

"I know," said Paean. "Mrs Flanagan read it to us. Really funny with that ancient English." She stared squarely at him. "Federi, this afternoon. That had nothing to do with Captain, am I right?"

"Course not!"

"And with Ailyss?"

He laughed cynically and shook his head. "Little luv, if it didn't mean that much to you I'd let her get what's coming to her. She deserves it."

Paean scowled. He was trying to veer off the topic! "It's all the blood?" she pushed.

"The killings – yes, always..." He smiled. " 's against the *romipen,* you know," he added. "Killing. Federi's an outcast. Can't return to my people."

She stared critically at him. It was a ruse, to throw her off track!

"But that's not the main reason," she observed.

His lack of a reply was enough of an answer. She was quiet for a second. So he didn't want to tell her.

"I was frightened," she said then.

"I'm sorry, little luv."

"Don't want a repeat of that!"

Federi gazed past her at the rolling waves and sighed.

"Then I'd better tell you, right? See, little luv. Federi's got this gift. Captain calls it a gypsy radar."

"I know," said Paean. "He called mine voodoo!"

Federi laughed. "So, your voodoo and my radar! Lovely! The point is, the gypsy radar's the reason Federi always gets away. I know when something bad is about to happen. Sometimes I walk into it with open eyes. Like back there at Atuona. Cor! Didn't think it would escalate like that though!"

"I know," said Paean. "I saw you pick something up, there at the pool."

"Was smelling the corpse," said Federi.

"Urgh!"

"Exactly. Actually surprised how Shawn could have thought that man was just asleep! Maybe he hasn't been around a lot of dead people."

"Yes, he's not," agreed Paean.

"That gypsy radar, little luv," Federi carried on. "You have no idea how it stretches a man to know something horrible is going to happen and not to know what, or when."

Paean shuddered. Her second sight was more a thing that kept tabs on loved ones.

"But it's over now, isn't it?" she asked.

Federi gave her a troubled glance. "Wish I could say yes, little sweetheart!"

"Ah," said Paean. "So the Rebellion is still on our tails!"

"And the Unicate too," completed Federi. "Think about it! We've now sunk a Rebellion flotilla! They want our blood. That freedom that you felt when we crossed over into the Pacific?"

"It's gone," said Paean. "We're hunted here too, now!"

"There's nowhere on Earth the Solar Wind can move in safety now," said Federi. "Captain bought us some time sinking that fleet. How long? Not very."

"Cor," muttered Paean.

"Worse than that," said Federi. "They're tightening the net. Captain does have a plan, but it relies on running and hiding. All hells, that's never going to be enough! So tired of running, little songbird! So tired of being an old coward!" He sighed.

"You're not an old coward, Federi!"

"Everyone around me gets killed," said the Romany darkly, "and Federi gets away. 's a curse!"

"And that's why you wanted to kill yourself," she said. Federi nodded and stared out over the black rolling waterscape.

"Och, Federi!" She wished she could somehow comfort him, give him hope. He was not afraid of dying. He was afraid of surviving! "And that's also why you hide your reminders?" she asked. "Even in hot weather, when even Ronan with his fair skin works without a shirt on?"

"Something like that." Of course he was hiding his concealed weapons too. He smiled. He ought to train her. She had that sharp element that was needed. Sheer!

"Well, it's not going to be, this time," said Paean resolutely. "This time, we're all going to get away. And Ailyss too. We need a bigger plan, don't you think?"

"A bigger plan," smiled Federi. "What did you have in mind, little pirate?"

"Well, *I* don't have one," said Paean. "Yet! But we'll work something out. We're fugitives too, don't forget!"

"That's right."

"Federi," said Paean seriously, "I want you to hang close."

"Oh?"

"Makes it easier to supervise you," she grinned.

"Little vixen! There's the Captain now, *isda!*"

Radomir Lascek and Jon Marsden came down from the bridge. Old Sherman took over at the console.

"All hands on deck," came his voice through the ship com. "On the dooble!"

The crew came trundling up out of the Solar Wind's interior.

Ailyss was clinging to her little brother's hand as though he might get lost in the crowd. She felt sick. Shawn Donegal and Rhine Gold, with Wolf Svendsson between them, were following her closely and took seats near her. She was aware of them, but it helped nothing. Captain's verdict would cut straight through them, and then they'd have to stand back and watch how she was going to be hanged...

She only hoped someone would take her little brother below deck!

"Ailyss," said Radomir Lascek. "Just for your record. The Solar Wind's crew feels unanimously that you and your brother should be kept aboard."

She glanced at them. She was thankful for that at least.

"The Law of the Pacific demands a life for treason," he continued. "By your treachery you have put us into an impossible position. You do understand, don't you."

She nodded. They couldn't keep her on. They couldn't put her ashore either. She was too dangerous. And Paean's little loophole – that didn't work because she was too young. Captain didn't even need to mention it.

Her life was up.

"So your life has been guaranteed by one of my officers."

She gasped. Had she heard right?

"This means that you are acquitted, provisionally," continued Radomir Lascek. "You're both staying on the Solar Wind. You are permanent crew. Your duties remain what they were; Keenan will be a cabin boy until he is of an age to take on bigger duties. I expect undivided loyalty from both of you!" He paused. "I'll take that as agreement," he said, as Ailyss covered her face and cried hysterically as the truth sank in. "Welcome aboard, Ailyss and Keenan Quinlan!"

The crew cheered. She heard it through the din in her head. She felt Wolf Svendsson's huge hand on her one shoulder, Shawn Donegal's smaller one on her other. She glanced up, and into the gypsy's face. He was holding something out to her. A glass. With something in it. Rum? She looked a bit further. Most of the crew were already holding a glass.

"Welcome aboard the Solar Wind, Ailyss!"

The terrifying assassin was actually smiling at her. Paean was next to him; as he moved on, she hugged Ailyss.

"Welcome home, my sister!"

I don't deserve this, thought the spy incoherently. I deserve death. Captain's given me my life back! She'd sail to hell for him too, she knew. Like all of his crew. And she'd find out who that officer was. She peered at Jon Marsden. He smiled at her.

"Ceilidh!" demanded Wolf.

"You!" Paean pointed a finger at the engineer. "You're now pushing the limits! You ought to be in Sick Bay!"

"Have mercy, Paean!"

"Oh well, you owe me," she said lightly. "Haven't named my condition yet."

"Urgh," said Wolf.

"So nice that Wolf Svendsson is honest and sticks to the rules," she added with an evil grin.

424

"Aargh!" groaned Wolf. "Lends itself to abuse!"

Federi stuck a glass of greengage jelly juice into Paean's hand. The two young boys had also received non-alcoholic drinks. It came with observing the Donegal house rules. As honorary Donegal he had this duty now. He waved a finger at Paean.

"Victimizing the Wolf again, are you?"

"My favourite hobby," laughed Paean.

"Listen, *dulciuri!*" Federi took her aside, to the prow, his long fingers around her wrist. Noisy place, this deck!

"Tomorrow," he said quietly, for her ears only, "we're landing at Prime Oil. Then I'll take you around the place and show you our Captain's plan! You're going to love Prime Oil, my little songbird!"

Paean smiled blissfully. Her gentle friend had guaranteed Ailyss' life by pledging his own! Her heart was singing. She suddenly knew the way forward for the Assassin. Step by step, one saved life at a time. And she was going to be right there supporting him.

The moon that peered through the rigging looked a bit like a silver dollar. With a sliver off of it. The Solar Wind ploughed on through the night.

*

Captain's Log, Solar Wind, 15 May 2116.

Nearly at Prime Oil Base.

Ailyss Quinlan has cracked. She is the Unicate agent, as we suspected. Some surprises though. Turns out she has a younger brother, Keenan, and the Rebellion captured him. Forced her hand into betraying herself. How does the Rebellion know about Ailyss and where did they find her brother? There are missing pieces in this picture too!

I'm personally extremely proud of my crew, especially the younger ones. Who would have thought? They came up for her in unanimous solidarity, shielding her from justice. Pirates! It saves me having to explain why I didn't want to put her to death in the first place.

Federi is not to be moved into getting involved with her in order to control her. Actually cut himself in anger when I suggested it. Or perhaps that was an accident. Wondering if I shouldn't take that stiletto away from him, he might hurt himself one day!

Concerning Ailyss, I hope the alternative plan, binding her to the ship by loyalty and friendship, is going to work – does she have it in her? Donegal Magic was mentioned in that context. And a complete surprise – Federi pledging his life to guarantee hers, although his instinct dictates that she should be executed. Wonder why he did that. It did give me the official loophole past Pirate Law though.

Tzigan went against my orders today, wonder what's eating the man. So did Verushka. Shall have to pull her up. Fraternizing with the new crew.

The Rebellion has been dealt a blow, we have eliminated six more of their Schooners. Admiral will be pleased. Also at the news of the Rebellion port on Hiva Oa. Will have to occupy that. I'll leave that coup to the Admiral. Got to leave some of the good bits for him!

New pirate, Captain Salvatore Rodriguez, best of luck to him. That makes two within three weeks. Great going!

R. Lascek (Pir. Capt.)

The National Hymn of Southern Free

Mahala[1]! Mahala!

Mahala sea, (uh-hum!)
Mahala sky, (uh-hum!)
Mahala sunshine!! (oh yeah!)

Mahala Freedom! (uh-hum!)
Mahala people! (uh-hum!)
Mahala Crime!! (oh yeah!)

We are the Free Free Country, Mahala…
We are the Southern Freebies…

No tax (uh-hum!)
No work (uh-hum!)
Mahala peace (and quiet, yeah!)

Plenty business (uh-hum!)
Ubuntu[2]! (uh-hum!)
God bless our freedom! (oh yeah!)

We are the Free Free Country, Ubuntu
We are the Southern Freebies…

(Ubuntu, uh-hum! Mahala, uh-hum!) x2
(uh-hum, uh-hum! Chicky-bum!)

---

[1] Mahala: For free, gratis
[2] Ubuntu: The concept of looking after each other, community

The Solar Wind sails on:

The Assassin (The Solar Wind II)

"They're tightening the net. Captain does have a plan, but it relies on running and hiding. All hells, that's never going to be enough!"

Federi foresees about three weeks of future for the Solar Wind, after which – the end. What is hiding in those data capsules makes the forecast worse. Even if the Solar Wind manages to escape the Unicate somehow, Earth won't.

The Solar Wind III: Freedom Fighter
The Solar Wind IV: Raider!
The Solar Wind V: The Morrigan

To send feedback, contact the author on <u>lrusso@pkaboo.net</u> *or visit* <u>www.pkaboo.net</u>.

www.ingramcontent.com/pod-product-compliance
Lightning Source LLC
Chambersburg PA
CBHW050915030726
47503CB00007BB/2309